Specters, Monsters, and the Damned

Specters, Monsters, and the Damned

Fantastic Threats to the Social Order in Nineteenth-Century Spanish Fiction

WAN SONYA TANG

VANDERBILT UNIVERSITY PRESS
Nashville, Tennessee

Copyright 2024 Vanderbilt University Press
All rights reserved
First printing 2024

Library of Congress Cataloging-in-Publication Data

Names: Tang, Wan Sonya, 1983- author.
Title: Specters, monsters, and the damned : fantastic threats to the social order in nineteenth-century Spanish fiction / Wan Sonya Tang.
Description: Nashville, Tennessee : Vanderbilt University Press, 2024. | Includes bibliographical references and index.
Identifiers: LCCN 2024016359 (print) | LCCN 2024016360 (ebook) | ISBN 9780826507129 (paperback) | ISBN 9780826507136 (hardcover) | ISBN 9780826507143 (epub) | ISBN 9780826507150 (pdf)
Subjects: LCSH: Fantasy fiction, Spanish--History and criticism. | Spanish fiction--19th century--History and criticism. | Marginality, Social, in literature. | Social structure in literature. | Social status in literature. | LCGFT: Literary criticism.
Classification: LCC PQ6147.F35 T36 2024 (print) | LCC PQ6147.F35 (ebook) | DDC 863/.50915--dc23/eng/20240808
LC record available at https://lccn.loc.gov/2024016359
LC ebook record available at https://lccn.loc.gov/2024016360

This book will be made open access within three years of publication thanks to Path to Open, a program developed in partnership between JSTOR, the American Council of Learned Societies (ACLS), University of Michigan Press, and the University of North Carolina Press to bring about equitable access and impact for the entire scholarly community, including authors, researchers, libraries, and university presses around the world. Learn more at https://about.jstor.org/path-to-open/.

Front cover images: Etchings by Francisco Goya, from the Los Caprichos series, 1799. Rosenwald Collection, courtesy National Gallery of Art, Washington, DC. Top, Que viene el coco (Here Comes the Bogey-Man); middle, Duendecitos (Hobgoblins); bottom, El sueño de la razon produce monstruos (The Sleep of Reason Produces Monsters).

Contents

Acknowledgments vii

Introduction. Unsettling National Narratives   1

Chapter 1. A Haunted Class: Denaturalizing the Bourgeois Worldview   19

Chapter 2. (En)Gendering Monstrosity: Questioning Gender Roles   55

Chapter 3. Accursed Peoples: Challenging Racial Stereotypes and Hierarchies   102

Coda: Fantastic Poetics and Politics   141

Notes 145
Bibliography 181
Index 197

ACKNOWLEDGMENTS

Completing a book is often compared to giving birth, but any academic who has done both will tell you that the two are nowhere near the same thing. Still, I found both experiences of gestation (one physical, one intellectual) and the moments of agony and joy that accompanied each to overlap in many ways. In my case, they literally overlapped, as I undertook archival research for this project shortly before I became pregnant, and finished the manuscript in moments I stole from my now four-year-old. Needless to say, I could never have written this book without the support of a small village, and I am eternally thankful for all those who helped to lift me up as I floundered between first-time book-writing and first-time parenting amid a global pandemic.

The journey that led me to write this book was winding, and it began long before I had read a single Spanish fantastic fiction. My sincerest thanks go to my eternally optimistic father, Yuan-Kai Tang, and to my capable and caring mother, Peng Yen Tang, who first came to the United States in pursuit of doctoral degrees and showed me the power of an education. I am especially grateful that, as two Taiwanese scientists, they allowed me to pursue my passion, even as they worried about my possibilities for gainful employment. Their support of my professional choices has encouraged me to become the best professor that I could be. Thanks, too, go to Wei Stephanie Tang, for forty years of incomparable sisterhood filled with love and the deepest belly laughs. I am enormously lucky to have been born into the Tang and Yen families, and only wish we didn't live on opposite sides of the country.

I am additionally grateful for all those professors that have formed part of my academic family. As an undergraduate at the University of Southern California, my passion for literature and cultural studies began with classes taught by Bruce Burningham (now at Illinois State University), Maite Zubiaurre (now at UCLA), Gabriel Giorgi (now at NYU), and Roberto Díaz, as well as an art history course taught in Madrid by the inimitable Francisco Gómez (now the director of American University's Center in Madrid). Special thanks go to Gabriel for introducing this clueless undergraduate to Foucault and explaining that Wikipedia is not a reputable academic source, and to Roberto, whose incredible warmth and generosity have accompanied me far beyond my undergraduate days. Whereas my professors at USC instilled in me a passion for learning, my professors at Yale filled the many gaps in my knowledge base, and taught me to set a high bar for my scholarship. Great thanks go to Rolena Adorno, Aníbal González, Roberto González Echevarría, Oscar Martín (now at Lehman College), Noël Valis, and the late María Rosa Menocal. As my thesis advisor, Noël was the ideal reader who both encouraged my interest in the fantastic and deepened my knowledge of nineteenth-century Spain. Although nearly nothing from the dissertation appears in this book, I could not have written it without the lessons I learned from her.

I am similarly indebted to two amazing unofficial mentors that I have found (or rather who have found me) in the field of nineteenth-century Spanish cultural studies: Linda Willem and Akiko Tsuchiya. Linda was the first *galdosista* to welcome me, a star-struck recent graduate, into the fold of Galdós scholars, and her unwavering faith in me has been a beacon of light throughout my career. Akiko has likewise been unbelievably giving with her time and expertise. I am in awe of her constant willingness to help me write new syllabi, hunt down sources, or talk through the pros and cons of different publishing venues, in spite of her own prodigious workload. I hope to one day pay forward the amazing mentorship these women have provided to me.

Specters, Monsters, and the Damned grew out of my experiences as a professor at Boston College. While teaching an undergraduate course on fantastic fiction, I realized that class discussions inevitably circled back to questions of class, gender, and race, which became the focal points of this study. I am grateful for the many undergraduate students who have taken iterations of "Haunted Modernity" with me, as well as for the MA students who took my seminar "Monsters, Specters, and the Supernatural in Nineteenth-Century Spain" via Zoom in the fall of 2020. Each of them helped me to think through the various arguments contained in this book, with special thanks to Ethan Hill for our many conversations on "El brasileño." If my students have pushed me to clearly articulate my ideas, it is the generous support of the Morrissey College of Arts and Sciences that made possible my multiple travels to consult nineteenth-century periodicals housed in the Biblioteca Nacional in Madrid, as well as to present my initial findings at conferences all over the US and in Spain. Thanks are due as well to my colleagues in the department of Romance Languages and Literatures, particularly the chair Franco Mormando, and my fellow Hispanic Studies professors: Sarah Beckjord, Ali Kulez, Irene Mizrahi, and Elizabeth Rhodes, who have always shown great interest in my research and its progress. I am, moreover, incredibly appreciative of the small army of research assistants that worked on various elements of this project, from those who helped me to pull the initial bibliography (Kinnell Douglas, Alyssa Pullin, Sydnee Blanco, Gisselle Haynes, and Ethan Hill), to those who painstakingly hunted down specific quotes (Sehyun Moon and Monika Stantcheva), with special thanks to Liam Stephanos for some unforgettable nineteenth-century finds (the *hombre tortuga* will never be forgotten).

The writing of this book would have been absolutely impossible without the aid of an American Fellowship from the American Association of University Women, which granted me the luxury of an entire year free from teaching responsibilities. I owe great thanks to Linda Willem, Leigh Mercer, and Leslie Harkema for writing letters of support for my project. Deeply heartfelt thanks also go to Jennifer Smith, David George, and Joyce Tolliver for reading early drafts of my book chapters, and to David and Joyce for additionally advising me on how best to tackle revisions. It is a true luxury to count on their expertise.

It was Zack Gresham who first expressed enthusiasm for my project on behalf of Vanderbilt University Press. I've since had the enormous pleasure of working with Gianna Mosser and Steven Rodríguez, who patiently guided me through each step of the publishing process. I am deeply grateful to each of them, as well as to every member of the Vanderbilt team who contributed in some way to the publishing of this book. I am likewise thankful for the two anonymous readers of my manuscript, whose careful reading and detailed recommendations have resulted in a more coherent and compelling study.

Book-writing is often solitary, but I have been blessed with friends who have ensured that I have never felt alone in the process. Sarah Thomas and Leslie Harkema were the first to sit with me, shoulder to shoulder in Boston, Providence, and New Haven, writing together and reminding me of why I love our profession. Aurélie Vialette and especially Julia Chang listened to the rough outlines of my project and shared sage advice both on book-writing and on the struggle of balancing the demands of the profession with those of motherhood. Sarah Thomas and Mary Kate Donovan went out of their way to procure some of the images that I analyze in this volume, and Lisandro Kahan sent photographs of the elusive Argentine variant of "Tropiquillos." Martin Repinecz provided me with hugely helpful bibliography on the question of race relations in Spain, and Nicholas Wolters deserves a medal for putting up with my endless flow of questions on the publishing process. Mattia Acetoso, Dean Allbritton, Joanne Britland, Catalina Iannone, Peter Mahoney, Anita Savo, and Amaury Sosa round out the group of friends who have cheered me on as I crawled toward the finish line.

I have reserved my final thanks for two individuals without whom I would never have finished this book. First, I owe at least a million thanks to Gaby Miller for the platonic ideal of friendship. Thank you for all the hours you spent working virtually with me, validating my ideas, reading and commenting on my drafts, recommending and sharing sources with me, and most importantly picking up the phone every time you sensed I needed a friend. Thank you for reminding me that I could do this, and for helping me to see it through.

And as my son Justin would say, I have saved the best for last. Thank you to my amazing husband, Timm Fair, who had no idea what a ridiculous roller-coaster ride book-writing would be, but who did every single thing in his power to help me through the process. Thank you for all the time and energy that you poured into our family. Thank you for being the solid rock that I could lean on when I was crumbling. Thank you for taking Justin on new adventures every weekend so I had time and space to write (shout-out to the Horne family for adopting Timm and Justin). Holding me and this family together was certainly not easy, and it was the greatest testament to love that I have ever witnessed. Thank you from the bottom of my heart.

Parts of Chapter 1 are derived from "La princesa, el granuja, y el obrero condenado: El retrato de las clases sociales en dos cuentos fantásticos de Galdós," *Anales Galdosianos* 49 (2014): 107–20, and sections of Chapter 2 originated in "'Yo no soy un hombre': Masculinity, Monstrosity, and Gothic Conventions in Galdós's *La sombra* (1871)," *Hispanic Review* 88, no. 3 (2020): 243–63. Copyright © 2020 University of Pennsylvania Press. All rights reserved.

INTRODUCTION

Unsettling National Narratives

To understand the intricacies of class, gender, and race as they were conceived in nineteenth-century Spain, literary scholars generally look to realist novels. A supposed mirror of contemporary society, the realist novel grew to become the dominant fictional form in Spain from 1870 through the century's end.[1] In contrast, this book examines the realist novel's apparent antithesis: fantastic short fictions featuring Gothic tropes. Like their lengthier realist counterparts, these tales of the supernatural are critically engaged with the historical context of nation building in which they were written, but they have traditionally been trivialized as serving only to scare, thrill, or perturb. *Specters, Monsters, and the Damned* challenges the near monopoly held by realist novels as the object of literary studies on late nineteenth-century Spain by demonstrating how a defining feature of fantastic fiction—the potential incursion of the supernatural into everyday reality—sheds light on the unnaturalness of the Spanish social order.

More specifically, the present study demonstrates how texts from a marginalized genre effectively illuminate and interrogate the marginalization of certain individuals and communities within Spanish society in the wake of the 1868 Revolution that deposed Bourbon queen Isabella II. Fantastic short fictions published in the final third of the nineteenth century (and a few from the early twentieth) engage with popular Gothic tropes to denaturalize the Spanish social pyramid that placed at its apex bourgeois men of the so-called Spanish race and relegated those of a different socioeconomic status, gender, and/or ethnicity to lower tiers. The narrative dynamics specific to fantastic storytelling breed instability within the text, which bleeds into the stories' treatment of class, gender, and race, thus unsettling society's classificatory schema at a pivotal moment in the construction of Spain's modern identity. For this reason, the fantastic literary production of the post-Isabelline period serves as an important counterpoint to the realist narrative that dominates discussions of Spanish letters in the age of nation building.

Consolidation of the Fantastic in Spain

The term "fantastic" as a literary classification is somewhat confounding, given the lack of consensus on its usage. As a point of departure, all readers can agree that fantastic writing requires the narration of something that is not of this world. For some, the criteria end there, resulting in an ample collection of texts that include everything from classical myths to futuristic science fiction. In 1970, Franco-Bulgarian scholar Tzvetan Todorov proposed a stringent definition of the fantastic based on the structural analysis of mostly French texts dating to the late eighteenth and nineteenth centuries. Despite a proliferation of fantastic theory over the past half-century, Todorov remains the most commonly cited authority on the genre. In his view, truly fantastic works, as opposed to the wholly marvelous or simply uncanny, follow a set narrative structure:

> In a world which is indeed our world, the one we know, a world without devils, sylphides, or vampires, there occurs an event which cannot be explained by the laws of this same familiar world. The person who experiences the event must opt for one of two possible solutions: either he is the victim of an illusion of the senses, of a product of the imagination—and laws of the world then remain what they are [as in the uncanny text]; or else the event has indeed taken place, it is an integral part of reality—but then this reality is controlled by laws unknown to us [as in the marvelous text].... The fantastic occupies the duration of this uncertainty.[2]

By this definition, the fantastic must evoke a sense of doubt in readers—a perpetual vacillation between acceptance as real or rejection as unreal of the seemingly supernatural occurrence narrated in the story. Although Todorov worked with French examples, each of the Spanish short fictions featured in the present study fits his basic framework regardless of authorship or subject matter: the stories are set in the contemporary world of the readers (generally post-Isabelline Spain), into which the supernatural unexpectedly erupts, and provide no definitive rationalization for the supposed breach with reality. Characters and readers alike must choose between multiple explanations for the impossible events that they have experienced or witnessed. In fact, the sense of epistemological uncertainty identified by Todorov as fundamental to the fantastic plays an essential role in how the selected narratives facilitate an interrogation of established social hierarchies, as we shall see.

Since Todorov's groundbreaking study, scholarship on the fantastic has flourished in every possible theoretical direction, much of which has challenged the narrowness of his vision. While reviewing competing definitions of the fantastic is not germane to this analysis, a helpful synthesis can be found in the introduction to Cynthia Duncan's *Unraveling the Real*, which walks readers through key figures in European and Latin American theorizations of the genre. This overview is logical within Duncan's study, as she argues for a broader, more inclusive conception of the fantastic as vital to the critical appreciation of Latin American works that have been overlooked in transnational scholarship for deviating from dominant theoretical models. While the texts examined here have likewise escaped transnational notice, they nevertheless follow the basic premise of Todorov's model by confronting the real with the otherworldly without favoring either a rational or a supernatural explanation of events. Thus, rather than proposing an expanded definition of the fantastic, which would not aid in revalorizing these Spanish short fictions, *Specters, Monsters, and the Damned* proposes a new way to read the selected texts: as a historically bound corpus that serves as a counterpoint to realist writing in terms of form, content, and subversive potential.

Because the narrative tension generated by reader uncertainty is difficult to sustain in the long term, fantastic writing as described by Todorov is particularly well suited to the short story and occasionally the novella. Not coincidentally, Todorov dates the consolidation of the fantastic genre to the nineteenth century, the same period in which the short story assumed its modern shape in Europe and the Americas. The rise of the short story form in the western world was largely conditioned by the explosion of periodical printing in the nineteenth century, which created a venue and a demand for shorter fictions with unity of action.[3] In Spain, the term *cuento* ("story") that came to designate the short story in the late 1800s originally bore the connotation of a fabulated tale that departed from the confines of reality; stories that narrated true events were described using other terms, such as *historia* ("story" and "history").[4] Given the conflation of terminology, the Spanish short story continued to be associated with a fantastical quality throughout the nineteenth century, and the expressly fantastic short story maintained popularity with Spanish audiences through century's end.

Fantastic short fictions first gained traction in Spain during the 1830s, amid the Romantic vogue for historical legends, regional folklore, and other narratives featuring the supernatural. As the century progressed, Spanish authors of the fantastic not only drew upon their own cultural heritage, but likewise gained inspiration in works from abroad, first in British Gothic novels and then in short stories by the German E. T. A. Hoffmann and the American Edgar Allan Poe.[5] Due to the censorship policies of the reactionary Ferdinand VII, translation of first-wave Gothic novels within Spain was highly selective, barring works deemed anticlerical, overly gruesome, or prurient in favor of those with a moralizing slant, such as the works of Ann Radcliffe. Nevertheless, censored novels often found their way to the black market either in the original language or via French translation, and Spanish literary production of the nineteenth century shows great familiarity with Gothic motifs, attesting to the popularity of Gothic fiction in spite of its limited availability.[6] The circulation of foreign models within Spain was greatly facilitated by the easing of draconian censorship laws upon the death of Ferdinand VII in 1833. This relaxation of repressive measures also produced an abundance of new periodicals in the 1830s and '40s, where the majority of Spanish fantastic production was published in the first half of the century, often with accompanying illustrations. Increased availability of fantastic narratives bolstered the popularity of the genre, which in turn encouraged its continued publication. In the century's final third, fantastic tales by Spanish authors not only appeared in the periodical press, but also in countless anthologies of single-authored short stories, including some by renowned realist authors. Notable examples include Pedro Antonio de Alarcón's *Narraciones inverosímiles* (1882; Unlikely narrations) and Emilia Pardo Bazán's *Cuentos sacro-profanos* (1899; Sacro-profane tales).[7] As David Roas, leading authority on the Spanish fantastic, acknowledges, fantastic short fiction was never the most preferred literary form in nineteenth-century Spain, but it was enthusiastically received by national audiences, who appreciated its evolution throughout the century.[8]

Reversing a Systematic Erasure

The fact that Spain produced noteworthy fantastic writing in the 1800s—or even at all—may come as a surprise, even to those well-versed in scholarship on the fantastic. Although in the nineteenth century English-language anthologies of supernatural fictions included short stories by Alarcón and Gustavo Adolfo Bécquer, Spain often disappeared from such archives in the following century.[9] Eric Rabkin's 1979 collection *Fantastic Worlds* provides a representative example. Touted by Oxford University Press as "the first international anthology to cover the entire scope of fantastic narrative" conceived in the broadest possible way, *Fantastic Worlds* includes more than fifty short fictions from thirteen countries worldwide.[10] It features such underrepresented nations in fantastic studies as Nigeria, Poland, and Switzerland alongside the usual suspects of Germany, England, and the United States; yet not a single text in the volume originated in Spain.[11] To take a European example, Italo Calvino's *Racconti fantastici dell'Ottocento* (1983; *Fantastic Tales: Visionary and Everyday*) contains more than five hundred pages of fantastic short stories from seven European countries and the US, but it does not feature a single Spanish text.[12]

Spain's gradual erasure from transnational discussions of the fantastic since their emergence in the nineteenth century can be attributed to a combination of external and internal factors. From the eighteenth century onward, power within Europe shifted from the Mediterranean states of Spain, Portugal, and Italy, to France, England, and what would later become Germany, epicenters of the industrial and social revolutions that ushered in a new era of European history.[13] This geopolitical change meant that Spain was increasingly evaluated against standards of modernity established by its northern neighbors and, more importantly, judged to fall short. Once an undeniable world power, Spain was now cast as a stagnant nation on the edge of Europe, with an underdeveloped economy and an overly influential Catholic Church.[14] A society in which miracles were still taken at face value was thought to be incapable of producing fantastic literature in its Todorovian guise, since the latter required some measure of reader skepticism.[15] Thus, Spain's deep-rooted religiosity was often viewed as an obstacle to the development of a modern fantastic tradition. In the prologue to his short story "La pasionaria" (1841; The passionflower), José Zorrilla describes German E. T. A. Hoffmann's fantastic fiction as a literature that "repugna nuestro país, que ha sido siempre religioso hasta el fanatismo" (disgusts our country, which has always been religious to the point of fanaticism).[16] Although Zorrilla speaks of Spain's near fanaticism as a point of pride, he unwittingly confirms contemporary stereotypes of Spanish obscurantism. Given Spain's nineteenth-century characterization as a peripheral backwater of Europe, Spanish fantastic literary production was automatically labeled a poor imitation of foreign—namely German, French, and Anglo-American—originals.

The charge that nineteenth-century Spanish cultural production is both derivative and inferior is not exclusively leveled at texts of the fantastic variety. Spanish realism has likewise, and for similar reasons, been relegated to a footnote in most histories of modern European literature.[17] Unlike realist fiction, however, fantastic writing from Spain has been doubly marginalized, both in the transnational context and within the nation's own borders. While nineteenth-century Spanish culture was increasingly dismissed by northern Europe and the United States as incapable of producing fantastic contributions of quality, the intelligentsia within Spain were actively invested in promoting realism as the national literary tendency. Benito Pérez Galdós's 1870 essay "Observaciones sobre la novela contemporánea en España" (Some observations on the contemporary novel in Spain) famously criticized the Spanish literary landscape as impoverished due to the lack of a "novela nacional" (national novel) based in the careful observation of present-day Spanish society.[18] Even before consolidation of the literary form in Spain, Galdós deemed the realist novel to epitomize national literary production and signal the modernity of Spanish letters, an assessment which would be repeatedly echoed by his peers. As the Spanish realist novel took shape, the nation's authors and critics consciously elevated the new literary form, often viewing contemporary novels to be the pinnacle of an autochthonous tradition of realism established with such illustrious works as *Don Quijote*.[19] In this manner, the nineteenth-century realist novel was born into a privileged position within Spain, and its prominence was cemented through immediate and sustained canonization. In spite of facing disdain from Spanish modernists in the early twentieth century, the realist novel's status was restored under the Francoist regime and endured through the transition to democracy, although the roster of celebrated authors and works changed in accordance with evolving sociopolitical circumstances.[20]

Prestige conferred within Spain upon the nineteenth-century realist novel was accompanied by a systematic devaluation of other literary forms dating to the same period, including fantastic short fiction. Consequently, in the preface to the 1890 edition of his fantastic novella *La sombra* (The shadow), which was accompanied by the fantastic short stories "Celín," "Tropiquillos," and "Theros," Galdós felt compelled to characterize these texts as "obrillas ... divertimientos, juguetes, ensayos de aficionado [de la creación fantástica]" (trifling works ... amusements, playthings, first attempts by a fan [of fantastic creation]) in spite of authorizing their republication.[21] Each of the texts had been published in leading periodicals prior to their collection in this volume, which contradicts the author's purported low opinion of them. Emilia Pardo Bazán similarly described the fantastic pieces reprinted in her short-story collection *Cuentos sacro-profanos* as intended "solo a divertir un rato" (only to amuse for a while).[22] As in the case of Galdós, the decision to reprint these works suggests that Pardo Bazán held her fantastic writing in higher esteem than she let on. Given that the enormous fame of both authors rested on their realist fiction, their disavowal of the fantastic in spite of an evident affinity for the genre appears to strategically distance them from a less respected form of literature. Fantastic writing from nineteenth-century Spain struggled against the prejudices of international and domestic critics alike, such that even renowned authors were reluctant to defend their fantastic creations. This same bias persists in Mariano Baquero Goyanes's seminal study *El cuento español en el siglo XIX* (1949; The Spanish short story in the nineteenth century), which declares the fantastic to have had few Spanish practitioners, all of whom are "muy inferiores . . . a los grandes creadores del género" (highly inferior . . . to the genre's great creators) identified as Hoffmann, Adelbert von Chamisso, Charles Nodier, and Poe.[23]

Though Baquero Goyanes's statement is understandable, it remains erroneous. As Joan Estruch Tobella beautifully articulated, "No es que tengamos una literatura fantástica pobre, sino más bien una visión pobre de nuestra literatura fantástica" (It is not that we [Spaniards] have a deficient fantastic literature, but rather a deficient vision of our fantastic literature).[24] Fortunately, in the four decades since Estruch's observation, Spanish scholars have made great strides in recuperating a fantastic corpus produced in Spain that dates back at least to the nineteenth century. Multiple anthologies of fantastic fiction specific to the period have been published, and critical studies of these texts have likewise gained momentum.[25] David Roas, director of the Barcelona-based Grupo de Estudios sobre lo Fantástico (Fantastic Literature Studies Group), has played a foundational role in tracing the development of the modern Spanish fantastic, discovering unknown writers and texts, and promoting their study. Montserrat Trancón Lagunas likewise provided an invaluable service to those interested in the nineteenth-century Spanish fantastic by compiling a comprehensive list of the fantastic theory, fiction, and artwork published in Spanish periodicals during the Romantic period.[26]

Most recently, Juan Jesús Payán's *Los conjuros del asombro* traces the nationalization of fantastic literature in Spain during the first two-thirds of the nineteenth century, highlighting for the first time the originality of Spanish fantastic authors. As he explains, fantastic fiction penned in Europe during the early and mid-nineteenth century varied from country to country as each nation engaged with the clash between reality and the supernatural in differing, culturally conditioned ways: "no cabría, por tanto, hablar de una única expresión fantástica, sino de una multitud de manifestaciones" (It would not be fitting, therefore, to speak of a single fantastic expression, but instead of a multitude of manifestations).[27] Recognizing an initial plurality of fantastic forms is pivotal for Payán, whose work revalorizes Spanish fiction that explores the confrontation with the otherworldly in complex and distinctly nationalistic ways that do not always fit Todorov's (or any other theorist's) mold. Broadening the category of the fantastic allows for the inclusion of Spanish examples among the genre's nineteenth-century pioneers, and in doing so, *Los conjuros del asombro* depicts Spain as contemporaneous to other European nations in the early theorization and practice of the fantastic, producing highly innovative formulations and even anticipating postmodern techniques as early as the 1840s.

Specters, Monsters, and the Damned builds upon this scholarship in two key ways. To begin with, it is the first book-length analysis of nineteenth-century Spanish fantastic fiction written for an English-speaking audience, which grants greater visibility to the texts under study and facilitates their inclusion in transnational debates and dialogues. Secondly, the present volume complements previous scholarship by concentrating on fantastic literature produced in Spain from 1865 onward. The selected works were written concurrently with the rise of realism in Spain, often by the same authors most closely associated with mastery of the realist mode. This simultaneity and shared authorship suggest that fantastic short fictions of the late nineteenth century were not merely a vestige of bygone Romantic tastes, but instead comprised a necessary foil to the modern realist novel. If the latter aided in consolidating—though not without criticism—the social order established in the process of nineteenth-century nation building, the former destabilized the hierarchies of class, gender, and race that emerged therein.

Literature and Nation Building

The nineteenth century has long been considered the age of European nation building, in which newly established nation states cultivated distinctive identities through a variety of means, including legislation, the founding of public institutions, and the promotion of a common culture with shared national symbols.²⁸ In addition to solidifying the nation as a geopolitical entity, these measures also constructed the nation as what Benedict Anderson deemed an "imagined community" composed of likeminded individuals bound in kinship by commonly held beliefs and values.²⁹ Prior to coalescing around a shared identity, "the various inhabitants of [any] national territory had little or no awareness of each other's existence, and did not expect to have anything—language, race, or culture—in common," as Jo Labanyi states.³⁰ The newfound sense of collective identity helped to unify the populace, but it also obscured the very real inequality that existed within national borders, in part as a result of the nation-building process. Emergent nations were inevitably shaped by a select few who modeled the ideal citizenry after themselves. Symbolic primacy within the national culture was thus conferred upon those with a hand in making laws, building institutions, and establishing cultural practices, whose interests were publicly represented, while less influential social groups were silenced and shunted to the periphery.³¹

These dynamics hold true in the case of Spain, where national consciousness in the modern sense first emerged during the Peninsular War (1808—1814) waged to oust French invaders from the Iberian Peninsula. During this time, the Cortes de Cádiz, a legislative body composed of representatives from all over Spain including overseas colonies, drafted the Constitution of 1812 in resistance to the French occupation. Although it was never fully implemented, the document nevertheless provided a blueprint for the definition of Spanish citizenship in the nineteenth century, effectively delineating whose voices were amplified and whose rights were privileged within the imagined Spanish community. Inspired in liberal ideology, Article 5 of the Constitution states that "Son españoles . . . todos los hombres libres nacidos y avecinados en los dominios de las Españas, y los hijos de estos" (all free men born and living in Spain's territories and their sons are Spaniards).³² However, the apparent inclusivity of this declaration belies the numerous groups that were excluded from Spanish citizenship due to their gender, race, and class. Susan Kirkpatrick observes that just as women were categorically omitted from "the civic and political universe represented in the Constitution," the *castas pardas*, or "free Americans with African ancestors" were barred from voting, as were those inhabiting Spanish territories who remained illiterate by 1830, which inevitably disenfranchised the working class.³³ Thus, from the inception of Spanish nation building, the model modern subject was imagined to be an ethnically *castizo* (a term which can be loosely translated as "authentically Spanish") man of some means, whose starring role in Spanish society was reinforced through contemporary cultural production.

While the Constitution of 1812 exemplified the legal definition of the Spanish state and its citizens, a shared image of nineteenth-century national life was most effectively created through the arts, particularly realist literature.[34] The "meteoric rise of the periodical press" that boosted circulation of the fantastic short story likewise bolstered the popularity of the serialized novel in the 1840s.[35] Although early nineteenth-century novels were criticized for their sentimentality and sensationalism, some liberal intellectuals recognized the novel's potential to convert the masses into Spanish citizens by propagating nationalism and modeling desired social behavior.[36] This potential would be realized with the birth and rise of the realist novel after 1870. Following the prescription for the national novel that Galdós set forth in "Observaciones sobre la novela contemporánea," authors like Leopoldo Alas, Pardo Bazán, and Galdós himself depicted the lives of middle-class protagonists across Spain in relation to their families and social networks. Equally important to the characters was the realist novel's implied reader, who was well-educated and civic-minded, and therefore presumed to be a bourgeois man residing in Spain.[37] The assumption of this specific audience not only "disinherited" the female reading public, as Catherine Jagoe argues, but given the association between novel and nation in the late nineteenth century, it cemented the image of the normative Spanish subject as middle-class, male, and metropolitan (as opposed to from the colonies).[38] Accordingly, even though realist novels "mostly illustrate the problems arising from modernity's homogenizing project, they nevertheless serve this same project" by normalizing the perspective of those individuals favored by the nation's new laws and institutions.[39]

Subverting the Social Order

The role of Spanish realist literature in upholding, albeit ambivalently, a definition of "Spanishness" centered around the bourgeois man has been meticulously studied since 1990, most notably in Jo Labanyi's *Gender and Modernization in the Spanish Realist Novel*. As Labanyi clearly articulates, the immediate consecration of the realist novel as a documentary art form perpetuated the illusion that the national society it depicted—one that privileged middle-class, male, and metropolitan perspectives—was an observable reality rather than a social construction.[40] In other words, the realist novel fortifies the social order by concealing its invented-ness behind the veneer of reality. Fantastic short fiction as described by Todorov does the exact opposite; it unsettles established social hierarchies by exposing the artificiality of reality itself. As Susana Reisz explains, fantastic storytelling dramatizes within the narrative a questioning of the "real," and in so doing exposes the inventedness of "todas las 'evidencias,' de todas las 'verdades' transmitidas en que se apoya el hombre de nuestra época y de nuestra cultura" (all the "evidence," all the transmitted "truths" upon which a man of our time and our culture stands).[41] If our conception of material reality, which is assumed to exist independently of us, occupies shaky ground within fantastic narrative, then the solidity and thereby legitimacy of social distinctions, which are man-made to begin with, become even more suspect. Accordingly, Rosemary Jackson argues that fantastic storytelling subverts dominant cultural narratives by "exposing the relative and arbitrary nature" of the "unifying structures and significations upon which social order depends."[42]

Whereas Jackson spoke generally of the challenge that fantastic writing posed to dominant value systems in "a post-Romantic, secularized [Western] culture," *Specters, Monsters, and the Damned* focuses specifically on the dynamics whereby the fantastic interrogates hierarchies of class, gender, and what nineteenth-century Spaniards considered "race" during the period of cultural consolidation that followed the Revolution of 1868.[43] Of the eleven short stories and single novella analyzed in the present study, only one text was published in the 1860s and two appeared just after the turn of the century; the majority date to the 1870–1900 period in which the realist novel emerged and rose to prominence on the national stage. The time span covered by the selected texts is not coincidental; examining fantastic works produced while realism gained traction in Spanish literary circles underscores how fantastic short fiction crafted a different narrative with respect to national identity, one that destabilizes affirmations of bourgeois, male "Spanishness."

To more effectively establish fantastic short fiction as a foil to the realist novel in nineteenth-century Spain, *Specters, Monsters, and the Damned* features authors who were proficient in both forms of writing: Alarcón, Galdós, and Pardo Bazán. Stacked against Galdós and Pardo Bazán, Alarcón is often considered a lesser novelist for his moralizing tendencies. Although he had fallen out of favor by the time of his death, Pardo Bazán was unequivocal in acknowledging Alarcón's contribution to the development of "el realismo más castizo y donoso" (the most pure-blooded and witty realism).⁴⁴ His fantastic tales "El amigo de la Muerte" (1852; Death's friend) and "La mujer alta" (1882; The tall woman) bookend his novelistic production, which spanned from 1855 to 1882, and in fact the fame of these disquieting narratives has come to eclipse that of Alarcón's lengthier writing. Contrarily, realist novels by Galdós and Pardo Bazán are thought to epitomize the genre in Spain. Nevertheless, both writers also demonstrated a commitment to fantastic storytelling throughout their careers. Galdós's twelve fantastic tales were few and far-between compared to his seventy-seven novels, but they were published at regular intervals over a thirty-year period (1865–1897).⁴⁵ Similarly, roughly half of the twenty short story collections that Pardo Bazán published between 1885 and 1922 feature at least one fantastic short story that meets Todorov's criteria; *Cuentos sacro-profanos* alone includes ten. The fact that Alarcón, Galdós, and Pardo Bazán felt repeatedly compelled to write in a fantastic vein suggests that such narrative fills a social function that the realist novel cannot. Particularly in the case of Galdós and Pardo Bazán, their fame as realist novelists paradoxically aids in legitimizing the genre of fantastic short fiction to which they were consistently drawn.

Alongside works by renowned authors, I analyze two short stories by Pedro Escamilla, a nineteenth-century writer from Madrid who has fallen into shocking obscurity, considering his prolific publication record of almost 400 short fictions, at least thirty-four novels, and thirty-some plays. Escamilla was rediscovered by Gisèle Cazottes in 1983; the dates of his birth and death, as well as most details of his life remain unknown, but his fantastic writing, which makes up a significant portion of his short stories, has enjoyed a revival thanks largely to the efforts of David Roas.⁴⁶ Precisely because so little is known about him, Escamilla provides an interesting counterpoint to Alarcón, Galdós, and Pardo Bazán. Judgments of his fantastic fiction must rest solely on the stories' quality, since the author's fame does not precede him and cannot condition reader expectations in the present day. Moreover, because Escamilla is not associated with the development of realism in Spain, his work serves to confirm that it is the form of the fantastic that facilitates interrogation of the social order rather than any particularity in the writing of primarily realist authors. While other late nineteenth-century authors such as Rafael Serrano Alcázar or José Selgas, each of whom published at least one collection of fantastic tales, could likewise have provided a counterpoint to Galdós and Pardo Bazán, the sheer quantity of fantastic short stories published by Escamilla, as well as their consistent quality, recommends his work for analysis.⁴⁷ Equally important to the present study, the lack of biographical data on Escamilla makes it nearly impossible to view his fantastic writing as a projection of the author's political convictions, a perennial impulse when reading the work of better-known writers. Each author's ideology inevitably informs to some degree his or her writing, fantastic or otherwise, but the aim of *Specters, Monsters, and the Damned* is not to investigate the extent of this influence, nor is it to parse out the authors' thoughts on thorny social questions based on a very limited selection of fantastic writing.[48]

Instead, I trace how the Todorovian structure of fantastic short fiction from nineteenth-century Spain imbues this literature with socially subversive potential, regardless of authorial intent. Although Alarcón, Galdós, Pardo Bazán, and presumably Escamilla held differing and evolving viewpoints concerning questions of social equity, their fantastic writing consistently calls into question the social structures that privilege certain subjectivities at the expense of others within Spanish society. It does so specifically through the fantastic treatment of distinct motifs popularized in Gothic literature. Thus, each chapter of *Specters, Monsters, and the Damned* analyzes the fantastic representation of a single facet of identity that could determine an individual's inclusion or exclusion from the imagined national community, focusing on how this marker of identity, be it class, gender, or race, is depicted in relation to a specific Gothic trope. Chapter 1 scrutinizes the use of ghostly imagery to explore questions of social class in late nineteenth-century Spain, Chapter 2 investigates how monstrous characterizations reflect established gender norms of the period, and Chapter 3 examines how curse stories by Spanish authors are informed by the nation's racial politics.

Given their reliance on Gothic motifs and cultivation of an "art of pleasurable fear," the works analyzed here can also be (and some have been) classified as Gothic texts.[49] This dual classification as both Gothic and fantastic does not pose a problem for the present study, as the selected fictions are thematically Gothic and structurally fantastic. The Gothic aesthetic has long been associated with a collection of recognizable tropes, characters, and circumstances intended to both frighten and titillate the reader, and the specters, monsters, and curses analyzed in the present study figure prominently in Gothic writing across national traditions. As Fred Botting explains in the succinct study *Gothic*, such recurrent motifs serve to express the "fascination with transgression and the anxiety over cultural limits and boundaries" at the heart of Gothic fiction.[50] This urge to transgress societal norms, however, is not inherently subversive, as numerous theorists of the

Gothic recognize. Although the transgressive impulse of Gothic writing can liberate repressed urges and desires at both the individual and societal level, Botting acknowledges that it can likewise "become a powerful means to reassert the values of society, virtue and propriety: transgression, by crossing the social and aesthetic limits, serves to reinforce or underline their value and necessity, restoring or defining limits."[51] Thus, the mere presence of popular Gothic motifs within a text does not necessarily interrogate social norms or the attitudes and beliefs that underlie them.

This is the case of the Spanish short fictions examined here, in which the characters' fear of ghosts, monsters, and curses is often rooted in a socially conservative ideology that scapegoats and demonizes already marginalized populations. As Allan Lloyd Smith describes of the British Gothic tradition, "The shadow at the edge of Victorian consciousness was the 'other' of social, sexual, or racial out-groups" embodied in such figures as "the anarchist, the gypsy, the sexual transgressor, [and] the colonial subject."[52] Painting these characters in an otherworldly light further excludes them from the social body, thus preserving existing social structures. This same dynamic appears in Spanish fantastic fictions of the period, in which the appearance of supernatural horrors is not itself subversive. Instead, what challenges the dominant ideology within the selected texts is their fantastic structure.[53] By casting unresolved doubt on the existence of the specter, the monster, or the curse within the story, these works defy a fixity of interpretation, challenging both a single, definitive reading of the text and a single, authoritarian vision of society. Thus, while each chapter of *Specters, Monsters, and the Damned* addresses both the Gothic and the fantastic elements of the featured works, primacy is granted to their fantastic structure as a destabilizing force. Within these fictions, the fantastic depiction of reality as unstable extends to Spain's social reality as well, gesturing toward the inhumanity not of the marginalized, but of the dominant social group.

Chapter 1 dissects the fantastic depiction of class-based anxieties through ghostly metaphor. An overview of the bourgeois ascendancy in late nineteenth-century Spain provides a backdrop for the textual analyses that follow, outlining how the nation's relatively small middle classes came to be the most culturally influential as of 1868. The chapter then establishes the popularity of spectral metaphors in contemporary European economic discourse and the recurrence of socioeconomic themes in ghost stories of the period. Conceptualizing the specter as a liminal figure that exists between the past and the present, visibility and invisibility, I examine how the specter's undecidability is amplified in fantastic texts that are themselves epistemologically ambiguous.

This dual uncertainty becomes a central feature of the specter's presentation and the social critique that it engenders within the selected short stories. The paradoxical nature of the ghost as both there and not there draws attention to the disconnect between appearances and reality in bourgeois society as depicted in various texts. Read in tandem, Pardo Bazán's "El antepasado" (The forefather) and "Los hilos" (The threads) challenges the equivalence drawn in realist literature between the bourgeois ascendency and the nation's modernity by revealing contemporary bourgeois society to be riddled with the specters of injustice and immorality thought to have been banished through liberal reform. Escamilla's "El número trece" (The number thirteen) and Galdós's "Una industria que vive de la muerte" (An industry that lives off of death) further exemplify how the specter's appearance underscores the penurious existence of those who aspire to a solidly middle-class status, while simultaneously exposing the bourgeois identity to itself be immaterial, based on false hopes and empty appearances. Across all four tales, doubt concerning the specter's reality forces various characters to choose for themselves whether or not to believe in the supernatural; their decisions reflect their level of integration into the dominant social group, which brings prestige and privilege but comes at a price.

Discussion of the consolidation of bourgeois values in Chapter 1 provides a foundation for the chapters that follow, which demonstrate how fantastic short fictions undermine bourgeois concepts of gender and race in nineteenth-century Spain. Chapters 2 and 3 show that contemporary conceptions of femininity, masculinity, and the so-called Spanish race were all anchored in the culturally dominant middle-class perspective. Consequently, the socioeconomic status of narrators and other characters conditions the treatment of gender and race in every text examined. Both the gender privilege afforded to men, as explored in Chapter 2, and the ethnic privilege extended to those deemed to be of the national race, as detailed in Chapter 3, are amplified for individuals who belong to the bourgeois elite. Thus, although each chapter foregrounds a separate aspect of identity, the analyses across chapters consider their inevitable intersection.

Bearing in mind this intersectionality, Chapter 2 examines how fantastic short stories challenge the limits of acceptable femininity or masculinity by casting doubt on society's designation of gender-deviant monsters. The chapter begins by briefly reviewing the now familiar figures of the "angel in the house" and the respectable gentleman as the respective ideals of nineteenth-century Spanish femininity and masculinity established by bourgeois society. The insistence on propagating these models reflects widespread cultural anxiety surrounding female empowerment as well as

Spain's perceived emasculation on the world stage. Within this fearful climate, the maintenance of clearly defined gender roles becomes paramount to establishing a sense of national stability, and the concept of monstrosity plays a key role in policing gender boundaries. In contrast to the shadowy specters of the previous chapter, the monster frightens due to the tangible, physical form it assumes, which provides a fitting analogy for those who fail to adequately embody dominant gender norms.

The short stories analyzed in this chapter depict in literal fashion the monstrosity of those who do not conform to prevalent standards for femininity and masculinity. In Galdós's "El verano" (The summer)/"Theros" and Alarcón's "La mujer alta" (The tall woman), women who deviate from the feminine ideal are portrayed as unnatural, otherworldly creatures. However, in these structurally fantastic narratives, belief in the monstrosity of unconventional women hinges on reader identification with the narrator's perspective. Acknowledging the storytellers' positionality as both bourgeois and male reveals how monstrosity is a subjective quality that serves to uphold traditional gender dynamics. In the case of male monstrosity as portrayed in Galdós's *La sombra* (The shadow) and Pardo Bazán's "Vampiro" (Vampire), the texts' fantastic element ultimately underscores the misogyny of Spanish society. Whereas the male protagonists of both works are publicly viewed as monsters for departing from the confines of normative masculinity, their true inhumanity lies in the deeply sexist and downright murderous treatment of their wives. This lack of regard for female lives remains reprehensible regardless of whether or not there is supernatural intervention; in fact, it is more disturbing as a purely human impulse. Thus, true monstrosity in all four fictions resides not in any outwardly aberrant male or female body, but in a society that encourages the (at times literal) erasure of vulnerable women.

Finally, Chapter 3 analyzes how the Gothic trope of the curse underlies the fantastic treatment of race as it was conceived within nineteenth-century Spain. In contrast to its current usage, which largely denotes phenotypical differences, for turn-of-the-century Spaniards the term *raza* or "race" generally designated an essentialized view of ethnicity. The chapter begins by synthesizing Spanish discussions of *raza* from the medieval obsession with *limpieza de sangre*, or purity of blood free from Jewish contamination, to turn-of-the-century concern over racial degeneration as a potential cause of the nation's imperial decline. The loss of Spain's American and Asian colonies when other European nations were bolstering overseas territories cast doubt on the vitality of "the Spanish race." In this moment of racial insecurity, the curse, which condemns certain groups to misfortune and even extinction, emerges as the ideal Gothic motif through which to explore questions of racialized alterity in intercultural encounters. In the short stories analyzed in this chapter, the curse is the central conceit that allows for an interrogation of the power dynamics between those who are considered Spanish and those who are racialized as Others within a context of Spanish imperialism.

More specifically, diverse groups of "non-Spaniards" both within Spain and in colonized lands are portrayed as simultaneously powerful and powerless upon cursing the protagonists of the selected fictions. On the one hand, their vengeful words appear to have a deleterious effect on the lives of the Spaniards who have exploited them; on the other, the fantastic structure of the narrative means that the efficacy of the curse is not guaranteed. It soon becomes clear that the protagonists' fear of the curse is contingent upon reducing the curser to an exoticized Other. Only when the accursed sees the curser as a savage with supernatural abilities does he give credence to the latter's words. Viewed in this manner, the curse confers no real power upon the utterer, who remains in a subordinate position. In both Galdós's "Tropiquillos" and Pardo Bazán's "El brasileño" (The Brazilian), wealthy Spanish men who profited from the imperial enterprise fear themselves to be jinxed by the indigenous peoples they had exploited. The cursers, in turn, remain doomed to extinction by continuing colonial practices. A similar dynamic runs through Pardo Bazán's "Maldición de gitana" (The gypsy's curse), in which a gypsy woman foretells death for the visibly "Spanish" noblemen who insult her, but is dealt physical and symbolic violence in return. Lastly, the Jewish character in Escamilla's "El cuadro de maese Abraham" (Master Abraham's painting) provides an interesting contrast to the racialized antagonists of Galdós's and Pardo Bazán's tales. His fabulous wealth and status as a man place him on par with the bourgeois protagonist whom he supposedly hexes, but his racialized ethnicity makes him an easy scapegoat when misfortune befalls the Spaniard. Taken together, these texts question who the cursed parties really are, revealing racial discrimination to rival occult powers as a source of evil.

As a final consideration, the historical context of where fantastic short fictions first appeared is revelatory for the study of this corpus. The story of fantastic literature is deeply intertwined with that of the periodical press in nineteenth-century Spain. Every fantastic work analyzed in this book first appeared on the pages of a contemporary periodical. A few of the selected tales were originally illustrated, and most were later modified in subsequent editions. All English translations of the stories' text are thus my own, since published translations, when they exist, have exclusively worked from posterior versions. Even for those stories without illustrations, or whose text remains untouched in subsequent editions, the original format of publication matters, since each of the works featured in *Specters, Monsters, and the Damned* once shared a space with other texts and images that inevitably affected the story's reception. In a concrete example, Pardo Bazán's short fictions generally appeared in "high-circulation, male-oriented periodicals" that reproduced the same patriarchal values contested in the author's work.[54] As Joyce Tolliver proclaims, "To ignore this physical and cultural context is to elide the inherently problematic nature of the discourse events these stories constitute."[55] Nevertheless, much scholarship produced in the United States studies nineteenth-century Spanish short stories as they appear in modern anthologies, without regard for their original form and context.

In the following chapters, fantastic short fictions by Alarcón, Galdós, Pardo Bazán, and Escamilla are examined as they were originally published in the periodical press. I have cited the original text directly, updating only the accent marks to meet the standards of current usage. The analysis of each work not only considers questions of content and narrative structure, but dissects any illustrations, notes where the original text varies significantly from later versions, and acknowledges the influence of neighboring texts and images on reader comprehension. The re-contextualization of these narratives enriches our understanding of them as literary products of their time, reminding readers that fantastic fictions were quite literally embedded in larger discourses of class, gender, and race in late nineteenth-century Spain. Notably, these discourses were far from monolithic and fixed, and as the present study demonstrates, their complexity and messiness found perfect expression in a literature rife with specters, monsters, curses, and above all, a sense of unease and uncertainty.

CHAPTER 1

A Haunted Class

Denaturalizing the Bourgeois Worldview

For as long as human beings have questioned the finality of death, they have traded ghost stories. A staple of oral and written traditions worldwide, ghost stories reached new literary heights in the 1800s, forming a considerable subset of the Gothic and fantastic fiction of the period. Thanks first to the Romantic revival of interest in the supernatural and then to a generalized "effort to unlock other worlds and dimensions" through the natural, social, and pseudo-sciences, ghosts experienced a true "heyday" throughout Europe and the Americas in the latter part of the nineteenth century.[1] This proliferation of specters in a time defined by scientific and technological advancement and sweeping societal change suggests that, as sociologist Avery Gordon states, "Haunting is a constituent element of modern social life."[2]

In late nineteenth-century Spain, modernity was often conflated with the adoption of a liberal political agenda—which dismantled the Old Regime and reordered social hierarchies under the premise of legal equality—and the establishment of greater economic freedom through the abolishment of guilds.[3] As a result of these and other developments discussed later in this chapter, Spanish modernity, like that of many other European nations, entailed the consolidation of bourgeois, or middle-class, culture as the national model. Consequently, "modern social life" generally referred to that of the newly established middle classes, and true to Gordon's assessment, the short stories examined below—Pardo Bazán's "El antepasado" and "Los hilos," Escamilla's "El número trece," and Galdós's "Una industria que vive de la muerte"—show this group to be haunted by endless anxieties and insecurities that assume a variety of ghostly forms.

From visions of a decapitated ancestor to a phantom web binding Madrid's high society, the specter appears in these texts as something perceptible and yet incorporeal that stalks one or more characters, often rendering life impossible. While no two specters featured in these stories are identical, each one reveals inconvenient truths about the social class of its victims, all of whom belong to the multiform middle classes, ranging from wealthy socialites to the nearly destitute. However, given that these tales are fantastic narratives, it is not just the specter's presence, but the ontological and epistemological crises that its appearance generates (Does the haunting figure exist outside of the character's mind? What is it, and how should readers interpret it?) that facilitate a closer inspection of bourgeois norms and lifestyles, the myths and structures that sustain them, and what or whom they exclude. The ghost's appearance thus brings to light contradictions in the bourgeois value system by granting visibility to the immaterial, and gestures toward the dehumanizing effect of a capitalist ethos in which wealth is viewed as the conduit to happiness and money mediates personal relations. Taken together, these stories by Pardo Bazán, Escamilla, and Galdós suggest that the ghost, regardless of the form it assumes, denaturalizes bourgeois logic within fantastic narratives, which always necessitate a choice between credence and skepticism. The decision to acknowledge or ignore the spectral presence at the center of each tale becomes a political act linked to different characters' investment in the dominant culture. Because readers, too, must decide whether to accept or dismiss the ghosts in each text, these fictions force readers out of passivity both in their reading practices and in the uncritical assumption of bourgeois values.

Spectrality and the New Social Order

As in much of Europe, a key component of Spanish modernization lay in the transition from the feudal society of the Old Regime to a more representative political system that favored the emergent middle classes. This sociopolitical shift would pave the way for the narratives of a haunted bourgeois society examined here. First framed in the Constitution of 1812 and gradually enacted throughout the century, Spain's liberal legislation did away with a number of longstanding aristocratic privileges while simultaneously increasing the decision-making powers of commoners. Major changes included the disentailment of lands held by the nobility, the abolition of seigneurial jurisdiction that endowed feudal lords with legal authority, and the subjection of aristocrats to state taxation from which they were previously exempt. The Constitution of 1812 likewise proposed to extend sovereignty to the Spanish public through the establishment of universal male suffrage.[4] Though not enacted until 1890, this expansion of voting rights was key to liberal political philosophy in nineteenth-century Spain. To better prepare the expanded electorate, politicians stressed the need for improved educational access, aspiring to have a primary school in every village.[5] This desire for educational reform culminated in the 1857 Moyano Law that mandated school attendance for children until the age of nine and subsidized studies for those of limited means.

Practically speaking, increased political representation and better preparation of the citizenry had few material effects on the lives of privilege enjoyed by the nobility. Nevertheless, liberal legislation constituted a symbolic toppling of the old ruling class. The new laws were so instrumental in consolidating middle-class influence that historian Adrian Shubert describes the shift from feudal to bourgeois society in Spain as "fundamentally a legal, and not an economic, revolution."[6] Yet legislation was not the sole factor favoring the bourgeois classes in Spain. Belated industrialization and the transition toward a market economy likewise played a part, particularly in Catalonia and the Basque Country.[7] In Madrid, where three of the four short stories examined in this chapter are set, the burgeoning bourgeois community reflected both the growth of state bureaucracy and urbanization in general as additional developments that bolstered the middle classes throughout the nineteenth century.

In this chapter, I use the terms "middle-class" and "bourgeois" interchangeably, as they were used within the context of nineteenth-century liberalism.[8] At the time when Alarcón, Escamilla, Galdós, and Pardo Bazán were writing, Spain's middle classes were small in size and far from uniform in composition.[9] Amongst their ranks, Shubert lists civil servants, shopkeepers, business agents, and stockbrokers, as well as the so-called liberal professions of doctors, lawyers, pharmacists and engineers.[10] Further highlighting the wide range spanned by Spain's bourgeoisie, Pardo Bazán explains that "cabe en ella desde la mujer del opulento fabricante—que es clase media sólo porque no es aristocracia—hasta la mujer del telegrafista o del subteniente—que es clase media sólo porque no es pueblo" (it includes both the opulent manufacturer's wife—who is middle class only because she is not of the aristocracy—and the wife of the telegraphist or of the second lieutenant—who is middle class only because she is not of the working class).[11]

All who fell between the nobility and manual laborers belonged to the middle classes, a diverse conglomeration that nevertheless shared tastes, social norms, and symbols.[12] It was thus a common culture, rather than a similar income level, that distinguished the Spanish bourgeoisie. This shared culture was clearly consumerist, promoting "aspirational and imitative lifestyles, which [we]re often financed through credit," and it soon spread through all sectors of Spanish society.[13] Although their numbers were modest, the middle classes wielded an enormous social influence in nineteenth-century Spain due to their active participation in the nation's political, legal, commercial, and academic institutions. As early as 1870, Galdós described Spanish modernity as "representada en la clase media" (represented by the middle classes) whom he deemed the directors of national politics and trade.[14] Unsurprisingly, then, the bourgeois way of life that had only recently appeared "became the hegemonic culture by the end of the century."[15]

Given the emergence of Spain's modern class system in the nineteenth century, class-based anxieties (how to ascend to a higher echelon or simply maintain one's social status and the veneer of respectability, how to relate to those above and below one's station, and what to do about poverty) abound in Spanish realist literature, particularly in the urban realism of Galdós's novels and many of Pardo Bazán's short stories. Notably, these works are generally narrated from a middle-class perspective, reflecting not only the authors' social milieu but also the bourgeois ascendency on the national stage, as well as specific economic conditions that produced a robust middle-class readership. On the one hand, realist fiction followed Galdós's directive to seek inspiration in the "fuente inagotable" (inexhaustible source) of the middle classes.[16] On the other, the dissemination of these texts was made possible by an economic boom from 1876 to 1886 that allowed for the commercialization of the publishing industry and gave rise to an affluent class with time for leisure reading.[17] Given the combination of subject matter and audience, these texts inevitably normalize bourgeois views and values, even while questioning and possibly contesting bourgeois lifestyles. Nevertheless, as Collin McKinney observes in *Mapping the Social Body*, "the normalized vision of society offered up by the middle class and its dominant discourses can be overcome by looking at the world with new eyes."[18] A new vantage point, I argue, is precisely what the fantastic short story offers. The works by Pardo Bazán, Escamilla, and Galdós examined here destabilize the middle-class worldview by drawing reader attention to spectral beings and relations that generally go unseen, thereby bringing into focus figures and forces whose existence bourgeois society glosses over, denies, or outright suppresses.

In light of the confluence between economic discourse and narratives of the supernatural throughout nineteenth-century Europe, it is unsurprising that specters abound in stories about wealth and the status that it affords. After all, the workings of liberal economies in which "invisible hands" adjusted supply and demand, and unseen stock market fluctuations could make or break fortunes readily lent themselves to supernatural analogy. The opening line of the *Communist Manifesto* (1848), "A specter is haunting Europe—the specter of communism," perfectly exemplifies how images of ghostliness colored economic philosophy of the period.[19] Marx's subsequent *Capital* (1867) further engages the language of spectrality in the discussion of fraught class relations under capitalism. In it, the German philosopher held that those objects commodified by bourgeois consumerism remain haunted by traces of the labor, and by extension of the workers, that produced them.[20] Thus, both Europe's fledgling free market economies and the social dynamics that they produced were often described as imbued with a spectral quality. At the same time, the "new, seemingly spectralised economy" played a key role in the Victorian ghost story, in which the pursuit of riches and social distinction often invoked the ghostly, as in the case of Dickens's *A Christmas Carol* (1843).[21] Just as the language of ghostliness enriched economic discussions in the nineteenth century, economic anxieties permeated supernatural fiction of the period.[22]

Whereas the ghosts of the Victorian Gothic tended to be literal spirits of the deceased, the Spanish stories featured here often engage with the questions of ghostliness and haunting in a wider sense, prefiguring the "spectral turn" of the 1990s, in which theorizations like Jacques Derrida's *Specters of Marx* (1993) employed the specter as a conceptual metaphor for any shadowy entity that might haunt the individual or community. Both "ghost" and "specter" have since come to be used interchangeably in the latter sense, which is how I employ them for the majority of this chapter. Key to this broadened concept of spectrality is the defiance of notions of certainty. Temporally speaking, specters are often described as an anachronism, "the appearance of something in a time in which they clearly do not belong."[23] Materially, the specter is defined as an "absent presence" that can be sensed, but not seized.[24] In both senses, these tenuous presences are marked by a sense of "undecidability."[25] They thus embody paradoxes that confound the structures we use to make sense of the world: the timelines and classificatory schema, including designations of social class.

Going one step further, María del Pilar Blanco and Esther Peeren describe the dividing lines between socioeconomic strata, as "themselves spectral, in the sense that they are based on retrospectively naturalized, performatively ingrained distinctions that require continuous rematerialization."[26] These boundaries are, like the ghost, an illusion of sorts, whose existence requires acknowledgment by others. The spectrality of class identity holds especially true for the Spanish bourgeois, who encroached on the aristocracy at one end of the social spectrum and bled into the working class on the other. Yet despite the invented-ness of class distinctions, socioeconomic status has an undeniable effect on people's lives, much like the power ghosts exert over the haunted. In light of these parallels, the ghost story has repeatedly been compared to Marxist discourse, in that both "provid[e] a paradigm for understanding the impact of unseen forces . . . their harm, and the constricting parameters within which they force us to live."[27] Without reducing the ghost story to economic philosophy, the tales discussed in this chapter further overlap with Marxist praxis in revealing the shortcomings of the capitalist ethos that informed middle-class practices in the nineteenth century.

Key to this social critique is the fantastic structure within which the ghost is introduced in each story. If the specter resists attempts at classification and understanding by simultaneously embodying opposing qualities (past and present, absence and presence), this fundamental "undecidability" is magnified in fantastic texts, which are by definition open-ended and ambiguous in their treatment of the otherworldly. The presence of the supernatural is neither fully confirmed nor denied outright, itself becoming a ghost-like possibility within the text. Fantastic ghost stories are thus doubly haunted, wrapping the fictional specter's ontological ambiguity in a layer of epistemological uncertainty. The story's characters, and with them the readers, must choose whether to believe in the supernatural intervention, and to do so requires scrutiny both of the specter and of the society that first produced and is now haunted by it.

The analyses that follow show that the ghost in and of itself does not necessarily challenge the existing social order, but that critical scrutiny of the ghost facilitated via fantastic framing reveals the cracks in dominant cultural narratives, signaling gaps and inconsistencies in bourgeois logic and hypocrisy in middle-class comportment. More specifically, the ghostly presences featured in "El antepasado" and "Los hilos" by Pardo Bazán challenge the idea that modernity as emblematized in the bourgeois classes is free from the injustices and immorality that had characterized feudal society, while the specters of Escamilla's "El número trece" and Galdós's "Una industria que vive de la muerte" reveal the social inequality endemic to nineteenth-century Spanish society by drawing attention to the material conditions of less privileged lives. Beyond their more obvious ghosts, the biggest haunting presence in these two stories is the promise of upward social mobility, which never materializes. Across these texts, the bourgeoisie fancy themselves haunted by decrepit aristocrats and diabolical workers, but they are largely haunted by their own moral corruption and refusal of introspection.

Haunted Narratives of Bourgeois Supremacy
PARDO BAZÁN'S "EL ANTEPASADO" AND "LOS HILOS"

In distilling the essence of the ghostly, spectral theory repeatedly emphasizes the quality of atemporality, commonly describing the specter as the ultimate anachronism. Ghosts are a vestige of the past appearing in the present "that seems to demand something of the future."[28] In nineteenth-century Spain, where the middle classes had recently risen to prominence, the past was often associated with the aristocracy, representatives of a toppled feudal order. In reality, Spanish nobles merged rather seamlessly with the bourgeois elite, intermarrying and mixing their finances to form an indistinguishable upper crust within Spanish society, but in the symbolic realm, they were obliged to cede before the new social order.[29] As Galdós describes in "Observaciones sobre la novela contemporánea en España," the aristocracy of the late nineteenth century lived "tan tranquila y pacífica en medio de una sociedad que ya no domina ni dirige, contenta de su papel" (so quietly and peacefully in the midst of a society that it no longer dominates nor directs, content with its role).[30] The middle classes were the nation's new protagonists, Galdós asserted, and bourgeois characters would signal the modernity of Spain's major realist novels, while the aristocracy were relegated to supporting roles.

In Spanish fictions of the supernatural, nobles often appeared in villainous roles, as was typical of the Gothic tradition starting with Horace Walpole's *The Castle of Otranto* (1764) and continuing through Bram Stoker's *Dracula* (1897).[31] Like these foreign examples, Gustavo Adolfo Bécquer's

Leyendas (1871; Legends) and Julia de Asensi's *Leyendas y tradiciones* (1883; Legends and traditions) are teeming with evil aristocrats, whose immoral behavior validated middle-class values by contrast.[32] Bécquer's "La cruz del diablo" (1860; The devil's cross), in which a wicked baron returns from the dead to terrorize his vassals, provides a classic example. The story is further notable for turning the aristocratic antagonist into a ghostly figure that simultaneously signals his outdatedness and his resistance to erasure. Like a specter, the nobleman belongs to a previous time but refuses to fade into obscurity.

Published almost forty years later, at the turn of the twentieth century, Pardo Bazán's "El antepasado," paints a similar picture of aristocratic degeneracy, but does so within a contemporary context. Though the protagonist reproduces the story of aristocratic decline and bourgeois ascendency in his family history, his life story, and even his own body, the transfer of power is depicted as far from simple and proves to be riddled with specters. "El antepasado" is almost exclusively known as part of Pardo Bazán's 1899 short story collection *Cuentos sacro-profanos*, but it first appeared the previous year in *Álbum salón* (Drawing room album), a Barcelona-based luxury periodical noted for the quality of its illustrations, although none accompany the text of Pardo Bazán's tale. Given that she was a frequent contributor there, Pardo Bazán's decision to publish "El antepasado" in *Álbum salón* is not exceptional. However, the story's message appears at odds with the journal's readership, described by the Spanish National Library as "la mayor parte de las familias aristocráticas y de la nobleza, incluida la Familia Real, las de los presidentes de casi todas las repúblicas hispano-americanas y . . . todas las personas de posición en España y América" (most of the aristocratic and noble families, including the royal family, those of the presidents of almost all the Spanish-American republics, and . . . all persons of standing in Spain and America).[33] What did these blue-blooded readers make of the story's less than flattering portrayal of the aristocracy?

Like most of Pardo Bazán's short stories, "El antepasado" contains multiple narrative layers. The main story is introduced within the context of a social gathering, in which Carmona, described as "nuestro proveedor de historias espeluznantes" (249; our provider of hair-raising tales), shares the account of his acquaintance with a young nobleman named Fadriquito Ramírez de Oviedo Esforcia, known to his friends as Fadrí.[34] Carmona describes him as a sickly gentleman with the eccentricity of never baring his neck in public, even while swimming. One day, Carmona manages to snatch Fadrí's neckerchief, uncovering a grotesque birthmark that resembles a bloody line encircling his friend's neck. Fadrí is then compelled to recount his family story. After five years of sterile marriage, his mother is sent far from the city to convalesce at Castilbermejo, an old castle owned by her husband's family. There, she grows obsessed with the rumor that an ancestor's decapitated head remains on the premises, eventually stumbling upon it just before her husband visits. Fadrí's mother suffers a nervous breakdown, and she is promptly removed from the estate. Nine months later, Fadrí is born with the unusual birthmark, which drives his mother mad. She dies under the care of Dr. Moyuela, "que prometió con su sistema, devolverle la razón" (250; who promised to restore her sanity with his system). Fadrí ends his narration by expressing fears about his own mental health.

"El antepasado" features three separate narrators: 1) a first-person narrator whose only intervention is to introduce Carmona, 2) Carmona, who describes Fadrí and their friendship, and 3) Fadrí himself, who reveals the secret behind his birthmark. Despite this multiplicity of voices, the text is clearly centered on Fadrí's family history, which can be read as an allegory for Spain's transition from the Old Regime run by the aristocracy to a liberal society based in bourgeois values. The first thing that readers learn about Fadrí is his noble lineage, as evidenced in his pompous family name Ramírez de Oviedo Esforcia. Carmona specifically emphasizes this mixed Spanish and Italian heritage as "evocador de nuestras glorias pasadas" (249; evoking our past glories), recalling Spanish rule over Naples, Sicily, Sardinia, and Milan during the Habsburg dynasty. Yet behind these "sonoros y heroicos apellidos" (249; resounding and heroic last names) lies a family history marked by domestic strife (Fadrí's father references an ancestor who had infamously poisoned his own mother) and egregious abuses of power (for which another ancestor was beheaded in the sixteenth century).[35] Thus, rather than view feudal society with nostalgia, the text foregrounds both the historic depravity of the nobility and the injustice of their status as above the law.

Moreover, if the nobility had once been tyrannical, in the present they are considered inconsequential in the face of the bourgeois ascendency. This shift is symbolized in the structure of Castilbermejo, which has transitioned from a medieval fortress and site of armed struggles to "una casa grande, cómoda, y apacible" (249; a large, comfortable, and placid house) typical of a bourgeois country estate.[36] "Ya no queda allí ni rastro de los tiempos crueles" (249; Not even a trace remains of the cruel [feudal] times), Fadrí's father assures his wife. Any holdovers from the castle's previous life languish in a state of disrepair: "En el estante más alto, hacinábanse objetos llenos de moho y de humedad, frascos de caza, monturas antiguas, papeles amarillentos" (250; On the highest shelf, there were heaped up objects full of mold and humidity, hunting bottles, antique mounts, yellowed papers). Clearly these decaying objects belong to a bygone era.

The same could be said of the aristocracy, which in the nineteenth century "came to be seen as ethereal, decorative, and otiose in relation to the vigorous and productive values of the middle class."[37] This "feminization of the aristocracy," as Eve Kosofsky Sedgwick describes it, is symbolized in Fadrí's debilitated physical condition, which is perceived by his peers as unmasculine.[38] For instance, Carmona contrasts Fadrí's illustrious family name with his physical state as an "organismo débil y exangüe" (249; weak and bloodless organism) bearing an "empobrecida complexión" (impoverished complexion). He further describes Fadrí as "una criatura endeble, anémica, clorótica, de afeminado semblante, de ojos claros y transparentes como el agua, de dulce carácter y exquisita finura" (249; a rickety, anemic, greenish creature, with an effeminate demeanor, eyes pale and transparent as water, a sweet character and exquisite delicacy). As Gabriela Pozzi explains, the characterization of Fadrí as a "criatura," a feminine noun in Spanish, means all subsequent adjectives take the feminine form, thereby highlighting the gender that is pejoratively assigned to the nobleman.[39] Moreover, Fadrí's description echoes the language used specifically to describe hysterical women, such that the nobleman channels not only the womanly, but a pathological, deviant femininity.[40] He thus serves as the double of his mother, who was herself "enfermiza, nerviosa y de una exaltada sensibilidad" (249; sickly, nervous and of an exalted sensibility). Clearly, Fadrí is not alone in signaling the nobility's downfall through his weakened constitution, and the initial childlessness of his parents' marriage—blamed on his mother, though his father may well be responsible—depicts in literal fashion the idea of the nobility as unproductive in the post-Isabelline years.

Just as "El antepasado" captures the aristocracy's decline, however, it likewise depicts the dethroned nobility's lingering influence through the metaphor of haunting. The story's most obvious specter is the image of the severed head that haunts Fadrí's mother during her stay at Castilbermejo: "la idea de la cabeza cortada empezó a preocuparla día y noche, — de noche especialmente.— La veía en sueños, destilando sangre, y se despertaba estremecida, a las altas horas, como si un fantasma acabase de tocarla con mano glacial" (250; the idea of the cut-off head began to worry her day and night, —especially at night.—She saw it in her dreams, dripping blood, and she would wake up shaken, in the wee hours, as if a ghost had just touched her with its glacial hand). What torments Fadrí's mother here is not the head's material presence (of which she still remains blissfully unaware), but the possibility of its existence, that is, its spectrality. This ghostliness is further cemented in the reference to an icy phantom's touch. When she eventually chances upon the head, Fadrí's mother falls physically ill in a hysterical fit that manifests as nervous convulsions. It is no longer the dread of potentially discovering the appendage that terrifies her, but the horror of its physical proximity. In its material form, the desiccated head serves as an inescapable reminder of the nobility's—specifically her husband's family's—past misdeeds and their extrajudicial punishment. The subsequent birth of Fadrí with the gruesome mark around his neck recalls the beheaded ancestor and cements the lamentable history of the Esforcia line as a haunting presence on their descendants. The image of decapitation that the unusual birthmark evokes additionally summons the specter of the guillotine from the French Revolution, the paradigmatic European uprising against the nobility. Like the conversion of Castilbermejo, his parents' prolonged sterility, and Fadrí's own frail constitution, the mysterious markings that encircle his throat represent the toppling of the aristocracy in favor of a new social order.

As a fantastic text, "El antepasado" does not offer a definitive explanation for Fadrí's birthmark. It could just as easily be the supernatural imprint of the family past as it could be a coincidental medical oddity. A potential hybrid explanation posits the mark as a psychosomatic manifestation of his mother's obsessive thoughts during pregnancy. More important than the accuracy or even plausibility of each explanation, however, is how the interpretation that each character favors indicates his or her feelings concerning the shift from the Old Regime to a modern, bourgeois society. Fadrís's mother, for example, seems to view the mark as the sign of a continued ancestral influence on the family's present and even future. For her, the birthmark serves as a constant reminder of the violent misogyny and more generalized inhumanity found in her husband's family. It is a physical representation of the long shadow cast by the sins of his forefathers. This is particularly distressing for her because she is deemed unsuited for modern—which is to say urban, bourgeois—life, and has been ordered to adopt the rustic lifestyle of "a simpler time" removed from the city, only to discover that the past is horrific rather than idyllic, rife with scenes of injustice and terror. Fadrí's mother seems destined to die not from a nervous affliction, but from an inability to either embrace the changing times or make peace with a horrifying family record. She fails to successfully "live with" ghosts, as Derrida prescribes, instead succumbing to the weight of their history.[41]

Unlike his mother, Fadrí chooses not to see the specter of the Esforcia imprinted on his skin. He gives no indication of believing the birthmark to be anything more than a physiological aberration, thus fashioning himself as a modern man who gives little credence to superstition. Accordingly, what haunts him is not his criminal forefathers, whose supernatural influence he denies, but the genetic predisposition to mental illness that he has supposedly inherited from his mother. He laments her death at Dr. Moyuela's convalescent home, specifically fearing that it sets a poor family precedent. Eager to avoid the same fate, Fadrí declares, "Yo necesito doble método y grandes precauciones . . . ¡Esas cosas se heredan!" (250, ellipsis in original; I need double the methodology and great precautions . . . These things are hereditary!).

In one of the story's revealing details, Fadrí's mother had tried to hide her obsession with the severed head from the service staff. "Comprendiendo, — porque era una señora de claro talento, — lo quimérico de estas figuraciones, no quería decir palabra de ellas a los que la rodeaban, ni preguntar por el cofre de terciopelo, recelosa de que se trasluciese su delirio en la pregunta" (250; Understanding, —because she was a woman of obvious talent,—the chimerical nature of these imaginings, she had not wanted to utter a word of them to those who surrounded her, nor inquire after the velvet box [containing the head], wary that her delirium be revealed in the question). Already subject to a regimen of boredom to increase her fertility, the pains she takes to conceal her all-consuming fears suggest resistance to further medical intervention, the most probable consequence of divulging her anxieties. Fadrí, on the other hand, has absolute faith in the medical establishment's restorative "systems," embracing the newly authoritative role of doctors in Spanish society. As Jennifer Smith explains, "medicine and hygiene became predominant forms of managing the population" in nineteenth-century Spain, such that doctors "began playing a larger role in social reform and politics."[42] In contrast with his progenitor, Fadrí's faith in the medical establishment shows his commitment to adopting a bourgeois mentality and adapting to bourgeois society. He is fully invested in eradicating any hold, spectral or otherwise, that the past may have on his existence, and chooses to tackle its most manageable manifestation. Thus, he fears the inheritance not of aristocratic immorality but of his mother's hysteria, which is certainly treatable and potentially curable. Ironically, however, Fadrí's mother meets her untimely end not in Castilbermejo, but under Dr. Moyuela's care, a turn of events that imparts a sinister tone to the doctor's ministrations. In spite of his promises to exorcise the ghosts that tormented her, his methods end up "curing" her to death, thus suggesting the price of progress by bourgeois standards.

In the story's first paragraph, Fadrí remarks that "no tengo quien me cuide . . . y he de cuidarme solo" (249, ellipsis in original; I have no one to care for me . . . and I must take care of myself). Not only is he orphaned in the literal sense, but the passing of his parents has symbolically dissolved his connection to any ancestors, whose ghosts he further banishes from his mind. Finding his mother's attempts to evade bourgeois society and its sanitary systems to produce disastrous, and in fact fatal, results, Fadrí fully embraces the present social order and its positivistic authorities, such as Dr. Moyuela. In so doing, Fadrí comes to represent the nineteenth-century nobility that melded with the upper middle class to form a blended "top layer of society."[43] Accordingly, Pardo Bazán's short story seemingly fortifies the bourgeois worldview by depicting the nobility's need to integrate into the new social order in order to survive.

As part of a fantastic fiction, however, the text's potential specters are never fully dismissed, and Fadrí's birthmark continues to suggest the intrusion of the past into the present. Historically speaking, the ghosts of the past were tenacious indeed, as the "aristocratisation of the bourgeoisie was more pervasive than the 'bourgeoisification of the imperious nobility.'"[44] The spectral elements of "El antepasado" reflect the messiness of attempts to separate aristocratic lifestyles from those of the emergent middle classes, thus challenging the nineteenth-century bourgeois narrative of a clean break with the past and clear deviation from previous structures of power and cultural norms. Fadrí's commitment to embrace bourgeois culture and trust its authorities, like Spain's dismantling of the Old Regime, is a conscious decision. Its dramatization within a fantastic narrative, which itself requires the reader to decide between the supernatural or the mundane, only emphasizes that the reality inhabited by Fadrí and his social circle is not the product of natural societal progression but of human choice, which inevitably bears flaws and contradictions.

Whereas "El antepasado" undermines notions of bourgeois modernity by introducing the ghosts of a lingering feudal order, "Los hilos" undermines any idealization of the bourgeois mentality by revealing the middle classes to harbor and thus be haunted by dark impulses and irrational fears. Notable among them was an incessant "preoccupation with social distinction" as befits a social group repeatedly described as amorphous and ill-defined, and that aped the aristocracy in the quest for cultural legitimacy.[45] As Leigh Mercer observes, "the production of the [Spanish] bourgeoisie is essentially one of outward display and visual perception; unlike the aristocracy, the middle class had to identify itself through external signs."[46] Anxiety surrounding the fledgling bourgeois identity could only be assuaged through the public affirmation of wealth and good taste, qualities thought to separate the middle from the working classes. Bourgeois distinction thus becomes a spectral quality that only exists in the eyes of others; it is perceptible but immaterial, all surface and no substance.

This lack of profundity further extends to public perception of the bourgeois lifestyle, particularly as enjoyed by the upper echelons of Spanish society. The bourgeois elites are repeatedly portrayed in literature of the period as occupied with a meaningless flurry of leisure activities designed to showcase economic privilege and cultural sophistication. Alongside emblematic realist novels such as Alas's *La Regenta* (1884–1885; The regent's wife) and Galdós's *Fortunata y Jacinta* (1886–1887), fantastic short fictions of the late nineteenth century likewise abound in well-to-do protagonists who are no more fulfilled for all the riches they possess or social engagements they attend. Pedro Escamilla's "La mosca" (1875; The fly), Julia de Asensi's "La casa donde murió" (1889; The house where she died), and Pardo Bazán's "La máscara" (1897; The mask) provide representative iterations of the bored bourgeois archetype.[47] Unlike their realist counterparts, however, these tales of the supposedly supernatural employ spectral language and imagery to denaturalize bourgeois legitimation of "a hedonistic culture that ultimately freed luxury of moral censure."[48]

For instance, Pardo Bazán's "Los hilos" employs an aesthetics of haunting to illuminate the materialism, commodification of human beings and relations, and self-interested hypocrisy plaguing the top tier of Spanish bourgeois society. Like "El antepasado," the story formed part of *Cuentos sacro-profanos*, but it first appeared in 1896 in the illustrated weekly *Apuntes* (Notes).[49] True to the prospectus of the publishing venue, which prided itself on its artistry, the original text featured three drawings by famed illustrator Álvaro Alcalá Galiano that have generally escaped critical notice.[50] The story begins with an intriguing piece of gossip: "Mucho se comentó la repentina *zambullida* de un hombre tan joven, festejado, rico e ilustre como Jorge Afán de Ribera" (italics in original; there was much discussion of the sudden 'plunge' of a man as young, celebrated, rich and illustrious as Jorge Afán de Ribera).[51] An unnamed first-person narrator then attempts to shed light on what had provoked his friend's sudden retreat from Madrid. After

Jorge meets an untimely end in a supposed hunting accident (pictured in the first illustration), the narrator uncovers a written confession (pictured in the second illustration) in which the deceased explains his social withdrawal. Following a spiritist session, Jorge had attended the theater (pictured in the third illustration, fig. 1.1), where he was haunted by visions of a web of strands connecting his various acquaintances and revealing their perverse passions and secret enmities. Horrified by the presence of these threads, Jorge chooses seclusion over a daily confrontation with "los bajos apetitos, las vilezas, las miserias de nuestra condición" (the dark desires, vile deeds, the miseries of our condition).

Prior to the theater scene, Jorge embodied the nineteenth-century archetype of the bourgeois gentleman afflicted by *ennui*. Like Fadrí from "El antepasado," he clearly belongs to society's top tier, bearing an illustrious lineage and socializing with the aristocratic and upper middle-class elite. Jorge possesses family wealth and the leisure time to spend it, such that he is known as "el más sociable de los vagos de Madrid" (the most sociable of Madrid's idle) who dedicate themselves only to "divertirse por todo lo alto" (amusement sparing no expense). His family's fortune is further signaled in the country estate to which he eventually retires, complete with spacious rooms and luxurious furniture. Even Jorge's seclusion does not preclude his reliance on a small army of service people, farmhands and shepherds who maintain the property.

However, despite being blessed with an enviable social position, Jorge's life lacks meaning. For one thing, his relationships are generally superficial. His two closest friends, the narrator and Paco Beltrán, laugh at the suggestion that Jorge might be in love, since "sus aventuras eran cosa pasajera, sin consecuencias" (his affairs were fleeting flings, of no consequence), and these same confidants admit to forgetting about Jorge after he leaves Madrid. Lacking authentic human connections, Jorge is consumed by boredom. This is what drives him to attend sessions for spiritism and hypnosis in the home of Kiriloff, secretary of the Russian Embassy, and when he tires of these, Jorge attends the theater in the story's climactic scene.[52] Ironically, in his quest for novelty, he gets more than he bargained for. Jorge begins to see the story's titular phantom threads, which haunt him with their revelation of the twisted wishes and rivalries that infest society's upper crust.

Through the disquieting strands, the hypocrisy of the bourgeoisie is placed on full display. The married Countess of Saravia, whose beauty is surpassed only by "su intachable reputación y la dignidad de su porte" (her impeccable reputation and the dignity of her bearing), is linked by a flaming red thread to Madrid's most degenerate Don Juan type, signaling an ill-fated love for him.[53] The politician X feels an intense hatred for and desire to betray his own mentor, as revealed in the black cord connecting the two. The newlywed Eloísa D is connected to an aged and decrepit general by a "repugnante" (repugnant) green thread, denoting her monstrous lust, and longtime friends A and B are revealed to be frenemies linked by an ominous strand that represents the deep-seated envy each feels toward the other. Across these examples, appearances turn out to be deceiving, bourgeois propriety is shown to be a façade, and the bonds of mentorship, marriage, and friendship are rendered meaningless.

This idea is heightened by the fact that Jorge first observes the threads while attending the theater, a space expressly designated for the performance of false sentiments and relations. By staging the appearance of the strands there, the text underscores the theatricality of bourgeois society itself, in which sincerity is scarce and playacting all too common. Jorge's eventual fear that he, too, may be the recipient of scandalous threads "de las personas a quienes creía yo inspirar algún afecto puro y generoso" (from those people in whom I believed I inspired some pure and generous affection) makes readers question the warm greetings extended to him by men and women alike upon his arrival at the theater. The speed with which he slips from the minds of even his closest friends once he retires from Madrid's social scene suggests that Jorge's fears are not unfounded.

Beyond shedding light on the falsity of human relations among the upper middle class, the space of the theater further highlights the bourgeois obsession with outward appearances, particularly as concerns the public performance of socioeconomic status. Contemporary critics were quick to note that the theatergoers themselves comprised a spectacle that at times surpassed the action on stage. Theater reviews of the period often included critiques of "the public attending the spectacle—if they displayed good or bad taste, civility or rudeness, elegance or vulgarity."[54] Evidently, the middle classes had entered "a new era of visuality and performativity" in which the correct enactment of theatergoing behavior could serve as confirmation of an attendee's social standing.[55]

All this is evident in Alcalá Galiano's third and final illustration for the story (fig. 1.1) that visualizes the space of the theater. Interestingly, this is the least faithful illustration of the series in that it does not expressly reproduce a scene from the text. Whereas in the story Jorge's horrific discovery of the phantom threads dominates the theater scene, the accompanying image showcases a quartet of contented youths in balcony seats, foregrounding

FIGURE 1.1. Illustration by Álvaro Alcalá Galiano from "Los hilos," in *Apuntes*, año 1, no. 17. Image courtesy of the Biblioteca Nacional de España, Madrid, Spain.

a young lady busy peering through binoculars. Each of the four individuals pictured is looking in a different direction, such that they appear less engaged with the performance on stage than with the scene comprised of their fellow attendees. The finery of their dress, intentionally selected to symbolize their wealth and good taste, suggests that they came not only to people watch, but to be seen as well. Thus, although the illustration does not correlate to any specific passage of Pardo Bazán's text, it strengthens the story's critique of a bourgeois "theater of behavior," in which distinction must be continually enacted within public view.[56]

Because the performance of bourgeois identity was so often tied to "public monetary displays" such as fancy dress or balcony seats, it is unsurprising that the middle classes should fixate on the acquisition of wealth to the detriment of cultivating genuine interpersonal relationships.[57] This is particularly evident in two of the ghostly threads that Jorge spies in the theater. In one instance, a golden thread originating in the forehead of Chuchú Cárdenas—a sixteen-year-old angel with "un rostro matizado por el rubor y aureolado por la candidez virginal" (a face tinged by a natural blush and surrounded by the halo of virginal naivety)—links her to the "opulento negociante" (opulent businessman) Rodón. The thread's color and its destination in Rodón's pocket denote that Chuchú is planning to trade her beauty (and likely her prized virginity) for riches, overlooking that the suitor in question is "calvo como una bola de billar y algo contrahecho" (bald as a billiard ball and somewhat hunchbacked). Aspiring neither to true love nor even to a lustful affair, Chuchú recognizes the social value ascribed to the possession of money, and chooses to parlay her looks into an advantageous financial standing.

In an even more chilling example, a dark and macabre thread runs from the youthful K to his own father, "que no acababa de morirse y dejarle su herencia" (who just would not die and leave him his inheritance). Even filial piety dissolves before the harsh reality of economic self-interest. Glossing Georg Simmel's *The Philosophy of Money* (1900), Michael Iarocci states, "To the extent that money increasingly mediates social relations . . . the social sphere in fact becomes a rationally intelligible web of connections."[58] However, "Los hilos" demonstrates that while a capitalistic emphasis on profit rationalizes human interactions by devaluing affective ties, doing so brings to the fore perverse instincts that society is not prepared to acknowledge. This is exemplified in Jorge's seclusion—and possible suicide—when faced with the revelatory threads.

As a true fantastic text, "Los hilos" allows readers to decide for themselves whether the threads that haunt Jorge exist outside of his mind. The story offers multiple possible explanations for the protagonist's vision. In one version, the threads are real. Hypnosis has allowed Jorge access to things that exceed the limits of current human comprehension, which he attributes to "causas físicas que ignoramos aún" (physical causes of which we remain ignorant). At the same time, the threads could be a product of Jorge's exalted imagination. In a placebo-like effect, Kiriloff's attempt at hypnosis could have produced Jorge's hallucinations through the sheer power of suggestion. The afflicted protagonist reflects, "sin duda la excitación que tales jugueteos con el mundo invisible causaron en mi sistema nervioso fue honda y funesta" (without a doubt the excitement that such dabbling with the invisible world caused in my nervous system was deep and terrible). As a final possibility, the threads could be the product of mental illness, which seems to be the explanation favored by Jorge's two friends. Disturbed by his written confession, Paco wonders, "¿Crees tú que estaba loco?" (Do you think he was crazy?). The narrator's answer of "loco lúcido" (a clearheaded madman) mitigates but does not deny the diagnosis.[59]

The suspicion of madness has long colored the duo's perception of their reclusive friend. They first write off his seclusion as the result of some mood disorder, "uno de esos males del alma que no tienen nombre conocido, y que así pueden impulsar al suicidio, como al claustro o al manicomio" (one of those illnesses of the spirit that lack a known name, and that could drive one to suicide, just as it could to the cloisters or the madhouse). This initial reference to suicide resonates throughout the entire text, as various passages suggest that Jorge's demise was no mere accident. First, there is the vague wording that announces his death: "se le había disparado la escopeta a Jorge Afán, había recibido el plomo en el vientre y se hallaba expirante" (a shotgun had gone off at Jorge Afán, he had received the shot in his abdomen and was on the verge of expiring). Although the passive construction of "se le había disparado" ("had gone off at") is common in Spanish, it generally indicates an attempt to skirt questions of responsibility. Its usage here leaves readers to wonder whether the wound was truly unintentional. The suspicion of suicide resurfaces at Jorge's wake, when the narrator expresses continued puzzlement that the deceased "voluntariamente había truncado su existencia social" (had voluntarily cut short his social existence). The narrator's particular wording here describes Jorge's withdrawal as a social suicide, seemingly foreshadowing his eventual demise. Further stoking this suspicion, the document in which Jorge describes the threads is couched as a postmortem confession, and expressly states that his seclusion is a means to "conservar algunas ilusiones, sin las cuales no es posible vivir, a no ser en el infierno..." (ellipsis in original; preserve some hope, without which it is impossible to live, unless it is in hell...). This foreboding final phrase, coupled with the murky circumstances of Jorge's accident, imply that the protagonist was ultimately unable to bear the presence of the phantom threads and the ugly truths about bourgeois society that they revealed. At the least, it allows the narrator and Paco to dismiss their friend's death as the understandable consequence of a disturbed mind.

In "History and Hauntology," Jo Labanyi lays out three ways in which individuals and societies respond to ghosts, which she defines as "victims of history who return to demand reparation."[60] She elaborates, "One can refuse to see them or shut them out, as the official discourses of the state have always done... One can cling to them obsessively..., allowing the past to take over the present and convert it into a 'living death.' Or one can offer them habitation in order to acknowledge their presence," making peace with the past and "liv[ing] with its traces."[61] The spectral threads haunting Jorge in "Los hilos" are not the ghosts of the disenfranchised that Labanyi references, but they elicit the same potential reactions of denial, obsession, or acknowledgment. And as a fantastic text, the story dramatizes both the obsessive and dismissive options, allowing for a choice between the two. Like Fadrí's mother in "El antepasado," Jorge cannot unsee the phantoms that disturb his peace, nor is he able to accept the unflattering reality that they expose. Instead, he appears overwhelmed to the point of death by the vision of hypocrisy running rampant through Madrid's high society. In contrast, his friend the narrator chooses to write off the ghostly web connecting their peers as a product of Jorge's mental instability, thus pathologizing the protagonist's vision much like Fadrí does with his mother. In both texts, the principal storytellers (Jorge's unnamed friend in "Los hilos" and Fadrí in "El antepasado") have little motivation to interrogate a socioeconomic system in which they form part of the privileged elite. Accordingly, they eschew critical examination of their social milieu and the introspection that such questioning entails.[62] Having seen the struggles of friends (Jorge) and family (Fadrí's mother) whose eyes were opened to inconvenient truths, they take the path of least resistance, rejecting the specter as a supernatural manifestation and favoring the explanation of madness, which can be cured or contained from within—and without detriment to—the bourgeois order. Thus, each story pits an unhealthy obsession with the specter and the societal shortcomings it visualizes against their outright denial. Like the story's characters, readers, too, may choose one or the other option, but standing outside the fiction, they alone are allowed the third alternative outlined by Labanyi: to acknowledge the ghosts plaguing bourgeois society without succumbing to them.

What Haunts the "Other Half"
ESCAMILLA'S "EL NÚMERO TRECE" AND GALDÓS'S "UNA INDUSTRIA QUE VIVE DE LA MUERTE"

In the two texts by Pardo Bazán examined thus far, the haunted individuals (and those who tell their tales) have belonged to the top tier of nineteenth-century Spanish society. The ghosts that plague them interrogate the premises of progress that underlie the bourgeois order, and the rejection of these phantoms by the stories' principal narrators serves as an act of affirmation that all remains well in their social circles. Nevertheless, readers are left perturbed by the stories' specters, the deaths they seemingly cause, and the societal tendency to rationalize them through the designation of madness.

There is something unsettling, both stories suggest, beneath the surface of bourgeois society. Indeed, as an optical illusion of sorts (the ghost appears, but has no real material presence), the specter complicates bourgeois narratives of modernity in part by signaling the gap between appearances and reality. This revelation is understandably disturbing for those belonging to the privileged middle classes, who are invested in maintaining their image as the champions of a new and improved social order.

For those of more modest fortunes, the disconnect between appearances and reality is felt more acutely in their daily lives, as illustrated in the following two tales: Escamilla's "El número trece" and Galdós's "Una industria que vive de la muerte." As the selection of short stories analyzed throughout this book attests to, the majority of fantastic fictions from late nineteenth-century Spain center on Madrid's high society. "El número trece" is thus exceptional for following a protagonist from the lower rungs of the bourgeoisie. Accordingly, the specter that haunts him exposes truths specific to the lower middle classes, illuminating in particular the fundamental contradiction between lofty bourgeois dreams and limited financial means that complicates the lower middle-class condition.[63]

As with almost all of Escamilla's fantastic writing, "El número trece" was published in one of the more affordable Spanish weeklies, the aptly named *El Periódico para todos* (The newspaper for everyone), in 1879.[64] The publication's accessibility to a broad readership may have affected the author's decision to feature a protagonist that would be more relatable to audiences outside of a limited social elite. Framed within a first-person narrator's musings on the irrationality of superstition, the story follows the life of Juan García, which is marked by a series of unfortunate incidents related to the number thirteen. Such is his aversion to the unlucky number that when he wins the lottery with a ticket numbered thirteen, he refuses to claim his prize of 32,000 *duros*, in spite of living in near indigence. In an effort to survive, Juan seeks employment, but to no avail. Cast out of his apartment and with nowhere to turn, he is eventually driven to claim his fortune, but with the prize money still fresh in his pocket, Juan's carriage is struck by another, and he is killed immediately.

"El número trece" could be summarized as a tale about an average Joe with terrible luck; at least, this is the story that the narrator seems intent on telling. From the first mention of his name, the generic Juan García, Escamilla's protagonist is painted as an everyman of average intelligence who "hizo todo aquello que hace la humanidad cuando viene al mundo" (187; did everything that humanity does when it enters the world). The one distinguishing factor in his life is his unwavering conviction that he is haunted by the ominous influence of the number thirteen. Every major misfortune that befalls him seems connected to the dreaded number: at thirteen, he breaks his leg, and spends over a month bedridden; as a grown man, he is shot thirteen times during military service, into which he was drafted with the number thirteen; his engagement to a lovely young woman aged twenty-six (which he views as thirteen doubled) is broken by her father; and he dies when his coach, paid for by the lottery prize from betting on thirteen, collides with carriage number thirteen.

However, the narrator goes to great lengths to dismiss any supernatural explanation for these events, assuring readers that Juan is victimized only by his own superstition. The narrator commences by explicitly stating that the story is not meant to confirm the veracity of Juan García's superstition. He declares, "voy a contaros una historia verídica, aunque no lo parezca, de la cual me guardaré muy bien de sacar la consecuencia de que el trece es un número siniestro" (187; I am going to tell you a true story, although it may not appear so, from which I will make very sure not to reach the conclusion that thirteen is a sinister number). In fact, he repeatedly speaks of the protagonist's fears as puerile, describing them as an "exageración hasta lo último" (187; exaggeration taken to the extreme) and "estúpida preocupación" (187; stupid preoccupation). At the same time, it is the narrator and not Juan who draws attention to the number thirteen painted on the out-of-control carriage that ends Juan's life. The protagonist is not even aware of this final coincidence, which the narrator proclaims in dramatic fashion through the use of capital letters and exclamation points: "El carruaje que había atropellado al suyo llevaba . . . ¡EL NÚMERO TRECE!" (188, ellipsis in original; The carriage that had trampled his own bore . . . THE NUMBER THIRTEEN!). This emphatic final utterance cements the story's fantastic nature, as it leaves readers unsure of whether the narrator now concedes a fatal influence to the dreaded number, or if he is merely aiming for a dramatic closing effect. Such uncertainty regarding the narrator's position forces readers to form their own conclusions, which requires closer examination of the causes underlying the calamities that befall Juan García.

While some of his misfortunes can be chalked up to bad luck (the broken leg) or paranoia (the broken engagement), Juan's socioeconomic status plays an undeniable role in the life-threatening incidents. Although the narrator universalizes Juan's childhood, the protagonist very clearly belongs to a specific social group: the lower middle class. Each of his life experiences that the narrator recounts reveals that Juan grew up in a family free from financial need, but modest in its expenditures. He first attends school at the age of six, where going hungry was a punishment for bad behavior rather than a circumstance of poverty. At the age of thirteen, he enjoys the luxury of free time, playing rather than working outside of school hours.[65] Moreover, he can afford to convalesce at home for more than a month upon breaking his leg. Juan even goes to the theater with his family, though it is a remarkable, rather than a regular, occurrence.[66] Beyond their financial solvency, however, Juan's family appears to wield no social clout. Although he is approved as a suitor for a respectable young woman, he has no family connections to fall back on when seeking employment.

This lack of wealth and status at the familial level is at least partially responsible for his near-death experience in the army. After all, the narrator prefaces Juan's stint as a soldier by explaining that military service is only obligatory for "todo aquel que no tiene ocho mil reales, o que no los quiere dar" (187; all those who don't have 8,000 *reales*. Or who don't want to hand them over). By drawing attention to the selective nature of the draft and noting that a generous payment was the sole means to elude it, the narrator underscores the role played by Juan's socioeconomic background in sealing his fate. Although not every soldier will be shot while in service, the danger of injury is real, particularly since Juan's service coincided with the start of the Hispano-Moroccan War. Juan may blame the thirteen shots that he eventually sustains on his draft number or the date on which he was discharged, but it is his lack of financial resources that first places him in harm's way.

Likewise, financial need drives him to play the lottery upon his reintegration into civil society. As a grown man no longer supported by his parents—an early allusion to older brothers suggests that perhaps there is not enough family wealth to go around—Juan is a prototypical *pobre vergonzante* (shameful poor person), described by Inma Ridao Carlini as an impoverished member of the middle class "defined by the discrepancy between their economic situation and their perceived social status."[67] Although he lives in a constant state of poverty, lacking the means to cover basic necessities, he does not eschew bourgeois social pretensions, maintaining both a disdain for manual labor and a taste for luxury that will contribute to his demise. In Juan's estimation, his death is foretold when he wins the lottery inadvertently betting on the number thirteen. Juan's landlady had placed the bet at his behest, choosing the number without his knowledge, and he is convinced that the money won by the ill-fated number "debía causar su perdición" (187; would lead to his ruin). Yet as in the case of his military service, where the protagonist fixates on the ubiquity of the number thirteen rather than the socioeconomic circumstances that landed him in the army, what compels Juan to play the lottery is likewise his lower middle-class condition.

Upon breaking his engagement to a modestly wealthy young lady, the protagonist loses the promise of economic security, and must seek alternate means of income. Logically, he searches for employment, but only considers positions that he deems appropriately dignified for a member of the middle classes. He first seeks a position as a doorman, "especie de ocupación para la que se consideran aptos todos los que han servido [en el ejército]" (187; a type of occupation for which those who had served [in the army] were considered suitable). When there are no vacancies, "Quiso ser cartero, repartidor de novelas y esquelas de funeral, criado de alguna congregación . . . Pero todas las puertas se le cerraban, porque aquella clase de destinos estaban entonces encomendados a personas dignas que no daban lugar a una cesantía" (187, ellipsis in original; He tried to be a mailman, a distributor of novels and obituaries, the servant of some congregation . . . But all doors closed on him, because that class of destinies were at the time entrusted to respectable people who were not moved by unemployment). Ironically, these socially acceptable positions barely rise above the manual labor that defined the working class. Yet there remains a dividing line, albeit tenuous, that Juan refuses to cross. In rejecting professions perceived to be beneath him, regardless of their ability to ameliorate his living conditions, Juan displays the pathological middle-class fear of downward slippage, which has material consequences for the protagonist's life.

Rather than betray his meager class status, Juan pins his hopes on the lottery—a risky endeavor with few chances of turning a profit. Even in times of pressing financial need, he plays the lottery religiously (187).[68] At one particularly low point, Juan indulges in an entire lottery ticket (generally split among several investors) in an act that the narrator likens to "quemar las naves" (187; a burning of the ships). Though at first he refuses to claim the prize, given his misgivings about the ticket number, Juan is eventually compelled to do so by his increasingly dire situation of homelessness and starvation: "Juan estaba hambriento, sediento, cansado, mal vestido, sin acostarse hacia ya algunas noches . . . ¿Qué importaba cobrar con el número trece, si de lo contrario iba a morirse de hambre y de miseria?" (188; Juan was hungry, thirsty, tired, poorly dressed, without sleep since a few nights ago . . . What did it matter if he got paid with the number thirteen, if otherwise he was going to die of hunger and misery?). Thus, it is his economic precarity that drives him to first play the lottery and then collect the winnings despite his superstitious reservations; and this sudden wealth finances the carriage ride that ends in his death.

While financial need motivates Juan to buy the lottery ticket that sets him on the path to his doom, his use of the proceeds to hire a carriage is almost entirely inspired by the bourgeois tendency toward conspicuous consumption. Juan's newfound wealth is meaningless without public acknowledgment, and the compulsion to flaunt his riches overrides even his hunger, as he immediately indulges in a previously inaccessible luxury. "La fiebre del dinero fue entonces superior en él a la fiebre del hambre" (188; The fever of money was at the time stronger in him than the fever of hunger), the narrator describes. "Quiso gastar, tirar, derrochar, desquitarse en un día de lo que había sufrido durante un año. Al efecto tomó un coche de plaza y se hizo conducir por Madrid sin dirección fija, sólo por el placer de insultar al que no tuviese tanto dinero como él" (188; he wanted to spend, squander, waste, recover in one day from what he had suffered during a year. To that effect he took a coach from the plaza and he ordered it to drive him about Madrid without any fixed direction, only for the pleasure of insulting he who did not have as much money).

Lacking a destination, Juan boards the vehicle purely as a public display of his recently acquired fortune, since carriage rides were an obvious signifier of socioeconomic status in nineteenth-century Spain.[69] Journalist Antonio Flores's 1853 article "El omnibus y la calesa" (The omnibus and the buggy) illuminates Juan's reasoning by stating that he who rented a private carriage instead of taking the omnibus "no tanto le [sic] alquilaba por ir de prisa y cómoda, cuanto por llevar pegado su cuerpo a una prenda de lujo y presentarse al público sobre un trono de esplendor y de magnificencia" (was not renting it so much to go quickly and comfortably, as to have a token of luxury pressed to his body and to present himself in public on a throne of splendor and magnificence).[70] What makes this conspicuous consumption particularly disturbing in "El número trece" is that Juan derives sadistic enjoyment from insulting the less fortunate through his ostentatious show of wealth. With money in his pocket, Escamilla's protagonist immediately disdains the have-nots, in spite of his own recent destitution, suggesting that the acquisition of wealth instantaneously perverts the individual's, and by extension his entire class's, sense of morality.[71]

Given the haughtiness that Juan develops upon claiming his prize money, it would be easy to read Escamilla's tale as moralizing. After all, the narrator judges the newly affluent Juan to be "loco, frenético" (188; crazy, frenetic), insinuating that the protagonist's downfall was not written in the stars, but instead resulted from his own poor choices. His death in the very vehicle that was meant to show off his rise in socioeconomic status thus seems an act of poetic justice. Readers should recall, however, that this same narrator does not register Juan's class status, but rather universalizes the protagonist's background as unexceptional. It follows that he should characterize Juan's questionable decision-making as an individual moral failing without considering his condition as a *pobre vergonzante* of limited means who is steeped in a superficial culture with lavish tastes.

However, "El número trece" does not merely censure Juan's bad behavior but shows his actions to be shaped by dominant cultural narratives, which the story exposes through fantastic means. The number thirteen looms phantom-like over the protagonist of Escamilla's tale, seemingly accounting for Juan's lifelong suffering, but no unearthly influence goes unquestioned within a fantastic text, particularly one in which the narrator explicitly warns against giving credence to superstition. The text thus encourages readers to seek alternate explanations for the misfortunes that befall Juan. Closer inspection reveals that the ill-fated number almost always appears while the protagonist partakes in activities dictated by his socioeconomic circumstances. Thus, the protagonist's lower middle-class status emerges as potentially wielding the most haunting influence over his life. Even when uncoupled from the number thirteen, the compulsion to keep up appearances and lack of economic resources characteristic of the lower middle classes spawn multiple ghosts that haunt petty bourgeois society as pictured in Escamilla's short story. Those who share Juan's station in life are constantly preoccupied with attempts to materialize phantasmal illusions and identities, whether it be through a quasi-superstitious belief in social mobility via the lottery, or the public performance of a constructed class identity. These fantasies of social ascent and even the bourgeois label itself turn out to be additional ghosts that the story's narrator cannot dismiss so easily.

Social mobility is similarly a pipe dream in Galdós's "Una industria que vive de la muerte," which like "El número trece" turns away from the socioeconomically privileged. By focusing on, and progressively spectralizing, a manual laborer within the context of a cholera epidemic, the story allows a particularly insightful glimpse into the marginalization of the working class, particularly in times of crisis. If bourgeois ascendancy required the unseating of the aristocracy, however nominal their toppling was, it likewise required the existence of a working class whose labor could sustain middle class consumerism in Spain's major cities. Inevitably, Spain's working class mirrored the bourgeoisie in numerous ways: it was small, predominantly urban, and far from uniform in composition.[72] Beyond the factory workers often associated with the term "working class" in the nineteenth-century context, there were artisans and other manual laborers working in specified workshops and within the home, where women in particular were often employed.[73] And just as the bourgeois emulated the aristocracy, the working class aspired to middle-class lifestyles. In fact, as "El número trece" illustrates, the line distinguishing the lower middle class from the working class was ill-defined at best.[74]

Even so, Escamilla's story also demonstrates that this distinction was crucial, since respectability was thought to end with the middle classes. Workers were often conflated with beggars and criminals to form a collective threat to Spanish society. Conceived as belonging to an unsavory lower class, workers were an integral part of the "social question" that was widely debated in the late nineteenth-century Spanish press, where opinions were constantly traded on the problem of urban poverty. Although Galdós's 1885 article "La cuestión social" (The social question) lamented the "estado aflictivo de las clases populares" (afflicted state of the popular classes) whom he depicted as "honrados obreros" (honest workers) seeking employment to no avail, Madrid's working class was often viewed as unhygienic and immoral, and described with a rhetoric of contamination.[75] The organization of labor and the occasionally violent confrontations that ensued only exacerbated public concern at the turn of the century.[76] Proposed solutions to urban poverty thus engaged "questions of social justice as well as of social control," and even as philanthropic reform sought to ameliorate the conditions of working-class life, it likewise served to contain the threat posed by the politicization of workers.[77] The question was, as Jo Labanyi states, "how could these excluded-but-included elements of the population be integrated ideologically without granting them full citizenship?"[78]

This dynamic of simultaneous inclusion and exclusion, or being selectively seen by mainstream society, lends the working class to spectral metaphor. Those who are relegated to society's sidelines for occupying nonnormative positions, including for socioeconomic reasons, have long been described in ghostly terms.[79] Moreover, since the publication of *Capital*, Marxist economic theory has "draw[n] attention to the occluded presence of labour within the production of commodities," such that the ghost of the worker could be thought to haunt all consumer societies.[80] Mainstream culture in post-Isabelline Spain was certainly obsessed with consumer goods and their display (both at points of sale and, once purchased, within the home/on the body), but manufacturing comprised a relatively small sector of the Spanish economy. As of 1877, only 11 percent of the Spanish workforce was employed in the creation of goods, as compared with around 48 percent in Great Britain.[81] Thus, whereas Bridget Marshall describes Gothic storytelling as "an effective means to depict workers struggling against the powerful forces of capitalism and industrialization" in the British tradition, the same cannot be said of Spain.[82] This is particularly the case for stories set in Madrid, which, unlike Barcelona or Bilbao, did not count among the nation's early industrial centers. The influx of migrants seeking opportunities in the Spanish capital was so poorly absorbed by Madrid's limited industrial structures that unemployment and mendicity skyrocketed there in the late 1800s.[83] Accordingly, Teresa Fuentes Peris observes that "most Madrid newspapers devoted more space to the beggar—or the unemployed forced into begging—than to the working classes."[84] Within this context, "Una industria" is noteworthy for featuring a working-class protagonist and employing spectral imagery to explore the role of labor within Spanish society.

"Una industria" was published only once in Galdós's lifetime, in 1865. It is often considered to be the author's first short story, and predates the appearance of his earliest novel *La Fontana de Oro* by five years.[85] Considering the story's content, its appearance on the pages of self-proclaimed "progressive daily" *La Nación* (The nation) is fitting.[86] Curiously subtitled "episodio musical del cólera" (musical episode of cholera), the story consists of three main narrative parts, divided into six sections. In part one (section I), the narrator explores the proposition that there is more beauty in unadulterated sound than in artful music, and illustrates this idea with examples of the evocative power of sounds such as the rustle of a silk dress or the twin thuds of a lady's shoes hitting the floor. Part two (section II) begins with the sound of a casket-maker's hammer, which leads into a lengthy description of the horrors caused by the very real cholera epidemic devastating Madrid in 1865. It is not until part three that the narrator states, "Entremos de lleno en nuestro cuento" (Let us fully delve into our story). What follows (sections III–VI) is the tale of a casket-maker who literally works himself to death, becoming the last case of cholera in the capital. Even in death, the hammer cannot be pried from his hands, and although at first the populace rejoices that the instrument's terrifying pounding has ceased, they are soon perplexed to hear the hammer's clang emanate from the casket-maker's grave as well as from the dead man's abandoned workshop.

Of all the short stories examined here, "Una industria" features the most traditional specter: the inexplicable hammering emanating from the defunct workshop is described as the product of an invisible hand, insinuating the deceased owner's continued presence there. At the same time, Galdós's tale deviates furthest from the traditional ghost story by focusing on the events leading up to the appearance of the ghost—that is, the cholera outbreak and its effect on the casket-maker's life—rather than on the subsequent haunting and its victims. In fact, the possibility of a ghost is not introduced until the story's conclusion (section VI). The theme of haunting, however, is a constant throughout the text. In a lighthearted and yet foreboding scene at the start of section III, the casket-maker's youngest son delights in draping himself with one of the black sheets in his father's workshop and scaring his siblings with phantasmal sounds. While such play is meant to demonstrate how little the casket-maker's chosen profession perturbs his family, it also foreshadows the man's impending death and potential conversion to a ghostly form.

The entire text of "Una industria" is further structured around a more metaphorical haunting—that of the capital by a deadly epidemic. Starting in section II, the short story narrates the plight of Madrid as besieged by the recent outbreak of cholera. In describing the city as "una población aterrada por una gran calamidad" (section II; a population terrified by a great calamity), the narrator casts the deadly illness as the tale's fearsome antagonist, which the casket-maker comes to personify.[87] His ceaseless hammering serves as a constant reminder of the cholera ravaging the community and, by extension, of the listeners' own mortality. Following the worker's demise, the narrator explicitly pronounces "aquel hombre era la personificación del cólera, y el cólera había muerto" (Section V; that man was the personification of cholera, and cholera had died), depicting his death as reflective of the epidemic's end.

The casket-maker's symbolic function is highlighted by his lack of individuality, an intentional move on the narrator's part. Although the creator of caskets is the clear protagonist of the story's second half, he is never named and is spoken of only through reference to his profession. The start of the story proper explicitly states that "nuestro personaje puede ser cada uno de los que esplotan [sic] la industria funeraria" (section III; our character can be each one of those who exploit the funerary industry), thus cementing the character's representative function. This declaration makes clear that beyond symbolizing the cholera running rampant through the capital, the casket-maker also stands in for those industries that have profited from the spread of the disease. Indeed, he is first presented in the text through the synecdoche of a disembodied "mano diabólica" (section II; devilish hand) occupied with "esplota[r] [sic] laboriosamente una industria que vive de la muerte" (laboriously exploit[ing] an industry that lives off of death) and "busca[r] la riqueza en el cólera" (seeking wealth in cholera) with an eye for "oro conquistado a la miseria" (gold conquered from misery). Each of these descriptors emphasizes the casket-maker's callous economic motivations, specifically criticizing the immorality of businesses seeking to profit from death and disease. It is therefore not his individual character that deserves censure, but his belonging to a "multitud de artesanos" (section II; multitude of artisans) who earn a living off of an "¡industria fatal, que florece al abrigo de la muerte!" (fatal industry that flourishes under death's wing!).[88]

Consequently, by the narrator's explanation, the casket-maker's diabolical hand was already haunting Madrid's populace long before his death. His incessant hammering stood for the cholera outbreak, as well as for unethical business practices driven by greed. From this perspective, readers can understand the narrator's proclamation that it is fair for those who survived the epidemic to rejoice at the casket-maker's death (section V); the man had served to represent both a physical and a moral plague upon the city. His potential reappearance in ghostly guise, then, could be read as an affirmation of his antagonistic nature. Even after death, the laborer will not leave Madrid's denizens in peace. Demonic in life, he becomes spectral after death.

However, despite the narrator's repeated reduction of the laborer to a symbolic role in a spectralization of sorts, the latter resists this narrative flattening. Both his words and his actions throughout the short story contradict his characterization as either cholera or avarice personified. Section III in particular individualizes and humanizes the laborer, rendering him sympathetic to the readers. For instance, the first full description of the character reads: "un hombre robusto y fornido . . . se ocupa en clavar unas tablas largas y estrechas de un extremo: su mano no descansa un momento: . . . su voz, trémula por el afán de concluir tareas interminables, interpela bruscamente a los oficiales que en torno suyo le prestan ardorosa colaboración" (a strapping and robust man . . . is busy hammering some boards that were long and narrow at one end: his hand does not rest for a moment: . . . his voice, tremulous due to the effort to finish interminable tasks, brusquely questions the apprentices who lend ardent collaboration around him). What we see is not a demonic being desirous of the death of his neighbors, but an industrious man of flesh and blood who is exhausted by his labor. He has, after all, worked ceaselessly without respite for the last eight days. Perhaps for this reason, the final description of the casket-maker's hand has evolved from the initial "diabólica" (section V; diabolical) to "pródiga" (prodigal), expressing awe for his productive capability.

The motives for the character's ceaseless construction further redeem him in the reader's eyes. The casket-maker reminds his daughters, "Vosotras aspiráis, sin duda, a salir de la posición en que nos encontramos. Queréis ser señoritas, vestir seda, ir a los teatros, arrastrar cola y llenaros la cabeza de perendengues" (section III; You aspire, surely, to get out of the position in which we find ourselves. You want to be ladies, dress in silk, go to the theater, sweep the train [of your skirts] and fill your heads with trinkets). This sense of paternal responsibility makes it difficult to view the protagonist as evil, and his supposed villainy is further contradicted by a sense of civic duty. When his daughters suggest that he at least reduce his workload, the father responds, "No: mi deber es equipar a todos los que mueren" (section III; No: my duty is to equip everyone who dies) further asking, "¿He de negar a mis semejantes este último mueble?" (Am I to deny my fellow man this final piece of furniture?). This response reveals the compulsion to provide a necessary good for his neighbors, rather than the desire for "oro conquistado a la miseria" (gold conquered from misery) that the narrator had described.

Given the commitment to serve his community, it seems particularly cruel that the casket-maker's neighbors, who work in "la industria que vive de la vida" (section III; the industry that lives off of life), refuse to construct a coffin for the man when he succumbs to the epidemic. Without a second thought, "los vecinos se meten en sus casas y los curiosos siguen su camino" (section IV; his neighbors enter their homes and the curious continue on their way). Not a single soul heeds the tearful pleas from the deceased man's daughters, who request assistance making a casket for their father. The narrator justifies this indifference by stating that "la vida no quiere encargarse de equipar a la muerte" (section V; life does not want to take charge of providing for death), but the neighborhood's postmortem treatment of the casket-maker nevertheless seems inhumane. He who dies aiding every deceased neighbor is denied the same consideration by his community.

Ultimately, the deceased worker is buried in his own handiwork, the most luxurious casket ever to emerge from his workshop. This masterpiece was intended for the Duke of X..., predicted to be the last case of cholera in the capital. The casket-maker had spared no effort in this creation, all the while lamenting, "Los ricos hasta en la muerte han de brillar más que nosotros" (section IV; Even in death the rich must outshine us). If he were himself wealthy, he would surely demand to be buried in "un ataúd tan suntuoso como este" (section IV; a casket as sumptuous as this one). Ironically, this wish is granted, since the laborer dies in the process of finishing the duke's order, while the nobleman unexpectedly recovers. Placed in his own magnificent creation, the protagonist seems to occupy it "con satisfacción" (section V; with satisfaction), or so states the narrator, suggesting that it is a fitting ending for the laborer.

Yet there is an undeniable poignancy in the story's final order of events. The fact that the duke survives the epidemic while the casket-maker does not is presented to readers as a surprising plot twist, but it is the expected outcome in a society where wealth and social status dictate each individual's possibilities, particularly during an epidemic.[89] As Nick Groom describes of cholera's stratifying potential, "It was the poor or seriously ill who were objectified in hospitals as collections of signs and symptoms; for the affluent infirm, private medicine at home remained the norm. In other words, medical treatment, good health and indeed life were an index of class and wealth."[90] Hence, the casket-maker's seemingly hyperbolic observation that even death distinguishes between those of differing social classes turns out to be accurate. At the same time, his dream of upward social mobility is shown to be pure fantasy, as it is only postmortem that he owns his first luxury good. Death precludes the casket-maker from enjoying any of the wealth that he has painstakingly accumulated during the pandemic and, more importantly, from watching his children do so.

Between fulfilling his parental and civic responsibilities, and the *pathos* of his demise, the casket-maker defies the unidimensional role assigned to him by the story's narrator. The latter's declaration that "justo era que los vivos se alegraran" (section V; it was just that the living rejoice) upon the protagonist's death likewise rings hollow. "Una industria" reminds readers, once again, that the storyteller in fantastic fiction should always be subject to scrutiny, as he or she shapes our interpretation of the story, and an awareness of inconsistencies in his or her account can drastically change our understanding of the recounted events. In the case of "Una industria," it is the narrator's elite bourgeois status, to which the casket-maker had futilely aspired, that leads readers to an alternate interpretation of the text.

Even if its narrative purpose remains up for debate, the discussion of sound that prefaces Galdós's story clearly serves to establish the narrator's class identity.[91] In this opening section, the speaker addresses "[al] amante de óperas y conciertos" (the lover of operas and concerts) familiar with German composers such as George Frideric Handel or Felix Mendelssohn. He goes on to mention operatic characters such as *La traviata* and literary figures from the works of Shakespeare, Goethe, and Hugo. Finally, the narrator illustrates the evocative power of sound with the image of a lady's silk dress gliding across the rug in a well-furnished abode. In each of these references, the narrator both affirms his identity as belonging to the upper middle class and directs himself to readers of the same social station. Clearly, he expects his audience to be familiar with both a lavish lifestyle and esteemed cultural references. This acknowledgment of the narrator's privileged status exposes potential biases in his judgments of the casket-maker, who occupies a much lower rung on Madrid's social ladder.

For instance, the narrator's bourgeois identity as revealed in textual references implies that both he and his imagined readers are steeped in a capitalist consumer culture driven by self-interest, which renders ironic any pejorative judgments of the casket-maker's business ethics. While the narrator singles out the casket-maker's profession as prioritizing profit above the collective well-being, the businesses that he does applaud are no less rapacious. At the start of section V, when the epidemic has ended and health and happiness have returned to Madrid, the city's convalescence is described as follows:

> El lujo reaparece en la tienda del joyero, del tegedor [sic] y del ebanista. Ostentan las flores artificiales su eterna frescura plantadas en un capote o en un sombrero, y los diamantes resplandecen sobre el fondo rojo de un estuche, cuyas dos tapas se abren como dos mandíbulas hambrientas. Desenvuélvense en los escaparates de la calle de Espoz y Mina pabellones de encaje, y blondas extendidas como una red, dispuesta a coger traviesos antojos femeniles . . .
>
> Luxury returns to the shop of the jeweler, the weaver, and the carpenter. Artificial flowers flaunt their eternal freshness on a cape or a hat, and diamonds shine against the red bottom of a jewel box, whose two sides open like two hungry jaws. In the shop windows on Espoz y Mina Street pavilions of lacework unfold and bits of silk lace extended like a net, arranged to catch restless feminine whims . . .

Although the creators and sellers of these decorative goods earn a living "off of life" and not "off of death," they are likewise depicted as predatory. The mandible-like sides of the jewel box are designed to devour the shopper's money, while the lace display is intended to ensnare unwitting passersby. In these descriptions, the consumer falls into the trap set by the merchant with the intent of taking shoppers' money. Nevertheless, "este despertar de las industrias que se alimentan de nuestra vida, se hace al compás alegre de martillos sonoros, cuyo timbre no nos horroriza, ni trae a nuestra mente otras imágenes que las de una felicidad" (Section V; this awakening of the industries that feed off of our life, takes place to the happy beat of resounding hammers, whose timbre does not horrify us, nor does it bring to mind other images than those of happiness). One wonders why these are described as happy rather than demonic hammers, if those businesses that profit "off of life" are no more scrupulous than the casket-maker's, and in fact seem less concerned with any sense of social responsibility.

No less provocative is the fact that the goods listed as products of the so-called "industries that live off of life" are decorative rather than essential, revealing the superficiality of bourgeois society, whose sole occupation appears to be the display of wealth. Moreover, the narrator describes the reappearance of plush furniture "elaboradas continuamente para satisfacer el capricho, la vanidad o la moda" (Section V; continuously manufactured to satisfy whims, vanity, or fashion trends) as indicating "la salud de la gran ciudad" (the health of the great city) thereby equating civic life with participation in the market for luxury goods from which their producers, like the casket-maker, are almost always excluded. It is therefore unsurprising that Galdós's narrator and his imagined peers show no empathy for the death of the working-class casket-maker. The laborer's lifestyle is wholly alien to the wealthy bourgeois, and even prior to his demise, he registers as more spectral than human in the narrator's eyes. Channeling the bourgeois perspective, Peñate Rivero sees Madrid as the victim of the casket-maker in "Una industria," concluding that "el relato presenta la oposición entre los intereses del fabricante y los de sus conciudadanos: la prosperidad del primero se asienta en la precariedad e incluso en la ruina de los segundos" (The story presents an opposition between the interests of the manufacturer and those of his fellow citizens: the prosperity of the former is secured by the precarity and in fact the ruin of the latter).[92] Yet considering the casket-maker's unending labor and eventual demise, we could easily argue that the opposite holds true: the well-being of bourgeois society, as measured in the availability of non-essential goods for purchase, depends on the economic precarity and ruin, oftentimes physical, of the worker. Viewed thusly, "Una industria" seems to allude to what Galdós would more explicitly articulate twenty years later, in his article "La cuestión social": "En estas catástrofes, el capital suele salvarse alguna vez, el obrero sucumbe casi siempre" (In these catastrophes [like a cholera epidemic], capital is sometimes saved, [but] the worker almost always succumbs).[93]

This reassessment of the narrator and the laborer that he judges so harshly inverts the story's purported victim and victimizer, which likewise affects how readers interpret the text's supernatural element. The seeming spectralization of the protagonist at the text's end can now be read as a symbolic act of resistance against a socioeconomic order that has no consideration for the working class. By this interpretation, the casket-maker may be invisible to society's upper echelons, but he defies erasure by announcing his presence through auditory means. Such a reading would align with Gordon's assertion that the ghost "has a real presence and demands its due, your attention," to notify us "that what's been concealed is very much alive and present."[94] Of course, as a fantastic text, "Una industria" does not favor any particular interpretation of the story's final specter. The phantom hammering could be caused by the casket-maker's malevolent or simply maligned spirit, but it could just as well be the projection of a community wracked with guilt for denying the deceased man assistance or even empathy. The possibilities proliferate, and once again it is each character or reader's investment in the dominant bourgeois culture that determines their response to the text's spectral figure. Whereas those who, like the narrator, subscribe to the bourgeois worldview may attribute a malicious intent to the protagonist, critical appraisal of the class dynamics between the narrator and his subject reveals the hypocrisy of Spanish bourgeois society, which values material goods but not their makers.

As the short stories analyzed in this chapter have shown, there is no set form for specters in nineteenth-century Spanish fictions. A disembodied head, a web of tangled relations, a number of ill omen, and even a disturbingly repetitive sound could all become haunting presences if they disturbed the peace of bourgeois society. What unifies them is not the shape they assume, but the victims they supposedly target. As Blanco and Peeren remind us, "ghosts are not interchangeable and it matters greatly (in terms of the effects and affects produced) in what guise they appear and to whom."[95] In the four tales featured here, the haunted individual or community has always identified itself with the dominant social group, whether they belonged to an aristocracy socially integrated with the bourgeois elite, or to the *pobres vergonzantes* on the verge of destitution. This is, of course, partially because their authors belonged to the middle classes and were most familiar with the bourgeois perspective. However, any sense of familiarity is quickly undermined by the fantastic storytelling in each text, which plants insurmountable seeds of doubt in the readers' minds. In the attempt to formulate their own interpretation of the haunting, readers must distinguish between the real and the unreal, truth and illusion, and at times victim and victimizer. Along the way, the myths of bourgeois modernity and exemplarity are also subject to scrutiny.

In unsettling these established narratives, the specter as featured in fantastic fictions becomes, in the words of Julian Wolfreys, "what is disorderly within an apparently straightforward temporal framework."[96] The specter not only embodies a past that will not be laid to rest, but also problematizes linear conceptions of progress at the societal level. This reading of the spectral as signifying a disrupted or disjointed modernity becomes particularly interesting in the context of nineteenth-century Spain, whose belated industrial development and comparatively small middle class has traditionally been perceived as "unmodern."[97] But rather than indicate a uniquely Spanish backwardness, the ghostly figures in "El antepasado," "Los hilos," "El número trece," and "Una industria que vive de la muerte" illuminate the pitfalls of equating modernity with the adoption of a bourgeois mindset that tends to pathologize or demonize one's family, friends, and neighbors in the quest to affirm an insecure—and indeed spectral—class identity.

CHAPTER 2

(En)Gendering Monstrosity

Questioning Gender Roles

If the specter is defined by incorporeality, the monster "inscribes alterity on the flesh," and nowhere were notions of alterity more obsessively discussed throughout nineteenth-century Europe than with regard to the question of gender.[1] Thus, monsters become an ideal vehicle through which to express fears of gender nonconformity in Victorian Gothic literature, as is well documented.[2] From Count Dracula's lascivious vampire harem to the bestial Mr. Hyde, Anglophone Gothic fiction of the late nineteenth century often portrayed a "slippage between sexual danger and supernatural danger," such that masculine or feminine deviance is itself viewed to be "as mysterious and frightening as the supernatural."[3] By demonizing these transgressive characters, the Victorian Gothic tended to reinforce traditional notions of masculinity and femininity, "us[ing] horror to encourage readers to stay on the normative path."[4]

This chapter traces how the trope of monstrosity likewise aids in establishing the limits of acceptable femininity or masculinity within fantastic short fictions from late nineteenth- and early twentieth-century Spain. First-person narrators in "El verano" / "Theros" by Galdós and "La mujer alta" by Alarcón cast women who deviate from the dictates of femininity as horrific, potentially inhuman beings. Yet because these stories are fantastic—refusing to definitively accept or reject the presence of the supernatural—any claims of monstrosity invoke a certain degree of skepticism, facilitating an interrogation both of the alleged monstrosity described and of the gender deviance that underlies it. Such scrutiny of both texts reveals the designation of monstrosity to be a misogynistic practice whereby women are judged against impossible standards. The sexism of Spanish society is confirmed in Galdós's novella *La sombra* and especially Pardo Bazán's "Vampiro," in which male characters are perceived to be monstrous for flouting masculine convention when their true inhumanity lies in their abhorrent treatment of women.

Whereas in realist novels the cover of mimesis draws reader attention to contemporary social ills, it is precisely the conjunction of nonmimetic elements in the works explored here—the interplay between otherworldly Gothic imagery and a fantastic narrative structure—that effectively captures the contradictions in dominant definitions of femininity and masculinity, and underscores problematic gender relations in post-Isabelline Spain. Through the suggestion, rather than certain knowledge, of the supernatural in these texts—the fantastic claim that "there *might* be a monster in this story"—these fictions depict a host of problems ranging from anxiety disorders to domestic abuse and even murder as rooted in a misogynistic gender binary shaped by bourgeois values that demonize nonconformists. Thus, in their spine-tingling aesthetics, the selected texts call into question the established hierarchies that shaped Spanish social life.

Gender Nonconformity as Monstrosity

In Spain, as elsewhere in Europe, men and women and their respective social roles were defined in rigid opposition to one another throughout the nineteenth and early twentieth centuries. As Thomas Laqueur details in *Making Sex*, a post-Enlightenment shift occurred in many Western societies from the classical one-sex model, which viewed women as imperfect versions of men, to a two-sex model, in which women became men's "incommensurable opposite."[5] Famed Catalan hygienist Pedro Felipe Monlau's *Higiene del matrimonio* (1853; Marital hygiene), which set the Spanish benchmark for marital guidebooks, confirms this oppositional binary in Spain by declaring an absolute "*polarización de los sexos*" (italics in original; polarization of the sexes).[6] Biological differences between men and women were thus believed to indicate an essential divergence between a rational male and sentimental female mind that predisposed each sex toward certain activities and primed them for gender-specific duties. This division was further reinforced by the consolidation of the separate spheres ideology, which accompanied industrialization and the establishment of liberal democracies across Europe. As cottage industries gave way to factories and storefronts, and notions of (male) citizenship were codified in new legislation, the home came to represent "an exclusively female, private, noncommercial space in opposition to an external, male, public world of work for wages."[7]

Women, viewed as the morally superior sex, were to embody the *ángel del hogar*, the Spanish correlate to the Victorian "angel in the house."[8] This entailed providing comfort for their spouses by maintaining the home as a clean, orderly and peaceful sanctuary from the outside world, while decorating it—and themselves—tastefully as a reflection of the family's financial and social status. Women's most important calling, however, was to bear and raise children, and to instill in them the sense of moral rectitude required of the next generation of Spanish citizens. Motherhood thus became the greatest civic duty of middle-class women in late nineteenth-century Spain, such that "until they exist[ed] as mothers, they d[id] not exist at all."[9]

Men, on the other hand, were expected to pursue professional endeavors outside of the home, and were judged on the basis of their "success in the marketplace and the accumulation of wealth."[10] While their financial standing influenced perceptions of their work ethic, productivity, and political and economic savvy, all qualities attached to bourgeois masculinity, success as a man also entailed communicating respectability in accordance with the social codes regulating polite society, including rules for fashionable dress.[11] However, even as bourgeois manhood was performed and confirmed in the public sphere, it maintained ties to the domestic refuge of the home. Men were expected to marry and engender offspring as "a patriotic duty," and their home lives and public accomplishments were assumed to reflect upon one another.[12]

The models outlined here were not the sole configurations of Spanish femininity and masculinity in existence from the dethronement of Isabella II through the early twentieth century. They were, however, the culturally dominant ones. Reinforced through medical and legal discourse, and reproduced in visual and print media, they were constructed as the most desirable iterations of manhood or womanhood within contemporary Spanish society.[13] Nevertheless, although these were the most visible gender models circulating during the period, they were not the most commonly embodied, and were in fact nearly "impossible for real bodies and subjectivities to achieve."[14] In an obvious example, working-class women lacked the material means to dedicate themselves solely to running the household; their need to generate an income precluded them from acting as domestic angels. Thus, Collin McKinney describes the reigning notions of gender within any society as "a socially endorsed fantasy" that reflect the desires of the most socially influential.[15] In late nineteenth-century Spain, the *ángel del hogar* and the respectable, self-made man were specifically male fantasies predicated on bourgeois values. As gender was codified in legal, medical, and cultural arenas run by men, the consolidation of normative gender roles became the story of middle-class men defining both the male selves that they aspired to be and the female companions that they aspired to have.

Though it may seem counterintuitive, the insistence on fixing idealized, bourgeois models of femininity and masculinity throughout the nineteenth century reveals the prevalence and persistence of challenges to the dominant gender ideology during the period. As Elaine Showalter proposes in *Sexual Anarchy*, "In periods of cultural insecurity, when there are fears of regression and degeneration, the longing for strict border controls around the definition of gender, as well as race, class, and nationality, becomes especially intense."[16] This was certainly the case in turn-of-the-century Spain, which continuously teetered on the verge of national crisis. Defending the status quo, including established gender norms, was perceived as a manner of staving off a Spanish downfall on the world stage. Some of the perceived threats to national stability explicitly questioned the reigning gender hierarchy, such as intensifying public debate on the state of women's rights (referred to as "the woman question"), and the nascent feminism of the late 1800s led by trailblazing figures like Concepción Arenal, Concepción Gimeno de Flacquer, and Emilia Pardo Bazán. As women slowly gained access to education and increased mobility in the public sphere, they distanced themselves from the myth of the *ángel del hogar*. At the same time, even the slightest female empowerment compounded a crisis of Spanish masculinity related to the nation's perceived decline as emblematized in its progressive loss of empire. As Joanne Nagel asserts, turn-of-the-century conceptions of masculinity in the United States and much of Europe "depended on a chauvinistic, militaristic nationalism" channeled into increased imperial pursuits.[17] Consequently, Spain's dwindling colonial holdings were equated with the nation's progressive effeminacy.[18] Additional factors common to Western Europe, such as the rise of socialism and anarchism in response to economic crises and labor unrest, or the appearance of new technologies, further destabilized traditional models of male dominance by threatening to collapse previously unchallenged boundaries, including class distinctions and even the space-time continuum.[19]

In *Marginal Subjects*, Akiko Tsuchiya details how pervasive fears of boundary collapse in nineteenth-century Spain found expression in an abundance of artistic representations of gender deviance.[20] Key among these were figures marked by gender indifferentiation, which Showalter describes as a form of "sexual anarchy" that was perceived as a harbinger of apocalypse.[21] As a symptom of generalized cultural anxiety, the effeminate man and the masculine woman were recurrent characters in literary production of the period. For instance, the uniquely Spanish figure of the *marimacho*, or "butch" woman, abounds in turn-of-the-century novels and periodicals that describe her as a "monstruosa combinación" (monstrous combination) of feminine and masculine traits.[22] To give one example, lawyer Pascual Santacruz derides *marimachos* as "seres incatalogables en los casilleros de la Zoología" (beings who cannot be classified within the categories of zoology), linking their non-traditional gender expression to the allegation of inhumanity.[23]

Both Santacruz's snide commentary and the stories discussed in this chapter highlight the fact that, given widespread belief in a biologically determined gender binary, femininity and masculinity in late nineteenth- and early twentieth-century Spain were defined not only in contrast to each other, but also in opposition to the concept of monstrosity. In addition to being perceived as unmasculine or unfeminine, aberrant gender embodiments were viewed as unnatural and even dangerous to society. Even those women whose defiance of the gender norm consisted of intellectual superiority were deemed "monstruos de talento y sensibilidad" (monsters of talent and sensibility) rather than prodigies.[24] In *Monsters by Trade*, Lisa Surwillo explains that the Western tradition designates as monstrous any individual "whom we wish to exclude from our community for physical, moral, or political reasons," categories that are commonly conflated with one another.[25] Those who deviated from established gender norms were considered monstrous for all three reasons listed by Surwillo: their gender nonconformity was expressed physically through the body (including dress and accoutrements, postures, and movements), perceived as a sign of moral perversion, and considered threatening to the traditional family structure that formed the basis of bourgeois society. Thus, figures such as the *marimacho* were easily viewed through a lens of monstrosity.

The link between gender deviance and monstrosity is not new to the nineteenth century. Dating back as far as classical antiquity, non-normative expressions of sex and gender were often associated with monstrosity and vice versa. On the one hand, supposedly aberrant displays of man- and womanhood were viewed as something to be feared. Throughout the Middle Ages, the hermaphrodite possessing both male and female genitalia was considered "a portent, a warning or an indicator of God's displeasure."[26] On the other hand, popular monsters of the oral tradition were often thought to violate existing gender norms. The predatory monstrosity of mythological sirens or werewolves of medieval lore was accompanied by an exaggerated distortion of gendered qualities, such as the dangerous sensuality of the former and uncontrolled aggression of the latter.[27] Notably, all these supernatural beings signaled their supposed inhumanity through the body, whether it be through the simultaneous possession of male and female sex organs or the merging of features from multiple species. This hybridity granted them "externally incoherent bodies" that resisted clear categorization and were thus viewed as threatening.[28] As monster theorist Jeffrey Cohen concludes, "And so the monster is dangerous, a form suspended between forms that threatens to smash distinctions" and throw the social system into disarray.[29]

The preoccupation with monstrous embodiments and their subversive power as articulated by Cohen runs through nineteenth-century Gothic fiction across national traditions. As Jack Halberstam argues, "the Gothic topos is the monstrous body," and such iconic figures as Frankenstein's monster, Dracula, and Mr. Hyde all emphasize "the horror of particular kinds of bodies" viewed as resistant to socialization.[30] The physical abnormality of these bodies prompts a visceral rejection in the reader, which is corroborated by the morally reprehensible and antisocial actions of each monster. In the texts by Galdós and Alarcón featured in this chapter, horror resides specifically in the unconventionally gendered body. Within these narratives, it is the failure to abide by the reigning rules of gender that marks certain bodies as aberrant and thus menacing in the public eye. Donna Heiland declares in the introduction to *Gothic & Gender* that "the transgressive acts at the heart of gothic fiction generally focus on corruption in, or resistance to, the patriarchal structures that shaped the country's political life and its family life."[31] The subversion of gender roles, as a challenge to the patriarchy on both the familial and national levels, thus becomes a commonplace occurrence in Gothic fiction. Yet the depiction of deviant femininity or masculinity is not progressive in and of itself. In the Spanish texts under study here, the Gothic aesthetic validates societal fear of gender deviance by rendering literal the perceived inhumanity of nonconformity. Terror and repulsion are, after all, logical responses in the face of individuals considered gender deviant when they truly are agents of evil.

Whereas the Gothic trope of monstrosity reinforces traditional gender norms in the selected stories by Galdós and Alarcón, their fantastic structure problematizes the fear of gender nonconformity. It does so by posing an interesting question: what happens if the alleged monster turns out not to be real? The hallmark of the fantastic is its refusal to confirm the existence of the supernatural. Readers are denied the certainty that something otherworldly has occurred and are privy only to the narrator's perception that he has fallen victim to malignant supernatural forces. As Cynthia Duncan observes, "The question of who speaks, who sees, and who controls our access to information in the narrative is central to these stories," because readers must identify with the narrator, adopting his perspective, if they are to find the story's supernatural element—here, the presence of a gender-bending monster—to be believable.[32] The male pronouns in the previous statements are intentional. The narrators of "El verano" / "Theros," "La mujer alta," and La sombra are young and well-to-do middle-class men. Identifying their gender biases, as well as the privileged position from which they recount their woes, undermines the speakers' claim to victimhood, and with it their perceptions of monstrosity and the preconceived notions of femininity and masculinity that inform them.

My reading of these three stories foregrounds the tension between narrative claims of monstrosity and the fantastic instability of the text by questioning who is deemed a monster within the story, by whom, and for what reason. This interrogation reveals how the discourse of monstrosity serves a patriarchal social system dominated by the bourgeois classes; it reaffirms the limits of acceptable (i.e., middle-class) femininity and masculinity by providing cautionary tales about those who do not conform. However, a reassessment of the story's narrative perspective, as facilitated by the fantastic structure, opens up possibilities for alternate interpretations that problematize existing norms. Given the unreliability of each text's narrator, the monstrous women of "El verano" and "La mujer alta" seem to be largely the projection of male anxieties and insecurities. In contrast, the male villain of La sombra is indeed a monster, though not because he fails to fulfill societal expectations of masculinity, as the narrator suggests; his true monstrosity lies in the egregious mistreatment of his wife, which is downplayed within the text. Finally, as a counterpoint to the works by Galdós and Alarcón, Pardo Bazán's "Vampiro" presents a more obvious critique of the socially constructed and thus contingent nature of the gender-deviant monster.

Within the story, power and privilege undeniably mitigate perceptions of monstrosity for men of sufficient means, thus elucidating the sexist and classist underpinnings for society's judgments that are more subtly alluded to in the texts by Galdós and Alarcón. Ultimately, the horrific element of these assembled texts is not limited to any specific body, but resides in the hypocritical and misogynistic social system, often personified in the narrator, that decries physical monstrosity but breeds moral monstrosity by enabling violence toward, and even the sacrifice of, underprivileged female bodies.

Re-thinking Wayward Women
GALDÓS'S "EL VERANO" / "THEROS" AND
ALARCÓN'S "LA MUJER ALTA"

Across the four works analyzed in this chapter, a fairly uniform description of the ideal woman emerges. In "La mujer alta," the protagonist's fiancée Joaquinita Moreda stands out for her "distinción, hermosura y garbo" (6; elegance, beauty, and grace).[33] Then there is Elena from *La sombra*, the protagonist's young wife whose physical beauty is matched by her comportment as a "modelo de amabilidad, de discreción, de prudencia" (610; model of kindness, of discretion, of prudence).[34] Fourteen-year old Inesiña from "Vampiro," wife to the elderly Don Fortunato, is likewise blessed with "ojos brillantes" (bright eyes), "carrillos como rosas" (rosy cheeks), and the desire to please.[35] Each of these women is lauded as prime marriage material for possessing physical beauty, impeccable morality, and a strong sense of decorum. Yet these exemplary ladies are relegated to a secondary if not minor role in the text, and none of them survives at story's end.

Instead, the women who dominate the narrative, capturing our attention and imagination, are those who fail to conform to the prevailing standard—the monstrous females. Depictions of aberrant femininity conceived as monstrosity abound in patriarchal societies such as that of modern Spain. Given that women were subjected to a particularly limiting definition of femininity in the late nineteenth and early twentieth centuries, the threat of falling short of the ideal was great, as was the judgment that nonconformity incited. Women were to abide by very specific rules dictating how they should look and behave, not to mention what spaces they might occupy, and even unintentional missteps could label them as deviant and thus dangerous. Socialized public scrutiny of female bodies further heightened awareness of any physical "defects" that might signal abnormal femininity. As Jo Labanyi generalizes of late nineteenth-century Spanish society, "Men had bodies but women were bodies"; and if Gothic monstrosity represented "embodied horror," then the fixation on women's bodies would logically produce a plethora of female monsters.[36]

Exemplifying this tendency, "El verano" / "Theros" by Galdós and "La mujer alta" by Alarcón are texts that present a threatening female archetype in supernatural guise: the femme fatale and the crone respectively. Although the latter is sometimes portrayed as a wise, maternal figure, here I refer to the more common depiction of an old, ugly, and often malicious hag, who may be a mother, but is markedly antimaternal. In this incarnation, the crone, like the femme fatale, has had a long and storied presence in oral and literary traditions worldwide. Just as Biblical figures like Salome or Delilah establish the femme fatale as an age-old antagonist, folkloric staples like the Slavic Baba Yaga or the child-devouring witch of "Hansel and Gretel" have cemented the crone as a mainstay in children's nightmares. Unsurprisingly, both the femme fatale and the crone are heavily featured in nineteenth-century Gothic texts, given the Gothic preoccupation with gender transgression.[37] Both figures are indicative of a lasting cultural obsession with supposedly aberrant femininity.

In *Idols of Perversity*, Bram Dijkstra examines the compulsive depiction of feminine evil in European and American *fin-de-siècle* culture, particularly the visual arts. Cataloguing image after image of alluringly dangerous women, Dijkstra concludes, "Woman became the victimizer of choice of the period's self-pityingly marginalized male."[38] Yet while Dijksta speaks of the entire female sex ("Woman"), he is alluding specifically to the femme fatale, young and sexually attractive by definition. *Idols of Perversity* makes no mention of less seductive yet equally threatening female figures, such as the aged and unsightly crone, who likewise haunted the collective imagination at century's end. The many witches featured in Francisco de Goya's *Caprichos*, published in 1799, provide ample visual representation of the Spanish post-Enlightenment characterization of elderly women as grotesque and diabolical beings, a depiction that would extend through the 1800s. Goya's prints likewise demonstrate that, though physically antithetical to the femme fatale, the crone provokes similar fears to those evoked by the deadly seductress. In particular, *capricho* 68 "¡Linda maestra!" (Pretty teacher; fig. 2.1), in which a physically enticing young woman and a wizened hag share a nocturnal broomstick ride, visualizes a certain continuity between the femme fatale and the crone as two females who defy patriarchal expectations and control. Since motherhood was expected to be Spanish women's greatest civic contribution, women were valued in large part for their reproductive capacity. Female bodies judged unfit for reproductive function, either through perceived promiscuity (e.g., the femme fatale) or infertility (e.g., the crone) became monstrous in society's eyes.[39] Moreover, the femme fatale and the crone's disturbing lack of maternal potential was compounded by the agency that each exercised. Theirs were not only undomestic, but also uncontrollable bodies that defied male authority.

The threat posed by the femme fatale resides largely in the power that she holds over her male victims, conveyed through their inability to resist seduction. She is problematic not because she is sexy, but because she renders men powerless with the onslaught of her charms. Given widespread concern about female empowerment throughout Europe and the Americas in the late 1800s, it follows that the femme fatale pervades turn-of-the century cultural production on both sides of the Atlantic. In Spain, the fixation on dangerous beauties was exacerbated by the collective anxiety over national emasculation, and femmes fatales became commonplace in literature of the period, from the green-eyed nymph of Gustavo Adolfo Bécquer's late-Romantic legend "Los ojos verdes" (1861; The green eyes) to the chilling widow of Carmen de Burgos's modernist novella *La mujer fría* (1922; The cold woman).[40] Within this context, Galdós's short story "El verano," later retitled "Theros," stands out for featuring a supernatural seductress in a period dominated by the realist-naturalist aesthetic, and moreover employs the menacing female figure self-reflexively. As the narrative unfolds, Galdós's text encourages scrutiny of the central femme fatale, providing unexpected insight into the cultural demonization of alluring women.

First published as "El verano" in the 1878 almanac to prestigious weekly *La Ilustración española y americana* (Spanish and American Illustration), the story was conceived as a seasonal allegory.[41] The tale was then republished at least three times during Galdós's life under the new title "Theros," which Peñate Rivero identifies as the ancient Greek term for summer.[42] The retitled text was appended to the 1890 edition of *La sombra*, appeared in the Mexican *Revista Moderna* (Modern Magazine) in 1901, and provided the sole representation of the author's work in a 1907 issue of *La República de las Letras* (The Republic of Letters) dedicated to Galdós as one of the periodical's founders.[43] Aside from the change in title, there are minimal differences across the story's four editions, which trace an unnamed male narrator's train ride through Spain, from Cádiz to Santander. En route,

FIGURE 2.1. "¡Linda maestra!" ("Pretty teacher!") by Francisco de Goya y Lucientes from the series *Caprichos* (1799; *Caprices*). Image courtesy of Brooklyn Museum, A. Augustus Healy Fund, Frank L. Babbott Fund, and Carll H. de Silver Fund, www.brooklynmuseum.org/opencollection/objects/47212.

the protagonist finds his train car occupied by a woman of "hermosura sobrehumana" (54; superhuman beauty), whose revealing tunic recalls the goddesses of antiquity, and whose body radiates unbearable heat.[44] Suffocating in his seat, the narrator complains to the train personnel, only to discover that all others see her as a perfectly normal lady in unremarkable dress. The mysterious dame eventually reveals to him that she is the embodiment of summer, and by the time they pull into Madrid, the two have begun to form an unlikely bond. In the capital, however, the narrator is put off by his companion's supernatural mischief-making. Fleeing the intense weather fluctuations that she has caused, he boards the train once more, but his escape is short-lived, as he is again joined by the otherworldly female. Unexpectedly, along their renewed travels, the narrator grows so enamored of his companion that he proposes marriage. The couple disembarks on Spain's northern coast and enjoys one another's company until one day the woman vanishes just as inexplicably as she had appeared. The narrator is left disconcerted and desolate.

In spite of multiple reprints during the author's lifetime, "El verano" / "Theros" has not enjoyed much posthumous fame. The story was routinely excluded from the few anthologies of Galdós's short fictions published before 2000, reflecting its lack of popularity among late twentieth-century literary scholars.[45] Any critical interest has focused on the story's central female figure, first identified as a femme fatale by Krisztina Weller and then viewed as the Earth Mother by Alan Smith.[46] Weller and Smith share an interest in uncovering the symbolism and archetypal value of the enigmatic female based on her interactions with the narrator. However, said interactions are focalized entirely through the narrator's eyes, such that the woman's identity matters little; what matters most is the speaker's perception of her and the role that he assigns her, which evolves as the narrative unfolds.[47] Thus, the characterization of the mysterious lady reveals more about the narrator (and his society) than about her, and the shifting of power between the two travelers determines the way in which the woman is described: first as an unearthly temptress, then as a mischievous lush, and finally as potential wife material. In scrutinizing the trajectory of her characterization, it becomes clear that the unnamed woman is described most monstrously when she is perceived as most powerful, or more accurately, when she renders the narrator most powerless.

When the lady in question first appears on the train, the narrator depicts her as a true femme fatale. Diametrically opposed to the asexual and subservient angel in the house, she is sexually tempting and defiant. "Cuasábanme estupefacción indecible su figura y su traje" (54; Her figure and dress caused me indescribable stupefaction), the narrator recalls, adding, "No podía decirse que el traje de la dama fuese extravagante, sino que no tenía traje alguno" (It could not be said that the lady's dress was extravagant, but rather that she had no dress whatsoever). His petition that she cover herself only meets with laughter. Although the narrator initially fixates on her scandalous attire, the unknown woman's most offensive qualities—and those that signal her inhumanity to the reader—are those that symbolically communicate her power over him: her unbearable body heat and literally burning gaze. Likening the intruder to "el mismo fuego" (55; fire itself), the narrator describes himself as uncontrollably sweating from the moment she steps foot in the train car. All attempts to alleviate his condition are in vain; the narrator destroys a fan in the futile attempt to fend off the "llamaradas insoportables" (55; unbearable flames) emitted by the scantily clad female. Subjected to this hellish company, the narrator feels that his brain boils, molten metal runs in his veins, and his entire body melts as if it were wax held to a flame (55). He is furthermore unable to meet the otherworldly female's gaze, or even look upon her for any length of time, since her eyes are "como pedazos del mismo sol" (54; like bits of the sun itself) that would blind the viewer who dared to stare.

While the narrator considers the bodily emanations of his traveling companion to be the cause of his physical discomfort, they likewise allegorize the power that she wields over him. On the one hand, the oppressive heat that her body supposedly radiates makes tangible the sexual attraction that the narrator feels toward her. In a telling moment halfway through the story, he describes her unclad state as "desnudez abrasadora" (56; scorching nudity), suggesting that her nudity is what really afflicts him, rather than any inhuman bodily effluvia. The inescapable heat that he so heroically battles becomes symbolic of the desire that surges within him, as perceived in his compulsive references to her incomparable physique and alluring body (54, 55, 57), visible beneath her sheer tunic. Worse still, the enflamed narrator finds himself not only powerless to satisfy his lust, but barred from staring at, and thus objectifying the woman before him. Given her luminosity, he is continually forced to look down or away from her, in an inversion of the patriarchal dynamic famously articulated by John Berger: "Men look at women. Women watch themselves being looked at. . . . Thus she turns herself into an object—and most particularly an object of vision: a sight."[48] This nonverbal display of male power and female powerlessness is inverted in Galdós's tale when the otherworldly female subjugates the male speaker's gaze with her flaming eyes, highlighting his impotence throughout their initial encounter.

Before long, she reduces him to an utterly passive state: "Yo caí exánime, sin fuerzas, todo sudoroso, desmayado, sin aliento; creo que mis facultades se alteraron visiblemente; perdí la noción de todas las cosas, se nubló mi juicio y apenas pude formular un pensamiento" (55; I fell lifeless, without strength, covered in sweat, in a faint, breathless; I think my faculties were visibly unsettled; I lost sense of all things, my judgment clouded, and I could hardly form a thought). The pathetic state detailed here illustrates the challenge that the femme fatale poses not only for the narrator, but for society at large. As an enticing and yet oppressive embodiment of summer, the mysterious lady threatens both the narrator's sense of self-control and a more general notion of masculine control over women. These challenges to male supremacy render her deviant and dangerous in the eyes of the narrator, who rationalizes her domination of him by casting her in a demonic light. While he does not explicitly deem her a monster, he refers to her variously as an "endemoniada ninfa" (55; devilish nymph), an "endemoniada aparición" (55; devilish apparition), and a "repulsiva diosa" (56; repulsive goddess), among other descriptors that likewise depict her as horrific and inhuman.[49] This can be no ordinary woman who has reduced him to a quivering heap.

Halfway through the story, however, the narrator's characterization of his companion changes dramatically upon witnessing comportment not befitting a supernaturally seductive female. While stopped in Madrid, he treats the peerless beauty to lunch, but is left speechless when she downs bottle after bottle of wine, convincing him that "no era mujer, sino más bien una bacante" (56; she was no woman, but an acolyte of Bacchus). Her behavior thereafter is erratic and tasteless in the narrator's view, and although she still displays superhuman abilities, these are less geared toward seduction than causing general mayhem. Her aimless running, hand flapping, and lunatic laughter through the city streets seemingly cause violent shifts in the weather that destroy public property and disturb the peace. Scandalized by her impropriety, the protagonist warns that she will be detained in a mental asylum if she continues such obnoxious behavior, but when he reboards the train seeking refuge, the mischief-maker reappears beside him.

Throughout the part of "Theros" that takes place in the capital, there is a notable difference in the story's tone that correlates with the narrator's shifting attitude toward the mysterious female at his side. Whereas he previously painted himself as the captive of a dangerous vixen, he now adopts the persona of the dismayed guardian of a capricious juvenile. In light of her drunken shenanigans, the unnamed woman is no longer perceived as a radiant goddess, but as a troublemaking child, a change that is reflected in the narrator's verbiage. In the paragraph describing her pranks throughout Madrid, his descriptions of her devolve from the initial "dama" (56; lady) to "niña" (girl), "pícara" (rogue), and "tunanta" (little rascal). Although her actions in Madrid still appear to produce supernatural effects, they detract from her fearsome aura due to their childishness. The narrator's apprehension evaporates when the supposed goddess's womanly wiles are upstaged by her misbehavior. If he had found her bodily emanations to be wholly foreign and thus distressing, he is all too familiar with the perils of immoderate drinking. The narrator begins "El verano" / "Theros" by imbibing one too many sherries in Jérez (54). Thus, her actions, though improper for a lady, humanize her for the narrator, such that his trepidation morphs into a paternalistic tone of disapproval.

This attitude shifts a third time when the two characters resume their journey north, and the story comes to approximate a sentimental novel. In the final moments, the unnamed woman is no longer characterized as a seductress or a scamp. Instead, she becomes the narrator's docile companion, deemed "compañera" (57; companion) five times on a single page, as well as "amiga" (57; friend) and "esposa" (57; wife). All threats of immolation or hints of immaturity in her have vanished, encouraging the now besotted narrator to propose marriage. Just before the dame herself vanishes at story's end, the text presents a beach montage in which the betrothed couple run through the waves, holding hands and locking eyes as the protagonist declares, "Nunca había visto a mi compañera tan hermosa ni tan alegre ni tan amable" (57; I'd never seen my companion so beautiful nor so happy nor so kind). However, this domestic bliss can only occur when the "goddess" loses her magical hold over the narrator. Even prior to the story's final act, a correlation is suggested between her waning powers and the narrator's growing romantic intent. Just prior to arriving in Madrid, the protagonist describes how the lady's body had ceased to burn so unbearably, and her increasingly tolerable gaze had begun to captivate him (56). This budding romantic interest is interrupted by the stopover in Madrid, but resumes as the two continue their travels to the Cantabrian coast. During the last leg of their journey, the narrator's companion no longer roasts him alive. Her eyes cease to shoot literal sparks, and her body stops flaming. Most importantly, the narrator relates, "pude acercarme libremente a ella" (57; I could freely approach her). With the reestablishment of the speaker's agency, the monstrosity of his companion dissipates. The man-eater is stripped of her debilitating power and thus demystified, although she maintains her superhuman beauty. She is, at last, ideal wife material.

By tracing the trajectory of relations between the narrator and his eventual fiancée alongside his changing vision of her, it becomes clear that monstrosity is not an ontological property that resides within the mysterious dame, but is instead a perceptual quality attributed to her by the narrator. The designation of "monster" is entirely subjective, a fact underscored by the story's narrative structure. As a fantastic text, Galdós's story neither confirms nor denies the lady's inhumanity. From start to finish, the narrator is the sole character who views her as otherworldly, and his testimony is undermined by his apparent inebriation. Just as the woman in question may be the physical embodiment of summer, there is ample evidence to suggest that the narrator drunkenly hallucinates the entire episode. At varying points in the story's opening moments, he describes himself as woozy, disoriented, and mentally incapacitated, and the stationmaster indulges him "como a un loco" (55; as he would a madman).

The speaker's reliability is further undercut by key contradictions in his account, particularly concerning the woman who perturbs him. While he introduces her as a diabolical agent of seduction, he adds that her comportment is perfectly modest, marked by "la castidad más perfecta y la más irreprensible decencia" (55; the most perfect chastity and the most irreproachable decency). One moment he likens her to a convent novice (55), only to call her an "endemoniada ninfa" (55; devilish nymph) two sentences later. Given the opposing nature of these consecutive descriptions, it seems unlikely that any female could simultaneously embody them. Such narrative inconsistencies render the protagonist's entire testimony to be suspect, suggesting that it is not female sexuality but the desirous and yet frustrated male gaze that creates an inhuman femme fatale. A woman's irreproachable comportment will not save her from being labelled a monster, so long as she is perceived as threatening by a man.

Thanks to its fantastic ambiguity, "El verano" / "Theros" posits that female monstrosity lies in the eye of the beholder. How then might we interpret the story's enigmatic end? At the height of the narrator's newfound domestic bliss, his companion evaporates, leaving him shrouded in "un frío que penetraba hasta [los] huesos" (57; a cold that penetrated [his] very bones). From an allegorical standpoint, the disappearance is clearly symbolic of the sunny season's end; the goddess of summer disappears on September 22, the first day of fall. Yet this facile reading does not preclude alternate interpretations. As one possibility, the sudden vanishing of the narrator's mate might signify the imagined nature of their entire affair. After all, her transformation from diabolical seductress to perfect spouse seems to be an alcohol-fueled projection of the speaker's insecurities and fantasies with little basis in reality. It is entirely plausible that the saccharine interactions he recounts, as well as their abrupt end, are likewise the product of his febrile imagination. Beyond denouncing the delusions of a single man, "Theros" may serve as a warning against reductive models of femininity at the societal level. Perhaps the perfect wife possessed of "hermoso cuerpo" (57; beautiful body) and "dulce y amoroso temple" (57; sweet and loving constancy) dissolves into thin air at the story's end because this paragon of domestic femininity has no place in reality. Read thusly, Galdós's short story demonstrates that monstrous women—and their perfectly virtuous counterparts—are largely the creations of their viewers, who are themselves the product of a misogynistic society in which real women of flesh and blood are subordinated to the ideals and stereotypes against which they are measured.

This is particularly true in the case of women past their childbearing prime, pushed to the margins of society by the inevitable act of aging. If young ladies faced the danger of being perceived as femmes fatales, their older counterparts were far likelier to be cast as terrifying crones, since "the aged female body, no longer able to engender or act on sexual desire, becomes a symbol of the abject, that which culture abhors and excludes as a way to sustain itself."[50] Deemed useless for their lack of reproductive potential, older women, including those who remained unmarried, retained social value only to the extent that they demonstrated maternal qualities. In an 1876 address delivered before the Academy of Medicine in Valencia, Catalan doctor Francisco de Paula Campá urged mature women, whom he defined as past the age of forty, to busy themselves with maternal—that is to say selfless—enterprises predicated on the care of others, such as the dedication to charity. Only in this way would they occupy "en la familia humana el lugar que a la mujer corresponde" (within the human family the place that corresponds to the woman)."[51] Thus, the abnegated spinster, or *solterona*, was grudgingly accepted as a "pejorative yet socially-acceptable category of non-normative femininity" during this period.[52] In contrast, older females who did not fit the motherly mold were judged to be not only unnatural, but antisocial and threatening to Spanish society, in light of their relative autonomy.

Whereas both the married homemaker and the young lady under her father's tutelage were subject to the authority of the men in their lives, the single woman over twenty-five years of age enjoyed some of the same legal privileges as the men around her in post-Isabelline Spain. These included full control of her own property, the right to act as a guarantor for a third party, and the ability to enter into legally binding contracts.[53] Single women of more advanced age additionally lived free from the moral scrutiny that dogged younger females, and could be out without a chaperone, a luxury that was widely discussed by Spanish authors of the period.[54] At liberty to traverse the public sphere and exercise rights generally reserved for men, old spinsters or widows were viewed to escape the confines that subordinated the female sex to male guardianship in Spain's patriarchal society.[55] This perceived autonomy imbued her with a disruptive quality, striking fear in those who defended traditional gender roles, and making her an ideal source of male terror to be explored in fantastic narratives.[56] Unmotherly and unmanageable crones abound in fantastic short stories from late nineteenth-century Spain, ranging from the little known "La casa donde murió" (1876; The house where she died) by Julia de Asensi and "Su retrato" (1881; Her portrait) by Pedro Escamilla, to Pardo Bazán's oft-anthologized "La santa de Karnar" (1891; The Saint of Karnar).

In a sea of stories featuring disquieting crones, "La mujer alta" by Alarcón stands out as one of few Spanish fantastic texts whose popularity has endured to the present, even transcending national borders. Subtitled "cuento de miedo" (a tale of fear), the story was first published serially in 1882 in the periodical *Ilustración Artística* (Artistic Illustration) and then as the closing text in the author's collected *Narraciones inverosímiles* (Unlikely Narrations) of the same year.[57] It was immediately popular with Spanish readers, including Emilia Pardo Bazán, who disliked the *Narraciones inverosímiles* as a whole, but praised "La mujer alta" as an exceptional contribution.[58] This positive reception further extended to contemporaries in the English-speaking world, who were generally ignorant of Spanish literary production. As early as 1890, a translation of the text appeared in George William Curtis's anthology *Modern Ghosts*, described as "the most modern and contemporary contribution to the literature of ghosts, selected from authors in various parts of Europe—Norway, France, Spain, Austria, Italy—all of them masters in their way."[59] It is therefore unsurprising that in the new millennium Juan Molina Porras named "La mujer alta" the epitome of nineteenth-century Spanish fantastic fiction.[60]

In Alarcón's celebrated tale, Gabriel narrates the sad fate of his friend Telesforo X, a bright young engineer who harbors a secret fear of lone women roaming the streets at night. Gabriel recounts his friend's two uncanny encounters with just such a female, "una mujer muy alta y fuerte, como de sesenta años de edad" (11; a very tall and strong woman some sixty years of age) who is nevertheless dressed in youthful attire, complete with a coquettish fan. The woman's appearance thoroughly disturbs Telesforo, and each of their run-ins is followed by a terrible revelation: first the notification that his father has died and then news of his fiancée's passing. For Telesforo, these deaths justify his phobia, which is exacerbated by his inability to identify the woman who haunts him: "¿Era una ladrona? ¿Era efectivamente un hombre disfrazado? ¿Era una vieja irónica, que había comprendido que le tenía miedo? ¿Era el espectro de mi propia cobardía? ¿Era el fantasma burlón de las decepciones y deficiencias humanas?" (19; Was she a thief? Was she actually a man in disguise? Was she an ironic old woman who had understood that I was afraid of her? Was she the specter of my cowardice? Was she the mocking ghost of human disappointments and shortcomings?). He receives no satisfying answers before succumbing to a sudden case of jaundice, but even after death, Telesforo does not seem free of the threatening figure. At his friend's funeral, Gabriel witnesses the gleeful cackling of a woman whose gaze fills him with dread. The short story ends with a coda in which an authorial voice asks each reader to judge for themselves whether the narrated events have a logical explanation.

In contrast with the evolving femme fatale of Galdós's allegorical piece, the tall woman in Alarcón's short story is presented as consistently disturbing from start to finish. Not only is she linked to the deaths of innocent people, but her appearance sends mixed gender signals. From the moment he spies the tall woman sheltered in a doorway, Telesforo is confounded by the contradictory aspects of her figure and dress: "Lo primero que me chocó en aquella que todavía denominaré *mujer*, fue su elevadísima talla y la anchura de sus descarnados hombros: luego, la redondez y fijeza de sus marchitos ojos de búho, la enormidad de su saliente nariz, y la gran mella central de su dentadura, que convertía su boca en una especie de oscuro agujero" (11; The first thing that shocked me in that so-called *woman*, was her extreme height and the width of her gaunt shoulders; next, the roundness and the fixedness of her withered, owl eyes; the enormousness of her protruding nose, and the great central gap in her teeth, which turned her mouth into a kind of dark hole). Though styled as a woman, the solitary figure's imposing stature and lack of traditionally feminine graces lead the young engineer to believe that she may actually be a man. As David R. George, Jr. and others have argued, these conflicting elements impede Telesforo's ability to confidently ascribe a gender identity to her, and the resultant sensation of impotence leads him to react with horror.[61]

In this manner, "La mujer alta" depicts Spain's pathological panic over gender indistinction at century's end. As Santacruz's descriptions of the *marimacho* demonstrated, deviation from fixed definitions of femininity produced discomfort and even disgust in those conditioned by Spain's patriarchal norms, and necessitated stripping the offending individual of their humanity. Although Telesforo does not refer to the tall woman as a monster outright, the language that he uses to describe her highlights a supernaturally aberrant nature. She is potentially an "espectro" (19; specter), a "demonio" (22; demon), and even "el Antecristo [*sic*]" (22; the Antichrist), among myriad other threatening possibilities. Tellingly, the descriptor that Telesforo most often settles upon is "bruja" (11, 19; witch). As she flees his grasp after their second, heated encounter, Telesforo views her not as running but flying away (22). For the young engineer, she is no different from the devil-worshipping hags pictured by Goya.

Thus identified with the haggard crone, the tall woman's gender is not the only characteristic that makes her a monster to Telesforo and his friends. Her advanced age likewise plays a key role in evoking the revulsion of the young men. After her imposing stature, the next three characteristics that catch the engineer's eye are her "marchitos ojos" (11; withered eyes) "saliente nariz" (11; protruding nose) and toothlessness, all characteristics stereotypically associated with old age.[62] Moreover, the tall woman draws attention to her physical deterioration by sporting the attire of a much younger female, and the contrast between her advanced age and youthful dress disturbs Telesforo and Gabriel greatly.[63] Scandalized by her self-presentation, Telesforo exclaims,

> ¡Nada más ridículo y formidable, nada más irrisorio y sarcástico que aquel abaniquillo, en unas manos tan enormes, sirviendo como de cetro de debilidad a giganta tan fea, *vieja* y huesuda! Igual efecto producía el pañolejo de vistoso percal que adornaba su cara, comparado con aquella nariz de tajamar, aguileña, masculina, que me hizo creer un momento (no sin regocijo) si se trataría de un hombre disfrazado . . .—Pero su cínica mirada y asquerosa sonrisa eran de *vieja*, de bruja, de hechicera, de Parca . . . (11, ellipsis in original, italics mine)

> (Nothing was more ridiculous and glaring, nothing more laughable and sarcastic than that tiny fan in such enormous hands, serving as a scepter of weakness for such an ugly, *old*, and bony giant! The same effect was produced by the gaudy cotton kerchief that adorned her face, compared with that cutwater-like, aquiline, masculine nose that made me believe for a moment [not without rejoicing] it might be a man in disguise . . . But her cynical stare and nauseating smile were those of an *old* woman, a witch, a sorceress, a Parca . . .)

He is clearly outraged that such a mannish woman should dare to style herself in a feminine manner, but he is equally offended by her age, which he references twice in this passage. Gabriel similarly mentions how old the woman is before acknowledging her stature (27), and fixates on those physical qualities that denote the tall woman's age just as much as they confuse his perception of her gender. Like Telesforo, he singles out "su enorme nariz" (27; her enormous nose) and "su asquerosa mella" (27; the disgusting gap in her teeth), in contrast with her headkerchief and dainty fan. More explicitly, the two men refer to the frightening figure as "la vieja" (the old woman) six times in the text of the story (11, 19, 22, 26, 27), only once fewer than they call her "la mujer alta" (the tall woman), thus strengthening the relation between her senescence and their abhorrence of her.

As noted previously, both engineers take particular offense at the tall woman's tiny fan. Beyond any phallic connotations, the mystery woman's fanning horrifies Telesforo and Gabriel because it is perceived as age inappropriate.[64] As Noël Valis details in *The Culture of Cursilería*, middle-class Spanish women of the eighteenth and nineteenth centuries were well-versed in the art of the fan, which was viewed as a symbolic extension of the female body. Its folding and unfolding, placement on the body, and varied movements formed a rich nonverbal language most often used in the expression of the bearer's sexuality.[65] For instance, a rapid waving of the fan communicated passion, which the intended male audience was trained to recognize.[66] Given its ability to both convey and incite desire, the fan in nineteenth-century art, both literary and visual, was almost always imagined in the hand of a young and attractive female for whom desire was still socially acceptable. When wielded by a woman deemed past her prime, the fan became a cause for ridicule. In her 1881 *costumbrista* sketch "La solterona" (The spinster), María del Pilar Contreras y Alba mocks the spinster who spends her evenings in the theater seeking a husband, fruitlessly signaling her availability through her "coquetón abanico" (flirtatious fan).[67] Thus, the tall woman's unapologetic display of the accessory is an abomination in the eyes of bourgeois gentlemen like Telesforo and Gabriel, not only due to the contrast between the diminutive feminine accoutrement and the woman's imposing and thus masculine stature, but also due to the perceived audacity of an older (and unattractive) female who engages in flirtatious behavior. This abhorrence of the tall woman's sexuality is confirmed in Gabriel's description of her departure from the cemetery, "abanicándose y saludándome a un propio tiempo, y contoneándose entre los muertos con no sé qué infernal coquetería" (27; at once fanning herself and waving to me, and swaying among the dead with a certain infernal flirtatiousness). Her attempts at sensuality are not only perceived to be offensive, but downright hellish.

As in the case of "El verano" / "Theros," the monstrous characterization of a female antagonist boils down to a matter of the narrators' perception. Gabriel in particular shares no verbal exchanges with the woman who horrifies him, and she is given no opportunity to challenge his vision of her. Thus, "La mujer alta" casts the older woman as a malevolent, monstrous being based entirely on the judgment of male speakers who are evidently biased as archetypal bourgeois gentlemen inculcated with traditional gender norms. From the start, Gabriel describes his friend as a paragon of normative masculinity. Not only was he "guapo, fuerte, animoso, con la aureola de haber sido el primero de su promoción" (6; handsome, strong, spirited, with the distinction of having graduated at the top of his class) but he was heavily sought after by private firms as well as "las mujeres por casar o mal casadas" (6; single or unhappily married women). The qualities that Gabriel highlights align well with Monlau's prescription for nineteenth-century Spanish masculinity: "El hombre es ardiente, altivo, robusto, velludo, osado, pródigo y dominador . . . su genio sublime e impetuoso le lanza a los altos y le hace aspirar a la inmortalidad" (Man is ardent, arrogant, robust, hairy, daring, generous, and dominating . . . his sublime and uncontrollable temperament launches him to great heights and makes him aspire to immortality).[68] By prevailing standards, men were to be proactive, passionate, confident, and strong, with notable accomplishments in the public sphere, conditions which Telesforo outwardly meets. His embodiment of ideal masculinity is rewarded with the admiration of his peers and the desire of the ladies around him, not to mention his engagement to the daughter of a marquis.

The only black mark against him is his phobia of solitary women, which he bears shamefully in secret, for fear of being ridiculed as unmanly. This fear is not unfounded, considering Gabriel's uncomfortable reaction when his friend shows signs of weakness (6). Telesforo must then re-establish his manhood, which he does by recalling situations in which he triumphed over male rivals or unruly subordinates through physical force or prowess (10). For good measure, he adds, "Toda mi vida . . . he andado a deshora por la calle, solo, sin armas, atento únicamente al cuidado amoroso que me hacía velar, y si, por acaso, he topado con bultos de mala catadura, fueran ladrones o simples perdona-vidas, a ellos les ha tocado huir o echarse a un lado, dejándome libre el mejor camino" (11; All my life . . . I have walked the streets at all hours, alone, unarmed, attentive only to the amorous errand that kept me up, and if by chance I ran into seedy-looking figures, whether thieves or simple thugs, they were the ones who had to flee or step aside, leaving the road clear for me). Not only is his masculinity displayed through physical intimidation in this account, but Telesforo additionally slips in a reference to his sexual exploits; his late-night wanderings unfailingly end in amorous encounters.

The fact that the two friends equate masculinity with the conquest of women implies a generally dismissive view of the female sex, which is confirmed at various points throughout their narration. When first describing Telesforo, Gabriel makes sure to mention the many ladies fighting for his attention, including "viudas impenitentes, y, entre ellas, alguna muy buena moza" (6; unrepentant widows, and amongst them, a certain very attractive girl). The speaker's attitude toward his friend's mistress is far from respectful; he would delve into salacious details if not called to order by his audience. A lack of consideration toward this "unrepentant widow" reflects nineteenth-century disdain for women considered to be morally loose, but Telesforo's fiancée Joaquinita, an angelic young noblewoman, hardly receives better treatment. She possesses the feminine charms deemed attractive by societal standards, and her comportment is above reproach, yet upon her death, Gabriel assumes that it is the loss of her fortune that renders Telesforo inconsolable (6). Nor does Joaquinita receive much consideration from her own fiancé, who only breaks off his affair with the widow when his engagement is made public. In simultaneously enjoying the company of both women, Telesforo demonstrates regard for neither.

Given the two engineers' patriarchal attitudes, their fear of the tall woman is primed by misogynistic social mores. These are on full display on the pages of *La Ilustración Artística* where "La mujer alta" first appeared. Across the four issues in which the story was printed, full-page feminine depictions, which comprise the majority of full-page illustrations, include the Virgen Mary, a beaming young mother, five impeccably dressed fashion plates, and two lovelorn beauties. No older women are featured. If young women were picture-worthy in their allotted roles of the virgin (e.g., Joaquinita) or the whore (e.g., the unrepentant widow), aged women were expected to disappear from view, or even to die. In the *costumbrista* sketch "Rosa la solterona" (Rosa the spinster), Sebastián de Mobellán writes that "la necesidad de la vejez la obliga a morirse, que es lo más acertado, o a perder la vergüenza, que es lo más frecuente" (the necessity of old age compels her to die, which is the correct course of action, or to become shameless, which is the most frequent).[69] Mobellán clearly disdains the shameless older woman, implicitly demanding that any self-respecting woman past childbearing age renounce her claim to sexuality. Similarly, though much kinder to older women, Carlos Rementería y Fica's bestselling conduct manual took for granted that aged ladies would be "libre de las pasiones de la juventud" (free from the passions of youth), just as Pedro de Madrazo's profile on "La señora mayor" (The older woman) describes her as retaining only "la ceniza de las ya estinguidas [sic] pasiones" (the ashes of long extinguished passions).[70] Because senescence has precluded the possibility of male desire toward her, she is expected to feel no desire in turn.

This harsh social reality explains why the tall woman's provocative fanning and swaying elicit revulsion and even outrage in Telesforo and Gabriel, but there is an additional element that makes her uncanny to the duo: her working-class background and apparent poverty. Telesforo's initial portrait of her does not explicitly reference her socioeconomic status, but he describes her outfit as that of a "mozuela del Avapiés [sic]" (11; a girl from Lavapiés), a low-income neighborhood on the outskirts of nineteenth-century Madrid. He then muses that she could be a homeless beggar (19), confirming her impoverished status. Later, when Gabriel spies her, he describes her as "una mujer del pueblo" (27; a working-class woman), immediately highlighting her class status. Her low socioeconomic standing thus becomes another factor that renders her appearance—in both senses of the word: her self-presentation and her presence in public—jarring for the story's male narrators. In a study of the marginalization of old women in medieval Spain, Joseph Snow concludes that the only positive depictions of the older female are those of women belonging to the highest social strata.[71] By the nineteenth century, little had changed. Madrazo's sketch on "La señora mayor" discusses the figure in aristocratic and middle-class contexts only, attesting to the culturally imposed invisibility of the older working-class woman. Thus, it is logical that the tall woman's socioeconomic background and her evident poverty disconcert Telesforo and Gabriel, two comfortably bourgeois gentlemen. It is ultimately her intersectional identity as an aged and poor woman from a disadvantaged social class that makes her refusal to renounce her sexuality so terrifying.

Speaking on Latin American fantastic literature, Duncan explains, "The males, who recognize themselves as victims of the fantastic, explain away the bothersome aspects of the female Other through supernatural events."[72] Telesforo and Gabriel exemplify this tendency in the Spanish context by comforting themselves through the insistence that an old and impoverished working-class woman who performs youthful, non-maternal femininity must be a monster. In doing so, they preserve their privileged, patriarchal worldview. In contrast with previous assessments that failed to question either gentleman's account of their perceived enemy, most recent studies of "La mujer alta" have acknowledged the narrators' bias in her characterization.[73] Upon denaturalizing the perspective of the two male speakers, their claim to victimhood becomes suspect, making way for the title character to emerge as the story's true victim.

Even if Alarcón's original audience, largely bourgeois males themselves, did not recognize the tall woman's suffering, present-day readers would be hard pressed to ignore Telesforo's gratuitous assault of her. Upon their second run-in, the protagonist attacks the unidentified female in a scene that has escaped critical notice: he recalls, "arrojéme sobre el corpulento vejestorio, tirélo contra la pared, echándole una mano a la garganta, y con la otra ¡qué asco! púseme a palpar su cara, su seno, el lío ruin de sus cabellos rucios, hasta que me convencí totalmente de que era criatura humana y mujer" (22; I threw myself upon that giant old bag, I shoved her against the wall, putting a hand on her throat, and with the other—how revolting!—I began to touch her face, her chest, and the contemptible mess of her gray hair until I was completely convinced that she was human and a woman). Ironically, Telesforo finds the objectionable part of this violent encounter to be the undesirability of the female body that he has manhandled. Following the assault, he interrogates the tall woman as to her identity, asking "¿quién soy para V.? ¿Quién es V. para mí?" (22; Who am I to you? Who are you to me?). To his two questions, Telesforo receives a single response: "¡El demonio!" (22; The devil!). The ambiguity in this answer is key. Existing criticism views the tall woman as admitting to her diabolical nature, but it is equally valid to assume that she has instead responded to Telesforo's first question, and that *he* is the devil she references.[74] He has, after all, just attacked her for the simple act of walking behind him on an otherwise abandoned street. Her true offense, however, is appearing in public as an old, ugly, and poor woman. Rather than be erased from view as befits her age and social condition, the tall woman dares to remain visible, in part by dressing as a younger female who might still matter to Spanish society. Monstrosity in this story is clearly not about the offending woman's actions, which are quite harmless, nor her motivations, about which readers know nothing. It is simply defined by the visibility of her non-normative body, triply marginalized by gender, age, and socioeconomic status.

In conjunction with "El verano" / "Theros," "La mujer alta" demonstrates that a discourse of monstrosity has long been a strategy by which society curtails women's agency. Both stories show that women are granted little leniency in the public eye. Those who deviate from the domestic angel mold, even if through the inevitable act of aging, are left with only two possibilities: invisibility or monstrosity. Consequently, the monstrosity of the fearsome women in these works is highly debatable, and the text indicates as much. Because these short stories are fantastic, they draw reader attention to the instability of the narrative and particularly of the narrators, reminding us that monstrosity is a quality designated from the normative position of a male, bourgeois speaker. The women here are nearly voiceless. Neither the femme fatale of "El verano"/"Theros" nor the crone of "La mujer alta" relate their own tales. The former might introduce herself as the goddess of summer, offering a lengthy description of the season, but she is quiet on why she travels, where she is headed, and what draws her to the narrator. While this is partially due to the work's origin as a seasonal allegory, Galdós's short story moves far beyond the formulaic genre, and yet the text's most intriguing character speaks sparingly. Alarcón's tall woman is allowed even fewer utterances; her direct speech is limited to a few lines in answer to Telesforo's questioning. Both stories are narrated by male voices, and their limited perspectives allow no access to the interiority of the female Other, who becomes a blank slate on which to pin accusations of monstrosity. By underscoring the subjectivity and fallibility of each story's narrator, the fantastic structure of these texts facilitates a questioning of the gender biases on display within them and allows for potential redemption of the female monster.

Monstrous Misogyny
GALDÓS'S *LA SOMBRA* AND PARDO BAZÁN'S "VAMPIRO"

In contrast, redemption is not possible for the male monsters that stalk Galdós's novella *La sombra* and Pardo Bazán's "Vampiro." This is not to minimize the pressures to embody the socially sanctioned model of masculinity that men faced throughout the late nineteenth and early twentieth centuries. Although men were viewed as superior to women in terms of physical and intellectual capacity—and received social, professional, and legal advantages accordingly—they were not exempt from gender rules, and suffered negative consequences upon deviating from the norm. As John Tosh observes, those who "fall short" of masculine expectations in a highly patriarchal society often "do not count in their own eyes as 'men.'"[75] Even Telesforo, lauded by his peers as the pinnacle of bourgeois masculinity in "La mujer alta," felt compelled to keep secret his phobia of solitary women, thus revealing the precariousness of his masculine identity and the insecurity provoked therein. Scholarship on masculinities has come to take for granted what Brian Baker deems "a fragmented, plural, performative or anxious subject (or range of subjectivities), constructed (incompletely) by contemporary cultural discourses," but this conceptualization was far from commonplace in the nineteenth century, when the fear of failing to "be a man" pervades the pages of novels like *Su único hijo* (1890; His only son) by Leopoldo Alas or Galdós's *Miau* (1888).[76]

Thus, Spanish men who fell short of the masculine ideal were also depicted as monstrous, though their monstrosity assumed different forms, with different stakes and implications. While women were reduced to maternal, that is, reproductive and caretaking, roles, men's identities in late nineteenth-century Spain, particularly in the capital, were tied to their civic duties as citizens. The modern man was tasked with maintaining the health of the economy through the accumulation, investment, and spending of wealth; fostering community and political ties through homosocial bonding in venues such as the casino; and engendering the next generation of Spaniards within the sacrosanct family unit. While they were undeniably judged against dominant physical standards, such as those articulated by Monlau, their bodies were additionally evaluated for evidence of the ability to successfully navigate and contribute to civic society. In the Introduction to *Horrifying Sex*, Ruth Bienstock Anolik affirms that in the Anglo-American Gothic tradition, "the horrifying male Other expresses anxieties that have as much to do with the body politic as with the sexual body."[77] This applies to late-nineteenth- and early-twentieth-century Spanish literature as well, in which physical expressions of male monstrosity could be viewed as indicative of antisocial attitudes and behaviors perceived to threaten societal stability.

In another key difference from female monstrosity, whereas the antagonists of "Theros" and "La mujer alta" are described in terms of long-standing archetypes, *La sombra* and "Vampiro" paint male monstrosity in relation to figures more closely associated with the nineteenth-century Gothic tradition: the mad scientist and the vampire respectively. In a world marked by paradigm-shifting scientific discoveries and technological innovation, the mad scientist reminded readers of the dangers in the quest for knowledge and advancement, ambitions coded as masculine given contemporary limitations on women's education. Science could destroy, in addition to creating, and proved dangerous without a strong moral compass. Mary Shelley's *Frankenstein* (1818) and Robert Louis Stevenson's *The Strange Case of Dr. Jekyll and Mr. Hyde* (1886) bookended the nineteenth century with Gothic tales of experiments gone wrong, and Goethe's play *Faust*, published in two parts in 1808 and 1832, provided a key referent for Galdós while writing *La sombra*.[78] The reappearance of the mad doctor in José Fernández Bremón's "Un crimen científico" (1875; A scientific crime) and Leopoldo Alas's "Cuento futuro" (Future story, 1886), signals continued interest in the figure among nineteenth-century Spanish readership.[79] Like the mad doctor, the vampire gained immense popularity in the Anglophone world during the nineteenth century, thanks first to John William Polidori's "The Vampyre" (1819) and then to Bram Stoker's *Dracula* (1897). As a suave and seductive aristocratic bloodsucker, the vampire in these examples expressed anxieties surrounding aberrant sexuality, the presence of foreigners within the nation, and questions of disease, infection, and contagion. Yet while these were all, to some degree, topics of concern in Spain, the figure of the vampire as a supernatural, life-draining fiend did not inspire Spanish variants until the early twentieth century.[80] "Vampiro" is thus one of the first noteworthy examples of modern Spanish vampire fiction.

Galdós and Pardo Bazán may not have read the specific works responsible for the popularity of these monstrous figures, given their dates of publication and translation.[81] Nevertheless, as well-read polyglots, both authors stayed cognizant of new developments in European and Anglo-American literature, including Gothic trends, and their engagement with the tropes of the mad doctor and the vampire suggest that Spain was synchronous to the rest of Europe and the United States in its use of fictional monsters to examine problematic relationships between society and the male subject. The fact that the female monsters explored in this chapter draw upon age-old molds while male beasts cut more contemporary figures recalls Pardo Bazán's assertion that Spanish women's roles had remained static for centuries, while men had gained political and legal ground in the age of liberalism.[82] Faced with new rights as well as new responsibilities, men were also in danger of underperforming masculine expectations in new ways related to Spain's shifting economic and social landscape and its changing imperial status.

Although they derive from more traditional models, the female monsters portrayed in Spanish fantastic fictions of the late nineteenth century are presented much more ambiguously than their male counterparts. "El verano"/"Theros" and "La mujer alta" call into question the threat posed by the femme fatale and the crone through the suggestion that female monstrosity is the product of society's sexist imagination. In contrast, the chilling aspect of male monsters like the deranged "doctor" of *La sombra* and the titular predator of "Vampiro" is only heightened by the gender dynamics at play in each text. To varying degrees, these stories reveal that society's fear of non-normative masculinity is misplaced; true monstrosity resides not in any deviation from the gender norm, but in the callous disregard for less-privileged, particularly female, lives as intimated in both tales. The protagonists of these two works are inarguably monsters, though not for the reason that society believes.

This disconnect between apparent and actual monstrosity lies at the heart of *La sombra*, Galdós's first foray into the novel genre and his only indisputably Gothic work.[83] Written around 1866 or 1867 in the author's recollection, the novella was published serially in the *Revista de España* (Journal of Spain) in 1871, and then issued in book form with minor revisions nearly twenty years later.[84] Although it has been consistently popular with Galdosian scholars, *La sombra* is far from the author's best-known work, partially due to its departure from his characteristically realist style. However, it is precisely the Gothic themes and fantastic structuring of *La sombra* that facilitate the text's exploration of monstrous male behavior. Motivated by a sense of masculine failure and identified as a mad scientist, the protagonist Anselmo enacts an increasingly troubled masculinity that ultimately costs him his wife. In its multiple narrative perspectives and their engagement with the question of monstrosity, Galdós's early novella problematizes the social pressures surrounding bourgeois masculinity that can drive men to violent misogyny, as well as society's tendency to turn a blind eye to the women who suffer the consequences.

The insecurities of the modern male subject are magnified through the narrative complexity of *La sombra*. Looking back from his old age, Anselmo recounts to an unnamed narrator the story of his failed marriage to the young and beautiful Elena, whom he suspected of having an affair. However, what forms the premise of many a realist novel takes a supernatural turn when Anselmo identifies his wife's alleged lover as Paris, the legendarily handsome Greek whose abduction of Helen launched the Trojan War. As the aggrieved husband recounts, the figure of Paris stepped out of one of Anselmo's prized paintings with the express purpose of tarnishing Elena's—which is to say Anselmo's—good name. While the supposedly sentient Paris taunts Anselmo for his weakness and inability to inspire love in his spouse, the plot thickens with references to Alejandro X, a gentleman of flesh and blood identical to the painted Paris who insists on entertaining the unhappy Elena in her home. Galdós never clarifies whether Paris and Alejandro are one and the same, or if Paris exists outside of Anselmo's frenzied imagination. What readers do learn is that, consumed by jealousy, Anselmo confines and even abuses his wife, who dies shortly thereafter. Without a target to seduce, Paris abandons the home, leaving a broken Anselmo to become the solitary mad "doctor" that readers meet at the novel's start.

While the word "monster" was absent from "El verano" / "Theros" and "La mujer alta," the text of *La sombra* is rife with explicit references to monstrosity. It is clearly a principal theme of the work, which includes multiple potentially monstrous figures. "Monstruo" (monster) or "monstruosidad" (monstrosity) appear twelve times in the original 1871 text, eight of which are uttered by Anselmo in reference to Paris.[85] The latter is additionally described as a "demonio" (demon) on fourteen occasions, related to the devil on seven, and called "infernal" six times.[86] More than as a monster, however, Paris is portrayed as a spectral figure who appears only to Anselmo and taunts him with a vision of unattainable masculine perfection.[87] In the protagonist's words, "Era hermoso, de una hermosura no común, un conjunto de todas las perfecciones físicas, tal como yo no lo había visto nunca, a no ser en las obras del arte antiguo. Vestía con una elegancia correcta y seria, como todos los que tienen el verdadero sentido y la exacta noción del bien vestir: era, en fin, perfecto en su rostro, en su cuerpo, en su traje, en sus modales, en todo" (423; He was beautiful, of an uncommon beauty, an ensemble of all physical perfections the likes of which I had never seen, except in works of ancient art. He dressed with a correct and serious elegance, like all those who have a true sense and exact notion of dressing well; he was, in sum, perfect in his face, in his body, in his clothing, in his manners, in everything). Paris is all that Anselmo is not, which is precisely what disturbs the latter. Beyond outshining Anselmo, however, Paris is hardly menacing. He never threatens any other characters, nor does he pose any danger beyond inciting adulterous thoughts in Elena; and in a society that had embraced José Zorrilla's *Don Juan Tenorio* (1844), the seduction of ladies hardly amounted to evil. It is thus logical that the narrator of *La sombra* views Paris with amusement rather than horror, and in labeling him "aquel travieso héroe de la antigüedad" (601; that mischievous hero of antiquity), the narrator assures readers that Paris is not to be feared.

What remains unresolved and potentially unsettling about Paris is the mystery surrounding his identity. Like all supernatural beings in fantastic texts, Paris's existence is never confirmed. On the lone occasion when he appears to be visible to everyone, Anselmo's narrative reliability is dubious at best. He recounts how one night Paris forcibly accompanied him along all of Madrid's busiest streets, and shamefully recalls the malicious smiles of acquaintances upon seeing Elena's husband in the company of her alleged lover. At the same time, Anselmo confides, "Según después me han contado, andaba por la calle con la vista extraviada, el andar inseguro y rápido, puestos el sombrero y los vestidos de muy singular manera. Hacía reír a las gentes; y aun los acostumbrados a ver en mí un hombre no parecido a otro alguno, se paraban a mi paso, señalándome como una curiosidad" (614; According to what I was later told, I wandered through the street with a deranged gaze, an unsteady and rapid gait, and my hat and clothes in a singular manner. I made people laugh; and even those who were accustomed to see in me a man unlike any other stopped as I passed, pointing me out as a curiosity). What he perceives as public titillation by the presence of Paris could well be observers' reactions to Anselmo's apparent lunacy. It is he, rather than Paris, who bears a monstrous semblance on the streets of Madrid. In fact, by the end of *La sombra*, the narrator is convinced that Paris is the brainchild of a compulsively insecure Anselmo, a possibility which only highlights the latter's aberrant nature.

From a visual standpoint, the unsightly Anselmo certainly makes a more convincing monster than the gorgeous Paris. When readers first meet him, Anselmo is described as unattractive, unkempt, and unsociable. His clothing is ill-fitting, his personal hygiene is suspect, his home is squalid, and he has no regard for the rules governing friendly conversation. Although Anselmo has evidently let himself go after the death of his spouse, the text implies that these deficiencies were always present to some degree. Even in his heyday, the protagonist was constantly plagued by feelings of inadequacy while in the company of his outwardly ideal nemesis. He recalls, "en su presencia mi alma se sobrecogía, mi palabra enmudecía, flaqueaban mis fuerzas. Páris ejercía sobre mí una fascinación irresistible. Desde que se ponía a mi lado, mi espíritu se sometía al dominio de aquel ser infernal; se doblegaba tristemente y angustiado como sintiendo su inferioridad" (614–15; in his presence, my soul cowered, my voice fell silent, my strength wavered. Paris exerted upon me an irresistible fascination. From the moment he came to my side, my spirit submitted to the command of that infernal being, yielding sadly and anguished as though sensing its inferiority). Yet while Paris may rattle Anselmo, Anselmo perturbs everyone else in the story, including the extradiegetic narrator with whom readers are positioned to identify.

Whereas the narrator views Paris through a generally benign lens, his image of Anselmo is far from flattering; his detailed descriptions of the protagonist, his habits, and his home are instrumental in characterizing Anselmo as a mad scientist. From the story's opening line, the narrator purports to paint Anselmo accurately, including the popular opinion that he was "loco rematado" (269; stark raving mad) as a consequence of his overactive imagination and manic-depressive tendencies. In this and multiple similar statements, the narrator claims to present public opinion without passing judgment, but his constant questioning of Anselmo's word suggests that he shares the community's contempt.[88] To his peers, Anselmo has lost the faculty of reason privileged by post-Enlightenment society and viewed as a marker of masculinity in opposition to a stereotypically illogical and capricious feminine nature. The equation between rationality and masculinity is made explicit when, reproaching his tyrannical acts against Elena, Anelmo's mother-in-law questions his sanity, asking "¿Es esto tener razón, es esto ser hombre?" (610; Is this rational behavior, is this acting like [a] man?). In the second question, the Spanish "ser hombre" is an ambiguous expression that may indicate either manliness or humanity more generally. Thus, a negative answer conflates the unmanly with the inhuman. Acknowledging the equivalence, the protagonist laments, "yo no soy un hombre, o, más bien dicho, soy como esos hombres repugnantes y deformes que andan por ahí mostrando miembros inverosímiles que escarnecen al Criador" (279; I am not a man, or better stated, I am like those repugnant, deformed men that walk around displaying unbelievable limbs that mock the Creator). Even in his own estimation, Anselmo's lunacy is not only a masculine shortcoming, but the mark of monstrosity.

This perceived freakishness is exacerbated by Anselmo's frenetic scientific activity, the other key element of the mad scientist persona. Holed up in a fourth-floor apartment worthy of "todas las brujas de un aquelarre" (270; all the witches in a coven) the protagonist occupies his days fiddling with an assortment of "aparatos de complicadas y rarísimas formas" (272; apparatuses of bizarre and complicated forms) that fill the room with unearthly sounds and smells. However, these experiments are only intended to keep their viewer busy. Anselmo expressly states that they will never lead to any scientific advancement (279). As Cyndy Hendershot explains in *The Animal Within*, the Gothic mad scientist is the "dark double" of the scientist, whose rationality and mastery of the natural world make him modernity's "ideal male subject."[89] In this sense, the mad scientist is a failed masculine icon. Yet while he is obsessive and unethical, the mad scientist is not unproductive. The experiments of Victor Frankenstein and Dr. Henry Jekyll are dangerous precisely due to their success. In contrast, Anselmo's research is intentionally fruitless, flouting the nineteenth-century expectation of masculine productivity and marking him as a failure on two fronts, both as a scientist and as a man.[90] Those who know him call him "doctor," but they do so ironically, firmly believing that "no existía un ser cuyo papel en la sociedad hubiera sido más pasivo" (278; there was no one whose role in society could have been more passive). Interpreted as a sign of innate passivity, the protagonist's deliberate lack of achievement designates him as aberrant and effeminate, thus reinforcing the perception of monstrosity as gendered failure.

Yet it is not only Anselmo's characterization as a lackluster and mad scientist that marks him as egregiously unmasculine and therefore monstrous.

His backstory as recounted by the extradiegetic narrator further establishes him as the antithesis of the bourgeois male ideal. In contrast to the self-made man thought to rise in social rank thanks to hard work and business savvy, Anselmo represents the self-ruined aristocrat.[91] Hailing from one of Andalusia's noblest families, he lost an impressive fortune through both his own carelessness and a minor lawsuit leveled against him, in which the lawyers made out like bandits (277). This story of financial ruin signals Anselmo's mismanagement of his assets, which runs contrary to the expectation of economic and political acumen in the male subject.[92] Fittingly, it is the lawyers who profit from Anselmo's situation, symbolizing the nineteenth-century bourgeois ascendency; and it is by bourgeois standards that Anselmo is deemed effeminate for proving incapable of safeguarding the material signs of a privileged social status. In contrast with the cultural fantasy of an upward financial and social trajectory, Anselmo devolves from a wealthy youth with a promising future to "el más desgraciado ser de la tierra" (283; the most wretched being on earth). He has lost his wife, his fortune, his manhood, and even his humanity in the public eye.

Between his bedraggled appearance, mental instability, bizarre comportment, and financial ruin, Anselmo is wholly repulsive to middle-class society; he is a monster to be shunned. This is clear at the start of *La sombra*, when Anselmo is described as a social pariah: "Pocos le trataban; apenas había un escaso número de personas que se llamaran sus amigos, desdeñábanle los más, y todos los que no conocían algún antecedente de su vida, ni sabían ver lo que de singular y extraordinario había en aquel espíritu, le miraban con desdén y hasta con repugnancia" (269; Few people had anything to do with him; there were hardly a handful who might call themselves his friends; the majority scorned him, and all those who knew nothing of his life story, and who did not know how to see the singular and extraordinary aspect of that spirit, viewed him with contempt and even with repugnance). Nevertheless, Anselmo still comes across as sympathetic because he controls much of his own narrative in *La sombra*. In this regard, he differs from the female figures examined in this chapter, who were rendered mute and thus inscrutable in the text, thereby accentuating their monstrosity. Although his account is framed by the narrator's thoughts, Anselmo is able to voice his anxieties and insecurities, and the profound sense of shame that he feels for deviating so spectacularly from masculine norms. He is quick to decry his aberrant mental life as "una enfermedad. . . una aberración, un vicio orgánico" (279; a sickness . . . an aberration, an organic vice), and is the first to brand himself a monster within the text, lamenting, "Yo no sé por qué vine al mundo con esta monstruosidad" (279; I don't know why I came into the world with this monstrosity). His abominable qualities are thus presented as beyond his control, and there is a certain pathos in the suffering that they cause him, particularly given the gleeful cruelty with which the outside world treats him.

Through its use of multiple and at times contradictory narrative perspectives, *La sombra* constructs Anselmo, rather than the otherworldly Paris, as both the story's principal monster and its victim. But as a fantastic text predicated on narrative instability, the novella invites readers to question all accounts of the narrated events, and doing so reveals Elena as the story's real victim. Apart from providing a catalyst for Anselmo's marital-turned-masculine crisis, Elena is easy to efface from *La sombra*, reflecting what scant regard she received both from her husband and society at large. Readers know little about her physical appearance or personality beyond that she was considered beautiful and virtuous, and she utters exactly one word in the entire text. Who Elena is as an individual is irrelevant to Anselmo's tale; all that matters is what she represents to the men around her. For her father, she is the ticket to financial stability; he promises her to a wealthy Anselmo to offset his own risky investments. For Anselmo, marrying Elena affirms his masculinity in the public eye. Her beauty becomes a point of pride for him, garnering him the respect, or at least envy, of his peers. It is for this reason that her suspected infidelity is so devastating for Anselmo; an affair would undermine any masculine legitimacy that Elena afforded him. Thus objectified by both the men in her life, her story is undeniably tragic: shortly after her arranged marriage, she is suspected of infidelity, imprisoned, terrorized, and physically assaulted by her paranoid husband. She comes to fear him, trembling at the sound of his voice, and falls physically ill, confined to her bed until she expires after prolonged agony. Elena's flimsy characterization and untimely end recall the silenced and confined damsel in distress typical of Gothic narrative; and if Elena is *La sombra*'s Gothic victim, then Anselmo is the monster that victimizes her.[93] However, by focusing on his struggles with intrusive thoughts and society's relentless judgment, the novel skims over his role as "a mad domestic tyrant and jailer" when this behavior is, or should be, what renders him most monstrous.[94]

On the one hand, Anselmo's mistreatment of his wife is indicative of his generally problematic reliance upon violence to solve interpersonal conflicts. Anselmo is the novel's only character who either threatens or enacts violence upon others: he promises to beat Paris and slit his throat, but he settles for challenging the apparition to a duel (430), and vows to kill anyone who has gossiped about his marriage (613). In these instances, violence serves as his recourse against perceived affronts to his masculinity, and he strikes out at those who confront him with his shortcomings. Ironically, however, the protagonist's violent turns only constitute further evidence of his deviation from the masculine ideal; they indicate a lack of emotional and physical restraint that is anathema for the bourgeois gentleman. Thus, beyond branding him as subhuman, Anselmo's supposed masculine inadequacy also leads him to lash out violently, which only confirms his monstrosity in the public eye.

While rooted in the same frustrations, the violence that Anselmo unleashes upon his wife differs from other instances. In comparison with the stated intent to hurt or kill any males that offend him, Anselmo's violence against Elena stands out as particularly horrendous for its spontaneous brutality. From breaking open her door and bursting into her room unannounced (418), to ransacking the space in search for traces of an imaginary lover (438), Anselmo's behavior escalates quickly to actual physical assault. Moreover, unlike the unrealized threats he makes to male rivals, his violence toward Elena has real, fatal consequences, which is particularly appalling given Paris's potential nonexistence. Nevertheless, his transgressions against Elena are almost entirely glossed over by Anselmo in the course of his narration. The protagonist mentions offhandedly, "creo que la maltraté" (438; I believe that I abused her), indicating his disregard for Elena's suffering both at the time of the assault and in his recounting of it. Worse still, upon hearing Anselmo's admission, the extradiegetic narrator of *La sombra* remains wholly indifferent to Elena's plight. Although he had repeatedly referred to her as an "infeliz" (418, 419; wretched woman), he shows no concern for her wellbeing in the wake of her husband's assault, instead feeling concern for "lo que padecía el infeliz en aquellos momentos en que traía a la memoria su funesta obsesión" (439; what the miserable man was suffering in those moments when he recalled his ill-fated obsession).[95] Within Elena's narrative arc, Anselmo is the monster who menaces and maims, but both his narration and his listener's reaction reveal something even more horrifying: society's inability to discern truly monstrous behavior when the victim is female.[96]

This is evident in the scenes describing Elena's death, which elicits no commentary from the narrator, in a departure from his typically opinionated style. As Anselmo describes her prolonged agony, the narrator inquires if Paris made any appearance (620), and after the narration of her passing, he asks about Alejandro's reaction (622). When he finally mentions Elena, he cares only whether she had in fact been unfaithful to Anselmo, and appears unconcerned by her premature passing, never mind Anselmo's role in her suffering (623). In this sense, the narrator represents a society that is horrified by effeminacy, but unmoved by domestic violence, particularly against a potential adulteress. According to the 1870 Spanish Penal Code, "a woman who *once* sleeps with another man can legally be killed by her husband if caught *in flagranti delicto*, while a man can have as much casual sex as he likes," provided it occurs outside of the home and without scandal.⁹⁷ This misogynistic double standard provides the backdrop against which Anselmo's abusive acts are ignored. None of the many negative opinions about Anselmo that the narrator shares in the story's exposition mention his abusive behavior, and while his apparent unmanliness publicly brands him a monster, his reprehensible treatment of Elena does not change his reputation as "el más afable e inofensivo de los seres" (272; the most affable and inoffensive of beings).

The only characters who protest Anselmo's attitude and actions toward his wife are her parents, the Count and Countess of Torbellino, whose authority is consistently undermined in the text. Although he introduces his father-in-law as a respectable personage, Anselmo's descriptions of the count portray him rather buffoonishly, as a noisy and corpulent "mastodonte" (605; mastodon) lacking both grace and good sense. The countess is dispatched as "una vieja coqueta" (421, 609; an old flirt) whose beauty has long faded, leaving only the now inappropriate desire to attend youthful social gatherings. Thus, when the two rebuke Anselmo as "el más fiero de los monstruos imaginables" (421; the most ferocious monster imaginable) for mistreating Elena, their allegation of monstrosity carries little weight. It would seem that in late nineteenth-century Spain, Anselmo's spousal abuse is only noteworthy in that it underscores how far he falls from the masculine ideal. Elena's distress, pain, and finally death are hardly taken into account, and have no bearing on society's judgment of her husband or their designations of male monstrosity.

As a complement to "El verano" / "Theros" and "La mujer alta," *La sombra* demonstrates that men, too, must abide by specific rules regarding their appearance and comportment, under threat of demonization in the public eye. The haunting presence of Paris suggests that prevailing masculine standards are impossible to meet for any man of flesh and blood. As the story's fantastical figure, Paris is either a supernatural homewrecker stepped out of a painting, or a figment of Anselmo's hyperactive imagination. Either way, he is not a real man, and yet in the quest to be like him, men like Anselmo end up enacting masculinity's most toxic variant. Nevertheless, if the novella shows masculine ideals to be damaging to the male psyche, it portrays them as even more harmful to those women whose battered bodies pay the price for their partners' pathological insecurity. In Galdós's portrayal of nineteenth-century Spanish society, men were judged by their looks, behavior, financial standing, and social status, but the hideous monstrosity of domestic abuse escapes public censure. Aside from his own guilt, Anselmo faces no consequences for facilitating if not outright causing Elena's death. Thus, beyond revealing the social pressures surrounding bourgeois masculinity that can drive men from perceived to real monstrosity, *La sombra* demonstrates how disposable women can be.

The insignificance of a woman's life alluded to in *La sombra* is more starkly represented in Emilia Pardo Bazán's "Vampiro," which depicts alarming marital dynamics in small-town Galicia, an economically depressed region of Spain throughout the nineteenth and early twentieth centuries. "Vampiro" first appeared in the popular periodical *Blanco y negro* (Black and white) in 1901, with two images by acclaimed illustrator Narciso Méndez Bringa.[98] It was later re-published with a few key edits in Pardo Bazán's 1907 *Cuentos de terruño* (Stories from the homeland). Surprisingly, both the original illustrations and the changes to the text have thus far escaped critical notice. The story itself, however, has incited interest as a compelling example of Spanish Gothic writing and as Spain's first contribution to vampire fiction.[99] While "Vampiro" shares a number of thematic overlaps with "El verano" / "Theros," "La mujer alta," and *La sombra*, the original treatment that Pardo Bazán gives them sets the story apart as a text that openly interrogates, rather than merely insinuating, society's contradictory and discriminatory expectations for men and women of different stations.

Much like *La sombra*, "Vampiro" offers an unconventional twist to the familiar Gothic narrative of a young woman's victimization at the hands of her husband.[100] As recounted through an omniscient narrator, the residents of Gondelle and surrounding towns could speak of nothing but the wedding between Inesiña, barely fifteen years old, and the decrepit Don Fortunato Gayoso, aged eighty-three and a half (re-written as seventy-seven in the revised edition).[101] Though the age difference is remarkable, the greater cause for alarm seems to be that Gayoso has not only paid a handsome bride price, but also declared Inesiña heir to the considerable fortune he has made in the Americas. The townspeople assume it will be a matter of days before Inesiña comes into this inheritance, but against all odds, Gayoso rejuvenates before their eyes, gaining health and vigor as Inesiña succumbs to a lengthy illness and dies before the age of twenty. Readers are privy to the old man's secret conviction gleaned from an English quack: that close physical contact with his youthful bride would result in an exchange of vital energies by which Gayoso would reanimate and Inesiña waste away. In its original form, "Vampiro" ends with the ominous announcement that "D. Fortunato seeks a wife," which is met by angry threats from the townspeople.

In exploring what comprises male monstrosity within a marital context, "Vampiro" provides an interesting contrast to *La sombra*. Whereas Galdós's novella liberally sprinkles references to monstrosity throughout the characters' dialogue, "Vampiro" shies away from any such discussions. The word "monster" appears only once in the text, in reference to the monstrous racket generated by protestors at Don Fortunato's wedding. Nevertheless, as the story's title establishes, monstrosity and its shifting definitions are a central concern of the work, and while there is no traditional bloodsucking within the narrative, there is an abundance of callous and predatory behavior that the text condemns. In this manner, Pardo Bazán's tale is much less ambiguous than Galdós's in its demonizing characterization. Unlike Anselmo, Don Fortunato Gayoso is indisputably the villain of the piece and garners no reader sympathy. However, exactly what constitutes his monstrosity depends on the viewer's perspective, as highlighted through the text's narrative style.

On the one hand, the townspeople view his intent to marry at the age of eighty-three to be nothing short of grotesque. Not only is it unnatural that he has clung to bachelorhood for so long, but it is even worse that he should aspire to take a wife in his old age.[102] The illustration on the story's second page (fig. 2.2) accentuates the gross disparity in the physiques of the two spouses: Gayoso is pictured as wizened, hunched over, and leaning heavily upon his wife, who is shown to be young, handsome, and of enviable posture. Furthermore, marriage was principally intended to produce children in turn-of-the-century Spain, and procreation is by now out of the question for Gayoso. Referencing the dolls that Don Fortunato has prepared for his young bride, the narrator confides, "no se concebía. . . que pudiesen venir otras criaturas más que aquellas de fina porcelana" (it was inconceivable . . . that there could be other babes beyond those of fine porcelain). In delaying marriage and eschewing children, the wealthy Don Fortunato flouts the expectations of middle-class masculinity, and his eventual wedding to an adolescent is protested by more than five hundred neighbors clanging pots and pans. In a footnote to his edition of the story, Juan Paredes Nuñez identifies this protest as a *cencerrada*, a custom in rural

FIGURE 2.2. Illustration by Narciso Méndez Bringa from "Vampiro" in *Blanco y negro*, no. 539 (August 31, 1901).

Galicia meant to express disapproval of marriages involving egregious age differences.[103] However, the protest subsides within twenty-four hours, and the newlyweds are soon left in peace.

What saves Don Fortunato from lasting allegations of monstrosity for marrying Inés is his financial standing and the narrative surrounding it. As opposed to Anselmo, who modeled the self-ruined aristocrat, Don Fortunato fully embraces his identity as an *indiano*, one who emigrates to and amasses a fortune in the Americas before returning to Spain. As James Fernández explains, "During Spain's uneven, hesitant entry into the modern world of the nineteenth century," the *indiano* "came to be one of Spain's few images of social mobility."[104] Thus, Don Fortunato seemingly epitomizes the bourgeois fantasy of the self-made man, and his ability to accrue wealth, as well as the money itself, grants him leniency in the public's judgment. There is no mistaking the tone of awe in the narrator's voice upon exclaiming that "que el Sr. Gayoso se había traído un platal, constaba por referencias muy auténticas y fidedignas; sólo en la sucursal del Banco de Auriabella dejaba depositado, esperando ocasión de invertirlos, cerca de dos millones de reales" (the fact that Mr. Gayoso had brought back with him a fortune was confirmed by very authentic and trustworthy references; in the branch of the Bank of Auriabella alone he left deposited, awaiting an occasion for investment, nearly two million *reales*). Although the townspeople laughingly refer to the *indiano* as a "viejo chocho" (senile old man) and "pasa seca" (dried raisin), they respect his financial success, and Gayoso is universally considered the better catch in his marriage: "a Inesiña le había caído el premio mayor" (Inesiña had won the biggest prize). His name could not be more fitting, since Don Fortunato's fabulous riches guarantee his manhood despite his evident physical decline and the unorthodox timing of his marriage. If in "La mujer alta," poverty is damning for an unladylike woman, here the protagonist's fortune shields him from allegations of monstrosity as aberrant masculinity, ironically revealing society's classist prejudices.

At the same time, however, Gayoso's great wealth, and more specifically his self-centered spending of it, designates him as antisocial and even menacing to the local way of life. The nineteenth-century *indiano* narrative did not end with the expatriate's return to his hometown, but with the investment of his riches in the surrounding community, beginning with extended family.[105] *Indianos* were known to commission extravagant mansions, but they were likewise expected to alleviate the material needs of any and all relatives, as well as fund educational, religious, and community constructions throughout the region, thereby securing "a moral legitimacy" for potentially ill-begotten gains.[106] Don Fortunato deviates from the social script by refusing to spread his wealth: "Cuantos pedazos de tierra se vendían en el país, sin regatear los compraba Gayoso" (However many plots of land were sold in the country, Gayoso bought them at full price). He finances construction of the requisite *indiano* palace, "decorada y amueblada sin reparar en gastos" (decorated and furnished without sparing any expense), but no mention is made of any investment in the public infrastructure of Gondelle or of neighboring towns. Nor does he appear to support any relatives, as this perceived slight fuels the protests at his wedding. Just prior to describing the angry objectors, the narrator relates the public outcry over Don Fortunato naming Inés his sole heir: "Los berridos de los parientes, más o menos próximos del ricachón, llegaron al cielo: hablaban de tribunales, de locura senil, de encierro en el manicomio" (The bellowing of relatives both close and distant to the rich man reached the heavens: they spoke of courts, of senile insanity, of confinement in a madhouse). Thus, the ensuing protest seems to be less motivated by concern for Inés, or even disgust with Don Fortunato's decision to marry, than by his unwillingness to take on the civic responsibilities implied in the *indiano* role. Rather than masculine inadequacy, as in the case of Anselmo, it is Don Fortunato's hoarding of wealth that offends and enrages his relatives and neighbors. In their eyes, Gayoso's self-interest is a destabilizing and thus monstrous force within Galician society.

Ironically, what the citizens of Gondelle find most objectionable in Don Fortunato only scratches the surface of his egoism. The townspeople are ignorant of the depths of depravity that the octogenarian displays within his marriage:

Sabía Gayoso que Inesiña era la víctima, la oveja traída al matadero... no sentía ni rastro de compasión. Agrrábase a Inés, absorbiendo su respiración sana, su hálito perfumado, delicioso... y si creyese que haciendo una incisión en el cuello de la niña y chupando la sangre en la misma vena se remozaba, sentíase capaz de realizarlo.

(Gayoso knew that Inesiña was the victim, the sheep led to the slaughterhouse; ... he didn't feel even a hint of compassion. He gripped Inés, absorbing her healthy respiration, her delicious, perfumed breath ... and if he had believed that he would rejuvenate by making an incision in the girl's neck and sucking her blood directly from the vein, he felt capable of doing so.)

In his intent to absorb Inés's life force for himself, Don Fortunato lives up to the story's title by exhibiting an egoism so extreme that he would kill another human to extend his own life. His willingness to sacrifice his wife in the name of self-preservation is particularly horrifying given the long and full life that he has already led. Whereas the average life expectancy for a Spanish man was only 33.9 years in 1900, Don Fortunato had already enjoyed an additional fifty years by the story's start, rich with experiences overseas.[107]

In contrast, Inesiña is a sheltered young orphan with her whole life ahead of her. Her tender age is emphasized in the story's repeated use of her nickname, the diminutive "Inesiña," rather than the adult "Inés," which only appears in the story's second half. Moreover, her innocence borders on naivete, as symbolized in the twin images of the lamb led to slaughter and the dolls "con caras de tontas" (with foolish faces) that await her in the marital chamber. Like the ill-fated lamb and clueless dolls, Inés is unaware of what her husband has in store for her, and dedicates herself wholeheartedly to his care: "¡Asistir al viejecito! Vaya: eso sí que lo haría de muy buen grado Inés. Día y noche... se comprometía a atenderle, a no abandonarle un minuto. ¡Pobre señor!" (Looking after the little old man! Wow: Inés would do that very willingly. Day and night ... she committed to assisting him, to not abandoning him for one minute. Poor man!). Whereas in previous texts readers were only granted access to the perspective of the male storytellers, the free indirect discourse of "Vampiro" allows an omniscient narrator to enter any character's thoughts at will, and the text's juxtaposition of Inés's guileless sentiments with those of her husband augment the monstrosity of Don Fortunato's designs for her. Whether or not his embraces effectively drain the girl of her lifeblood, his stated intent is to kill. Inés's compassion for her ailing husband is met with unfeeling cruelty that is nothing short of sociopathic.

This lack of regard for human life—not his feeble body that must be carried to the altar, nor his unapologetic tightfistedness—is what strikes the reader as most monstrous about Don Fortunato. Yet his callous self-interest should come as no surprise, considering that his identity as an affluent *indiano* likely implies collusion with the transatlantic slave trade. Of the thousands of Spaniards who set sail for the Americas in hopes of improving their lot in life, only a select few amassed any true wealth overseas.[108] Those who were most successful acquired their fortune financing the slave trade through direct or indirect means.[109] Although "Vampiro" does not specify the source of Don Fortunato's money, the narrator does place its provenance into question upon mentioning that "El sería bien ganado o mal ganado, porque esos que vuelven del otro mundo con tantísimos miles de duros, sabe Dios qué historia ocultan entre las dos tapas de la maleta" (it could have been earned by fair means or foul, because those who return from the other world with so very many thousands of *duros*, God knows what story they hide between the two sides of their suitcase). The allusion to slavery, while subtle, would not have been lost on Pardo Bazán's original readers, who were well-aware of the polemics surrounding the trafficking, sale, and ownership of individuals throughout the nineteenth century.[110]

Within this context, Don Fortunato's treatment of Inesiña echoes his probable exploitation of captured Africans across the Atlantic Ocean. She, like the enslaved bodies sold overseas, is not considered a person, but a good that has been rightfully purchased to be used and abused at will.[111] In his casual rationalization of "¿No había pagado? Pues Inés era suya" (Hadn't he paid? Well then Inés was his), Don Fortunato claims ownership of the girl as his property, and the young wife spends her days attending to her husband's every need, while she slowly succumbs to "consunción, fiebre ética, algo que expresaba del modo más significativo la ruina de un organismo que había regalado a otro su capital" (consumption, tubercular fever, something that expressed in the most significant way the ruin of an organism that had gifted its capital to another). The use of the word "capital" here is particularly evocative, as it underscores the ruthless capitalism that informs Don Fortunato's—and his surrounding society's—worldview. The financial success of his business endeavors abroad has provided him with social prestige back in Spain, rewarding the quest for profit as a guiding principle. At the same time, the marriage market dictates that a penniless woman's worth lies in her beauty and reproductive potential, transitory properties contingent on youth. Economically speaking, it is unsurprising that Gayoso should view his marriage to Inés as the exchange of his riches for her youth, which he hopes to literally consume.

As a man of innumerable resources, Gayoso feels entitled to deal in what he considers less-worthy lives, and the larger community generally enables his behavior. Thus, the terrifying aspect of "Vampiro" lies not only in the actions of a single man, but in the complicity of an entire social system that devalues the lives of certain individuals, which the text does not shy away from demonstrating. Though the neighbors suspect the sordid origin of Don Fortunato's earnings, they do not care to investigate further. Instead, they tacitly condone any connection to the slave trade by asking, "¿quién se mete a investigar el origen de un fortunón? Los fortunones son como el buen tiempo: se disfrutan y no se preguntan sus causas" (Who busies themselves with investigating the origin of an enormous fortune? Enormous fortunes are like good weather: they are enjoyed without inquiring as to their cause). Similarly, they turn a blind eye to any red flags surrounding the *indiano*'s marriage to Inesiña. While they protest the union on the wedding day, no one thinks to intervene or even criticize the husband-to-be in the weeks leading up to the event. Instead, Inesiña's "luck" in attracting the eye of Gayoso is discussed in "los casinos, boticas y demás círculos" (the casinos, pharmacies and other circles) coded as male spaces, as well as in "los atrios y sacristías de las parroquiales" (the atria and sacristies of the parishes), considered the domain of women and priests. This is visually expressed in the opening illustration for "Vampiro," in which an elderly couple dressed in regional clothing discuss and pass judgment on Gondelle's most newsworthy couple (fig. 2.3). Behind the pair, groups of men, women, and children huddle to gossip before what appears to be a church door. The image emphasizes the universal nature of the sentiment that Inesiña had come out on top in the unbalanced union.

The visual representation of the church, as well as the reference to the sacristy, a space reserved for the clergy, further highlight the role of powerful local institutions in condoning and even promoting the exploitation of impressionable young women in rural Galicia. Notably, it is Inesiña's uncle, the parish priest, who brokers her marriage to Don Fortunato and blesses the union. Thus, both the informal and formal institutions of the town and surrounding area, including those endowed with moral authority, approve what amounts to the sale of desirable young women to wealthy suitors, particularly *indianos*, regardless of exaggerated differences in age or physical condition.[112] Apart from the initial *cencerrada*, there are no subsequent interventions in the *indiano*'s marital relations, nor any evidence of concern for Inesiña's deteriorating health as the marriage wears on. The only public commentary reproduced in the story's text concerns Don Fortunato's miraculous rejuvenation, whereas his wife's alarming decline is relegated to two sentences in the story's final paragraph, reflecting her social status as expendable. This dismissiveness echoes the narrator's initial introduction of Inesiña when, voicing the opinion of the townspeople, (s)he remarks that in spite of the girl's beauty, "¡hay tantas así desde el Sil al Avieiro!" (there are so many like her from Sil to Avieiro!). To what degree, then, would the denizens of Gondelle have protested Gayoso's plans had they known his marital intentions were murderous rather than amorous?

The story's closing sentence offers some hope in this regard when the townspeople express vehement disapproval of Don Fortunato for the first time. In response to the proclamation that the octogenarian—by now eighty-seven or eighty-eight—seeks a new wife, the neighbors demand that "o se marcha del pueblo, o la cencerrada para en quemarle la casa y sacarle arrastrando para matarle de una paliza" (either he leaves town, or the protest ends by burning his house and dragging him outside to beat him to death). This threat of extreme violence, a considerable escalation from the banging of pots and pans at Gayoso's first nuptials, appears to be motivated by Inesiña's premature passing, though she is neither mentioned nor alluded to. The 1907 revised edition adds "¡Estas cosas no se toleran dos veces!" (Such things are not tolerated twice!), implying that the people of Gondelle will not condone a repeat performance of the *indiano*'s brutally self-serving marriage.[113] Nevertheless, the final sentence of the revised text suggests that neither public condemnation nor the threat of punishment affect Don Fortunato in the least: "Y don Fortunato sonríe, mascando con sus dientes postizos el rabo de un puro" (And Don Fortunato smiles, chewing with his false teeth the end of a cigar).[114] He obviously considers the community's ultimatum to be performative posturing, and can quite literally afford to call the town's bluff. Armed with wealth that is unimaginable to those around him, Don Fortunato has faced no consequences for his probable participation in the slave trade, and will likely face none for procuring

FIGURE 2.3. Illustration by Narciso Méndez Bringa from "Vampiro" in *Blanco y negro*, no. 539 (August 31, 1901).

a wife who dies under mysterious circumstances. As "Vampiro" posits, a man of unlimited means and nonexistent morals is the most frightening monster of all.[115]

Unlike Don Fortunato, previous figures dissected in this chapter have been deemed monstrous for their deviation from the socially sanctioned gender norms of female domesticity or male authority and achievement. These characters unsettled and at times repulsed those around them for their supposedly freakish nature. Yet in "El verano" / "Theros" and "La mujer alta," readers are offered alternative interpretations thanks to the texts' fantastic nature. Galdós's lady traveler is either a diabolical seductress or simply a highly attractive female, and Alarcón's tall woman is either a witchlike harbinger of death or a disadvantaged older lady. Reader perception of these figures changes dramatically upon either accepting or rejecting their status as not of this world, and the decision hinges on the reader's level of identification with narrators of questionable reliability. Filtered through a normative male perspective, "El verano" / "Theros" and "La mujer alta" capture the profound sense of shame and even existential crisis generated by feelings of impotence in a middle-class man. Thus, these narratives could be read psychoanalytically as the fragile male ego's attempt to externalize the source of discomfort by casting beings perceived to be emasculating as literal monsters with superhuman abilities. *La sombra* complicates this dynamic by creating multiple monstrous figures in Paris and Anselmo. Given that the very human Anselmo is also a source of terror within the text, denying the supernatural does not negate the monstrosity depicted, though competing narrative claims do mitigate the horrendous nature of the protagonist's actions. Neither the existence of a perfect, invincible rival nor a diagnosis of mental illness absolves him of abusing Elena, but both possibilities validate to a certain extent Anselmo's claim to victimhood, thereby suggesting that the quixotic quest for bourgeois masculinity can itself result in monstrous behavior.

"Vampiro" takes the relationship between normative masculinity and monstrosity one step further. Whereas Anselmo's frustrated masculinity finds expression in abhorrent outbursts, it is precisely the measure of Don Fortunato's success as a man, that is, his money, that enables him to indulge in truly inhuman acts. Furthermore, it is not merely his appearance or comportment, but his character that is monstrous, as revealed in the *indiano*'s fiercely guarded secret. The fantastic uncertainty over whether he has indeed stolen years off Inés's life through occult means leads readers to wonder if it truly matters whether he possesses preternatural powers. Ultimately, the possibility of superhuman abilities is not what makes Gayoso terrifying. Instead, it is his callous claim of ownership over Inés's life. Of all the monsters we have encountered thus far, Don Fortunato alone is unequivocally predatory.

Thus, Pardo Bazán's short story draws reader attention away from monstrosity's physical forms to dwell on its manifestation as immorality. In so doing, she implicates the whole of Spanish society in the systematic devaluation of female lives. Both Don Fortunato and Inés are fully committed to the gender ideals that equate masculinity with the accumulation of wealth and femininity with care-taking; in fact, they each embody these roles to excess.[116] The disparate fortunes that result—rejuvenation and potential remarriage for the one, and suffering and death for the other—reflect the inherent inequity in the contrasting expectations for men and women and the forms of capital in which each is permitted to deal. As Beatriz Trigo asserts, women have always been "vampirizada[s] por la sociedad patriarcal" ("vampirized" by patriarchal society), and "Vampiro" exposes the gross imbalance of power that all too easily breeds male monstrosity and encourages female sacrifice.[117] This criticism can be found in the texts by Galdós and Alarcón as well, since each female character who dutifully fulfills the assigned feminine role dies prematurely in the home, suggesting that life as an obedient, selfless wife without free will or bodily sovereignty is itself a symbolic death. Nevertheless, in allowing access to the female character's interiority through the use of free indirect discourse, "Vampiro" is an outlier. Not coincidentally, there is not even a whiff of victimization in Don Fortunato's characterization. Inés is the sole sufferer in Pardo Bazán's work, regardless of whether her demise is due to supernatural influence or to the more mundane cause of ceaseless caregiving. From start to finish, it is clear that Don Fortunato's perceived identity as a self-made man grants him privileges that an impoverished young girl will never experience.

Whereas the use of the monstrous and the supernatural to explore the oppression of women was common in nineteenth-century Anglophone writing by female authors—famously deemed the "Female Gothic" by Ellen Moers, the general dearth of women writers experimenting with this aesthetic in Spain precluded the development of such a subgenre there.[118] Pardo Bazán stands out from other Spanish authors for her otherworldly depiction of female victimization, and although neither the author's sex nor her gender identity determines the form of her fantastic or other writing, her experiences as a woman who faced chauvinism allowed her an alternative perspective on gender nonconformity and monstrosity. Unsurprisingly, "Vampiro" is particularly explicit in its indictment of society's hypocrisy for condemning physical monstrosity but condoning violent attitudes and behavior toward women. Unlike most texts belonging to the "Female Gothic," however, the social commentary in "Vampiro" is tied to its fantastic open-endedness. Most famously exemplified in the works of Ann Radcliffe, the "Female Gothic" is often characterized as a literature of "the supernatural explained," in which bizarre happenings are fully and rationally accounted for by the story's end.[119] In contrast, "Vampiro" maintains its fantastic narrative ambiguity: Inés's life force may be consumed through magical means or just through the daily toil of caring for an infirm and pathologically egocentric husband. Either way, the mere possibility that her demise has a supernatural cause suggests that the self-sacrifice demanded of Spanish women is, contrary to public opinion, unnatural. Fully articulating what "El verano" / "Theros," "La mujer alta," and *La sombra* insinuate, Pardo Bazán's vampire fiction reveals misogyny as the greatest monstrosity harbored both by the individual and society in turn-of-the-century Spain.

CHAPTER 3

Accursed Peoples

Challenging Racial Stereotypes and Hierarchies

In Chapter 2 of *Monsters by Trade*, Surwillo asserts that "for a contemporary bourgeois novel to function, certain secrets cannot be stated, lest the novel reveal society's basic monstrosity. Race is one of these secrets."[1] Notably, Surwillo speaks only of the Spanish realist novel, eliding other literary forms that were popular during the post-Isabelline period. This chapter expands on Surwillo's observation by turning to fantastic short fictions from late nineteenth- and early twentieth-century Spain, shedding light on how allusions to the supernatural allow for more explicit engagement with the question of race obliquely explored in more canonical texts. Specifically, I examine four short stories that follow the unexpected misfortune of a first-person narrator seemingly cursed by one or more racialized Others: various indigenous peoples in Galdós's "Tropiquillos" and Pardo Bazán's "El brasileño," a young Romani woman in Pardo Bazán's "Maldición de gitana," and a Jewish shopkeeper in Escamilla's "El cuadro de maese Abraham." Whereas a twenty-first-century reader would likely classify these individuals as ethnically rather than racially distinct, in the context of post-Isabelline Spain, indigenous peoples, the Roma, and Jews were all viewed in opposition to the "Spanish race," itself an ethnic category described in racial terms. My analyses thus contribute to a recent body of scholarship, anchored in Joshua Goode's 2009 study *Impurity of Blood*, on the literary and visual depiction of race as it was conceived in late nineteenth-century Spain.[2]

Compared with the themes of social class and gender examined in previous chapters, the question of race and particularly racial alterity in their aforementioned acceptation is central to relatively few fantastic short stories of the period. Due to the expulsion of ethnic minorities from Spain in the medieval and early modern periods (Jews in 1492 and *moriscos*, or Muslims who had converted to Catholicism, in 1609), and the lingering obsession with *limpieza de sangre* (purity of blood) as a prerequisite for many social privileges, the Spanish state had long prided itself on a racialized ethnic homogeneity.[3] Even contact with numerous indigenous peoples throughout Spain's colonial history was thought to have fused these groups into Spanish bloodlines without diluting a supposed national essence, rather than resulting in any racial pluralism.[4] This official discourse of sameness meant that questions of racial difference were nowhere near as ubiquitous within Spain as "the woman question" or "the social question" in the late 1800s.

Nevertheless, interracial relations were discussed with regularity in Spanish public fora, given the reach of Spanish colonialism and the presence of a highly persecuted Roma population within Spain, and were foregrounded across a wide range of literary works, particularly those intended for mass consumption. For instance, black- and yellowface were commonplace in popular theater of the late 1800s, serving to both provide comedic effect and reaffirm Spain's colonial policies—as well as its whiteness.[5] Novels of the same period varied widely in their approach to race relations. In celebrity author Faustina Sáez de Melgar's melodramatic serial novel *Los miserables* (1862–63; The miserable), the protagonist's mixed race is essential to the narrative intrigue, driving the plot to reflect the author's feminist and abolitionist agendas.[6] In contrast, realist works penned for bourgeois audiences frequently portrayed racial difference as divorced from biology or ethnicity. Although a handful of realist novels featured prominent characters of Jewish heritage, racial alterity was often projected upon white female protagonists perceived as threatening by bourgeois society, as in the working-class heroines of Pardo Bazán's *La tribuna* (1883) and Galdós's *Fortunata y Jacinta* (1886–1887). These portrayals of race have only recently received scholarly attention and may not even have registered with many of the novels' readers.[7] However, the question of race is harder to ignore in contemporary fantastic fictions in which heavily stereotyped indigenous Asians and Americans, gypsies, and Jews appear as antagonists.

This chapter highlights how those fantastic short stories from the late nineteenth and early twentieth centuries that reflect upon racial relations within the Spanish nation and empire repeatedly do so through the Gothic trope of the curse. Analyzing shared elements across a range of such curse stories yields unexpected insights into popular conceptions of the Spanish race in relation to a wide array of racialized Others. In particular, the threat of a curse in narratives of cross-cultural relations allows for meditations on individual and collective agency and autonomy as they relate to ethnic difference. Each text invites readers to consider: who wields the power in an interracial exchange? Is that power temporary or lasting, and what are its limits? Whereas the curse is often thought of as recourse for the disadvantaged (here, the non-Spaniard), the fantastic quality of these texts—which leaves the efficacy of the curse in doubt—reveals the potentially illusory nature of any reversal in the position of the downtrodden, thereby indicating the limitations of the curse as an exercise of power. Readers are left pondering who is truly doomed to suffer: the Spaniard who may be hexed, or the racially distinct adversary who is incapable of changing his or her marginal position?

The Curse of Racial Difference in History and Literature

Matthew Jacobson reminds readers in *Whiteness of a Different Color* that "races are invented categories," whose basis lies "not in nature but in politics and culture."[8] Thus, both the concept of race itself and the criteria for racial classification change considerably across sociohistorical contexts. Even within a single society, such as that of Restoration Spain, the term "*raza*," or "race," could harbor multiple meanings. Particularly for Spaniards writing in the late nineteenth century, race was a hazy construct whose definition shifted from one usage to the next, alternately denoting ethnicity, nationality, or even social class.[9] Tracing Pardo Bazán's references to *raza* across a range of short stories, Lou Charnon-Deutsch can only generalize that the term "designated groups with homologous characteristics," drawn together through shared affinities or estranged from one another in antipathy.[10]

Publicly, racial discourse in Spain in the late 1800s often centered around *la raza española* (the Spanish race) or *la raza ibérica* (the Iberian race) as an essentialized national character in line with Romantic notions of *volkgeist*.[11] Reporting on the 1892 Congreso Geográfico Hispano-Portugués-Americano (the Hispanic-Portuguese-American Geographic Conference) celebrating the quadricentennial of Columbus's arrival to the Americas, prominent geographer Ricardo Beltrán y Rózpide observed that the conference "sirvió para mostrar una vez más el valor de las virtualidades y energías que la raza hispana atesora" (once again demonstrated the value of the Iberian race's potentialities and energies), reminding participants "que aun estamos llamados a grandes hechos en los futuros destinos de la humanidad" (that we are still called to do great things in the future destinies of humanity).[12] Spain's historical greatness was attributed to racial superiority throughout the conference proceedings, as well as in numerous other commemorative writings from 1892.

For instance, in one of her many reflections on the quadricentennial celebrations, Pardo Bazán praises Martín Alonso Pinzón, captain of the Pinta, as "impulsivo, sublime en su terquedad—español" (impulsive, sublime in his obstinacy—Spanish) thus nationalizing those personal attributes that ensured his success.[13] Doubling down on this essentialization of the Spanish character, she contrasts the Spanish sailor to the Genovese Columbus, noting the former's intrepidness and resolve as holdovers of "la ardiente tenacidad de la raza íbera, que se agiganta en presencia de lo imposible" (the fiery tenacity of the Iberian race, that rises up in the presence of the impossible).[14] Allegedly Spanish qualities are thus viewed as enduring elements of a collective identity with roots in an ancient civilization. They are thereby racialized, fulfilling the three criteria Goode ascribes to turn-of-the-century conceptions of race: "That it was transmitted, that it lingered through time, and that it was unique to Spain."[15] The fact that these racial ruminations were inspired by the Spanish commemorations of 1492 further confirms Goode's assertion that modern states were most apt to hone in on questions of racial distinction "in service of nationalism."[16]

Although talk of a Spanish race ramped up considerably at the turn of the century, this emphasis on an inherited ethnic singularity dates back to the Middle Ages, when the concept of a Spanish *casta* (caste) characterized by *limpieza de sangre* was first used to separate "true" Spaniards of Catholic ancestry from Muslims, Jews, and their descendants. That religion be viewed as "a transmitted inheritance" carried in one's blood rather than as a matter of personal faith marked the discourse of *casta* as racial in nature.[17] Unsurprisingly, Catholicism remained a cornerstone of Spain's racial heritage, in spite of the secularization of public policy in the nineteenth century.[18] Catholic fervor had further granted the Spanish *raza* with a distinctive imperial calling, noteworthy for its supposedly civilizing objective. Thus, throughout the 1800s, the term *raza* "crystallized around the idea of Spain's legacy as a conqueror, empire builder, and unifier of different peoples" under the banner of Catholicism.[19] Additional attributes deemed inherent to an abiding Spanish identity included a strong sense of honor, "courage, faith, perseverance, [and] wisdom."[20]

Clearly, the concept of race in question was not grounded in phenotypical characteristics such as skin color, and yet belonging to the Spanish race entailed a certain degree of "whiteness," as evidenced in the debates surrounding colonial legislation to deny citizenship to the *castas pardas*, free Americans of African ancestry.[21] This disenfranchisement was largely rooted in the fear that granting votes to the *castas pardas* would shift the balance of power away from Spaniards in their Caribbean territories. However, discrimination against the *castas pardas* inevitably drew attention to the visible difference of their darker skin tones, which cast Spaniards as fair-skinned by contrast. The bourgeois emphasis on "una limpieza y blancura corporal" (a bodily cleanliness and whiteness) as depicted in novels like *Fortunata y Jacinta* was furthermore imagined to affirm Spain's position in a Europe defined to consist of white imperialists dominating darker-skinned colonial subjects.[22] The whitening of the Spanish race in the late nineteenth century is amply captured in multiple references to swarthy and therefore foreign complexions in the short stories examined in this chapter.

Because race came to the forefront of public discussion within larger debates concerning Spanish nationhood, it was a topic of growing interest in the final decades of the nineteenth century, when forging a cohesive collective identity became a top priority in the wake of the 1868 Revolution. In contrast to political affiliation, regional identity, or social class, which were thought to divide the Spanish populace into potentially antagonistic sectors, race was evoked by liberal politicians to create a sense of national belonging.[23] Conservative statesman Antonio Cánovas del Castillo, architect of the 1874 Bourbon restoration in Spain, exemplified the tendency in his 1882 *Discurso sobre la nación* (Address on the nation), in which he described the nation as a group of men living in a set territory under a single government, joined by the bonds of race and language.[24] Yet while it promoted a sense of unity, the concept of a Spanish race did not include all inhabitants of the nation. For instance, the Roma community continued to be viewed as foreigners of separate racial lineage in spite of having an established presence in Spain since the fifteenth century. Blind to its own role in exacerbating Romani insularity, mainstream Spanish society condemned the Roma for resisting integration with Spanish bloodlines, while persecuting them in relentless and at times violent fashion.[25] Thus, even as the construct of race endowed many Spaniards with a sense of belonging, perceived racial differences were used to justify discrimination and even physical oppression within Spanish borders.

If fixing the contours of the Spanish race was an integral part of liberal nation building in the final third of the nineteenth century, a preoccupation with national decline at the century's end—as encapsulated in the Regenerationist movement—led some Spanish intellectuals to seek a racial basis for the loss of empire and diminished prestige occasioned by the Spanish-American War of 1898. Concurrent with the popularity of Max Nordau's *Degeneration* (1892) throughout Europe, a number of Spanish social scientists concluded that the nation's decline could be traced to the enervation of its citizenry, blaming political and social ills on a debilitated Spanish race.[26] Early criminal anthropologists like Rafael Salillas fanned the flames of this racial rhetoric by bemoaning the infiltration of gypsy blood into the Spanish population as one cause of the latter's degeneracy. Although turn-of-the-century racial theorizations generally began as an introspective examination into Spanish decline, all too often they ended up scapegoating perceived outsiders for the nation's shortcomings.

That discussions of race in Restoration Spain easily veered into meditations on alterity made the subject prime material for Gothic representation. In societies fixated on classifying individuals into separate groups along inherited bloodlines, Gothic fiction provides an outlet for anxieties over the permeability of boundaries between the self and the Other. Speaking of the wider European and Anglo-American traditions, Eugenia DeLamotte observes that "the rise and proliferation of [Gothic literature . . .] coincides historically with the rise of conceptions of 'race,'" attesting to their shared fear of "dark, mysterious Others."[27] H. L. Malchow further argues that racial thought and Gothic fiction were mutually constitutive discourses in nineteenth-century Britain; just as race was described in Gothic terms, Gothic literature often capitalized on society's racial fears. Thus, "*racism* required a 'demonization' . . . of difference," and British Gothic novels abounded in swarthy villains, as sinister Moors, Italians, and Spaniards stalked the pages of many popular works.[28]

Previous scholarship on Gothic portrayals of racial difference, largely interested in British and Anglo-American cultural production, have focused on the trope of the monster, attesting to how frequently those of other races were literally demonized.[29] In the North American tradition, a subset of nineteenth-century Gothic literature painted racialized Others who were the victims of colonization, particularly Native Americans, not as monsters but as specters. Never fully repressed nor erased from history, they haunted the dominant group from the margins of society.[30] In the Spanish case, the trope most often associated with interracial encounters during this time period is that of the curse. This distinction is logical, given Chris Baldick's declaration of the curse as the principal structuring motif of shorter Gothic fiction.[31] Although the novel is generally privileged as the paradigmatic Gothic genre, Spain's engagement with the Gothic occurred almost exclusively in short stories during the post-Isabelline period.[32]

At its heart, the Gothic curse narrative involves a plea for supernatural intervention to ensure an individual or entire group's earthly suffering and/or eternal damnation. Some texts include the enunciation of the curse, highlighting the intention to harm, while others strictly focus on its consequences. In both variations, the curse story is tied to questions of power. The cursed party is powerless to change his or her destiny, which seems to be under the curser's control. Accordingly, the curse is often presented as a mechanism of resistance for the disenfranchised; one need only possess the faculty of language to deploy it.[33] In the words of Karen Stollznow, "curses are a kind of linguistic vigilante justice where the victim tries to take back the power."[34] Stollznow's statement not only underscores the shifting power relations underlying curse stories, but further raises the theme of justice as broached in these texts. True to the Old Testament proverb that "the curse causeless shall not come" (Proverbs 26:2; King James Version), Gothic curse stories tend to provide some justification for the curse, though readers may debate whether or not it is warranted. Finally, although the curse confers power upon the curser, it may also prove dangerous for him or her, at times backfiring in spectacular fashion. Each of these attributes of the Gothic curse story—a narrative trajectory of inescapable misfortune for the cursed party and potential harm to the curser, and an engagement with the complex themes of power and justice—are endowed with a racial dimension in the short stories featured in this chapter.

Despite the scarcity of scholarship on the subject, the trope of the curse is well-suited to capturing racial stereotypes and hierarchical conceptions of different races, ethnicities, and cultures. Popular folklore worldwide has long cast marginalized racial or ethnic groups as accursed peoples, often justifying their mistreatment thusly, as in the case of the Curse of Ham.[35] Within the biblical context, Brian Britt suggests that curses played a role in consolidating ancient notions of ethnicity by erecting a supernatural boundary between groups "that were uncomfortably similar to each other."[36] Clearly, the curse was imagined and employed as a racially and ethnically divisive force long before the Gothic took shape. Later, in the Victorian Gothic vogue, the trope of the curse commonly appeared in mummy fictions, inspired both in nineteenth-century archaeological expeditions and the 1882 British invasion of Egypt to secure control of the Suez Canal.[37] While these tales most immediately questioned the British military presence in Egypt and British claims to the nation's artefacts, they inevitably addressed perceived differences of appearance, character, and culture separating the British invaders from the Egyptians they encountered. In this manner, the nineteenth-century Gothic curse story maintained the racialized tensions of folkloric and Biblical traditions.

As curse stories, the Spanish texts analyzed in this chapter capture the power differential between protagonists of the "national race" and diverse racial Others considered to be inferior, as well as the apparent inversion of this hierarchy through magical means. Yet because these texts are structurally fantastic, they question the reality of narrated events, including the efficacy of the curse at the story's center. Neither characters nor readers can be certain that the protagonist's suffering is indeed caused by occult intervention, which facilitates scrutiny of the power dynamics proposed in the text. If it is unclear whether the curse functions as articulated, it is likewise questionable whether the curser actually wields any power. Instead, this power may be purely illusory, producing no real change in the curser's disadvantaged situation. To what extent, then, is the protagonist truly victimized within the narrative?

The discussion of class and gender in Chapters 1 and 2 demonstrates that uncertainty surrounding the presence of the supernatural in a fantastic text is often tied to skepticism toward the narrative perspective. In the tales by Galdós, Pardo Bazán, and Escamilla featured here, those who recount their cursed status are similarly suspect. Across the board, we hear the voices of men who have enjoyed a privileged status, racially and otherwise, in life. As native Spaniards who either possess family wealth or fortunes amassed through colonial endeavors, they appear as exemplars of the enterprising, "civilizing" Spanish race, brought down only by exotic peoples practicing dark arts. But if the curse is empty rhetoric, then the protagonists' misfortune may just as well be the result of their own excessive hubris or karmic retribution for past wrongdoing. In undermining the narrative authority of these texts, the fantastic reveals the curse to be a smokescreen that deflects attention from Spanish racism and deeply unethical colonial practices that themselves have pernicious effects. Thus, belief in the curse reaffirms the prevalent narrative that pits the cultured Spanish race against darker-skinned, backward and barbaric peoples, and skepticism toward the curse's power allows for alternate, more complex racial narratives. Ultimately, the uncertainty of the fantastic in the selected stories encourages questioning of how race is presented in the text and within Spanish society as a whole.

Cursing the Colonizer
GALDÓS'S "TROPIQUILLOS" AND PARDO BAZÁN'S "EL BRASILEÑO"

In Galdós's "Tropiquillos" and Pardo Bazán's "El brasileño," the curse is pronounced in faraway colonized lands, though its effects are felt long after the protagonists return home. This context of Spanish colonialism facilitates the development of racial themes in both texts, since colonizing activities abroad necessarily entailed interracial encounters. Spanish colonialism in particular placed representatives of the nation in contact with diverse peoples across multiple continents, given that Spain retained possessions in the Americas and Asia until 1898, and Africa through the 1950s. Although Spain referred to its colonies as *la España ultramarina* (overseas Spain), conferring upon them national status, the privileges granted therein were not applied equally to all inhabitants. Not only were the *castas pardas* disenfranchised, but the enslavement of Africans was legal in Cuba until 1886. While these discriminatory practices served the political ends of maintaining Spanish dominance in the colonies, they were often justified through arguments of Spanish racial superiority.

Beyond discrimination against specific populations, racism more generally sustained the entire colonial project in Spain and elsewhere. In *A Missionary Nation*, Scott Eastman describes how "nineteenth-century politicians and statesmen spilled a great deal of ink explaining how culture, ethnicity, and race differentiated Europeans from Africans and Asians" in an attempt to rationalize the latter's subjugation.[38] Spanish belief in a civilizing mission was likewise based in prejudiced conceptions of American, Asian, and African primitiveness. Yet if Spain's racial superiority was assumed in comparison with the indigenous populations of foreign lands, the nation's loss of nearly all its colonial holdings by the turn of the century cast Spain's own racial health into doubt. As the imperialist fervor reached a zenith in other European nations, the status of each empire was equated with the colonizer's racial strength, which was constantly measured against that of other imperial powers.[39] Spain's imperial defeat was made particularly glaring in the face of British imperial ascendency, seemingly indicating degeneration of the national race.

Consequently, reflections on empire frequently entailed meditations on race in the time when Galdós and Pardo Bazán were writing, as captured in "Tropiquillos" and "El brasileño." Somewhat surprising in these texts, however, is the use of Gothic imagery and fantastic storytelling to explore colonial race relations. Beyond the plethora of *indianos* gracing the pages of works like Pardo Bazán's "Vampiro," analyzed in Chapter 2, few Gothic tales or truly fantastic stories from late nineteenth-century Spain feature the colonial context as a major plot point.[40] Nevertheless, as Mary Coffey details in *Ghosts of Colonies Past and Present*, "the 'hauntology' of Spanish colonialism hovers over nearly all nineteenth-century Spanish literature."[41] Her description of Spain's colonial past in spectral terms illustrates how the nation's singular experience of unparalled imperial splendor and early colonial loss easily lent itself to supernatural treatment.

Spain's unique perspective as a waning world power clinging to the vestiges of empire is undeniably gothicized in Galdós's "Tropiquillos" and Pardo Bazán's "El brasileño," which share a number of structural and thematic similarities. More concretely, I deem both texts to be "imperial curse stories," conceived as a subset of what Patrick Brantlinger terms "imperial Gothic" or a "literature of terror as it becomes obsessed with the perceived 'dusk' of an empire."[42] Brantlinger's conception stemmed from the British tradition and has, at times, been considered a strictly English literary phenomenon. However, the essence of "imperial Gothic" as a literature written from the colonizer's perspective to express fear of imperial decline through contact with contaminating native forces also maps onto the texts by Galdós and Pardo Bazán studied here. While inspired in Brantlinger's classification, my analysis of "Tropiquillos" and "El brasileño" follows James Procter and Angela Smith's assertion that imperial Gothic fiction not only represents colonized lands and cultures as a source of horror, but may also "offer a critique of the empire from within," problematizing colonial practices even as it fears their end, which was imminent in the Spanish case.[43]

In the fictions by Galdós and Pardo Bazán examined below, ambivalence toward Spanish colonialism is amplified by the story's form; the open-ended narrative structure of fantastic storytelling provides no certainty for readers already disoriented by contradictory attitudes present in the text. Homi Bhabha gestured toward the interrogative power of speculative fictions upon observing that, in its desire to fix the colonized in a recognizable and thus controllable form, the discourse of the colonizer strategically "employs a system of representation, a regime of truth, that is structurally similar to realism" and precludes alternate interpretations.[44] But as Coffey notes of Spanish literature post-1898, "the kind of truth associated with the realist mode" no longer sufficed to capture the nation's complex and conflicting feelings surrounding its imperial downfall.[45] Accordingly, she finds that Galdós's later fiction, including "Tropiquillos," turns toward the closure-defying fantastic to broach the subject.[46] True to Coffey's observation, both "Tropiquillos" and Pardo Bazán's "El brasileño" present readers with unstable texts in which the impossibility of discerning truth from superstition is matched by the moral ambiguity surrounding Spanish imperialism and the colonial practices it inspired. Although both protagonists represent the colonizing perspective, their attitudes of racial superiority are placed in question by inconsistencies in their own accounts of past colonial exploits, and the uncertainty surrounding the curse each man supposedly bears highlights the inequities perpetrated in the name of imperialism. It is thus the fantastic treatment of the Gothic curse narrative that casts doubt upon the colonizer's racialized cultural superiority.

Galdós wrote "Tropiquillos" long after Spain's colonies in continental America had declared their independence (1810–1826), but over a decade before the so-called Disaster of 1898, when Spain lost its remaining Asian and Caribbean holdings. Situated between these colonial losses, the short story provides a unique perspective on the nation's lingering imperial aspirations. Originally titled "Fantasía de otoño" (Autumnal fantasy), the tale first appeared in 1884 on the pages of Argentine periodical *La Prensa* (The press), where Galdós contributed a column on European current events.[47] In a note to the director printed as the story's prologue, Galdós apologized for eschewing his typical reporting in favor of an exclusively literary piece, although the act of replacing the news with this short fiction likely underscored the story's political dimension for South American readers. On Spanish soil, the story first went to press alongside Galdós's novella *La sombra* in 1890. Retitled "Tropiquillos," the work was again dismissed by its author as a trifling and formulaic autumnal allegory.[48] Yet Galdós published the text a third time in December of 1893 in *Los lunes de El Imparcial* (The Impartial's Mondays), the literary supplement to the leading liberal periodical of post-Isabelline Spain.[49] Just one month later, the revised "Tropiquillos" was reprinted in *La Prensa*, and a fragment titled "Boceto vino" (Wine sketch) ran in the Canary Islands' *El diario de Las Palmas* (The Las Palmas daily) in 1895. A decade of appearances in varied contexts and media belies the author's dismissal of the text, suggesting that "Tropiquillos" offers far more than mindless entertainment.

Given the rare combination of prestige and popularity enjoyed by *Los lunes de El Imparcial*, "Tropiquillos" likely reached its broadest Spanish readership when it was published there.[50] Of further interest for this study, Spanish imperial sentiments were on full display in both *El Imparcial* and its literary supplement on the day that Galdós's story appeared, providing an interesting paratext for the tale. For instance, the newspaper's lead story involved a scuffle in the Spanish-occupied city of Melilla between Moroccan pirates and the Spanish troops who opened fire upon them. The jingoistic report recounts Prime Minister Práxedes Mateo de Sagasta's enthusiastic applause of the Spanish military response, while describing the Moroccans as "semisavage."[51] Imperialist pride likewise permeates the pages of the issue's literary supplement. The cover features color engravings of smartly dressed Spanish soldiers deployed in Morocco, and later images include a uniformed General Arsenio Martínez Campos inspecting Spanish troops on horseback, in contrast to dark-skinned, turbaned Moroccans in traditional *djellabahs* and slippers, who are idly sitting or standing by. The strong presence of imperialist ideology and imagery throughout *El Imparcial* and its literary accompaniment draws reader attention to the depiction of imperial decline in "Tropiquillos," which clashes with the self-congratulatory tone of surrounding material.

Surprisingly, "Tropiquillos" has attracted little critical attention in spite of the steady growth of scholarly interest in Galdós's treatment of Spanish imperialism, culminating in Coffey's *Ghosts of Colonies Past and Present*.[52] The story begins with Zacarías Tropiquillos's return to Spain after first amassing and then losing an enviable fortune overseas. Although the text does not explicitly name the lands in which he has prospered, references to his dealings in spices, ivory, opium, and tea place him mainly in Asia.[53] Now destitute and dying of tuberculosis, Tropiquillos has returned to the abandoned family vineyard, where *mestre* (Master) Cubas, an old employee of his father's, rescues him. Under the Cubas family's care, the protagonist convalesces through the winemaking season, recovering both health and optimism, and marrying Cubas's daughter. However, the tale takes a disturbing turn when the happily-wed Tropiquillos suddenly finds himself collapsed on the floor, seemingly in a drunken heap. In the story's closing line, a servant hands him a steaming mug, stating that "eso va pasando" (this will soon pass) with the aid of strong coffee. The text offers no further explanation for this abrupt ending, only intimating that some, if not all, of what has transpired has been a figment of the protagonist's imagination.

Unlike the imperial Gothic texts outlined by Brantlinger, "Tropiquillos" does not actually depict the protagonist's adventures abroad. Yet though his colonizing endeavors have concluded by the story's start, they play a key role in his characterization as a man whose psyche and person have been ravaged by the pursuit of wealth and power through the ruthless exploitation of foreign lands and peoples. In line with the *indiano* Don Fortunato Gayoso that we saw in the previous chapter, Tropiquillos's trajectory suggests that "wealth gained in the empire is somehow disreputable," and "implies a certain stain on the character," but whereas the antagonist of "Vampiro" faced no consequences for his immorality, Tropiquillos's actions abroad have taken a substantial toll on his well-being.[54] Within the context of Spanish Regenerationism, which sought to diagnose and remedy the ailing nation, the protagonist's moribund state invites allegorical interpretations.[55] Tropiquillos's debilitated state easily comes to symbolize what Surwillo describes as a "terminally ill [Spanish] imperialism."[56]

At both the individual and national level, then, "Tropiquillos" depicts colonizing activities as producing negative consequences for the colonizer, and it does so in the guise of a Gothic curse story. Although the text does not specifically contain the word "curse," it nevertheless suggests that some kind of supernatural vengeance on the part of the colonized has caused the protagonist's (and his family's) downfall. Moreover, the curse is conceptually present in the narrator's reference to the litany of insults levied against him by different racialized Others that he had encountered—and exploited—in foreign lands: "una confusión espantosa de injurias dichas en inglés, en portugués, en español, en tagalo, en cipayo, en japonés" (a frightening confusion of insults in English, Portuguese, Spanish, Tagalog, the Sepoy language, Japanese).[57]

As the least conventional curse story presented in this chapter, "Tropiquillos" still contains all the key elements associated with the trope. To begin with, there is the sudden and dramatic reversal of fortune typical for cursed individuals. The protagonist describes, "Después de verme enaltecido por el respeto y la envidia, amado por quien yo amaba, rico, poderoso, vime herido súbitamente por la desgracia" (After seeing myself elevated by respect and envy, loved by whom I loved, rich, powerful, I saw myself suddenly wounded by misfortune). When the tale begins, Tropiquillos is already penniless, depressed, and terminally ill; not even the tunic he wears belongs to him. Adding to the scope of his suffering, the protagonist's impending death signals the end of his entire family line. His father's passing was preceded by that of Tropiquillos's two younger brothers in the fictional Battle of Zarapicos, and vague references to a subsequent fire and flood in the family estate underscore the cataclysmic doom faced by the entire clan.[58] Their shared misfortune is moreover emphasized by the almost exclusive use of the family name Tropiquillos to refer to the decrepit main character, including in the story's revised title. His given name of Zacarías appears only once in the text, uttered by his father just prior to death. The extension of the protagonist's ill fortune to his kin not only marks his ruination as total and devastating, but additionally recalls Old Testament curses condemning the descendants of those who invoked the Lord's fury, thereby strengthening the curse motif in Galdós's short story.

Furthermore, "Tropiquillos" ties the protagonist's downfall to the themes of power and powerlessness that are customary in curse narratives. Most obviously, the protagonist has toppled from a position of authority to a state of utter impotence. Even his return to Spain was contingent upon the charity of others, thus highlighting the transitory nature of power. Adding insult to injury, Tropiquillos attributes his downward trajectory at least partly to the machinations of his colonized subordinates. Though his fortunes are lost in fires, explosions, and shipwrecks that could be accidental, he associates these calamities with the "aliento de traidores" (breath of traitors), "alaridos de salvajes sediciosos" (shrieks of seditious savages), and "horribles garabatos de escritura chinesca" (horrible scribbles of Chinese writing), faulting native populations for the catastrophes that have befallen him.[59] While he recognizes the role that his own "profit fever" played in bringing about his lamentable current state, Tropiquillos shifts some blame to those impersonalized and inscrutable subordinates from whom he had expected obedience. His condescension toward the colonized is clearly evidenced in the aforementioned description of the stream of foreign insults hurled at him "por bocas blancas, negras, rojas, amarillas, cobrizas y bozales" (by white, black, red, yellow, coppery, and black slave mouths). Far from granting the colonized any individuality, Tropiquillos does not even appear to view them as human beings, but as disembodied, racialized mouths speaking in unintelligible tongues. It is precisely this lack of comprehension that gives their words a sinister, possibly supernatural, edge.

In light of the colonizer's disregard or outright disdain for the colonized, it is unsurprising that his subordinates should indeed sabotage him, inverting the colonial power dynamic in an act of retributive justice. By the protagonist's reckoning, the colonized lands themselves appear to exact revenge on the Spaniard who defiled them. Every element of nature that Tropiquillos encounters abroad is described as doing him harm: "el sol irrita el cerebro y envenena la sangre" (the sun irritates the brain and poisons the blood) and the colonizer is beset by the "fragancia mortífera de flores tropicales, en atmósfera espesa de epidemias asiáticas" (lethal fragrance of tropical flowers, in an atmosphere thick with Asian epidemics). Even the flora in Asia is pathogenic to the outsider, attacking his system with malevolence, and although he returns to "el temple benigno de la madre Europa" (the benign constancy of Mother Europe) he laments, "Tengo el fuego del trópico en mis entrañas, el tifón en mi cerebro" (I have the fire of the tropics in my bowels, the typhoon in my brain). The places that he has invaded have now invaded him.

Highlighting the racial dimension of this unorthodox reverse colonization, Susana Bardavío Estevan observes that in Pardo Bazán's short stories the colonies often corrupt "los cuerpos ya débiles de los españoles" (the already weakened bodies of the Spanish) and in doing so reveal the latter's degeneration.[60] Her conclusion that "todos los que regresan de los territorios de ultramar lo hacen enfermos, contaminados o heridos por esa naturaleza que no han sabido domesticar" (all who return from the overseas territories do so sick, contaminated, or wounded by that nature that they have not known how to domesticate) extends to "Tropiquillos" as well.[61] In Galdós's tale, the protagonist's susceptibility to Asian contagion not only suggests a weakening of Spanish racial stock, but also propagates an exoticized image of Asia, and other colonized lands, as savage and dangerous spaces. However, the power that Tropiquillos attributes to these places, their peoples, and their languages—conceived as wielding the supernatural ability to debilitate and ultimately eject him—ironically stems from reductive stereotypes that reflect the colonizer's ignorance of and disdain for the indigenous. These simultaneous and yet contradictory perceptions of native populations as powerful but contemptible exemplify Bhabha's assertion that "it is the force of ambivalence that gives the colonial stereotype its currency," indicating the fundamental lack of logic behind colonial thinking.[62] Stories like "Tropiquillos" demonstrate how the Spanish curse narrative, as filtered through the colonizer's perspective, underscores the danger presented by the colonized while at the same time denying them any subjecthood. The hex doubles back on them, reducing them to caricatures.

In an interesting twist to the typical curse story, the action of "Tropiquillos" revolves not around the protagonist's decline abroad but his joyful convalescence in the Spanish countryside. Nevertheless, the exuberance that characterizes his stay with the Cubas clan, a stark contrast to the pathos of his initial condition, is cut short when the text's ending suggests that Tropiqiullos's miraculous recovery was merely an illusion. As a fantastic text, "Tropiquillos" offers multiple possible interpretations of the story's closing lines, in which the disoriented protagonist abruptly awakens beneath a table. The simplest is that all that has transpired previously in the text—financial ruin, deathly illness, and miraculous recovery—has been the inebriated dream of Zacarías Tropiquillos, who remains wealthy enough to maintain a manservant.[63] It is also possible that the protagonist's illness and impending death are real, but that his rejuvenation under the care of *mestre* Cubas has been the product of his desperate imagination. The cruelest option, most fitting for a Gothic curse narrative, is that all recounted events are real, and that the evaporation of his newfound happiness as Cubas's son-in-law is the full extent of Tropiquillos's punishment for subjugating racially distinct foreign peoples and exploiting their resources with avaricious intent. Regardless of which option most appeals to the reader, the fantastic existence of multiple possibilities confounds the readers' sense of reality, and just as the bewildered protagonist feels the floor in search of some tactile certainty at the story's end, readers retrace Tropiquillos's steps though the text, trying to separate fact from fiction.

The only certainty across all potential interpretations is that Galdós's story does not have a happy ending, nor is there any positive reading of the colonial enterprise as depicted within the text. Whether the protagonist is a wealthy and discontented dreamer or a rapacious colonizer at death's door, his pitiful final state suggests that his loving marriage has been illusory, as is any redemption from a life of rapine overseas. The story's final and potentially single true scene further dispels any notions of European cultural or moral superiority as a justification for colonization. Throughout the text, Tropiquillos adopts the colonizer's patronizing gaze, describing the indigenous peoples he had encountered as vice-ridden in their affinity for opium, and uncultured for their ignorance of European wine. Yet at the story's end, it appears that his own overindulgence in the supposed drink of civilization has left him prostrate on the floor in a stupor not unlike the opium-addled haze he so openly disdained in Asia. Whether or not Galdós intended for this irony, Tropiquillos's hypocrisy as revealed in the text's closing lines casts doubt on his value judgments and the racial preconceptions upholding colonialism in general.[64]

In wrapping the Gothic premise of the curse in a fantastical structural ambiguity, "Tropiquillos" facilitates an interrogation of the racial hierarchies inherent to colonization and lays bare the inconsistencies therein. Yet although the tale may present a compelling national allegory, the critique of empire and colonization present in "Tropiquillos" is generalized rather than specific to the Spanish case. While most of the protagonist's colonizing activities take place in Asia, where Spain controlled the Philippines, the text's Asian references specifically allude to India and China, targets of Britain's imperial project.[65] Accordingly, even as his weakened body may be symptomatic of Spanish racial degeneration, Tropiquillos's immoral actions abroad are not necessarily reflective of the national character, but of the imperialist mindset in general. This same distancing appears in Pardo Bazán's "El brasileño," which sidesteps Spanish immorality by setting the colonial action in Brazil, formerly part of the Portuguese empire.

As in the case of Galdós, scholars of Pardo Bazán have increasingly turned their attention to the author's engagement with Spanish imperialism.[66] In fiction and nonfiction alike, Pardo Bazán was particularly vocal on the topic in the years preceding and following the 1898 loss of Cuba, Puerto Rico, the Philippines, and Guam. Given her unapologetic participation in the commemorative events of 1892 and the profusion of journalistic writing she dedicated to Spain's waning empire, existing studies have generally read the author's short stories through the lens of her essayistic pieces, often characterizing Pardo Bazán as an outspoken apologist of the nation's imperial interests.[67] As Charnon-Deutsch reminds readers, however, Pardo Bazán's fiction is not a straightforward rendering of her own political beliefs.[68] Moreover, her thoughts on empire, the colonies, and the colonized were ambivalent and far from static throughout her literary career.[69] Thus, rather than scrutinize "El brasileño" for what it may reveal about the author's attitude toward Spain's colonizing history, this study turns to how the trope of the curse, as developed within a fantastic narrative frame, serves to capture the complex dynamics driving intercultural, interracial encounters from the perspective of the colonizer.

In contrast with "Tropiquillos," "El brasileño" was published only once in the author's lifetime. It appeared in the prestigious *La Ilustración española y americana* (The Spanish and American Illustration) in 1911, but was not included by Pardo Bazán in any of her subsequent short-story collections, which may explain why the work has yet to be the object of critical study.[70] Additionally, whereas Galdós's tale anticipated the loss of Spain's final colonies in the Caribbean and Asia, "El brasileño" was published more than a decade after the Spanish-American War effectively put an end to Spain's imperial pretensions. The colonizing impulse, however, remains alive and well on the pages of *La Ilustración española y americana*, where the text of "El brasileño" is interrupted by photos of Spanish soldiers aboard steamboats departing for Melilla, ostensibly to defend Spain's mining rights there.[71] This lingering imperial consciousness comes to the fore in Pardo Bazán's literary contribution.

Published at least twenty years after Galdós's short story, "El brasileño" nevertheless bears a number of striking similarities to its predecessor in its Gothic exploration of the fraught relations between colonizer and colonized. But whereas readers only infer that the title character of "Tropiquillos" is damned, the narrative intrigue in "El brasileño" revolves around a curse whose enunciation is vividly depicted within the text. In Pardo Bazán's tale, Don Jacobo Vieira, a former slave trader, explains the provenance of an extraordinary diamond that he proudly wears. By his account, the jewel came in a talisman from a besotted indigenous queen named Baraní. The captive of an enemy tribe, she had begged the Spaniard to take her to Europe, and cursed him upon his refusal. Don Jacobo has since lived a comfortable life, but none of his amorous relationships have prospered. He is uncertain as to whether the diamond is truly hexed, but refuses to part with it nonetheless. "El brasileño" thus becomes a paradigmatic example of an imperial curse story that explores the questions of damnation, justice, power differentials, and racial or ethnic stereotypes within a colonial setting.

Unlike the protagonist of "Tropiquillos," Don Jacobo suffers no dramatic reversal of fortune, material or otherwise, after the curse. He returns to Spain a rich man, lives in the *barrio de Salamanca* (the poshest neighborhood of Madrid), and enjoys luxury goods like the exquisite cigar that he offers the narrator at the story's end. Rather than engendering an all-around decline, the curse that plagues Don Jacobo affects only one area of his life: his ability to marry and procreate. Nevertheless, although he seems perfectly content in his bachelorhood, marriage and fatherhood are key signifiers of success for middle-class men, as discussed in Chapter 2. Without them, Don Jacobo falls short of his masculine potential in the public eye. His anguished cry of "¡No conseguir lo que cualquiera consigue: un hijo, una mujer!" (186; To not attain what anybody attains: a son, a wife!) laments above all the perception of impotence, anathema to a man who takes great pains to broadcast his womanizing past.[72] A lack of wife and progeny not only place Don Jacobo's masculinity into question, but likewise foretell the end of his family line. The queen's curse effectively sentences Don Jacobo to sterility, and without an heir, the legacy of self-made success that the *indiano* has built up "corriendo peligros y jugándo[se] a cada momento la vida" (183; running risks and gambling with his life at every moment) dies with him. As a former slave trader of both Africans and indigenous Brazilians, the aged Don Jacobo remains unapologetic about his role in damning others to a life of objectification and servitude. It is thus fitting that for the crime of separating families and robbing individuals of their futures, the Spaniard should himself be barred from forming matrimonial or parental bonds and denied any sense of familial legacy.

Given the subtext of slavery in "El brasileño," autonomy and agency are major themes in Pardo Bazán's story, which depicts the curse as conferring some semblance of power upon those who are disenfranchised. The curser Baraní is a marginalized individual in terms of race, sex, and circumstance: she is an indigenous woman forced into concubinage by the leader of a rival tribe (183), and yet the curse she utters challenges the dominance of a white, male slave trader. The gross power differential between them is clear in her initial attempt to sway Don Jacobo into rescuing her. Rather than petition him as equals, she begs him on her knees, literally objectifying herself by offering to serve as a footstool and slave (183), before resorting to the curse. The hex she places on her potential savior thus appears to be the desperate act of a captive woman with little agency or bargaining power, but her power play is effective in that Don Jacobo believes in the occult influence that she wields. Although he dismisses Baraní as an individual, refusing to take her with him, he begrudgingly accepts the curse's power, eventually resigning himself to a life of solitude.[73]

As was illustrated in "Tropiquillos," however, the curse is a flawed means of resistance when wielded by the colonized, as it often reinforces the same stereotypes used to rationalize colonization in the first place. Don Jacobo's apprehension is contingent upon the conviction that a "savage" queen like Baraní possesses occult powers wholly foreign to the supposedly civilized. Her words are powerful only insofar as she fits the stereotype of indulging in primitive magical practices thought to be long eliminated from rational, scientific-minded, post-Enlightenment Europe. Thus, although the queen's hex deters the retired slave trader from persisting in his search for a wife, it also confirms his prejudice against the indigenous as superstitious and atavistic. Don Jacobo therefore feels justified in his disdainful treatment of Baraní, from his refusal to free her during his own escape—in spite of the instrumental role that she played in saving his life—to his unfavorable description of her as smelling of ants (183). Beyond the misogyny so typical of the imperial gothic, the Spaniard's actions and words display a steadfast contempt for those native to Brazil that facilitates their continued subjugation.[74]

This contemptuous exoticization of the indigenous is particularly evident in Don Jacobo's depiction of the Tapuya—the enemy tribe holding Baraní captive—as war-mongering, cruel, and vice-ridden.[75] By the *indiano*'s account, they regularly indulged in polygamy, alcohol-infused orgies, and the worst transgression of all, cannibalism. His rhetoric echoes that of the original Spanish colonizers in the Americas, specifically recalling Bernal Díaz del Castillo's *Historia verdadera de la conquista de la Nueva España* (The True History of the Conquest of New Spain). Written in 1568 and published in 1632, the *Historia verdadera* painted the indigenous peoples of Mexico as bloodthirsty savages poised to butcher and feast upon Cortés and his men, in a bid to justify their decimation by the Spaniards.[76] Accordingly, Don Jacobo's fixation on the Tapuya's allegedly immoral and inhumane practices aligns him ideologically with ruthlessly colonizing predecessors.

Much like "Tropiquillos," however, the text of "El brasileño" interrogates the protagonist's hierarchical views. The fantastic nature of the text, in particular, draws attention to the racism that Don Jacobo, and the European colonizer more generally, espouses. On the one hand, if the curse is indeed effective, its wording—"¡El Tupá (ellos llaman así al Espíritu que adoran) hará que ninguna blanca sea tu compañera, ni viva a tu lado bajo tu techo!" (183; The Tupá [they call thusly the Spirit that they adore] will ensure that no white woman is your companion, nor lives at your side under your roof!)—offers a potential loophole. Longtime readers of folklore and fairy tales are conditioned to think of curses and prophecies as bound to the letter of the law. In this case, the curse prohibits Don Jacobo from seeking marriage or even long-term companionship with a white woman—that is, a woman of European descent, but it does not preclude the possibility of miscegenation. One might argue that it is ultimately not the magic of the curse that dooms Don Jacobo to a solitary life, but his own discriminatory attitudes, as racial prejudice makes it impossible for the social-climbing *indiano* to imagine a future with a nonwhite wife. On the other hand, the questionable efficacy of the curse allows readers to see through the protagonist's gothicized characterization of the Brazilian queen. If the curse has no real effect except on Don Jacobo's psyche, then Baraní is not a threatening Other invested with supernatural powers, but a bound woman whose only access to power lies in her words. Because Don Jacobo refuses to free her from captivity, the reader may assume that she is doomed to suffer far more than he does.

Beyond the story's fantastic structuring, the narrative framing of "El brasileño" as a conversation between Don Jacobo and a dubious first-person narrator further casts the protagonist's account into doubt. Although the narrator intervenes little in the *indiano*'s storytelling, principally asking questions to move the narration along, his queries continually undermine the speaker's narrative authority, particularly with regard to his seductive prowess. When the ex-slave trader purports to have been a veritable Don Juan irresistible to all women, the narrator takes note of "la bravía y atezada fealdad del anciano" (183; the uncouth and tanned ugliness of the old man), pausing to survey "los pelos cerdosos que emergían rígidos de las fosas de su nariz y de la oquedad de sus oídos." (the bristly hairs that emerged rigidly from his nostrils and the cavity of his ears). Like the narrator, readers are left incredulous that Baraní should have fallen head over heels for such a specimen. Any doubts concerning Don Jacobo's self-awareness are compounded by the fact that nearly every woman he mentions as a prospective partner: his niece, a maid of his, and Baraní herself, occupies a subordinate position relative to the *indiano*, such that she is not at liberty to reject his advances. Moreover, although he describes his second betrothed as "¡una chiquilla formalísima!" (186; a most serious young girl), she ends the engagement by running off to the Americas with another man. Her actions directly contradict Don Jacobo's word, showing him to be either a poor judge of character or an unreliable storyteller. Either way, readers are moved to adopt the extradiegetic narrator's skepticism toward his wealthy acquaintance.

In addition to revealing Don Jacobo's self-aggrandizing tendencies, the critical distance from which the narrator appraises the *indiano* approximates the latter's condescension toward his curser, Baraní. Both men approach their subject as a curious and foreign object of anthropological study. Moreover, Don Jacobo's comportment and physical appearance are described in a manner analogous to his own perception of indigenous Brazilians. From the story's opening line, the narrator judges the *indiano* to be ill-mannered and poorly dressed. He is uncultured, unrefined, and downright uncivilized, all adjectives that the protagonist would ascribe to the native peoples he had encountered. Most notably, the narrator fixates on Don Jacobo's skin, tanned through continuous sun exposure abroad and anomalous among Madrid's high society. In drawing attention to the protagonist's lack of social graces and his swarthy countenance, Pardo Bazán's portrayal of the retired slave trader aligns with the stock image of the *indiano* from the late nineteenth and early twentieth centuries as a self-made man whose struggles to integrate socially are signaled through physical signs of difference like unfashionable clothing or a darkened skin tone.[77]

At the same time, in a story about a Spaniard who has built his fortune trafficking Africans and native Brazilians, the cultural differences and suncured skin that characterize Don Jacobo are easily racialized. In their analyses of Galdós's novel *Tormento* (1884) and his play *La loca de la casa* (1892; The crazy woman of the house), Luisa Elena Delgado and Eva María Copeland each observe the racialized characterization of the *indiano* characters, respectively referred to as "caribe" (Caribbean) and "negro" (black) within the text. Delgado and Copeland read these two *indianos* as embodying a racially hybridized identity within metropolitan Spanish society.[78] No longer fully Spanish nor entirely colonial, they straddle the supposed divide between European "civilization" and American "barbarism."[79] In "El brasileño," Don Jacobo, too, appears to have absorbed some of the alleged savagery of the Tapuya by association, insinuating that perhaps the curse upon him consists not only of eternal solitude or the termination of his family line, but also of contagion by those peoples whom he had always viewed as subhuman.

In this sense, the title "El brasileño," which refers to the exotic diamond at the story's center, could likewise allude to the evolution in Don Jacobo's identity after a lifetime of colonial exploits. No longer representing the Spanish culture or race, he now belongs to Brazil, like the slaves he brought over from Africa or the tribes he plied with *aguardiente* in the Amazon. That the story of the protagonist's slave trading escapades be set in Brazil, rather than the formerly Spanish-owned Cuba is noteworthy. While Brazil was the last Western nation to put an end to the institution of slavery in 1888, abolition had occurred in Cuba only two years prior, which makes it a similarly compelling locale for a story featuring a slave trafficker. Practically speaking, however, an early twentieth-century story about a diamond bestowed by an enslaved indigenous queen could only take place in Brazil, where both diamonds and indigenous tribes could be found in abundance.[80]

Conveniently, displacing Don Jacobo's nefarious business practices to a Brazilian setting allowed Spanish readers to contemplate the most objectionable aspects of colonialism, particularly slave trading, from a safe distance, free from the influence of imperial nostalgia. A foreign locale makes possible the critique of colonizers' greed, cruelty, and self-glorification as divorced from national history, although racist attitudes follow Don Jacobo home to Spain. Just as the reigning racial hierarchy of early twentieth-century

Spain plays a role in dooming the *indiano* by precluding the possibility of a mixed-race marriage, his punishment is in part to suffer the same racism that he has always practiced. If the Tapuya and their captive queen struck Don Jacobo as dark-skinned primitives, he represents the same for the story's first-person narrator, a white male Spaniard from the social class to which the *indiano* has only ascended by dint of his barbaric transatlantic activities.

Compared to "Tropiquillos," "El brasileño" more explicitly challenges the colonizer's worldview and its racist premises. Although the protagonists in both works share a contempt for colonized, nonwhite peoples, the prejudice that underlies Don Jacobo's commodification of African and Brazilian lives far overshadows Tropiqillos's discriminatory views of Asian immorality and simplicity. Thus, it is poetic justice that retribution against the ex-slave trader includes a racial dimension. Whereas in Galdós's story the colonizer's moral shortcomings are exteriorized as physical decay, Pardo Bazán's tale racializes the *indiano* and subjects him to prejudices similar to those he espouses, isolating him socially.

In both stories, it is unclear whether the protagonist's suffering is truly caused through supernatural means, and it is ultimately this uncertainty—the fantastic quality of the text—that opens up a space for critical scrutiny of the premises and practices of colonization. On the one hand, belief in the curse's magical power is shown to be contingent upon racist stereotypes that characterize indigenous populations as savage and superstitious. On the other hand, skepticism toward the curse casts responsibility for the colonizer's misfortune back upon himself, both as a morally flawed individual and as a representative of a prejudiced and prejudicial colonial system that could not possibly produce happy endings.[81] It is thus the threat of the curse within the text rather than the curse itself that blurs the distinction and upends the hierarchy between Spanish "civilization" and the "barbarism" of those who are exploited through colonization.

A Gypsy Scorned
ANTI-ROMANI SENTIMENT IN PARDO BAZÁN'S "MALDICIÓN DE GITANA"

In many ways, the power dynamics that underlie the exchanges between colonizer and colonized in "Tropiquillos" and "El brasileño" are echoed in Pardo Bazán's "Maldición de gitana," in which the trope of the curse likewise functions to interrogate a racialized cultural hierarchy. This similarity is logical if we consider Spain's historical treatment of the Roma community to be a case of internal colonization.[82] First used by Leopold Marquard in 1957 to describe South African apartheid, internal colonization refers to situations in which certain racial minorities within the nation face discrimination and economic exploitation akin to that which indigenous populations experienced in the colonies. Viewed as second-class citizens, these minorities are effectively rendered "domestic colonies" and treated as "nations within a nation," as were the Roma throughout much of Spanish history.[83] Since their arrival to Spain in the fifteenth century, the Roma were continually subjected to discriminatory policies restricting their movement and cultural practices with the objective of limiting their influence and forcing their assimilation into mainstream Spanish society.[84] Most egregiously, the Great Round-Up of 1749 imprisoned more than 9,000 Roma in one fell swoop, in an intent to eliminate their presence from Spain entirely. The planned raid further intended for the economic exploitation of the Roma. As conceived by the Council of Castile, incarcerated Romani men and women were destined for forced labor, while their possessions were seized by the State. In this manner, they were denied sovereignty of their belongings and even of their own bodies, much like indigenous populations under the oppressive rule of invading colonizers. And as in colonization overseas, discrimination against the Roma was justified via arguments of racial inferiority.

While the Roma were always viewed as ethnically distinct within Spain, this difference was most clearly racialized in the nineteenth century, when competing tendencies in the arts and social sciences alternately romanticized or criminalized the figure of the gypsy for flouting bourgeois behavioral codes.[85] As María Sierra-Alonso discerns, "the way of observing and relating to the Gypsy type, even when it was of admiration, was unmistakably colonial and involved multiple practices that created subalternity."[86] Lingering Romantic interest in exoticized foreigners led to a sort of "gypsyphilia" throughout Europe that inspired a proliferation of highly sensualized literary and artistic renderings of dark-skinned and raven-haired female gypsies.[87] Compounding this Orientalizing obsession, the popularity of bohemianism, *majismo* (which elevated the traditional customs of commonfolk as national heritage), and *flamenquismo* (a fondness for the art of flamenco and associated Spanish customs such as bullfighting) within Spain contributed to an ethnographic interest in Romani culture, which increasingly came to represent Andalusia as a whole.[88] Yet if the popular imaginary was rife with seductive gypsy dancers, emerging social sciences like criminal anthropology were busy typecasting the Roma as "criminals who possessed 'polluting bodies' and the destructive potential to destabilize the integrity of the Spanish social body."[89] In works like Salillas's *El delincuente español* (1896; the Spanish delinquent) and Constancio Bernaldo de Quirós's *Las nuevas teorías de la criminalidad* (1898; the new theories of criminality), the gypsy was portrayed as an antisocial danger to the Spanish race. More specifically, Salillas and like-minded colleagues argued that Spanish criminal tendencies originated in racial contamination by the Romani, and yet maintained that the Roma's "biological deficiency and atavism" stemmed from their refusal of racial fusion with the larger community.[90] Paradoxically, then, the Spanish Roma were criticized both as overly endogamous and as spreading racial contagion. Simultaneously depicted as alluring and pathogenic, turn-of-the-century Roma were equally "admired and despised," evoking the same ambivalence that Bhabha noted in the colonial context.[91]

Given the fascination they provoked, the Roma were a mainstay in Spanish cultural production throughout the nineteenth century, from images of gypsy sirens in the illustrated press to scenes of raucous gypsy revelry in realist novels by Armando Palacio Valdés and Vicente Blasco Ibáñez.[92] In realist literature, lawless gypsies provided a foil for bourgeois respectability, but it was another stereotype—that of the Roma's magical abilities—that bolstered their popularity in Spanish fantastic and Gothic short fictions.[93] Old gypsy fortune-tellers seemingly doom those seeking material gain in stories like Serafín Estébanez Calderón's "Los tesoros de la Alhambra" (1832; The treasures of the Alhambra) or Pardo Bazán's "Los zapatos viejos" (1899; The old shoes), and the half-gypsy Constanza of Gustavo Adolfo Bécquer's "La corza blanca" (1863; The white deer) is an unearthly femme fatale. Whether as soothsayer or temptress, the gypsy appears as a one-dimensional figure characterized by the possession of otherworldly powers and questionable morality. Notably, in these tales of the supernatural, the gypsies depicted are generally women. Their combined alterity of race and gender is key to mystifying the traditionally middle-class male narrators whose perspectives shape the texts in question.[94]

Pardo Bazán's "Maldición de gitana" offers a more nuanced portrayal not only of a Romani woman, but also of the Roma's racialization within Spanish society. The story first appeared in 1897 on the front page of popular periodical *El Liberal*, occupying prime real estate in a Sunday edition.[95] It was reprinted twice in the following year: in the Cuban weekly *El Eco de Galicia: Diario de la tarde* (The Echo of Galicia: Evening Paper), and as part of Pardo Bazán's short story collection *Cuentos de amor* (1898; Love stories).[96]

Like "El brasileño," "Maldición de gitana" recounts both the enunciation of the curse and its potential effects. It, too, frames the tale of the curse within a larger conversation, this time between a first-person narrator and Gustavo Lizana, a "mozo asaz despreocupado" (very happy-go-lucky lad) whose uncharacteristic apprehension during a meal with thirteen guests piques the narrator's curiosity.[97] Once probed, Lizana recalls the last meal that he had attended with thirteen diners, after which he and his dear friends, the brothers Leoncio and Santiago Mayoral, encountered a young gypsy offering fortune-telling services. Santiago declines them contemptuously, insulting her, and the wounded gypsy retorts, "¡que vayas montado y vuelvas tendido!" (May you leave mounted and return lying down!). The shaken gentlemen proceed to go hunting, where Leoncio accidentally shoots his brother, killing him on the spot and fulfilling the gypsy's prophecy. Leoncio is never the same thereafter.

Whereas "Tropiquillos" and "El brasileño" boast ambiguous titles, "Maldición de gitana" openly announces that it is a curse story, and the malediction that it features is fairly straightforward. By the gypsy's pronouncement, Santiago will either return from the hunt gravely injured or dead. He does indeed die during the hunt, and his downfall likewise topples Leoncio, who goes mad from the guilt of killing his brother and turns to a life of debauchery. Consequently, Santiago's death likely signals the extinction of his family line, a repeated element of the curse stories analyzed thus far. As orphans, the Mayoral brothers bear the responsibility of perpetuating their lineage, but Santiago's premature passing and his brother's subsequent lunacy suggest that there will be no heirs to the family's considerable wealth. Given that Zacarías Tropiquillos built his fortune through the labor of indigenous subordinates and Don Jacobo sold men into slavery, Santiago's transgression of insulting a gypsy, however caustically, does not seem to warrant his death and the obliteration of his family. Unlike in "Tropiquillos" and "El brasileño," there is no sense of poetic justice here. However, the vehemence of the titular curse is not unfounded if we examine the power relations between the Mayoral brothers, particularly Santiago, and the unnamed gypsy woman who hexes him.

Recalling Baraní's situation in "El brasileño," the gypsy in "Maldición de gitana" is multiply disadvantaged in terms of class, gender, and racialized ethnicity, particularly when juxtaposed with Santiago and Leoncio, carefree Spanish gentlemen of leisure. Born into "una familia extremeña antigua y pudiente" (an old and wealthy family from Extremadura) with multiple properties across various provinces, the brothers did not lack for money, and dedicated themselves to aristocratic pursuits like dinner parties and hunting. Though they are not directly involved in colonizing activities, their class status is in part signaled by access to products that represent a history of Western imperial interests, such as Japanese furniture or chocolate, which originated in Mexico. Possessing none of these luxury goods, the gypsy woman that the brothers encounter is repeatedly described as dirty and unkempt. The lengthy description of Santiago's stylish riding outfit contrasts with references to her bare feet and tattered dress, placing her indigent state into relief.

In addition to the gypsy's obvious lack of purchasing power, she is furthermore subject to discriminatory treatment based on her gender. She is clearly contrasted with the feminine mold exemplified by Santiago's cousin and love interest, a "dulce" (sweet) and "encantadora" (charming) young lady. The gypsy, in contrast, breaks with bourgeois gender conventions upon brazenly flirting with Santiago, and in so doing evokes his repugnance. As evidenced in Chapter 2, unwomanly women were viewed as monsters in the public eye, and the mere suggestion of the gypsy's attraction toward Santiago offends his conventional sensibilities. Yet at the same time that she faces Santiago's rejection, the unabashed woman is thoroughly objectified by Lizana, who finds her to possess "cierto salvaje atractivo." (a certain savage appeal). Though put off by her observable poverty and supposed primitivity, Lizana nevertheless lingers on each element of her exoticized appearance, from head to toe: "los ojos brillaban en su faz cetrina como negros diamantes, los dientes eran piñones mondados y el talle un junco airoso. Los pingajos de su falda apenas cubrían sus desnudos y delgados tobillos" (her eyes sparked in her olive skin like black diamonds, her teeth were shelled pine nuts, and her waist a graceful reed. The tatters of her skirt hardly covered her naked and slender ankles). As a female in a male-dominated society, the gypsy incites sexual desire in others, but may never express any herself.

If her identity as a poverty-stricken woman were not enough to marginalize the gypsy in "Maldición de gitana," her racialized ethnicity, signaled through her dark complexion, designates her as an outsider in Restoration Spain. This is made clear in the physical contrast between Santiago, named after the Moor-slaying patron saint of Spaniards, and the exoticized woman who curses him, referred to by Lizana as an "egipcia" (Egyptian).[98] Whereas the idealized Santiago is "rubio y blanco" (blonde and white), his admirer turned adversary is "atezada" (tanned), of "faz cetrina" (olive complexion). Not only does her swarthy countenance communicate foreignness by

Lizana's account, but Santiago further denigrates her coloring, conflating her darkness with ugliness as he exclaims, "¡Si tuvieses ventura, no serías tan fea y tan negra, chiquilla!" (If you had any good fortune, you wouldn't be so ugly and so black, little girl!). By his pronouncement, the gypsy's skin tone marks her not only as racially distinct from the blue-blooded Mayoral brothers, but also relegates her to a position of inferiority. Nevertheless, there is a certain irony in Santiago's disparagement of the gypsy's dark visage. At the end of Gustavo Lizana's account, the unnamed first-person narrator who has listened to his testimony finally recalls the Mayoral brothers. He remembers Santiago as the blonde that Lizana had described, but characterizes Leoncio to be a lively "moreno," an ambiguous Spanish term which may refer to either a brunette or a dark-skinned person. By this description, Leoncio may well share the gypsy's coloring, which, in Jennifer Smith's words, "points to skin (dark vs. fair) as un unreliable sign of race."[99]

Perhaps for this reason, in the subsequent version of "Maldición de gitana" that appears in *Cuentos de amor*, the gypsy's racial alterity is expressed not only via skin color, but also linguistically within Lizana's narration. Intentional misspellings in the transcription of her dialogue denote that the gypsy's pronunciation deviates from standard Castilian.[100] Her original retort from the 1897 text: "¿No quieres buenaventuras, hermoso? Pues, toma maldiciones ... Permita Dios ... permita Dios ... ¡que vayas montado y vuelvas tendido!" (You don't want good fortune, handsome? Then, take curses ... God willing ... God willing ... may you leave mounted and come back lying down!) now reads "¿No quieres buenaventuras, *jermoso*? Pues, toma *mardisiones* ... *Premita* Dios ... *premita* Dios ... ¡que vayas *montao* y vuelvas *tendío*!" (italics mine).[101] Whereas previously the gypsy had spoken what was considered proper Spanish, her revised speech includes both a marked Andalusian accent, often conflated with the Romani identity and viewed pejoratively within Spain, and a number of mispronunciations.[102] This transformation in the gypsy's speech widens the divide separating her from the Mayoral brothers by simultaneously indicating her ethnic Otherness and her lack of formal education, thereby revealing the intersectional nature of her marginalization. Taken individually, the gypsy's race, gender, and class are each judged to be inferior to that of Santiago and Leoncio by mainstream—that is to say white, patriarchal, and middle-class—Spanish society. In conjunction, the young woman's Romani heritage, female sex, and low social class relegate her to a hopelessly disempowered social position, which is met with condescension from those judged to be superior. Accordingly, the virulence of her curse toward Santiago can be read as targeting the privileged status that he represents rather than targeting him as an individual.

Any resentment that the gypsy might feel toward the Mayoral brothers and their social milieu is not misplaced. Their encounter may be brief, but Lizana's account of it is rife with passing remarks that reveal deep-seated discriminatory attitudes toward the Roma. While only Santiago patronizes her openly, calling her the diminutive "chiquilla" (little girl), Lizana is likewise incapable of seeing past her racialized identity. Given her fleeting appearance in the text, the gypsy's name is never revealed, but this anonymity suits the storyteller, who repeatedly denies her individuality by speaking of her as one of "ellas" (them), "los de esa casta" (those of that race) that Lizana animalizes as "cornejas agoreras" (ominous crows). The automatic attribution of ill-intent that such a characterization entails is further displayed in the storyteller's repeated characterization of the young gypsy as "malvada" (wicked) and a "bruja" (witch), in spite of knowing very little about her.

As in the case of "Tropiquillos," it is precisely Lizana's lack of knowledge surrounding the gypsy and his reliance on racial stereotypes that allows him to ascribe malevolent magical powers to the young woman before him. References to his incomprehension abound throughout his descriptions of her. In the storyteller's words, there are "no sé qué amuletos" (I don't know what amulets) strung around her neck, her eyes sparkle "de un modo raro, que no supe definir" (in a strange manner, that I could not define), and when she finally pronounces the curse upon Santiago, Lizana recalls, "Yo no sé con qué tono pudo decirlo la malvada, que nos quedamos fríos" (I don't know with what tone she could have said it that left us chilled). Shortly afterward, when she escapes, "nadie supo por dónde" (no one knew where), and an exasperated Lizana exclaims, "¡Quién sabe a dónde vuelan esas cornejas agoreras!" (Who knows where those ominous crows fly!). Nearly every time that Lizana mentions the gypsy, he underscores what a mystery she is, and this aura of the unknown is what leads the aristocratic trio to consider her words threatening.

Nevertheless, the efficacy of the titular curse remains unconfirmed in "Maldición de gitana." A true fantastic short story, the narrative offers multiple explanations for Santiago's sudden death. Aside from the possibility that the aggrieved woman harnessed supernatural gypsy powers to strike down her offender, the story likewise posits that Santiago's untimely end is the result of having attended a dinner for thirteen guests the previous evening.[103] After all, the entire account of Santiago's demise is part of the explanation for Lizana's fear of dining in the company of twelve others. Additionally, there is the more mundane explanation of a simple hunting accident, particularly since Leoncio was perturbed by the gypsy's invocation and likely distracted from the activity at hand. Finally, Smith reads Santiago's death as a racially motivated murder; by her analysis, the darker-skinned Leoncio, already resentful of society's adulation for his fair-skinned brother, is inexorably triggered by Santiago's insult concerning the gypsy's complexion.[104]

In light of the many potential causes for the accidental shooting, it is telling that Lizana seems reluctant to absolve the gypsy of responsibility. His insistence upon associating the young woman with the occult speaks to his inculcation with a Manichean view of "bad, dark female Other and good, fair, male self."[105] However, the facts of the story show how warped Lizana's (and potentially the readers') vision of good and evil, victim and victimizer, is, particularly within a racially charged context. The curse and its inscrutable utterer temporarily disturb the three hunters, but what transpires next reminds readers that this assertion of power is fleeting. While in the majority of curse stories, the curser disappears from the narrative after articulating the fateful words, here we see Leoncio advance menacingly toward the gypsy, which instigates the hunting dogs to attack her, threatening to maul her to death. Her audacity is punished with potentially deadly consequences, and although the three hunters quickly move to call off the hounds, both the gypsy and the story's readers are reminded of the precarity of her physical circumstances, which are symbolic of her subaltern social position. Even if it results in Santiago's death, the curse she hurls does not alter the gypsy's helplessness before the Mayoral and their similarly privileged friend, nor does it affect the larger social hierarchy that insists upon the Roma's marginalization.

In Smith's reading of the story, "the violence of patriarchy and racism competes with that of the savagery of the racial[ized] Other."[106] In their confrontation, no one emerges victorious. On the one hand, the gypsy's curse reflects a highly questionable sense of justice. Do Santiago's insulting remarks and the bigotry that infuses them merit grievous bodily harm or even death? On the other hand, vengeance enacted on an individual scale, even if aided by occult forces, cannot overcome discrimination at the systemic level. Even as the Mayoral brothers are made to suffer, the gypsy continues to occupy a subordinate position within Spanish society, and the power that Lizana attributes to her cursing words only reaffirms longstanding stereotypes of the Roma. Thus, the fantastic ambiguity surrounding the gypsy's curse brings the story's racial dynamics (and those of late nineteenth-century Spain) to the fore. A supernatural reading of the text can only be sustained through prejudice against the Roma.

Ultimately, readers are left wondering who the story's truly accursed party is. Is it the Mayoral, a pair privileged in nearly every way, who are destined for extinction? Or is it the gypsy, who allegedly bears "the curse of Semitic/Oriental blood?"[107] As Smith rightly observes, the story's title is ambiguous in this regard. "Maldición de gitana" may either be read as a curse uttered by the gypsy or as a curse that she herself suffers. In the egregiously racist *costumbrista* sketch "La gitana" (1881; The gypsy), the aristocratic author Blanca de los Ríos describes how the mere sight of a gypsy clairvoyant evokes "todo el peso del impenetrable estigma que gravita sobre los suyos" (the full weight of the impenetrable stigma that bears down upon her people), such that "se siente la maldición de Dios, cayendo sobre su raza" (one feels God's curse, falling upon her race).[108] Yet "Maldición de gitana" suggests that the true curse borne by the gypsy is not her bloodline, but the unrelenting discrimination that she must continually suffer for being a visibly impoverished woman and belonging to a race deemed undesirable by Spanish bourgeois society. As Pardo Bazán's fantastic rendering of the Gothic curse motif illustrates, racism is almost always imbricated with classism and sexism, particularly with regard to the Roma.

Return of the Jewish Necromancer
ESCAMILLA'S "EL CUADRO DE MAESE ABRAHAM"

No discussion of Spanish curse stories as reflecting tensions between racialized ethnic groups would be complete without accounting for the fantastical treatment of Jews, given their history of relentless persecution on the Iberian Peninsula. As Bienstock Anolik pronounces, "Jews have the dubious distinction of being the first group set up as the Other, and the demonic Other, in the Western tradition."[109] In medieval Spain, Jews famously lived alongside Muslims and Christians in a state of *convivencia* (coexistence), though they faced discrimination, forced conversions, and finally expulsion in 1492. Thereafter, those who had previously converted were viewed as an internal threat to the nation (much like the Roma) and thus hounded by the Inquisition, and a slew of new statutes required *limpieza de sangre* to occupy any prestigious state-sponsored positions. No officially Jewish population remained in Spain after the edict of 1492, and even four centuries later, Jews comprised a tiny minority on the Iberian Peninsula, with only

406 registered in Spain by the 1877 census.¹¹⁰ In spite of these paltry numbers, the so-called Spanish race continued to be constructed in opposition to the racialized Otherness of Jews, as evidenced in the 1884 dictionary of the Real Academia Española (Royal Spanish Academy), where the term "limpio" (clean) is defined as free of "mezcla ni raza de moros, judíos, herejes o penitenciados" (mixture or race of Moors, Jews, heretics, or prisoners of the Inquisition).¹¹¹ Regardless of how few Jews inhabited Spain at the time, they remained ever-present in the collective imagination.

At the same time, a confluence of events worldwide thrust Jews back into the Spanish public eye. First, the Hispano-Moroccan War of 1859–1860—in which Spain sought to fortify its holdings in Africa in light of other colonial losses—brought to the nation's attention the community of Sephardic Jews residing in Morocco. Spanish liberals in particular were intrigued by this exiled population that nevertheless maintained elements of the national culture, including its language.¹¹² Later, during the universally decried Russian pogroms of 1881–1882, Spain offered asylum to the Jews who were being persecuted. Finally, the Dreyfus affair in neighboring France shined a spotlight on Jews and antisemitism once more, from 1894 through the early 1900s. Consequently, Jews and the discrimination that they continued to face were a consistent topic in Spanish news cycles throughout the second half of the nineteenth century.¹¹³ However, the lack of any real Jewish presence within Spain during the period in question meant that national discussions generally considered Jews in symbolic terms, as stand-ins for distinct political values rather than as a real community subject to government policy as in the case of the Roma.

Not surprisingly, these "imaginary Jews," as Hazel Gold deems them, represented different things for Spanish conservatives and liberals.¹¹⁴ Whereas the former viewed Jewish subjects as a threat to national unity, the latter considered them a group wronged by Spain's Catholic intransigence, to whom restitution should now be made. Many left-leaning Spanish intellectuals, most notably senator Ángel Pulido, even pushed for the repatriation of Sephardic Jews as a manner of rejuvenating the ailing nation and boosting Spain's international standing.¹¹⁵ As Gold describes, Jews in Restoration Spain functioned as "a blank signifier, infinitely malleable and continually rewritten in the service of liberal and conservative agendas alike."¹¹⁶

This polyvalence of the Jewish figure in Spanish political discourse also extended to the nation's literature. Noteworthy for its firsthand observations of Morocco's Sephardic community, Alarcón's widely read *Diario de un testigo de la Guerra de África* (1859; Diary of a witness to the War in Africa) painted these Jews through a heavy veil of prejudice. Most other authors who conceived Jewish characters lacked Alarcón's direct experience, and produced a wide variety of representations ranging from benevolent depiction in Galdós's *Gloria* (1877) to more stereotypical characterizations in Pardo Bazán's novels *Una cristiana* (1890; A Christian woman) and *La prueba* (1890; The test), and play *El becerro de metal* (1906; The metal calf).[117] While Galdós and Pardo Bazán provide examples from realism, the nineteenth-century "imaginary Jew" was likewise rendered in supernatural terms, with plenty of inspiration from biblical folklore and the Gothic literary tradition.

For centuries, Jews had been cast as a cursed people for their alleged role in deicide, most prominently in the legend of the Wandering Jew, a Jew who had taunted Jesus on his way to the Crucifixion and was thus doomed to wander the earth until the Second Coming. By the late eighteenth and particularly the nineteenth century, the Wandering Jew had come to symbolize the entire Jewish diaspora, inspiring several Gothic fictions, including such popular works as Matthew Lewis's *The Monk*, Charles Maturin's *Melmoth the Wanderer* (1820), Eugene Sue's *Le Juif errant* (1844, The wandering Jew), and George du Maurier's *Trilby* (1894). While the Wandering Jew is comparatively scarce in the Spanish Gothic tradition and certainly in works by celebrated authors, Jewish characters frequently appear as caricatures informed by anti-Semitic folklore such as the Blood Libel, a legend accusing Jews of kidnapping and killing innocent Christians, particularly children, as part of perverse religious rites.[118] Key examples include Gustavo Adolfo Bécquer's "La rosa de pasión" (1864; The passion flower) and multiple stories by Pardo Bazán, including "Corpus" (1899) and "El buen judío" (1910; The good Jew). Though sensational, these short stories are frequently narrated as factual, eschewing any semblance of supernatural intervention beyond the work of God.

Within this context, Escamilla stands out for crafting multiple fantastic stories featuring more sympathetic Jewish characters, such as the lovelorn Maritana of "La mosca" (1873; The fly) or doting grandfather Abraham in "El reloj" (1874; The watch).[119] Of his stories, "El cuadro de maese Abraham" (1873) most closely adheres to the typical curse story model. Not coincidentally, the story's portrait of Jewish antique dealer Abraham is also the most stereotypical. Like Escamilla's other short fictions analyzed in this study, "El cuadro de maese Abraham" was published in *El Periódico para todos,* which speaks to the popular appeal of otherworldly Jewish figures.[120] The text opens with a description of the elderly Abraham as an unscrupulous antique dealer before launching into the story of the narrator and protagonist's inexplicable compulsion to buy a mysterious canvas from Abraham's store. Before heading home, the narrator receives and promptly ignores a letter from his uncle Celedonio, requesting that he comply with an advantageous arranged marriage. Back at home, the narrator hangs the canvas in the window, as Abraham had suggested, and dreams of his uncle and his proposed fiancée, whose face is obscured, with an eerily laughing Abraham in the distance. He awakens to discover that the canvas now reveals a beautiful female countenance worthy of Murillo. The following night, he again dreams of Celedonio's house, this time aglow with a sinister aura of death, but puts it out of his mind until his uncle's unannounced arrival a month later. The narrator excuses his negligence, insisting that he has fallen in love with the woman in the painting that he contemplates day and night. An incredulous Celedonio identifies her as Teresa, the narrator's would-be fiancée, who has died awaiting her nuptials. Upon learning the news, the narrator collapses, "lanzando una maldición al judío Abraham y a su lienzo" (617; launching a curse at the Jew Abraham and his canvas), which the narrator blames for ruining his chances at earthly happiness.

In contrast with "El brasileño" or "Maldición de gitana," in which the curse is clearly articulated, in Escamilla's tale it is merely intimated that Abraham has sold the narrator a cursed painting, possibly even hexing the canvas himself. The shopkeeper purports that the scroll came from the Holy Land, which automatically imbues it with an otherworldliness, and as the narrator stands transfixed by it, "Abraham [lo] contemplaba [a él], dirigiéndo[le] miradas oblicuas por encima de los anteojos que descansaban en la punta de su afilada nariz" (616; Abraham contemplated [him], directing [at him] sideways glances above the glasses that rested on the tip of his sharp nose). In his description, the narrator links Abraham's disconcerting gaze to the stereotypically Jewish quality of a prominent nose, thus characterizing the shopkeeper's ethnicity as unnerving by association. This unsettling quality is further developed in the protagonist's observation that "en aquel momento estaba pasando alguna cosa extraña entre Abraham, el cuadro y yo; algún misterio de esos que solamente se explican por el fluido-magnético de lo desconocido" (616; in that moment something strange was happening between Abraham, the painting, and myself; some mystery of the type that are only explained through the magnetic flow of the unknown). The idea of Abraham's occult abilities as part of his Jewish heritage is thus planted in readers' minds, and strengthened by the multiple references to curses and cursing elsewhere in the story. First, Celedonio's letter threatens the narrator with eternal damnation should he ignore the summons to meet his intended wife (616). Later, upon learning of Teresa's death, the narrator curses Abraham as culpable of the tragedy (617). The explicit use of the word "maldición" (curse) in both instances, toward the start of the story and in its final lines, establishes the curse as undergirding the entire narrative.

Nevertheless, the misfortune that befalls the narrator in Escamilla's tale is presented as far less grave than the terminal illness or death that awaited other protagonists featured in this chapter. Unlike the concrete losses suffered by Tropiquillos or the Mayoral brothers, the narrator of "El cuadro de maese Abraham" loses his ideal mate before ever making her acquaintance. Consequently, his sorrow is based entirely on hypotheticals. It is furthermore difficult to view Teresa's death in tragic terms, seeing as readers know nearly nothing about her or the circumstances of her passing. The text reveals only that she was young and beautiful, and met Celedonio's expectations for a niece-in-law, but these impersonal facts do not facilitate any emotional attachment to her. Even the narrator's stricken response to his betrothed's unexpected death seems disingenuous. Earlier in the story, he admits to having "negado mil veces" (616; denied a thousand times) his uncle's plea to meet the girl, demonstrating no interest whatsoever in her well-being until he learns that she resembles the portrait that he has been idolizing. Given the limited characterization of Teresa and the narrator's previous dismissal of her, there is little pathos in her sudden passing.

As opposed to "Maldición de gitana," where a death sentence for insulting a young Romani woman seems disproportionately severe, in "El cuadro de maese Abraham," the loss of a love interest seems a fitting comeuppance for the self-centered protagonist. His haughty refusal to consider the match that his uncle had secured appears rightly punished with the impossibility of wedding her, though markedly unfair for the innocent girl whose life is sacrificed as collateral damage. Her demise underscores the disposability of women's lives in Gothic and fantastic fiction elaborated in Chapter 2. Although the narrative ends at the protagonist's discovery of Teresa's premature passing, it seems unlikely that he will mourn her for long, given the lack of sentimentality that has governed his previous conduct. Instead, Teresa's death will at most teach the narrator a lesson about heeding his uncle's word. Celedonio's visit at the story's end further suggests that the offended uncle will not make good on the threat to disinherit his nephew, though he could do so blamelessly, considering the fair warning offered in his letter.

Escamilla's short story does not include the egregious wrongs of colonial exploitation or slave trading, nor does the curse it depicts result in calamitous ruin or the protagonist's death. It does, however, allow for an interesting meditation on the dynamics of power and blame as related to perceived racial differences. In the other texts analyzed in this chapter, the protagonist occupies an overwhelmingly dominant social position in terms of class, gender, and race that appears to be resisted or even temporarily inverted through a curse by the obviously disadvantaged. In contrast, the balance of power between the narrator and his curser is more ambiguous in "El cuadro de maese Abraham." To begin with, both characters are men, which eliminates any obvious hierarchy of gender. Additionally, Abraham is known to be one of the wealthiest men in town (615), potentially possessing more riches than the narrator. While the latter is certainly a man of means who can afford to spend his days rifling through knickknacks at an antiques store, the store's owner is allegedly a millionaire (615). However, his purported wealth stands in stark contrast with his humble dress and tiny home/store, which the text relates to his ethnicity through recourse to the stereotype of Jews as both obsessed with material gain and paranoid in the hoarding of riches.[121] This racist portrayal reveals that the shopkeeper, though wealthy, remains marginalized by his identity as part of an exiled group rendered nearly nonexistent in Spain but nevertheless suspected of sabotaging "the economic and spiritual health" of the nation.[122]

That Abraham's characterization revolves around his racialized religious affiliation is clear from the story's start. He is introduced in the text's opening words as "el judío Abraham" (615; the Jew Abraham), and the rest of the story alternates between calling him Abraham, the Jew, or the Israelite, often in combination. His identity thus largely consists of his ethnic alterity, which is visualized in the text's first illustration (fig. 3.1). In the image, Abraham's swarthy complexion and long beard contrast starkly with the narrator's pale, mustached countenance. Dressed to reflect this difference in physiognomy, the Jew's dark and exotic clothing (what appear to be a tunic and a Fez-like hat) are juxtaposed with the narrator's light-colored garb, the bourgeois gentleman's uniform of suit and tie. He furthermore stands back, lurking in the shadows, while the protagonist sits directly below the illuminating glow of a lamp. This imagery recalls DeLamotte's observation that "by the late nineteenth century the one unproblematized, emphatically stable boundary in that [Anglo-Gothic] genre was the color line" that separated light, associated with virtue, from dark, which connoted immorality and evil.[123]

As a contemporaneous Spanish text, the overwhelming darkness of both Abraham's skin and his outfit in the illustration for "El cuadro de maese

FIGURE 3.1. Illustration by Mariano Urrutia from "El cuadro de maese Abraham," in *El Periódico para todos*, año II, no. 39. Image courtesy of the Biblioteca Nacional de España, Madrid, Spain.

Abraham" not only casts doubt upon his intentions, but further suggest a connection to the occult, revealing the unstated stereotype that underlies Escamilla's tale: that of the *judío nigromante*, or Jewish necromancer dating back to the Middle Ages. Because Jews were viewed as antithetical to Christianity in medieval times, they were frequently associated with Satanism, sorcery, and the dark arts, a characterization that remained popular in Spain thanks to canonical works like Don Juan Manuel's celebrated story collection *El Conde Lucanor* (1335; *Tales of Count Lucanor*). This association was so pervasive that even in the age of Spanish realism Jewish characters could still be plausibly linked to the occult. Harkening back to the necromancers of old, Abraham is set apart both textually and visually as a potentially dangerous racialized Other. Once again, it is precisely the perception of

Abraham as representing an exotic, non-Spanish race capable of summoning the supernatural that casts him under suspicion of having cursed the narrator's love life. Here, as elsewhere, the culpability of the racial Other is predicated upon the narrator's prejudiced perspective, which is reproduced in the story's illustration.

However, as in any fantastic text, "El cuadro de maese Abraham" allows multiple potential explanations for the recounted events aside from what the narrator believes to have transpired. There is, for instance, an entirely mundane option in which the resemblance between Teresa and the painting is purely coincidental, the narrator's dream was inspired by his uncle's letter (and a guilty conscience), and Teresa died of natural causes, albeit prematurely. More intriguing perhaps is a third alternative: that Teresa's death is the actualization of Celedonio's hex upon his nephew for the latter's continued disrespect. Although the narrator never entertains this idea, Celedonio explicitly threatens to curse his nephew should the latter fail to come meet Teresa. In fact, Celedonio's is the only curse against the narrator that is articulated within the text. Even so, the lovelorn protagonist fixates on Abraham as the origin of his ills, thus revealing society's, and his own, prejudices against the Jew. Although the protagonist shows great familiarity with the shopkeeper, and admits to frequenting Abraham's home on nearly a daily basis, he nevertheless continues to view the Jew with distrust, and it is through his eyes that readers perceive Abraham as an ominous figure when none of his words or actions in the text are outright objectionable.

In the face of fantastical uncertainty, the narrator of "El cuadro de maese Abraham" immediately engages age-old racial stereotypes, demonstrating that it is far easier to cast blame on another whose ethnicity is reviled than to find fault in a family member or in oneself. By shifting responsibility to a racialized Other already under suspicion of sorcery, the protagonist need not consider his own role in Teresa's passing, and the fatalistic nature of a curse absolves him from wondering what he could have done to save her. These questions, however, linger in reader minds, feeding the doubt concerning just who the accursed party is in Escamilla's tale: the idle gentleman who had spent most of the story indifferent to his intended, or the Jewish antique dealer who is blamed for her passing. If the first has been denied marriage to a physically ideal mate, the second is doomed never to belong in Spanish society. Abraham may run a successful business and possess an enviable fortune, but he will always be defined by an exoticized racial alterity, and be the first to take the fall when misfortune strikes.

The short stories by Galdós, Pardo Bazán, and Escamilla examined in this chapter demonstrate how fantastic treatment of the curse story allows for an interrogation of the power dynamics governing intercultural exchanges both within the Spanish nation and in colonial holdings worldwide. Together, they reveal how belief in the power of the curse obscures individual autonomy and agency, as well as the lack thereof. Each of the four selected works is narrated by a privileged white male narrator who nevertheless views himself as a victim of forces beyond his control. It is no coincidence that "Tropiquillos," the only story in which the narrator connects his present misery to his own past immorality, is also the text in which the idea of the curse is least clearly articulated. At the same time, belief in the curse as depicted in these works indicates belief in racist stereotypes that attribute the non-white, non-Catholic, essentially non-Spanish curser with dark magic and malevolent intent. Thus, the curse functions as an effective scapegoating mechanism in a society that harbors misgivings about racialized Others, particularly those who are poverty-stricken and female.

Yet though Tropiquillos, Don Jacobo, the Mayoral brothers, and Celedonio's unnamed nephew at least partially attribute their suffering to the insidious machinations of those judged to deviate from the *raza española*, their word is far from final. Each of the selected tales entertains one or more alternate readings that contradict the narrator's judgments, particularly regarding the possibility of occult intervention. And if claims of supernatural meddling are spurious, then the curse grants a mere semblance of power to the curser. The indigenous peoples of Africa, Asia, and the Americas in "Tropiquillos" and "El brasileño" may pronounce menacing words, but their utterances have little effect on their colonized status, as their exploitation does not end with an individual colonizer's downfall. Likewise, a gypsy's curse cannot save a Romani woman from physical attack or elevate her social status in "Maldición de gitana," and in "El cuadro de maese Abraham," even the wealthiest of Jews is still regarded with suspicion by his Spanish neighbors. The curse, these fantastic texts suggest, may be no more than a great, Gothic lie that allows the powerful—the white, Catholic men of means who share their stories—to skirt moral responsibility, while granting those who are disenfranchised with illusory power tied to their acceptance of racial stereotypes. In uncovering the lie, fantastic storytelling not only places into question the narrators' perceptions of the supernatural, but likewise interrogates the cultural hierarchies that pit "civilized and Enlightened" Spaniards against "atavistic" Others, revealing such characterizations as equally fictitious.

CODA

Fantastic Poetics and Politics

In one story, bourgeois society shuns an industrious casket-maker who works himself to death during an epidemic. After his passing, his neighbors are perturbed by his persistent memory. Another tale narrates the gossip-worthy nuptials between a wealthy, octogenarian *indiano* returned from the Americas and a mere child from rural Spain. She soon dies from the physical toll of the ceaseless care that she provides her new husband. In a third fiction, the aristocratic male protagonist insults a Romani woman's dark complexion before dying in a hunting accident. When we remove the supernatural element from these and similar works, they become instantly recognizable as meditations on class, gender, and race; but because they entertain the possibility of ghosts, monsters, and curses, they are dismissed as frivolous escapism.

As seen in the preceding chapters, however, the supernatural element of the selected short fictions, and particularly their fantastic treatment within the narrative, allows for incisive commentary on the social landscape of late nineteenth-century Spain. Chapter 1 explored how the specter's dubious existence sheds light on the artificiality and superficiality of the bourgeois lifestyle, which further scrutiny reduces to a game of smoke and mirrors. Chapter 2 demonstrated how restrictive gender norms are challenged when the allegations of monstrosity hurled at nonconforming individuals are called into question. Chapter 3 examined how curses of indeterminate efficacy expose the invariable power differential between "true Spaniards" and the racialized Others who wish them harm from a subordinate position. As a whole, *Specters, Monsters, and the Damned* highlights the subversive potential of fantastic storytelling to destabilize the prevailing social order through the manipulation of reader uncertainty.

If, as contemporary Spanish literati argued, "only realist novels could represent 'lo español' [the Spanish]," then the fantastic short story served to contest this "Spanishness."[1] More specifically, the fantastic treatment of familiar Gothic tropes in short fictions by Alarcón, Galdós, Pardo Bazán, and Escamilla reveals the artificiality of the national identity constructed by and therefore favoring bourgeois men of the *raza castiza* (authentically Spanish race). Within these texts, he who is granted a voice wields the power of definition, and it is from the normative position that alterity is defined. Thus, distinct Gothic motifs in the featured stories call attention to those individuals and groups relegated to the margins of the imagined national community on the basis of social class, gender, or ethnicity as conceived in racial terms. Both the old aristocratic order and the emergent working class become specters that haunt bourgeois society, those who defy established gender roles morph into literal monsters, and anyone viewed as outside of—and inferior to—"the Spanish race" must be an irrational, mystical being that wields the dark arts with vengeful intent. However, the fantastic structure of each text leaves characters and readers alike uncertain as to the reality of these supernatural characterizations, and if these attributions are not set in stone, then neither is the privilege afforded to *castizo* bourgeois males. The doubt sown within fantastic tales concerning the nature of reality in the material sense spreads to existing social realities as well.

Both the epistemological and ideological uncertainty produced within these fantastic fictions depends in large part on their narrator, whose perspective proves to be highly subjective. In almost all the short fictions featured in *Specters, Monsters, and the Damned*, the narrative is focalized through the viewpoint of an explicitly middle-class, male storyteller whose Spanish identity is taken for granted; yet although he belongs to the most legally and symbolically privileged social group, he nevertheless fancies himself to be the story's victim. Conversely, the alleged victimizers are impoverished, female, ethnically Othered, or some combination thereof, but their marginalization within the national community is obscured by the narrators' belief in their possession of supernatural powers. These dynamics are laid bare within the fantastic text, where the confines of reality—viewed as synonymous with the narrator's testimony and his underlying worldview—are unceremoniously called into question. And if reality is revealed to be man-made, then the categories and hierarchies that define Spanish social life are even more obviously (biased) social constructions.

Although each chapter focuses on a different marker of identity to facilitate the book's organization, analyses across chapters acknowledge the impossibility of separating any one quality from the others. In "El antepasado," Fadrí's sickly constitution may render him effeminate in the public eye, but this emasculation is compounded by the decadence of his aristocratic line. Contrarily, Don Fortunato's accumulation of fabulous riches initially mitigates the community's perception of the misogynistically murderous old man in "Vampiro." As a final example, the nameless, poverty-stricken women in "La mujer alta" and "Maldición de gitana" are doubly terrifying to wealthy male protagonists, even without adding old age or racial difference to the equation. All these stories show that it is the intersection of class, gender, and race that accounts for an individual's inclusion or exclusion from the bourgeois-dominated, highly patriarchal, and increasingly nationalistic society of nineteenth-century Spain.

The intention of *Specters, Monsters, and the Damned* has been to show how fantastic narratives expose the social structures governing post-Isabelline Spain that privileged select individuals at the expense of many others. Nevertheless, this book has unwittingly reproduced some of the very hierarchies that it seeks to deconstruct, by focusing largely on bourgeois male authors. While this is in part a function of the disproportionately small percentage of women-authored works published in Spain's mainstream periodical press during the late 1800s, there are undoubtedly talented female writers whose contributions to fantastic literature have yet to be recognized. For instance, Julia de Asensi's *Leyendas y tradiciones en prosa y verso* (1883; Legends and traditions in prose and verse) and *Novelas cortas* (1889; Short novels) have only recently incited critical interest.[2] Although their tendency to situate the supernatural in medieval settings placed them outside the parameters of the present study, Asensi's stories are a treasure trove of aesthetic and ideological riches awaiting discovery. If little is known about women writers of the fantastic, even less is known about fantastic writing from Spain's final colonies, particularly the Philippines and pre-independence Cuba. How might fantastic writing from a colonial context contest the narratives of specters, monsters, and curses imagined from the metropolis? Answering this question will surely confront a different set of demons, both literal and figurative.

Specters, Monsters, and the Damned helps pave the way for these studies by shining light on the social commentary facilitated specifically through fantastic storytelling. Thus, the preceding analyses follow Rosemary Jackson's footsteps in "extend[ing] Todorov's investigation from being one limited to the *poetics* of the fantastic into one aware of the *politics* of its forms."[3] In the Spanish stories selected for study, Gothic motifs such as the specter, the monster, and the curse are repeatedly deployed within the narrative to make individuals of a certain class, gender, or ethnicity appear unnatural, but thanks to the fantastic ambiguity of each text, the normative position ends up emerging as equally if not even more unnatural. Thus, the possible appearance of the supernatural within Spanish fantastic fictions of the late nineteenth century ultimately serves to denaturalize those attitudes, beliefs, and social structures taken for granted in a nation busy constructing its ideal citizen as male, middle-class, and "authentically Spanish" both through its laws and its realist literature. Close scrutiny of the multiple layers of ambiguity within the fantastic text reveals a disquieting picture of Spanish society as plagued not by otherworldly forces, but by all-too-real individuals who, complacent with their social influence, prefer scapegoating and blame-shifting over introspection or societal reform.

Notes

INTRODUCTION

1. Although in *The Red and the Black* (1830), Stendahl famously compared the novel to a mirror carried along the road, this vision of realism as purely mimetic is now considered to be overly simplistic. Lilian Furst's study *All Is True: The Claims and Strategies of Realist Fiction* (1995) broke new ground by uncovering the tension between "the claims of referentiality . . . and those of textuality" in realist writing, and the past thirty years have seen a proliferation of scholarship on the realist novel as simultaneously reflecting and constructing the social reality it portrays. Mary Coffey and Margot Versteeg, introduction to *Imagined Truths: Realism in Modern Spanish Literature and Culture*, ed. Mary Coffey and Margot Versteeg (Toronto: University of Toronto Press, 2019), 12.
2. Tzvetan Todorov, *The Fantastic: A Structural Approach to a Literary Genre*, trans. Richard Howard (Ithaca, NY: Cornell University Press, 1975), 25.
3. Andrew Kahn, *The Short Story: A Very Short Introduction* (Oxford: Oxford University Press, 2021), 1. In *El cuento español en el siglo XIX* (The Spanish short story in the nineteenth century), Mariano Baquero Goyanes states that "Era, pues, obligado acudir al siglo XIX para estudiar lo que el cuento es como género literario . . . acudir al momento mismo en que el cuento comenzó a adquirir jerarquía literaria, asistiendo a su evolución a lo largo del siglo XIX hasta su rotundo triunfo en los años finiseculares" (It was, then, obligatory to go to the nineteenth century to study what the short story is as a literary genre . . . to go to the very moment in which the short story began to figure in the literary hierarchy, attending to its evolution throughout the nineteenth century up until its resounding triumph at the turn of the century). Mariano Baquero Goyanes, *El cuento español en el siglo XIX* (Madrid: CSIC, 1949), 14.
4. Baquero Goyanes, *El cuento español*, 68.
5. For more on reception of the Gothic novel in Spain, see Miriam López Santos, *La novela gótica en España (1788–1833)* (Vigo: Academia del Hispanismo, 2010). For a concise summary, see Xavier Aldana Reyes and Rocío Rødtjer, "The Gothic in Nineteenth-Century Spain," in *The Cambridge History of the Gothic*, vol. 2, *Gothic in the Nineteenth Century*, ed. Dale Townshend and Angela Wright (Cambridge: Cambridge University Press, 2020), 285–302. Hoffmann was first translated for Spanish audiences in 1831, while Poe was first translated in 1857. On the popularity and impact of both authors in Spain, see David Roas's *Hoffmann en España: Recepción e influencias* (Madrid: Biblioteca Nueva, 2002) and *La sombra del cuervo: Edgar Allan Poe y la literatura fantástica española del siglo XIX* (Madrid: Devenir, 2011).
6. Abigail Lee Six studies the presence of Gothic motifs across a wide range of Spanish literature from the nineteenth century onward in *Gothic Terrors: Incarceration, Duplication, and Bloodlust in Spanish Narrative* (Lewisburg, PA: Bucknell University Press, 2010).

7. For a more comprehensive list of single-authored volumes of fantastic fiction, see David Roas, prologue to *El Castillo del espectro: Antología de relatos fantásticos españoles del siglo XIX* (Barcelona: Círculo de lectores, 2002), 15.
8. Roas, prologue to *El castillo del espectro*, 6.
9. For instance, Alarcón and Bécquer provided two of the seven short stories in the 1890 anthology *Modern Ghosts*, edited by American writer and public intellectual George William Curtis. In the volume's introduction, Curtis specifically singled out Bécquer as an author whose name "will have great interest for many readers," thus attesting to the quality of the Spanish author's fantastic writing. George William Curtis, Introduction to *Modern Ghosts* (New York: Harper & Brothers Publishers, 1890), xiv.
10. This marketing blurb comes from the website of Oxford University Press, https://global.oup.com/academic/product/fantastic-worlds-9780195025415?cc=us&lang=en&.
11. Rabkin does, however, include two short stories originally written in Spanish by Argentine authors Jorge Luis Borges and Julio Cortázar, thus reflecting the larger trend of ignoring Spain in favor of Latin America, the birthplace of magical realism, in studies of the fantastic.
12. At the end of the introduction, Calvino excuses this absence by stating, "Among the other national literatures I've omitted, Spanish writing has one very well known [sic] author of fantastic tales, Gustavo Adolfo Bécquer. But this anthology does not pretend to be exhaustive." Italo Calvino, introduction to *Fantastic Tales: Visionary and Everyday*, ed. Italo Calvino, trans. Alfred MacAdam (Boston: Mariner Books, 2015), xvii.
13. It is not coincidental that Roger Callois omits the Mediterranean countries from his account of nineteenth-century fantastic literature: "From the Ukraine to Pennsylvania, in Ireland and England as in Germany and France, that is to say throughout the range of western culture, with the exception of the Mediterranean, on both sides of the Atlantic, and in the space of about thirty years, from 1820 to 1850, this new genre produced its masterpieces." Roger Callois, "The Fantastic," *Forum* 2, no. 3 (May 1958): 54.
14. For a succinct explanation of how Spain came to be perceived as "unmodern" in the late eighteenth and early nineteenth centuries, see chapter 1 of Michael Iarocci's *Properties of Modernity: Romantic Spain, Modern Europe, and the Legacies of Empire* (Nashville, TN: Vanderbilt University Press, 2005). As Iarocci explains, the depiction of Spain as obsolete served the interests of the newly dominant European powers, whose ascendancy required both the "material and discursive defeat" of the original European powerhouse. *Properties of Modernity*, 8.
15. Callois explains, "The fantastic is posterior to the image of a world without miracle and under the law of a rigorous causality." "The Fantastic," 53.
16. José Zorrilla, prólogo a "La pasionaria," in *Cantos del Trovador*, vol. 3 (Madrid: Ignacio Boix, 1841), 8.
17. Mary Coffey and Margot Versteeg identify France and England as "the countries considered primary producers of realist fiction," whereas Spain "was widely considered a nation slow to adopt economic, political, or artistic innovation." They cite Peter Brooks's classic *Realist Vision* as a representative critical study of nineteenth-century European realism that exclusively examines French and British texts (with some mention of the Irish Joyce at the end). Coffey and Versteeg, *Imagined Truths*, 6, 27n2.
18. Pérez Galdós, Benito. "Observaciones sobre la novela contemporánea en España," in *Ensayos de crítica literaria*, ed. Laureano Bonet (Barcelona: Ediciones Península, 1999), 125.

19. In the preface to *Un viaje de novios* (1881; *A Wedding Trip*), for instance, Emilia Pardo Bazán exalts "nuestro realismo nacional" (our national realism) as "tradición gloriosísima del arte hispano" (the most glorious tradition of Hispanic art). She classifies as early examples *La Celestina, Don Quijote*, paintings by Velázquez and Goya, and the work of playwrights Tirso de Molina and Ramón de la Cruz. Emilia Pardo Bazán, prologue to *Un viaje de novios* (Alicante: Biblioteca Virtual Miguel de Cervantes, 2000), no pagination, https://www.cervantesvirtual.com/nd/ark:/59851/bmckk977.
20. Naturally, not all realist authors or works were promoted under the dictatorship. For instance, while Pardo Bazán's ardent Catholicism was celebrated, Galdós's work was generally decried as anticlerical, with the exception of the *Episodios nacionales* (National episodes), which were thought to promote Spanish patriotism. In contrast, Galdós was held up as the paragon of nineteenth-century realism in democratic Spain, thanks to his socially progressive views.
21. Benito Pérez Galdós, prologue to *La sombra* (Madrid: La Guirnalda, 1890), 7.
22. Emilia Pardo Bazán, prologue to *Cuentos sacro-profanos* (Madrid: V. Prieto y Compañía, 1899), 10. The three fantastic stories that she singles out with this statement, "Los hilos," "Desde afuera" and "La máscara," were all published previously in the periodical press.
23. Baquero Goyanes, *El cuento español*, 235. Juan Jesús Payán offers a brilliant rebuttal to this statement in the Coda of *Los conjuros del asombro: Expresión fantástica e identidad nacional en la España del siglo XIX* (Newark, NJ: Juan de la Cuesta, 2022), 337–38.
24. Joan Estruch Tobella, introduction to *Literatura fantástica y de terror española del siglo XVII*, ed. Joan Estruch Tobella (Barcelona: Fontamara, 1982), 11.
25. General anthologies of fantastic writing from nineteenth-century Spain include Roas's previously cited *El Castillo del espectro* and his *Cuentos fantásticos del siglo XIX (España e Hispanoamérica)* (Madrid: Marenostrum, 2003), as well as Juan Molina Porras's *Cuentos fantásticos en la España del realismo* (Madrid: Cátedra, 2006). Anthologies of single-authored fantastic work include: Benito Pérez Galdós, *Cuentos fantásticos*, ed. Alan E. Smith (Madrid: Cátedra, 2008) and Emilia Pardo Bazán, *Cuentos fantásticos*, ed. Ana Abello Verano and Raquel de la Varga Llamazares (León: Eolas, 2020). For an early anthology of scholarly work on the nineteenth-century Spanish fantastic, see Jaume Pont, ed. *Narrativa fantástica en el siglo XIX (España e Hispanoamérica)* (Lleida: Milenio, 1997).
26. Montserrat Trancón Lagunas, *La literatura fantástica en la prensa del Romanticismo* (Valencia: Institució Alfonse el Magnànim/Diputació de València, 2000).
27. Payán, *Los conjuros del asombro*, 18.
28. José Álvarez Junco describes the nineteenth century as "a period characterized by the frenzied affirmation of cultural identities [throughout Europe]; in other words, the construction or invention of myths, symbols and discourses referring to the collectivities called nations which, in order to lay claim to political sovereignty, had to demonstrate that they were the protagonists of history." A large part of nineteenth-century nation building thus consisted of establishing a sense of identification between "a [single national] culture and a polity." José Álvarez Junco, *Spanish Identity in the Age of Nations* (Manchester: Manchester University Press, 2011), 122.
29. Benedict Anderson, *Imagined Communities: Reflections on the Origin and Spread of Nationalism*, revised edition (London: Verso, 2006).
30. Jo Labanyi, *Gender and Modernization in the Spanish Realist Novel* (Oxford: Oxford University Press, 2000), 8.

31. Marieta Cantos Casenave and Daniel Muñoz Sempere, "Introduction: Otherness and National Identity in 19th-Century Spanish Literature—Spaniards on the Margins," in *Otherness and National Identity in 19th-Century Spanish Literature*, ed. Marieta Cantos Casenave and Daniel Muñoz Sempere (Leiden: Brill, 2022), 5.
32. *Constitución Política de la Monarquía Española* (1812), art.V, https://www.congreso.es/docu/constituciones/1812/ce1812_cd.pdf.
33. Susan Kirkpatrick, "Constituting the Subject: Race, Gender, and Nation in the Early Nineteenth Century," in *Culture and the State in Spain 1550–1850*, ed. Tom Lewis and Francisco J. Sánchez (New York: Garland Publishing, 1999), 231, 232, 237.
34. As Labanyi observes, "The attempt to write the nation into existence through the law is paralleled by the attempt to construct it in fiction." *Gender and Modernization*, 3.
35. Catherine Jagoe, "Disinheriting the Feminine: Galdós and the Rise of the Realist Novel in Spain," *Revista de Estudios Hispánicos* 27, no. 2 (May 1, 1993): 226.
36. Jagoe, "Disinheriting the Feminine," 228.
37. Examining the case of *La desheredada* (1881; *The Disinherited Lady*), Jagoe observes, "The implied reader of Galdós's novel possesses an education in the classics, is sexually and politically knowledgeable, and will follow the subtleties of a narrative strategy that works by implication rather than declaration. He will understand the skillful use of symbolism through the cumulative depictions of material details and enjoy the jibes at [the protagonist] Isidora's foolishness without being made too uncomfortable by them." "Disinheriting the Feminine," 240.
38. Jagoe, "Disinheriting the Feminine," 241.
39. Labanyi, *Gender and Modernization*, 6.
40. Labanyi, *Gender and Modernization*, 13. Antonio Risco made this same observation a few years prior, noting, "La superchería del realismo—movimiento a través del cual la burguesía pretendía expresarse de la manera más cabal y completa—consistía entonces en esta ocultación del signo como tal, o sea en querer hacer pasar por *naturaleza* una mera imaginación simbólica" (The trick of realism—a movement through which the bourgeoisie sought to express itself most exactly and completely—consisted then of this concealment of the sign as such, that is to say, of wanting to make pass as *nature* a mere symbolic imagination). Antonio Risco, *Literatura fantástica de lengua española* (Madrid: Taurus, 1987), 18.
41. Susana Reisz, "Las ficciones fantásticas y sus relaciones con otros tipos ficcionales," in *Teorías de lo fantástico*, ed. David Roas (Madrid: Arco/Libros, 2001), 194.
42. Rosemary Jackson, *Fantasy: The Literature of Subversion* (London: Methuen, 1981), 70, 69.
43. Jackson, *Fantasy*, 4–5.
44. Emilia Pardo Bazán, "Pedro Antonio de Alarcón. Necrología." *Nuevo Teatro Crítico* 1, no. 9 (1891): 24. Noël Valis describes Alarcón's waning popularity thusly: "Once wildly popular, even critically esteemed, he is now largely ignored. When measured against such giants as Galdós, Pardo Bazán, and Clarín, he falls short." Noël Valis, review of *Pedro Antonio de Alarcón (prensa, política, novela de tesis)*, by Ignacio Javier López, *Hispanic Review* 78, no. 3 (Summer 2010): 449. Even during his lifetime, Alarcón had slowly faded from view. Pardo Bazán begins his obituary by stating, "La noticia de la muerte de Alarcón ha levantado gran clamoreo, y, por espacio de media semana, llenó la prensa un nombre que iban deshabituándose de componer los cajistas de periódico" (News of the death of Alarcón has incited great clamoring, and during the span of half a week, a name that

newspaper typesetters had lost the habit of composing filled the press). Pardo Bazán, "Pedro Antonio de Alarcón," 22.
45. I follow Alan Smith's classification of Galdós's fantastic production in *Cuentos fantásticos*.
46. See Gisèle Cazottes, "Contribución al estudio del cuento en la prensa madrileña de la segunda mitad del siglo XIX. Pedro Escamilla," *Iris* 4 (1983): 14–15. This article provides a taxonomic study of Escamilla's many short stories. Roas first observed the quantity and praised the quality of Escamilla's fantastic stories in "Entre cuadros, espejos y sueños misteriosos. La obra fantástica de Pedro Escamilla," *Scriptura* 16 (2001): 103–18. He then included Escamilla's short stories in his two anthologies of fantastic short stories from nineteenth-century Spain. Since then, two new anthologies of Escamilla's fantastic writing have appeared: *La casa maldita y otros casos insólitos* (Torrelavega: Quálea, 2015) and *La pesca del diablo y otros relatos extraños* (Madrid: Diábolo Ediciones, 2021).
47. Rafael Serrano Alcázar published *Cuentos negros o historias extravagantes* in 1874, while José Selgas published *Escenas fantásticas* in 1876 and *Mundo invisible* the following year.
48. Lou Charnon-Deutsch cautions readers against ascribing biases to Pardo Bazán based on the interpretation of specific texts when the author penned a total of over six hundred short stories, in which "she explored all alternatives." Lou Charnon-Deutsch, "Evolutionary Logic and the Concept of Race in Pardo Bazán's Short Fiction," in *Approaches to Teaching the Writings of Emilia Pardo Bazán*, ed. Margot Versteeg and Susan Walter (New York: Modern Language Association of America, 2017), 65. Akiko Tsuchiya elaborates more generally that "characters and narrators cannot be seen as mere repositories of authorial ideology, even assuming this ideology is easily identifiable." *Marginal Subjects: Gender and Deviance in Fin-de-Siècle Spain* (Toronto: University of Toronto Press, 2011), 26
49. Xavier Aldana Reyes, *Spanish Gothic: National Identity, Collaboration, and Cultural Adaptation* (New York: Palgrave Macmillan, 2017), 6. Specifically, Aldana Reyes includes Alarcón's "La mujer alta," Galdós's *La sombra*, and Pardo Bazán's "Vampiro" in his account of Spanish Gothic literature.
50. Fred Botting, *Gothic* (London: Routledge, 1996), 2.
51. Botting, *Gothic*, 7.
52. Allan Lloyd Smith, "The Phantoms of *Drood* and *Rebecca*: The Uncanny Reencountered through Abraham and Torok's 'Cryptonymy'," *Poetics Today* 13, no. 2 (Summer 1992), 290.
53. I concur with Jackson's judgment that "an understanding of the subversive function of fantastic literature emerges from *structuralist* rather than from merely *thematic* readings of texts." Jackson, *Fantasy*, 175.
54. Joyce Tolliver, *Cigar Smoke and Violet Water: Gendered Discourse in the Stories of Emilia Pardo Bazán* (Lewisburg, PA: Bucknell University Press, 1998), 44. Charnon-Deutsch describes the nineteenth-century periodical press in Spain as a "male cultural system" featuring images "painted by men, etched, photographed, and engraved by men, published by male magazine editors for an overwhelmingly male readership." Lou Charnon-Deutsch, *Hold That Pose: Visual Culture in the Late-Nineteenth-Century Spanish Periodical* (University Park: Pennsylvania State University Press, 2008), 21. This assessment tracks with the fact that 81.2 percent of Spanish women were illiterate as of 1887. Jo Labanyi, introduction to *Galdós*, ed. Jo Labanyi (London: Longman, 1993), 8.
55. Tolliver, *Cigar Smoke*, 44.

CHAPTER 1

1. María del Pilar Blanco and Esther Peeren, "Introduction: Conceptualizing Spectralities," in *The Spectralities Reader: Ghosts and Haunting in Contemporary Cultural Theory*, ed. María del Pilar Blanco and Esther Peeren (London: Bloomsbury, 2013), 2. One indication of this late nineteenth-century interest in ghosts was the 1882 creation of the Society for Psychical Research, which sought to study paranormal phenomena through scientific methods. Attesting to the organization's perceived legitimacy, William James served as the organization's president from 1894–95.
2. Avery Gordon, *Ghostly Matters: Haunting and the Sociological Imagination* (Minneapolis: University of Minnesota Press, 2008), 7.
3. As Isabel Burdiel states, "Between 1808 and 1843 the entire socio-economic order of the Spanish Ancient Regime was dismantled," as liberal legislation brought sweeping changes to the nation. "The nobility and the clergy lost their legal privileges and the equality of all male citizens before the law was proclaimed. Entails, seigneurial rights and the tithe were abolished. The lands of the Church were disentailed and sold at public auction, the guilds were suppressed and economic freedom established. The Inquisition was dissolved and the Church's legal jurisdiction in civil affairs eliminated. The absolute power of the monarch was replaced by a parliamentary system based on popular sovereignty." Isabel Burdiel, "The Liberal Revolution, 1808–1843," in *Spanish History since 1808*, ed. José Álvarez Junco and Adrian Shubert (London: Arnold, 2000), 17. Spanish liberalism thus prided itself on driving "the programme of political and social modernisation of the country." José Álvarez Junco, "The Nation-Building Process in Nineteenth-Century Spain," in *Nationalism and the Nation in the Iberian Peninsula: Competing and Conflicting Identities*, ed. Clare Mar-Molinero and Angel Smith (Oxford: Berg, 1996), 97.
4. In reality, voting rights only applied to free "whites and indigenous Americans" in Spain and its colonies, and was subject to a literacy requirement envisioned for 1830. Kirkpatrick, "Constituting the Subject," 237. Since the Constitution of 1812 was abrogated by Spanish king Ferdinand VII upon his return to the throne after the ousting of the French in 1814, universal male suffrage would not be implemented in Spain until 1890.
5. Shubert, *A Social History of Modern Spain* (London: Unwin Hyman, 1990), 182.
6. Shubert, *A Social History*, 5.
7. Although the extent of Spain's industrialization lagged behind other European nations such as France or England in the nineteenth century, what industrial development there was created opportunities for growth of the middle classes. Noël Valis further reminds readers that "awareness of being middle class and the adoption of certain life styles and attitudes can and do exist even when the economic structure lags behind, that is, when there is a perception of being modern despite insufficient modernization." Noël Valis, *The Culture of Cursilería: Bad Taste, Kitsch, and Class in Modern Spain* (Durham, NC: Duke University Press, 2002), 11.
8. Jesús Cruz, *The Rise of Middle-Class Culture in Nineteenth-Century Spain* (Baton Rouge: Louisiana State University Press, 2011), 10. Valis similarly asserts, "The truth is, throughout Europe, the terms *bourgeoisie* and *middle class* were often used synonymously for practical purposes, since both occupy the same indeterminate ground between rank and the common people." Valis, *The Culture*, 10.
9. Although Jo Labanyi reminds readers that "in most European countries the middle classes were still relatively small" at the time of their bourgeois revolutions, Cruz sin-

gles out the Spanish bourgeoisie for its small size. Labanyi, *Gender and Modernization*, 24. Cruz, *The Rise*, 12.
10. Shubert, *A Social History*, 111–13. Cruz further explains that the composition of the middle classes varied widely from city to city. Whereas Madrid's bourgeois largely comprised a "group connected to the bureaucracy, to provisioning the city, and to state contracts and finances," Barcelona had a more traditional "urban class dedicated to commerce and industry." Cruz, *The Rise*, 13.
11. Pardo Bazán, Emilia. "La mujer española," in *La mujer española y otros escritos*, ed. Guadalupe Gómez-Ferrer (Madrid: Cátedra, 2018), 99–100.
12. Cruz, *The Rise*, 11.
13. Inma Ridao Carlini, *Rich and Poor in Nineteenth-Century Spain: A Critique of Liberal Society in the Later Novels of Benito Pérez Galdós* (Woodbridge: Tamesis, 2018), 8.
14. He proclaims: "Esa clase es la que determina el movimiento político, la que administra, la que enseña, la que discute, la que da al mundo los grandes innovadores y los grandes libertinos, los ambiciosos de genio y las ridículas vanidades: ella determina el movimiento comercial, una de las grandes manifestaciones de nuestro siglo, y la que posee la clave de los intereses, elemento poderoso de la vida actual, que da origen en las relaciones humanas a tantos dramas y tan raras peripecias." (That [middle] class is the one that determines political movement, that administers, that teaches, that debates, that gives the world the great innovators and the great libertines, the ambitious geniuses and ridiculous vanities: that class determines commercial movement, one of the great manifestations of our time, and possesses the key to economic interests, a powerful element of life today, that gives origin to so many dramas and such strange changes of fortune in human relations.) Pérez Galdós, "Observaciones," 130–31.
15. Cruz, *The Rise*, 13.
16. Pérez Galdós, "Observaciones," 130.
17. Jo Labanyi, Introduction to *Galdós*, 6–7.
18. Collin McKinney, *Mapping the Social Body: Urbanisation, the Gaze, and the Novels of Galdós*, (Chapel Hill: University of North Carolina Press, 2010), 13.
19. Karl Marx and Frederick Engels, *The Communist Manifesto*, trans. Samuel Moore (London: Pluto Press, 2017), 47.
20. Marx states in section 1 of chapter 7 that "By the purchase of labour-power, the capitalist incorporates labour, as a living ferment, with the lifeless constituents of the product." Karl Marx, *Capital: A Critique of Political Economy*, vol. 1, *The Process of Capitalist Production*, trans. Samuel Moore and Edward Aveling, ed. Frederick Engels (Chicago: Charles H. Kerr & Company, 1906), 206.
21. Andrew Smith, "Hauntings," in *The Routledge Companion to Gothic*, ed. Catherine Spooner and Emma McEvoy (London: Routledge, 2007), 150.
22. Andrew Smith examines the British ghost story in relation to economic policies and practices of the nineteenth century in *The Ghost Story, 1840–1920: A Cultural History* (Manchester: Manchester University Press, 2010).
23. Peter Buse and Andrew Stott, "Introduction: A Future for Haunting," in *Ghosts: Deconstruction, Psychoanalysis, History*, ed. Peter Buse and Andrew Stott (London: Macmillan, 1999), 14.
24. Smith, "Hauntings," 147.
25. Alberto Ribas-Casasayas and Amanda L. Petersen, "Introduction: Theories of the Ghost in a Transhispanic Context," in *Espectros: Ghostly Hauntings in Contemporary Transhispanic*

Narratives, ed. Alberto Ribas-Casasayas and Amanda L. Petersen (Lewisburg, PA: Bucknell University Press, 2016), 2.

26. Blanco and Peeren, "Introduction," 20.
27. Gordon, *Ghostly Matters*, 196. Andrew Smith likewise states, "Making visible what is invisible is an issue shared by the ghost story and Marxist praxis." Smith, *The Ghost Story*, 14.
28. Ribas-Casasayas and Petersen, "Introduction," 1.
29. Ridao Carlini describes in particular how the aristocracy "adapt[ed] their finances to the new economic conditions" imposed by bourgeois liberalism, and further consolidated their fortunes by accepting intermarriage with financially successful members of the up-and-coming class. Practically speaking, there emerged a new "dominant class formed by a symbiosis between the old and new aristocracy and the bourgeoisie." Ridao Carlini, *Rich and Poor*, 81–82.
30. Pérez Galdós, "Observaciones," 127–28.
31. Botting states that in early Gothic literature, "The anxieties about the past and its forms of power are projected on to malevolent and villainous aristocrats in order to consolidate the ascendancy of middle-class values." Botting, *Gothic*, 6.
32. Some examples include Bécquer's "Creed en Dios" (1862; Believe in God), "El miserere," (1862; The Miserere), and "La promesa" (1863; The promise). Julia de Asensi's "El encubierto" (1883; The Shrouded One) provides a particularly interesting example for contrasting heroic guildsmen with greedy nobles against the backdrop of the 1521 Revolt of the Brotherhoods in Valencia. Other stories of hers that feature evil aristocrats include "La sombra de don Luis Arce" (The shadow of Don Luis Arce) and "La hija del diablo" (The devil's daughter), from the 1883 collection *Leyendas y tradiciones en prosa y verso* (Legends and traditions in prose and verse), although the noble antagonists of these works are mainly concerned with harming other nobles, rather than commoners.
33. Quote from "*Álbum salón*," Hemeroteca Digital, Biblioteca Nacional de España, accessed June 28, 2024, https://www.bne.es/es/colecciones/prensa-revistas/album-salon. *Álbum salón* ran from 1897 to 1907.
34. All passages quoted from the story come from the 1898 version published in *Álbum salón*. Emilia Pardo Bazán, "El antepasado," *Álbum salón*, July 1, 1898, 249–50. The character Carmona reappears as the narrator of Pardo Bazán's short story "Así y todo" (Even so), included in the collection *Cuentos de Amor* (1898; Love stories).
35. The Esforcia family history was inspired by the historical figure of the Milanese Galeazzo Maria Sforza (1444–1476). Accused of poisoning his mother, Bianca Maria Visconti, Sforza was by all accounts a terrible, cruel man, who was ultimately killed and beheaded by conspirators seeking justice.
36. According to José Monleón, analogous country homes depicted in works by Guy de Maupassant and Henry James "did not project, of course, any sense of a medieval or feudal world. They are images of leisure, of unproductive retirement, places of rest where the bourgeois can escape from the unbearable social conditions that he himself created in the urban centers." José Monleón, *A Specter Is Haunting Europe: A Sociohistorical Approach to the Fantastic* (Princeton, NJ: Princeton University Press, 1990), 88.
37. Eve Kosofsky Sedgwick, *Between Men: English Literature and Male Homosocial Desire* (New York: Columbia University Press, 1985), 93.
38. Kosofsky Sedgwick, *Between Men*, 93.
39. Gabriela Pozzi, "Madres histéricas, médicos y la sexualidad en tres cuentos fantásticos de Emilia Pardo Bazán," *Letras femeninas* 26, no. 1-2 (Spring-Fall 2000): 162.

40. Pozzi, "Madres histéricas,"162.
41. Jacques Derrida, *Specters of Marx: The State of the Debt, the Work of Mourning, and the New International*, trans. Peggy Kamuf (New York: Routledge, 1994), xviii.
42. Jennifer Smith, *Women, Mysticism, and Hysteria in Fin-de-Siècle Spain* (Nashville, TN: Vanderbilt University Press, 2021), 14.
43. Ridao, *Rich and Poor*, 81.
44. Ridao, *Rich and Poor*, 83. Valis further states that "The middle classes prized newness, progress, and individual achievement, but in Spain, as elsewhere in Europe, many of them also looked to the aristocracy as social and cultural models. They looked, that is, to the past." Valis, *The Culture*, 49.
45. McKinney, *Mapping*, 48. In his 1897 speech before the Real Academia Española (Royal Spanish Academy), Galdós describes "la llamada clase media" (the so-called middle class) as an "informe aglomeración de individuos procedentes de las categorías superior e inferior, el producto, digámoslo así, de la descomposición de ambas familias: de la plebeya, que sube; de la aristocrática, que baja" (a shapeless mass of individuals coming from superior or inferior classes; the product, let's say, of the decomposition of both families: of the plebeian, which is ascending, and of the aristocratic, which is dropping). Benito Pérez Galdós, "La sociedad presente como material novelable," in Bonet, *Ensayos de crítica literaria*, 222.
46. Leigh Mercer, *Urbanism and Urbanity: The Spanish Bourgeois Novel and Contemporary Customs (1845–1925)* (Lewisburg, PA: Bucknell University Press, 2013), 5–6.
47. The protagonist of Escamilla's "La mosca" provides a paradigmatic example of this bourgeois *ennui*: "Andrés vivía en Madrid con una pensión de doce mil reales que le pasaba su tío . . . si no asistía a la Universidad, contraía deudas y no faltaba a ninguna primera representación. Era poco docto en el Fuero juzgo, es verdad; pero el estudio no podía conciliarse con las combinaciones del *golfo* y de la *ruleta*. Además, Andrés tenía conocimientos prácticos en el *billar*; sabía destapar como ninguno una botella de *champagne*, y fumaba cigarros de tres cuartos, que, disfrazados de *brevas de Cabañas*, le costaban dos reales cada uno." (Andrés lived in Madrid with a pension of twelve thousand *reales* that his uncle passed to him . . . while he did not attend university, he did incur debts and he never missed a premiere. He was poorly versed in *fuero juzgo* [a codex of medieval Spanish laws], in truth; but he could not reconcile his studies with combinations for *golfo* [a Spanish card game] and for *roulette*. Moreover, Andrés had practical knowledge of *billiards*, he knew how to uncork a bottle of *champagne* like no other, and he smoked three-quarter cigars, which disguised as Cuban cigars, cost him two *reales* each.) Italics in original. Pedro Escamilla, "La mosca," *El Periódico para todos*, February 8, 1875, 611.
48. Cruz, *The Rise*, 4.
49. *Apuntes* was printed in Madrid from March 22, 1896 to February 27, 1897, at which point it was re-baptized *La Revista Moderna* (The modern magazine). In some issues, such as no. 23 (August 23) and no. 30 (October 11), *Apuntes* featured a section directed to the readers, which explicitly described the publication as "rehuyendo cuanto no tenga relación directísima con la índole artística y literaria que le informa" (fleeing from all that does not have a direct relation with the artistic and literary nature that informs the publication). This disclaimer suggests that its readership may have been primed to ignore the political dimension of any texts included in the periodical.
50. The only critic to acknowledge these illustrations is Ángeles Quesada Novás, who notes their number, size, and content. See Quesada Novás, "Nuevos cuentos ilustrados de

Emilia Pardo Bazán," in *Literatura ilustrada decimonónica: 57 perspectivas*, ed. Borja Rodríguez Gutiérrez and Raquel Gutiérrez Sebastián (Santander: Universidad de Cantabria, 2011), 677–90.
51. All quotes come from Emilia Pardo Bazán, "Los hilos," *Apuntes*, July 12, 1896. The periodical does not have numbered pages.
52. A female character similarly named Kriloff, also described as the secretary of the Russian embassy, appears in the short story "El té de las convalescientes" (1919; The convalescents' tea), in which she possesses a magic mirror that can tell fortunes. In the revised version of "Los hilos" that appears in *Cuentos sacro-profanos*, the name Kiriloff has been replaced with Mirovich, although the man's post at the Russian embassy remains the same.
53. In the original 1896 text, the womanizer is named Julio Tovar, but in the 1899 revision, he becomes Tresmes, a notorious Lothario who appears regularly in Pardo Bazán's short fictions.
54. Cruz, *The Rise*, 175.
55. Mercer, *Urbanism and Urbanity*, 45.
56. Valis, *The Culture*, 147.
57. Mercer, *Urbanism and Urbanity*, 5.
58. Iarocci, *Properties of Modernity*, 87.
59. The figure of the "loco lúcido" is an archetype of Spanish literature most famously embodied in Don Quijote.
60. Jo Labanyi, "History and Hauntology; or, What Does One Do with the Ghosts of the Past? Reflections on Spanish Film and Fiction of the Post-Franco Period," in *Spanish Culture from Romanticism to the Present: Structures of Feeling*, ed. Jo Labanyi (Cambridge: Legenda, 2019), 304.
61. Labanyi, "History and Hauntology," 303–4.
62. In doing so, they confirm Valis's observation that "a culture in which credit runs rampant encourages self-interest and discourages the virtue of self-knowledge." Valis, *The Culture*, 141.
63. Valis links this contradiction to the Spanish concept of *cursilería*, stating that "Lo cursi is, more than anything else, particularly lower middle class, reflecting the need to keep up appearances and the inability to do so in a satisfactory way." Valis, *The Culture*, 11.
64. According to David Roas, all but three of Escamilla's fifty-nine fantastic short stories were published in *El Periódico para todos*. Roas, "Entre cuadros," 104. *El Periódico para todos* was less concerned with reporting current news than with entertaining the reader, as evidenced in a section devoted to lively anecdotes and "tasteful" jokes. See "El Periódico para todos," Hemeroteca Digital, Biblioteca Nacional de España, accessed July 18, 2022, http://hemerotecadigital.bne.es/details.vm?q=id:0003433857&lang=en. All quotes from the story cite the original version in *El Periódico*. Pedro Escamilla, "El número trece," *El Periódico para todos*, January 12, 1879, 187–88.
65. Adrian Shubert explains that in the late nineteenth century, "Working class childhoods were ephemeral." He elaborates that it was not uncommon for children to begin working "at the tender age of 7." Adrian Shubert, *A Social History*, 137, 138.
66. Mercer describes the theater as "the pastime par excellence of bourgeois Spain." Mercer, *Urbanism and Urbanity*, 42.
67. Ridao Carlini, *Rich and Poor*, 175.

68. In this practice, Juan was not alone, as the lottery was criticized throughout the nineteenth century for "distract[ing] workers from productive work." Ridao, *Rich and Poor*, 191.
69. Collin McKinney notes that "If the wealthy travelled about the city in private carriages, others, who perhaps could not afford to buy their own carriages, would rent them in order to be seen parading down the same streets." *Mapping*, 50. This imitative posturing describes Juan's carriage ride to a tee.
70. Antonio Flores, "El ómnibus y la calesa," in *Ayer, hoy y mañana o la fe, el vapor y la electricidad*, vol. 2 (Barcelona: Montaner y Simón, 1893), 336.
71. Andrew Smith observes this same effect across British ghost stories of the nineteenth and early twentieth centuries, in which "the acquisition of money becomes like a disease" and "money generates immorality." Smith, *The Ghost Story*, 22. This same dynamic plays out on a more extreme scale in Pardo Bazán's "Vampiro," discussed in Chapter 2.
72. As Shubert describes, "The Spanish working class was small in relative terms . . . It was unevenly distributed across the country, forming a series of concentrated enclaves buried in a predominantly agricultural society . . . [and] highly fragmented: by work experience, regional identity and language, religion and, eventually, ideological affiliation." Shubert, *A Social History*, 119.
73. Aurélie Vialette, *Intellectual Philanthropy: The Seduction of the Masses* (West Lafayette, IN: Purdue University Press, 2018), 8.
74. Galdós describes the urban working class as having lost its distinctive character, "muy modificado ya por la influencia de la clase media" (much changed already through the influence of the middle class). Pérez Galdós, "Observaciones," 128.
75. Benito Pérez Galdós, "La cuestión social," in *Obras inéditas*, ed. Alberto Ghiraldo, vol. 6, *Cronicón (1883–1886)* (Madrid: Renacimiento, 1924), 148. McKinney explains that "the prevailing hypotheses on the subject of hygiene linked the increase in filth and disease with the growth of Madrid's lower-class population. Madrid, or at least the ideal Madrid of the bourgeoisie, was under siege and nowhere was this more apparent than in the discourse on public health and hygiene." McKinney, *Mapping*, 30.
76. The Spanish section of the First Workers' International was founded in 1868, and the Spanish Socialist Party in 1879. At the century's end, anarchists resorted to terrorist tactics in Barcelona with the assassination attempt on General Martínez Campos and the bombing of the Lyceum Theater in 1893, and the 1896 bombing of the Corpus Christi procession. This particular act of terrorism set off "a wave of arrests, torture, executions and deportations" that rocked all of Spain. Labanyi, introduction to *Galdós*, 11.
77. Ridao Carlini, *Rich and Poor*, 145. Ridao's statement reconciles what seem to be opposing interpretations of the philanthropic movement in nineteenth-century Spain. On the one hand, Valis argues that "Foucauldian approaches do not do justice to the philanthropic turn of these texts, reductively insisting on the sole rationale of social control of the lower classes as the overriding reason for such moral and practical reforms." Noël Valis, *Sacred Realism: Religion and the Imagination in Modern Spanish Narrative* (New Haven: Yale University Press, 2010), 113. On the other hand, Aurélie Vialette shows how "philanthropy was presented as a form of providing assistance to workers, which would help maintain social order and avoid a revolution of the masses." Vialette, *Intellectual Philanthropy*, 15. In spite of the apparent contradiction, both Valis and Vialette acknowledge a mix of self-interest and genuine concern for the Other as motivating bourgeois philanthropic projects.

78. Labanyi, *Gender and Modernization*, 53.
79. Clearly articulating this idea, Blanco and Peeren observe that "certain subjectivities have been marginalized and disavowed in order to establish and uphold a particular norm [. . . and] such subjectivities can never be completely erased but insist on reappearing to trouble the norm." María del Pilar Blanco and Esther Peeren, "Spectral Subjectivities: Gender, Sexuality, Race / Introduction," in Blanco and Peeren, *The Spectralities Reader*, 310. Speaking specifically of the Hispanophone context, Ribas-Casasayas and Petersen add that "Modernity in the Transhispanic world is haunted by the Other who is segregated, disenfranchised, and excluded by processes of colonization and modernization." Ribas-Casasayas and Petersen, "Introduction," 6.
80. Smith, *The Ghost Story*, 14.
81. Shubert, *A Social History*, 119.
82. Bridget M. Marshall, *Industrial Gothic: Workers, Exploitation and Urbanization in Transatlantic Nineteenth-Century Literature* (Cardiff: University of Wales Press, 2021), 5.
83. Teresa Fuentes Peris, *Visions of Filth: Deviancy and Social Control in the Novels of Galdós* (Liverpool: Liverpool University Press, 2003), 9.
84. Fuentes Peris, *Visions of Filth*, 10n2.
85. I follow Alan Smith's classification of "Una industria" as Galdós's first short story. Smith, introduction to *Cuentos fantásticos* by Benito Pérez Galdós, ed. Alan E. Smith (Madrid: Cátedra, 2008), 14. Both Oswaldo Izquierdo Dorta and Yolanda Arencibia designate Galdós's first short story as "Un viaje redondo por el bachiller Sansón Carrasco" (A circular travel by the learned Sansón Carrasco), written in 1861, but this work was never published in the author's lifetime, and appears unfinished. Benito Pérez Galdós, *Obra Completa*, vol. 1, *Los cuentos de Galdós*, ed. Oswaldo Izquierdo Dorta (Las Palmas de Gran Canaria: Cabildo Insular de Gran Canaria/Centro de la cultura popular canaria, 1994). Benito Pérez Galdós, *Cuentos*, ed. Yolanda Arencibia (Las Palmas de Gran Canaria: Cabildo Insular de Gran Canaria, 2013).
86. The periodical featured the subtitle "diario progresista." Galdós began reporting for *La nación* in February of 1865, and went on to become the periodical's most prestigious collaborator. "Una industria que vive de la muerte" first appeared in two installments, on December 2 and 6, 1865. As the periodical's pages were not numbered, and each installment of the story's text, though lengthy, occupies less than a single page, I cite instead the section of the story in which each quote appears. Benito Pérez Galdós, "Una industria que vive de la muerte," *La nación*, December 2 and 6, 1865.
87. This was not the first time that Galdós presented cholera under a supernatural guise. In an article published several months earlier, on August 13, 1865, he called the illness "el más temible de los huéspedes" (the most fearsome of guests), further likening it to a "genio pestilente, errante, ebrio de cadáveres que hace algunos años abandonó el Asia, su cuna, para pasearse por Europa dejando una huella de muerte, luto y esterminio [sic]" (pestilent genie, nomadic, drunk off of cadavers, that abandoned Asia, its cradle, some years ago to stroll through Europe leaving a trail of death, mourning, and extinction). Benito Pérez Galdós, "13-VIII-65. Revista de la semana," in *Los artículos de Galdós en "La Nación,"* ed. William H. Shoemaker (Madrid: Ínsula, 1972), 117.
88. Julio Peñate Rivero judges the narrator to harbor an "intenso odio" (intense hatred) toward the casket-maker, which is motivated by the latter's "obsesión fatal por la riqueza [a] toda costa" (fatal obsession with wealth at all costs) and all-consuming desire for luxury. Peñate Rivero, *Benito Pérez Galdós y el cuento literario como sistema* (Zaragoza: Libros

Pórtico, 2001), 128. However, since this same narrator repeatedly underscores the casket-maker's symbolic role, we should not read his statements as reflecting too personally on the protagonist's moral failings, but rather as a critique of certain economic practices.
89. The influence of socioeconomic status on health outcomes has been proven once again with the recent COVID pandemic. See J. A. Patel et al., "Poverty, Inequality and COVID-19: The Forgotten Vulnerable," *Public Health* 183 (2020): 110–11.
90. Nick Groom, *The Vampire: A New History* (New Haven, CT: Yale University Press, 2018), 168.
91. Rodolfo Cardona argues that rather than a short story, "Una industria" is instead an essay on sound, and that sections II-VI of the story are merely an elaborate illustration of the essay's thesis, established in section I. Rodolfo Cardona, "1865 Galdós en *La Nación*: 'Variedades,'" in *A Sesquicentennial Tribute to Galdós 1843-1993*, ed. Linda M. Willem (Newark, NJ: Juan de la Cuesta, 1993), 261–68.
92. Peñate Rivero, *Benito Pérez Galdós*, 136.
93. Pérez Galdós, "La cuestión social," 149.
94. Gordon, *Ghostly Matters*, xvi.
95. Blanco and Peeren, "Spectral Subjectivities," 309.
96. Julian Wolfreys, *Victorian Hauntings: Spectrality, Gothic, the Uncanny and Literature* (New York: Palgrave Macmillan, 2002), 5.
97. Monleón describes, "By the eighteenth century, the 'backwardness' of Spanish society had become an irrefutable fact, and the Peninsula lay at the periphery of Europe, in the shadows of the northern economic powers." Monleón, *A Specter*, 104. More recent scholarship describes this dismissal or outright denial of Spanish modernity as a geopolitical maneuver that would solidify "the ascent of the *Kulturwelt* of Britain, France, and Germany as the new European powers." Iarrocci, *Properties of Modernity*, 8. For examples of newer scholarship that dismantle the stereotype of Spain as resistant to progress, see Mónica Burguera and Christopher Schmidt-Nowara's edited volume *Historias de España contemporánea: Cambio social y giro cultural* (Valencia: Universitat de València, 2008) and Jesús Astigarraga, ed. *The Spanish Enlightenment Revisited* (Oxford: Voltaire Foundation, 2015). Attempts to demarginalize Spain within the history of (Western) European modernity often focus on Spain's imperial policies. See for example Christopher Schmidt-Nowara and John Nieto-Phillips, eds. *Interpreting Spanish Colonialism: Empires, Nations, and Legends* (Albuquerque: University of New Mexico Press, 2005); Gabriel Paquette, *Enlightenment, Governance, and Reform in Spain and Its Empire 1759-1808* (New York: Palgrave Macmillan, 2008); and Josep Fradera, *La nación imperial: Derechos, representación y ciudadanía en los imperios de Gran Bretaña, Francia, España y Estados Unidos (1750-1918)* (Barcelona: Edhasa, 2015).

CHAPTER 2

1. Joseph M. Pierce, "I Monster: Embodying Trans and *Travesti* Resistance in Latin America." *Latin American Research Review* 55, no. 22 (2020): 308.
2. For a good overview of scholarship on the topic, see Ruth Bienstock Anolik, "Sexual Horror: Fears of the Sexual Other," in *Horrifying Sex: Essays on Sexual Difference in Gothic Literature*, ed. Ruth Bienstock Anolik (Jefferson, NC: McFarland & Company, 2007), 1–24.
3. Bienstock Anolik, "Sexual Horror," 5, 4.
4. Bienstock Anolik, "Sexual Horror," 16.

5. Thomas Laqueur, *Making Sex: Body and Gender from the Greeks to Freud* (Cambridge, MA: Harvard University Press, 1992), viii.
6. Pedro Felipe Monlau, *Higiene del matrimonio o el libro de los casados* (Madrid: M. Rivadeneyra, 1858), 113, https://babel.hathitrust.org/cgi/pt?id=ucm.5322558049&view=1up&seq=7.
7. Catherine Jagoe, *Ambiguous Angels: Gender in the Novels of Galdós* (Berkeley: University of California Press, 1994), 16.
8. The term "angel in the house" was popularized by Coventry Patmore's 1854 narrative poem of the same name, while the Spanish term first gained traction in María Pilar del Sinués de Marco's domestic novel *El ángel del hogar* (1857; The angel in the house). Sinués later directed a weekly magazine for women by the same name from 1864 to 1869. Lisa Nalbone provides a sociohistorical overview that is particularly accessible for undergraduate students in "The Legal, Medical, and Social Contexts of the Angel in the House" in *Approaches to Teaching the Writings of Emilia Pardo Bazán*, ed. Margot Versteeg and Susan Walter (New York: Modern Language Association of America, 2017), 49–57.
9. Bridget Aldaraca, *El ángel del hogar: Galdós and the Ideology of Domesticity in Spain* (Chapel Hill: University of North Carolina Press, 1991), 66.
10. Collin McKinney, "'Enemigos de la virilidad': Sex, Masturbation, and Celibacy in Nineteenth-Century Spain." *Prisma social: Revista de ciencias sociales* 13 (December 2014–May 2015): 100.
11. Both Eva María Copeland and Collin McKinney have worked extensively on nineteenth-century notions of respectable masculinity in Spain. See especially Collin McKinney, "How to Be a Man," in *Spain in the Nineteenth Century: New Essays on Experiences of Culture and Society*, ed. Andrew Ginger and Geraldine Lawless (Manchester: Manchester University Press, 2018), 147–73. For more on the guidelines of nineteenth-century urbanity, see chapter 2 of Cruz's *The Rise of Middle-Class Culture in Nineteenth-Century Spain*. With respect to men's fashions, Nicholas Wolters details how a fixation on outward appearances linked middle-class masculinity to an ethos of consumption thought to drive the Spanish economy, such that men's self-fashioning became conflated with the processes of modernization and nation-building in nineteenth-century Spain. See Nicholas Wolters, *Masculine Figures: Fashioning Men and the Novel in Nineteenth-Century Spain* (Nashville, TN: Vanderbilt University Press, 2023).
12. Gabrielle Miller, "¡Mi hijo es mío, puñales! Excessive Paternal Devotion in Benito Pérez Galdós's *Torquemada* Novels," *Decimonónica* 17, no. 2 (Summer 2020): 65–66.
13. For a comprehensive study of norms for nineteenth-century Spanish women, including primary sources from the medical and legal fields, see Catherine Jagoe, Alda Blanco, and Cristina Enríquez de Salamanca, eds. *La mujer en los discursos de género: Textos y contextos en el siglo XIX* (Barcelona: Icaria, 1998). Collin McKinney provides an overview of norms for men in "How to Be a Man."
14. Tsuchiya, *Marginal Subjects*, 113.
15. McKinney, "Enemigos," 76.
16. Elaine Showalter, *Sexual Anarchy: Gender and Culture at the Fin de Siècle* (New York: Viking, 1990), 4.
17. Joanne Nagel, "Masculinity and Nationalism: Gender and Sexuality in the Making of Nations," *Ethnic and Racial Studies* 21, no. 2 (1998): 251.
18. For more on the relation between imperial failure and masculine crisis in Spain, see Nerea Aresti, "La hombría perdida en el tiempo. Masculinidad y nación española a finales del siglo XIX," in *Hombres en peligro: Género, nación e imperio en la España de cambio*

de siglo (XIX–XX), ed. Mauricio Zabalgoitia Herrera (Madrid: Iberoamericana Vervuert, 2017), 19–38, and Christian von Tschilschke, "La crisis de la masculinidad como crítica al colonialismo en *Aita Tettauen* (1905) de Benito Pérez Galdós," in *El otro colonialismo: España y África, entre imaginación e historia*, ed. Christian von Tschilschke and Jan-Henrik Witthaus (Madrid: Iberoamericana Vervuert, 2017), 149–70.

19. George Mosse, *The Image of Man: The Creation of Modern Masculinity* (New York: Oxford University Press, 1996), 79. Rail travel challenged previous understandings of space and time with its rapidity of transport, and was seen as one cause for "the shattering of men's nerves" and male decadence in general. Mosse, *The Image of Man*, 82.
20. Tsuchiya's comprehensive study, which examines both canonical and little-known texts, focuses particularly on the figure of the female deviant as the embodiment of "the complex negotiations of gender, class, race, and nationality taking place in Spain at the turn of the century." *Marginal Subjects*, 27.
21. Showalter, *Sexual Anarchy*, 4. In one example from nineteenth-century Spain, sexologist Vicente Suárez Casañ employed "doomsday language" to paint lesbianism as a threat that could destroy society. Jennifer Smith, "(De)Pathologizing Lesbian Desire in Late Nineteenth-Century Spain," *Anales Galdosianos* 56 (2021): 193.
22. Joyce Tolliver, "La voz antifeminista y la amenaza 'andrógina' en el fin de siglo," in *Sexualidad y escritura (1850–2000)*, ed. Raquel Medina and Barbara Zecchi (Barcelona: Anthropos, 2002), 106. The *marimacho* was also a staple figure of medical literature, where she was often conflated with the masculine lesbian and described as a pseudo-hermaphrodite possessing an enlarged clitoris. Smith, "(De)Pathologizing Lesbian Desire," 187, 191.
23. Pascual Santacruz, "El siglo de los marimachos," *La España Moderna* 19, no. 227 (November 1, 1907): 80.
24. Santacruz, "El siglo," 81.
25. Lisa Surwillo, *Monsters by Trade: Slave Traffickers in Modern Spanish Literature and Culture* (Palo Alto, CA: Stanford University Press, 2014), 22. In classical philosophy, moral monstrosity was often assumed to manifest itself in some bodily deformation, such that individuals who fell short of normative standards of beauty were regularly ascribed negative or even monstrous character traits, a practice popularized through the pseudoscience of physiognomy.
26. Dana Oswald, "Monstrous Gender: Geographies of Ambiguity," in *The Ashgate Research Companion to Monsters and the Monstrous*, ed. Asa Simon Mittman and Peter J. Dendle (Farnham: Ashgate, 2012), 358. Even in nineteenth-century Spain, hermaphroditism maintained its association to the monstrous, as seen in the 13th edition of Monlau's *Higiene del matrimonio*. Noël Valis, "Homosexuality on Display in 1920s Spain: The Hermaphrodite, Eccentricity, and Álvaro Retana," *Freakish Encounters: Constructions of the Freak in Hispanic Cultures*, ed. Sara Muñoz-Muriana and Analola Santana. *Hispanic Issues on Line* 20 (2018): 196.
27. Oswald provides an excellent analysis of the gender of mythological beasts like sirens and werewolves in "Monstrous Gender."
28. Jeffrey J. Cohen, "Monster Culture (Seven Theses)," in *Monster Theory: Reading Culture*, ed. Jeffrey J. Cohen (Minneapolis: University of Minnesota Press, 1996), 6.
29. Cohen, "Monster Culture," 6.
30. Judith Halberstam, *Skin Shows: Gothic Horror and the Technology of Monsters* (Durham, NC: Duke University Press, 1995), 11, 3.

31. Donna Heiland, *Gothic and Gender: An Introduction* (Malden, MA: Blackwell Publishing, 2004), 5.
32. Cynthia Duncan, *Unraveling the Real: The Fantastic in Spanish American Ficciones* (Philadelphia, PA: Temple University Press, 2010), 44.
33. All quotes are from "La mujer alta" as it first appeared in *La Ilustración artística* on January 1, 8, 15, and 22 of 1882. Page numbers are continuous across issues. Although Robert Fedorchek has an English translation of the tale, it is based off the later edition of "La mujer alta," and at times deviates from the original text. Thus, I have provided my own translations. For Fedorchek's translation, see Pedro Antonio de Alarcón, "The Tall Woman: A Tale of Fear," in *The Nun and Other Stories*, trans. Robert M. Fedorchek (Lewisburg, PA: Bucknell University Press, 1999), 153–69.
34. All quotes come from the original version of *La sombra* that appeared in *Revista de España* across issues 70, 71, and 72 in 1871. As in the case of Alarcón, there exists an English translation of the work, but it is based on the 1890 edition, with enough differences in wording that I have provided my own translations. For the existing translation, see Benito Pérez Galdós, *The Shadow*, trans. Karen O. Austin (Athens: Ohio University Press, 1980).
35. All quotes are from Emilia Pardo Bazán, "Vampiro," *Blanco y negro*, August 31, 1901, no pagination. The story appears on the periodical's first two pages.
36. Jo Labanyi, *Gender and Modernization*, 217; Halberstam, *Skin Shows*, 2–3.
37. Notable examples of late Gothic femmes fatales include the titular siren of Anne Bannerman's "The Mermaid" (1800), the sultry Victoria in Charlotte Dacre's *Zofloya* (1806), the sorceress Ayesha in H. Rider Haggard's *She* (1886–7), and the vampire harem in Bram Stoker's *Dracula* (1897). For detailed analyses of the femme fatale in *She* and *Dracula*, see Rebecca Stott, *The Fabrication of the Late-Victorian Femme Fatale: The Kiss of Death* (London: Macmillan, 1992). Memorable Gothic crones include the cruel Prioress of Matthew Lewis's *The Monk* (1796) and Marchesa Vivaldi of Ann Radcliffe's *The Italian* (1797). For more on the Gothic crone, see Avril Horner and Sue Zlosnik, "No Country for Old Women: Gender, Age and the Gothic," in *Women and the Gothic: An Edinburgh Companion*, ed. Avril Horner and Sue Zlosnik (Edinburgh: Edinburgh University Press, 2016), 184–98.
38. Bram Dijkstra, *Idols of Perversity: Fantasies of Feminine Evil in Fin-de-Siècle Culture* (Oxford: Oxford University Press, 1988), 371.
39. As Virginia Allen poetically states, "The femme fatale, no matter how amorous, does not conceive. Sin alone may feed at her luscious breast." *The Femme Fatale: Erotic Icon* (Troy, NY: Whitston Publishing Company, 1983), 4.
40. For more on literary representations of the femme fatale in nineteenth-century Spain, see Marina Cuzovic-Severn's "Imperialist Seductions: A Genealogy of the *Femme Fatale* in Spanish Literature from Romanticism to Modernism (1845–1908)," (PhD Diss., Michigan State University, 2014). Similarly, Lou Charnon-Deutsch's *Fictions of the Feminine in the Nineteenth-Century Spanish Press* (University Park: The Pennsylvania State University Press, 2000) provides an invaluable resource on visual depictions of the femme fatale.
41. Galdós describes that these allegorical pieces "sirve[n] para ilustrar y comentar las naturales divisiones del año, literatura simpática, aunque de pie forzado" (serve to illustrate and comment upon the natural divisions of the year, amusing literature, although a bit forced). Pérez Galdós, prologue to *La sombra*, 7. According to Lou Charnon-Deutsch, the *Ilustración Española y Americana* was founded as a "modern 'museum' for the bourgeois class" intended for a cultured audience. Lou Charnon-Deutsch, *Hold That Pose*, 85.

42. Peñate Rivero, *Benito Pérez Galdós*, 521n1.
43. Peñate Rivero, the only critic to acknowledge the 1901 edition of "Theros," lists the story as appearing in the second issue of *Revista Moderna de México* from that year, but it actually appears in the year's first issue. Peñate Rivero, *Benito Pérez Galdós*, 521n1. In his bibliography, Hernández Suárez mentions an additional appearance of "Theros" in the June 14, 1883 issue of *La Correspondencia de Canarias* (The Correspondence of Canarias), but no other sources corroborate this edition, and I could not locate the short story in the number listed. Manuel Hernández Suárez, *Bibliografía de Galdós*, (Las Palmas: Cabildo Insular de Gran Canaria, 1972), 1:405.
44. All quotes come from the original version of "El verano" as published in the *Almanaque de La Ilustración española y americana para 1878*.
45. Examples include Oswaldo Izquierdo Dorta's edited collection *Ocho cuentos de Galdós* (Las Palmas: Cabildo Insular de Gran Canaria, 1988), republished with Akal in 2001, and German Gullón's collection titled *La conjuración de las palabras* (Barcelona: EDHASA, 1991). The more recent *13 cuentos* by Galdós, edited by Esteban Gutiérrez Díaz-Bernardo (Madrid: EDAF, 2001), likewise omits "Theros." Additionally, at a time when criticism of Galdós's work centered on his realist novels was flourishing, evaluations of "Theros" were generally brief and unflattering. In 1971, Walter Oliver set the tone for future scholarship by designating the story Galdós's "least interesting" and lambasting the work's "utter lack of intellectual or emotional content." The dismissive attitude displayed by Oliver and subsequent likeminded critics has largely been rooted in taking the tale at face value as a seasonal allegory. Walter C. Oliver, "The Short Stories of Benito Pérez Galdós." (PhD Diss., University of New Mexico, 1971), 242.
46. Krisztina Weller, "The Mysterious Lady: An Enigmatic Figure in the Fantastic Short Story of Nineteenth-Century Spain," *Scripta Mediterranea* 8-9 (1987-88): 59-68. Alan Smith, *Los cuentos inverosímiles de Galdós en el contexto de su obra* (Barcelona: Anthropos, 1992), 146. Examples of scholarship that have followed Smith's reading include: Paloma Andrés Ferrer and Miguel Jiménez Molina, "'Theros,' la cosecha de la vida, cuento inverosímil de Galdós," in *Homenaje a Alfonso Armas Ayala*, ed. Lourdes Acosta González (Las Palmas: Cabildo Insular de Las Palmas 2000), 2:75-97 and Andrés Sánchez Martínez, "La cara oculta de la realidad: Elementos fantásticos en *La princesa y el granuja* de Benito Pérez Galdós," *Philobiblion: Revista de Literaturas Hispánicas* 11 (2020): 121-37.
47. Peñate Rivero was the first to note this in *Benito Pérez Galdós*, 535-36.
48. John Berger, *Ways of Seeing* (London: Penguin Books, 1990), 47.
49. The use of the term "nymph" in this story is particularly evocative. In chapter 7 of *Idols of Perversity*, Bram Dijkstra relates the propensity to paint wantonly frolicking nymphs during the nineteenth century with the coining and popularity of the term "nymphomaniac" in the 1860s as a description of pathological female sexuality. Dijkstra, *Idols*, 249. Jennifer Smith further elaborates on the diagnosis of nymphomania in the Spanish context, explaining how the establishment of the disorder as "a female perversion worked to control the female subject in several ways" including the pathologization of female pleasure, the corroboration of procreation as the "natural" objective for women, and the inculcation of a self-policing impulse in women to negate their own wishes and desires. Smith, *Women*, 42.
50. Duncan, *Unraveling*, 177.
51. Francisco de Paula Campá, "Las dos edades críticas de la vida de la mujer," in *Discursos pronunciados en la inauguración de las sesiones de la Academia de Medicina de Valencia en*

el año 1876 (Valencia: Imprenta de Ferrer de Orga, 1876), 43, https://www.google.com/books/edition/_/G30B1FY8WzgC?hl=en&gbpv=0.

52. Gabrielle Miller, "Unveiling the *Beata*: Feminine Aging and Subjectivity in *El doctor Centeno* (1883) and *Tormento* (1884)," *Anales Galdosianos* 55 (2020), 41.
53. Geraldine Scanlon, *La polémica feminista en la España contemporánea (1868–1974)*, trans. Rafael Mazarrasa (Madrid: Akal, 1986), 123. Cristina Enríquez de Salamanca discusses some of the ways in which in which unwed adult women were nevertheless legally restricted in "La mujer en el discurso legal del liberalismo español," in Jagoe, Blanco and Enríquez de Salamanca, *La mujer*, 240.
54. Carlos Rementería y Fica's popular conduct manual *El hombre fino al gusto del día* (*The Refined Gentleman by Current Tastes*) reminds the nineteenth-century man aspiring to bourgeois urbanity to seek the counsel of the elderly woman who, in her mature age, has grown to be "a cubierto de la murmuración; tiene la libertad de recibir bien a las gentes de cualquiera clase que sean" (protected from murmurings; she is at liberty to receive visits from any class of people). *El hombre fino al gusto del día, o Manual completo de urbanidad, cortesía y buen tono* (Madrid: Imprenta de Moreno, 1829), 3. Similarly, Pedro de Madrazo's contribution on "La señora mayor" (The older woman) to the 1844 edition of *Los españoles pintados por sí mismos* (*Spaniards as Painted by Themselves*), describes that "la Señora Mayor se halla por su edad al abrigo de las hablillas de la gente ociosa" (the Older Woman is found due to her age to be sheltered from the gossip of idle folk). Pedro de Madrazo, "La señora mayor," in *Los españoles pintados por sí mismos*, ed. Ignacio Boix, vol. 2 (Madrid: Ignacio Boix, 1844), 357.
55. Ana Rueda contrasts the literary representation of Spanish widows with their lived experience in the long eighteenth century, noting that in spite of their relative freedom, widows were nevertheless subject to patriarchal controls, such as an 1851 Penal Code that threatened to arrest and fine women who remarried within 301 days of losing their husbands. Ana Rueda, "At the Crossroads of Age and Gender: Widowhood in the Spanish Long Eighteenth Century," in "Intersections between age and gender in Enlightenment society," ed. Hanna Nohe, special issue, *Das achtzehnte Jahrhundert* 44, no. 2 (2020), 233. This prohibition remained in effect in the Civil Code of 1889. "Código Civil de 1889," in Jagoe, Blanco and Enríquez de Salamanca, *La mujer*, 263.
56. Gabrielle Miller explores this same dynamic in two of Galdós's realist novels, concluding that the character Marcelina Polo's "espousal of the *beata* identity is enabled by her advancing age, which paradoxically empowers her to adopt a lifestyle of unprecedented agency and autonomy," much to the dismay of the men around her. Miller, "Unveiling the *beata*," 41.
57. The first installment of Alarcón's short story ran in the inaugural issue of *La Ilustración Artística* on January 1, 1882, and the story unfolded over the next three issues, ending on January 22.
58. Emilia Pardo Bazán, "Pedro Antonio de Alarcón. Las novelas," *Nuevo Teatro Crítico* 1, no. 10 (1891): 36.
59. Curtis, introduction to *Modern Ghosts*, xiii–xiv. Alarcón's story appears in at least one other English-language anthology of the period: *Stories by Foreign Authors: Spanish* (New York: Charles Scribner's Sons, 1898).
60. Juan Molina Porras, introduction to *Cuentos fantásticos*, 20.
61. In George's reading, informed by the work of Judith Butler, the ambiguity of the tall woman's gender points to the constructed-ness of gender itself, which destabilizes Telesforo's

own identity as a supposed paragon of bourgeois masculinity. David R. George, Jr., "The Tall (Wo)Man: Crossing Heterosexual Gender Identities in Pedro Antonio de Alarcón's *La Mujer Alta*," *Romance Languages Annual* 7 (1995): 473-77.

62. Gabrielle Miller studies the visual portrayal of elderly women in satirical publications such as *Madrid cómico* (Comical Madrid) in her upcoming book *Aging into Agency: Spinsterhood in Nineteenth-Century Spain*, where she observes an outsize proboscis as a repeated feature of such caricatures.

63. Only Ramón Espejo Saavedra explicitly acknowledges this fact: "Lo que le produce tanto horror a Telesforo es la contradicción entre el traje que sugiere juventud, lozanía y oportunidad sexual y la visión de desgaste del cuerpo de la mujer vieja" (What produces such horror in Telesforo is the contradiction between her dress that suggests youth, vitality, and sexual opportunity, and the vision of deterioration in the body of the old woman.) In "El terror y el deseo en 'La mujer alta' de Pedro Antonio de Alarcón," in *Perversiones decimonónicas: Literatura y parafilia en el XIX*, ed. Jorge Avilés Diz (Valencia: Albatros, 2018), 70.

64. Laura de los Ríos refers to the fan as a magic wand that symbolizes the tall woman's power and authority. Laura de los Ríos, "Análisis de los cinco cuentos de esta selección," in *La Comendadora, El clavo, y otros cuentos*, by Pedro Antonio de Alarcón, ed. Laura de los Ríos (Madrid: Cátedra, 2003), 86. Both David R. George Jr. and Colleen Combs draw out the phallic connotations of the accessory. George, Jr., "The Tall," 476; Colleen J. Combs, *Women in the Short Stories of Pedro Antonio de Alarcón* (Lewiston: The Edwin Mellen Press, 1997), 109.

65. Valis, *The Culture*, 88. This can be clearly seen in Juan Meléndez Valdés's late eighteenth-century ode "El abanico" (The fan) in which the speaker describes a young woman's sensuous use of the fan to provoke male desire.

66. Valis, *The Culture*, 108.

67. María del Pilar Contreras y Alba, "La solterona," in *Las mujeres españolas, americanas y lusitanas pintadas por sí mismas*, ed. Faustina Saez de Melgar, vol. 1 (Barcelona: Juan Pons, 1881), 370.

68. Monlau, *Higiene del matrimonio*, 114.

69. Sebastián de Mobellán de Casafiel, "Rosa la solterona," in *Las españolas pintadas por los españoles*, ed. Roberto Robert, vol. 1 (Madrid: J.E. Morete, 1871), 104.

70. Rementería y Fica, *El hombre fino*, 3. Madrazo, "La señora," 350. Florencio Moreno Godino's sketch on "La vieja verde" (The dirty old woman) is one of the few male-authored texts of the period that recognizes the cruelty of censuring the older flirt: "si el hombre no debe ser nunca ridículo, la mujer está en su derecho pretendiendo agradar el mas tiempo posible, puesto que el hombre la ha repartido este papel en la comedia de la vida" (if the man is never to be ridiculous, the woman is within her rights to intend to be pleasing for the longest possible time, given that the man has assigned her this role in the comedy of life). In *Las españolas pintadas por los españoles*, ed. Roberto Robert, vol. 2 (Madrid: J.E. Morete, 1872), 117.

71. Joseph Snow, "Viejas marginadas en el patriarcado medieval español," in *Actas del XVI Congreso de la Asociación Internacional de Hispanistas: nuevos caminos del hispanismo*, ed. Pierre Civil and Françoise Crémoux, (Madrid: Iberoamericana Vervuert, 2010), 128.

72. Duncan, *Unraveling*, 42-43.

73. José B. Monleón, Ezequiel González Mas, and Consuelo Puebla all view the tall woman harshly. Monleón first described the tall woman as, "without any doubt, the monster

through which the unreasonable forces of society destroyed [Telesforo's] promising life." *A Specter*, 129. Similarly, González Mas refers to her as "grotesca" (grotesque), "estantigua" (freakishly tall), and "horrible vieja" (horrible old lady) in "En torno a *La mujer alta*, de Alarcón," *Salina: Revista de Lletres* 7 (1993): 57. As recently as 2003, Puebla considered the title character to be a "horripilante aparición nocturna" (hideous nocturnal apparition), "causa de desgracia para el joven" (source of misfortune for the young man), and "una mujer de aspecto hombruno y ademanes diabólicos" (a woman of manly appearance and diabolical gestures). Consuelo Puebla, "La deformación del personaje Alarconiano," in *Monstruosidad y transgresión en la cultura hispánica*, ed. Ricardo de la Fuente Ballesteros y Jesús Pérez Magallón (Valladolid: Universitas Castellae, 2003), 246. In contrast, Aldana Reyes recognizes that the story "allows for a reading that dispels [the tall woman's] presence as a bad and deadly omen" in *Spanish Gothic*, 117. Most recently, Espejo Saavedra proposes that she appears as an aged prostitute to remind Telesforo of the physical toll that the exploitative institution of sex work takes on women. Espejo Saavedra, "El terror y el deseo," 72.

74. Studies that read the tall woman's response as self-referential include: George, Jr., "The Tall," 476; González Mas, "En torno," 58; and Mohamed Ben Slama, "El género femenino como elemento amenazante: 'La mujer alta', de Pedro Antonio de Alarcón, y 'La mujer sin cara', de Emilio Carrere," *Brumal* 4, no. 2 (Autumn 2016): 256.
75. John Tosh, "Hegemonic Masculinity and the History of Gender," in *Masculinities in Politics and War: Gendering Modern History*, ed. Stefan Dudink, Karen Hagemann, and John Tosh, (Manchester: Manchester University Press, 2004), 47.
76. Baker, Brian. "Gothic Masculinities," in Spooner and McEvoy, *The Routledge Companion to Gothic*, 164.
77. Bienstock Anolik, "Sexual Horror," 11.
78. The German character is referenced in the early pages of Galdós's novella (270), attesting to the author's familiarity with the figure.
79. For more on the presence of the mad doctor in nineteenth-century Spanish fiction, see Aldana Reyes, *Spanish Gothic*, 121–28.
80. As Abigail Lee Six points out, supernatural beings with vampiric traits such as bloodsucking or holding victims in thrall are well-established in traditional Spanish folklore, particularly in the Galician region. However, these monsters were generally described as witches, such as the Galician *meiga*, rather than specifically as vampires. Abigail Lee Six, *Spanish Vampire Fiction since 1900: Blood Relations*, (London: Routledge, 2019), 162. Monleón argues that vampirism did not excite the Spanish imagination in the nineteenth century due to the immense popularity of the Don Juan figure, who fulfilled the same function of destabilizing the family and the nation through seductive methods. José B. Monleón, "Vampiros y donjuanes (Sobre la figura del seductor en el siglo XIX)," *Revista Hispánica Moderna* 48, no. 1 (June 1995): 19–30.
81. Polidori's "The Vampyre" was first translated into Spanish in 1824, and new editions appeared in 1829, 1841, and 1843. Roas, *De la maravilla al horror*, 123. Goethe's *Faust* and Stevenson's *The Strange Case of Dr. Jekyll and Mr. Hyde* were first translated into Spanish during Galdós's and Pardo Bazán's lifetimes, in 1882 and 1891 respectively. For more information on the former, see Stefan Beyer, "Goethean Rhymes and Rhythms in Verse Translations of Faust into Spanish," *MonTI: Monografías de Traducción e Interpretación* 5 (2013), 349–63.

82. "La distancia social entre los dos sexos es hoy mayor que era en la España antigua, porque el hombre ha ganado derechos y franquicias que la mujer no comparte... Cada nueva conquista del hombre en el terreno de las libertades políticas, ahonda el abismo moral que le separa de la mujer... Libertad de enseñanza, libertad de cultos, derecho de reunión, sufragio, parlamentarismo, sirven para que media sociedad (la masculina) gane fuerzas y actividades a expensas de la otra media femenina" (The social distance between the two sexes is greater today than it was in Spain before, because men have gained rights and privileges that women do not share... Each new conquest by man in the terrain of political liberties, deepens the moral abyss that separates him from woman... Freedom of schooling, freedom of religion, the right to gather, suffrage, parliamentarianism, serve so that half of society [the male half] gains in strength and activities at the expense of the other, feminine half). Pardo Bazán, *La mujer española*, 89.
83. While *La Fontana de Oro* was the first novel that Galdós published in 1870, *La sombra* was the first that he penned. Although previous scholars had alluded to a Gothic influence on the text, Sylvia López was the first to analyze in detail the many Gothic conventions employed in the novella, in "The Gothic Tradition in Galdós's *La sombra*," *Hispania* 81, no. 3 (Sept. 1998), 509–18.
84. Pérez Galdós, prologue to *La sombra*, 5.
85. The revised 1890 text contains the words "monster" or "monstrosity" eleven times, seven of which are references to Paris.
86. Paris is described in devilish terms as a "diablo" (devil), "diabólico" (devilish), and "endiablado" (awful).
87. For more on Paris's spectral nature as a commentary on the impossibility of bourgeois ideals, see Wan Sonya Tang, "'Yo no soy un hombre': Masculinity, Monstrosity, and Gothic Conventions in Galdós's *La sombra* (1871)," *Hispanic Review* 88, no. 3 (2020): 243–63.
88. The extradiegetic narrator's role within *La sombra* was hotly debated throughout the 1970s and 80s. Harriet Turner was the first to examine the subject in depth, describing the narrator, whom she identifies to be Galdós himself, as guiding readers to slowly sympathize with Anselmo. Harriet Turner, "Rhetoric in *La sombra*: The Author and His Story," *Anales Galdosianos* 6 (1971): 5–19. Marcy Shulman later viewed the narrator as unreliable in "Ironic Illusion in *La sombra*," *Anales Galdosianos* 17 (1982): 33–38, and Karen Austin viewed Anselmo to usurp the author/narrator's role within the novel in "Don Anselmo and the Author's Role," *Anales Galdosianos* 18 (1983): 39–47. Finally, Thomas Franz viewed Anselmo's storytelling and that of the narrator's as competing accounts that gesture toward the metafictional aspect of the text. Thomas Franz, "The Concentrated Metafiction of Galdós's *La sombra*," *Revista de estudios hispánicos* 21, no. 3 (Oct. 1987): 51–66. Nearly all subsequent scholarship has made some mention of the narrator's role in reader interpretation of the novella and its protagonist.
89. Cyndy Hendershot, *The Animal Within: Masculinity and the Gothic* (Ann Arbor: University of Michigan Press, 1998), 69.
90. Ana Martínez Santa tellingly deems Anselmo's workspace an "anti-laboratory" in "La influencia de E. T. A. Hoffmann en *La sombra*," in *Actas del IV Congreso Internacional de Estudios Galdosianos* (Las Palmas: Cabildo Insular de Gran Canaria, 1993), 2:161.
91. Although the term "self-made man" is most closely associated with the Anglo-American tradition, the man who owed his success to economic prudence and an unwavering work ethic was likewise an aspirational model in nineteenth-century Spain. The overwhelming

success of British author Samuel Smiles's book *Self-Help* (1859), which illustrated every man's potential for success with a lengthy list of self-made men, spread to Spain and inspired public intellectuals such as politician and author Rafael María de Labra. Teresa Fuentes Peris, *Galdós's Torquemada Novels: Waste and Profit in Late Nineteenth-Century Spain* (Cardiff: University of Wales Press, 2007), 19.

92. Anselmo seems conscious of this expectation, as he praises his father-in-law for this very knowledge: "En algunas cosas, sin embargo, era fuerte, sobre todo en cuestiones de política y de hacienda. Ocupábase mucho de la alza y baja de los fondos públicos, y negociaba con el crédito del Estado, tomando parte juntamente con los primeros capitalistas en las más arriesgadas operaciones mercantiles, lo cual fortalecía y aprovechaba sus conocimientos en Hacienda" (606; He was, nevertheless, strong in some matters, especially in politics and finance. He was very concerned with the rise and fall of public funds, and traded with the credit of the State, taking part with the major capitalists in the riskiest of commercial ventures, which strengthened and leveraged his knowledge of finance).

93. Sylvia López, Abigail Lee Six, and Leigh Mercer have explicitly linked the novel's Gothic aesthetic to a discussion of gendered violence. Viewing Elena as a powerless victim, all three authors link her abuse to Anselmo's masculine insecurities rooted in the outmoded practice of arranged marriage and exacerbated by an obsession with an antiquated concept of honor. Sylvia López, "The Gothic," 510; Lee Six, *Gothic Terrors*, 77; Leigh Mercer, "Shadowing the Gothic: Rosalía de Castro's *La hija del mar* and Benito Pérez Galdós's *La sombra*," *Decimonónica* 9, no. 1 (Winter 2012), 41–42.

94. Mercer, "Shadowing," 41.

95. In the 1871 text, the narrator describes Anselmo's violent outbursts as "martirios para aquella infeliz" (419; martyrdom for that wretched woman) though this description is omitted in the 1890 text, downplaying the young wife's suffering.

96. Throughout the nineteenth century, domestic abusers faced few consequences. Carolina Coronado's 1843 poem "El marido verdugo" (The executioner husband) strongly censures Spanish society for enabling wife-beating. According to the 1870 Penal Code, men who abused their wives were only sentenced to "arresto y reprensión" (arrest and public warning) for five to fifteen days. "Código Penal de 1870" in Jagoe, Blanco, and Enríquez de Salamanca, *La mujer*, 262.

97. Anja Louis, *Women and the Law: Carmen de Burgos, an Early Feminist* (Woodbridge: Tamesis, 2005), 57.

98. Lou Charnon-Deutsch describes *Blanco y Negro* as "Spain's first moderately priced illustrated weekly magazine." Intended to appeal to a broad and diverse audience, the magazine enjoyed "sudden and meteoric success" after its founding in 1891. Charnon-Deutsch, *Hold That Pose*, 85. Méndez Bringa was one of the periodical's longtime illustrators, whose name became synonymous with *Blanco y Negro*. His illustrations graced the pages of stories by numerous acclaimed writers, including both Galdós and Pardo Bazán. For more on Méndez Bringa, see "Méndez Bringa: la vision de la España de entresiglos," *Descubrir el arte*, April 22, 2015, https://www.descubrirelarte.es/2015/04/22/mendez-bringa-la-vision-de-la-espana-de-entresiglos.html.

99. Aldana Reyes, *Spanish Gothic*, 119.

100. Michelle Massé deems this the "marital Gothic," in which the protagonist's husband "become[s] the avatar of horror who strips voice, movement, property and identity itself from the heroine" in "Gothic Repetitions: Husbands, Horrors, and Things that Go Bump in the Night," *Signs: A Journal of Women in Culture and Society* 15, no. 4 (1990): 682.

101. Although it is not known why Pardo Bazán made this change, the possibility of rehabilitating an octogenarian likely seemed too fantastical even for the author.

102. Monlau insisted that "los célibes, en fin, hasta cuando se arrepienten causan daño al Estado. Ellos son en mayoría los que forman los matrimonios de edad desproporcionada; y ya hemos visto que tales matrimonios son un escándalo fisiológico, porque ni pueden ser dichosos, ni pueden procrear hijos robustos" (celibate men, in short, cause harm to the State even when they repent. They are in large part those that form marriages of disproportionate ages; and we have already seen that these marriages are a physiological scandal, because they can neither be happy, nor can they generate robust children). Monlau, *Higiene del matrimonio*, 58.

103. Juan Paredes Nuñez, ed. *Cuentos completos de Emilia Pardo Bazán* (Vigo: Fundación Pedro Barrié de la Maza, 1990) 2: 450n2 under "Vampiro."

104. James Fernández, "America Is in Spain: A Reading of Clarín's 'Boroña,'" in *Bridging the Atlantic: Toward a Reassessment of Iberian and Latin American Cultural Ties*, ed. Marina Pérez de Mendiola (Albany: State University of New York Press, 1996), 34.

105. Surwillo, *Monsters*, 132.

106. Lisa Surwillo, "Inscribing *Indianos* into Modern Imperial Histories," *Empire's End: Transnational Connections in the Hispanic World*, ed. Akiko Tsuchiya and William Acree (Nashville, TN: Vanderbilt University Press, 2016), 195.

107. Marta Guijarro and Óscar Peláez, "La longevidad globalizada: un análisis de esperanza de vida en España (1900–2050)," *Scripta Nova: Revista electronica de geografía y ciencias sociales* 12, no. 260 (March 2008), http://www.ub.edu/geocrit/sn/sn-260.htm.

108. Surwillo, *Monsters*, 130.

109. Surwillo, "Inscribing *Indianos*," 193. As Surwillo poetically states, "those who met with success thrived in the candyland of the slave economy. It is all but impossible to untangle a single occupation—for example, that of shopkeeper—from the larger economic framework." *Monsters*, 137.

110. Slave trade to the Spanish colonies was made illegal in 1817, although the ban was hardly enforced, and the 1845–1867 period saw what Martin Rodrigo-Alharilla describes as a boom in the activity of Spanish slaving ships. Martin Rodrigo-Alharilla, "Spanish Sailors and the Illegal Slave Trade to Cuba, 1845–1867," *Journal of Iberian and Latin American Studies* 27, no.1 (2021): 94–117. Surwillo further states that "even the most canonical realist novelists wove slavery and the slave trade into their works seamlessly, without complicated introductions or weighty ideological pronouncements: such polemics were unnecessary, as the presence and relevance of slavery and the slave trade in the late nineteenth century were amply understood by contemporary readers." *Monsters*, 13.

111. The analogy between women and slaves was famously explored in Gertrudis Gómez de Avellaneda's 1841 abolitionist novel *Sab*. Interestingly, this analogy was also employed by those who argued against women's emancipation in the Spanish context. Santacruz's invective against the *marimacho* concludes, "La mujer no ha nacido para ser libre, y mucho menos en el sentido que el feminismo pregona. La fuerza de la mujer está en seguir siendo *esclava* para el *derecho público* y en reservar su señorío para el privado" (Woman was not born to be free, and much less in the sense that feminism preaches. The strength of a woman lies in continuing to be a *slave* by *public law* and in exerting her dominion in private). Santacruz, "El siglo," 89, italics in original.

112. As Fernández describes, a frequent plot of *indiano* fictions entails marriage as a mutually beneficial contract between "the indiano, who returns with wealth but without lin-

eage" and "a proud but impoverished aristocracy, which has lineage but alas, no wealth" in "America Is in Spain," 35. Even without aspiring to the rank of nobility, *indianos* sought social prestige through marriage to the town's most attractive bachelorettes, paying generous bride prices in exchange for their wives' beauty to visibly signify their masculine prowess, much like Anselmo did in *La sombra*. This is the most common marital economy depicted in Pardo Bazán's short fictions. In stories like "El voto" (1892; The vow) or "Saletita" (1898), both the *indiano* and the object of his fancy understand the unstated terms of the deal.

113. Emilia Pardo Bazán, "Vampiro" in *Cuentos completos*, ed. Juan Paredes Nuñez (Vigo: Fundación Pedro Barrié de la Maza, 1990) 2:354.
114. Pardo Bazán, "Vampiro," in *Cuentos completos*, 2:354.
115. Ironically, given his questionable morality, Don Fortunato does not truly embody the self-made man in the original sense of the term. As Fuentes Peris explains, "One of the fundamental virtues of the self-made man as conceptualized by Smiles [and other nineteenth-century intellectuals] was, in fact, moral fiber. In Smiles's view, elevation of character and moral worth was more important than material prosperity and worldly success." *Galdós's* Torquemada *Novels*, 22. Thus, Don Fortunato represents a perversion of the archetype, and "Vampiro" could be read to critique Spanish society's embrace of materialism without a moral compass.
116. Beatriz Trigo observes that Inés is the angel in the house "llevada a sus extremos" (taken to extremes). Beatriz Trigo, "El espacio fantástico en tres cuentos de Emilia Pardo Bazán o la reafirmación de la sociedad patriarcal," *Cuaderno Internacional de Estudios Hispánicos y Lingüística* 2 (2002): 126.
117. Trigo, "El espacio," 126.
118. Ellen Moers, *Literary Women: The Great Writers* (New York: Doubleday, 1976).
119. For an excellent discussion of "the supernatural explained" and why it became commonplace for women writers, see chapter 7, "The Supernatural Explained" in E. J. Clery, *The Rise of Supernatural Fiction 1762–1800* (Cambridge: Cambridge University Press, 1995), 106–14.

CHAPTER 3

1. Surwillo, *Monsters by Trade*, 101.
2. Much of this work has appeared in the form of edited volumes, such as Akiko Tsuchiya and William G. Acree, Jr., eds., *Empire's End: Transnational Connections in the Hispanic World* (Nashville, TN: Vanderbilt University Press, 2016); Jennifer Smith and Lisa Nalbone, eds., *Intersections of Race, Class, Gender, and Nation in fin-de-siècle Spanish Literature and Culture* (New York: Routledge, 2017); and N. Michelle Murray and Akiko Tsuchiya, eds., *Unsettling Colonialism: Gender and Race in the Nineteenth-Century Global Hispanic World* (Albany: State University of New York Press, 2019).
3. The Congreso Geográfico Hispano-Portugués-Americano (the Hispanic-Portuguese-American Geographic Conference) of 1892 concluded, for instance, that based on studies of the cephalic index of the current Spanish population, "cabe considerer a dicha población como la más homogénea de Europa" (we should consider said population to be the most homogenous in Europe). Ricardo Beltrán y Rózpide, "Los congresos del centenario," *La Ilustración española y americana*, December 30, 1892, 458.
4. Alda Blanco traces descriptions of such racial fusion across the speeches delivered at the Congreso Geográfico Hispano-Portugués-Americano. In one prominent example, Ángel

Rodríguez Arroquia, former president of Madrid's Geographic Society, commented on the exceptionality of the Spanish race as "easily fus[ing] with other races without diminishing the virility of its blood and its physical conditions, even inspiring their way of thinking and creating empires of peoples that are eminently Spanish." Quoted in Alda Blanco, "Theorizing Racial Hybridity in Nineteenth-Century Spain and Spanish America," in Tsuchiya and Acree, Jr., *Empire's End*, 88–89.

5. See Mar Soria, "Colonial Imaginings on the Stage: Blackface, Gender, and the Economics of Empire in Spanish and Catalan Popular Theater," in Murray and Tsuchiya, *Unsettling Colonialism*, 135–69; and David R. George, Jr., "'Playing Japanese' in *fin-de-siècle* zarzuela," in Smith and Nalbone, *Intersections*, 123–45.

6. See Ana Mateos, "A Black Woman Called *Blanca la extranjera* in Faustina Sáez de Melgar's *Los miserables* (1862–63)," in Murray and Tsuchiya, *Unsettling Colonialism*, 107–33.

7. Jo Labanyi first proposed that Fortunata, painted in *Fortunata y Jacinta* as a "'savage' and superior breeder," is racially Othered as a "'native' female" in need of "civilization" with imagery borrowed from colonial discourse. Labanyi, *Gender and Modernization*, 192. Ana Mateos similarly discusses the racialized portrayal of factory worker Amparo within a colonial framework in "Fantasies of Race: A Transatlantic Approach to Class and Sexuality in Emilia Pardo Bazán's *La Tribuna*," *Bulletin of Hispanic Studies* 92, no. 5 (2015): 531–49. More recently, Julia Chang analyzes the colonial and oriental tropes surrounding titular characters in Valera's *Doña Luz* (1879) and Galdós's *Fortunata y Jacinta* (1886–87) in *Blood Novels: Gender, Caste, and Race in Spanish Realism* (Toronto: University of Toronto Press, 2022).

8. Matthew F. Jacobson, *Whiteness of a Different Color: European Immigrants and the Alchemy of Race* (Cambridge, MA: Harvard University Press, 1998), 4, 9.

9. Jennifer Smith and Lisa Nalbone, introduction to *Intersections of Race, Class, Gender, and Nation in Fin-de-siècle Spain*, 3.

10. Charnon-Deutsch, "Evolutionary Logic," 66.

11. David Félix Fernández Díaz describes this discourse as a "nuevo mito que se forja en la Guerra de Independencia [1808–1814]" (new myth forged during the Peninsular War), during which the Spanish race was defined in opposition to the French occupier. David Félix Fernández Díaz, "Fisonomías de lo invisible: raza y nación en la literatura decimonónica española (1808–1843)," *Cuadernos de Ilustración y Romanticismo* 25 (2019): 17.

12. Beltrán y Rózpide, "Los congresos del centenario," 458. English translations from Alda Blanco, "Theorizing Racial Hybridity," 87.

13. Emilia Pardo Bazán, "El descubrimiento de América en las letras españolas: (1.a) Libros de Fernández Duro, el p. Cappa y el p. Coll," *Nuevo Teatro Crítico* año 2, no. 20 (August 1892): 87.

14. Emilia Pardo Bazán, "El descubrimiento de América en las letras españolas: Las conferencias del Ateneo. (Primera serie.)," *Nuevo Teatro Crítico* año 2, no. 21 (September 1892): 41.

15. Joshua Goode, *Impurity of Blood: Defining Race in Spain, 1870–1930* (Baton Rouge: Louisiana State University Press, 2009), 29.

16. Goode, *Impurity of Blood*, 4.

17. George Mariscal, "The Role of Spain in Contemporary Race Theory," *Arizona Journal of Hispanic Cultural Studies* 2 (1998): 17. Goode states that "most recent studies of race in European history usually point to the Iberian Peninsula as the first center of racial thought and even racial policies" in *Impurity of Blood*, 11.

18. Goode concludes that even in 1918 "the Spanish race was fundamentally a religious entity, united by common religious principles and values." *Impurity of Blood*, 21.
19. Goode, *Impurity of Blood*, 20.
20. Javier Krauel, *Imperial Emotions: Cultural Responses to Myths of Empire in Fin-de-Siècle Spain* (Liverpool: Liverpool University Press, 2013), 14.
21. For more on discrimination against the *castas pardas* and the role of skin color in evolving racial thought, see Albert Garcia-Balañà, "Racializing the Nation in Nineteenth-Century Spain (1820–65): A Transatlantic Approach," *Journal of Iberian and Latin America Studies* 24, no. 2 (2018): 265–77.
22. Lisa Surwillo, "Pituso en *blackface*: Una mascarada racial en *Fortunata y Jacinta*," *Hispanic Review* 78, no. 2 (Spring 2010): 197–98.
23. Goode, *Impurity of Blood*, 13, 15. The tendency to promote a single, immutable "Spanish race" was infused with an "esencia castellanófila inquebrantable" (an unshakeable Castilianphilia) biased toward North-Central Spain and dismissive of alternate regional identities. Fernández Díaz, "Fisonomías de lo invisible," 12. Ironically, however, the discourse of race also served regional nationalisms within Spanish borders. Andalusian, Galician, Catalan and Basque nationalists often resisted centralizing tendencies and bolstered their claims for autonomy with racial arguments, claiming a difference in bloodlines that rendered them "an entirely separate national category from their Castilian neighbors." Angel Smith and Clare Mar-Molinero, "The Myths and Realities of Nation-Building in the Iberian Peninsula," in *Nationalism*, 8.
24. "¿Qué otra cosa entendemos, en general, por nación hoy día sino un conjunto de hombres reunidos por comunidad de raza, o parentesco, y de lengua, que habitan un territorio o país extenso, y que por tales o cuales circunstancias históricas, están sometidos a un mismo régimen y gobierno?" (What else do we understand, in general, a nation to be today if not a group of men gathered together by a commonality of race, or kinship, and of language, who inhabit an extensive territory or country, and who for whatever historical circumstances are subject to the same regime and government?). Antonio Cánovas del Castillo, *Discurso sobre la nación: Inauguración del curso del Ateneo en Madrid, noviembre de 1882* (Madrid: Biblioteca Nueva, 1997), 68.
25. For a succinct history of this discrimination, see David Martín Sánchez, *Historia del pueblo gitano en España* (Madrid: Catarata, 2018).
26. Ricardo Campos Marín, José Martínez Pérez, and Rafael Huertas García-Alejo, *Los ilegales de la naturaleza: Medicina y degeneracionismo en la España de la Restauración (1876–1923)* (Madrid: CSIC, 2000), 161.
27. Eugenia DeLamotte, "White Terror, Black Dreams: Gothic Constructions of Race in the Nineteenth Century," in *The Gothic Other: Racial and Social Constructions in the Literary Imagination*, ed. Ruth Bienstock Anolik and Douglas L. Howard (Jefferson, NC: McFarland, 2004), 18.
28. H. L. Malchow, *Gothic Images of Race in Nineteenth-Century Britain* (Stanford, CA: Stanford University Press, 1996), 3. Obvious examples of racialized Gothic villains can be found in Ann Radcliffe's *The Italian*, Matthew Lewis's *The Monk*, and Charlotte Dacre's *Zofloya*.
29. See for example: Steven Jay Schneider, "Mixed Blood Couples: Monsters and Miscegenation in U.S. Horror Cinema," in Bienstock Anolik and Howard, *The Gothic Other*, 72–89; Karen Kingsbury, "Yellow Peril, Dark Hero: Fu Manchu and the 'Gothic Bedevilment' of Racist Intent," in Bienstock Anolik and Howard, *The Gothic Other*, 104–19; Ruth Bienstock Anolik, "The Infamous Svengali: George du Maurier's Satanic Jew," in Bienstock Anolik and Howard, *The Gothic Other*, 163–93.

30. See particularly Renée L. Berland, *The National Uncanny: Indian Ghosts and American Subjects* (Hanover, NH: University Press of New England, 2000). For a similar approach to more recent US Gothic fiction, see Kathleen Brogan, *Cultural Haunting: Ghosts and Ethnicity in Recent American Literature* (Charlottesville: University Press of Virginia, 1998).
31. Chris Baldick, "The End of the Line: The Family Curse in Shorter Gothic Fiction," in *Exhibited by Candlelight: Sources and Developments in the Gothic Tradition*, ed. Valeria Tinkler-Villani and Peter Davidson, with Jane Stevenson (Amsterdam: Rodopi, 1995), 147.
32. Roas states that while Spanish authors rarely produced Gothic novels, "los cuentos góticos españoles recorren todos los temas y motivos típicos de esa clase de historias" (Spanish Gothic short stories ran through the entire gamut of themes and motifs typical of that kind of tales). Roas, Introduction to *Cuentos fantásticos del siglo XIX*, 18.
33. Brian Britt, *Biblical Curses and the Displacement of Tradition* (Sheffield: Sheffield Phoenix Press, 2011), 5, 6, 59. Max Weber holds that even "the last and the poorest could avail himself of this 'weapon of democracy'" in *Ancient Judaism*, trans. and ed. Hans H. Gerth and Don Martindale (Glencoe, IL: The Free Press, 1952), 257.
34. Karen Stollznow, *Language, Myths, Mysteries and Magic* (New York: Palgrave Macmillan, 2014), 16.
35. In the early modern period, the story of the Curse of Ham recounted in Genesis 9:18–27 was appropriated to rationalize slavery. Deviating from the biblical text, pro-slavery Christians cast Africans as the descendants of Ham, cursed by Noah to serve his brothers in perpetuity. For more on the Curse of Ham as a justification for human bondage, see David M. Whitford, *The Curse of Ham in the Early Modern Era: The Bible and the Justifications for Slavery* (New York: Routledge, 2009).
36. Britt examines specifically the curses on Canaan and Gibeon. *Biblical Curses*, 77.
37. Andrew Smith describes that "between 1860 and 1914 there were approximately 100 mummy stories published in the British periodical press, and that around two-thirds of these could be classified as curse narratives." Andrew Smith, "Gothic Imperialism at the Fin de siècle," in *The Cambridge History of the Gothic*, vol. 2, *Gothic in the Nineteenth Century*, ed. Dale Townshend and Angela Wright (Cambridge: Cambridge University Press, 2020), 470. For more on this corpus, see Roger Luckhurst, *The Mummy's Curse: The True History of a Dark Fantasy* (Oxford: Oxford University Press, 2012).
38. Scott Eastman, *A Missionary Nation: Race, Religion, and Spain's Age of Liberal Imperialism, 1841–1881* (Lincoln: University of Nebraska Press, 2021), 8.
39. Susana Bardavío Estevan, "'¡España es también aquí!': Nación e imaginario colonial en los cuentos de Emilia Pardo Bazán," *Castilla: Estudios de Literatura* 9 (2018): 178.
40. One particularly compelling example from the science fiction genre is understudied author José Fernández Bremón's "Gestas, o el idioma de los monos" (1872; Gestas, or the language of monkeys), in which a man tries to educate and impart Spanish culture on a monkey in hopes of using the simian as part of a civilizing mission in Africa.
41. Mary Coffey, *Ghosts of Colonies Past and Present: Spanish Imperialism in the Fiction of Benito Pérez Galdós* (Liverpool: Liverpool UP, 2020), 48.
42. Johan Höglund, *The American Imperial Gothic: Popular Culture, Empire, Violence* (Surrey: Ashgate, 2014), 8. Patrick Brantlinger first coined the term "imperial gothic" in *Rule of Darkness: British Literature and Imperialism, 1830–1914* (Ithaca, NY: Cornell University Press, 1988). See also Patrick Brantlinger, "Imperial Gothic," in *Teaching the Gothic*, ed. Anna Powell and Andrew Smith (Basingstoke: Palgrave Macmillan, 2006): 153–67.
43. James Procter and Angela Smith, "Gothic and Empire," in Spooner and McEvoy, *The Routledge Companion to Gothic*, 97, 99. For his part, Joseba Gabilondo generalizes that all

Gothic novels question the premises of imperialism, stating that "The shortest definition of the Gothic novel would describe it as *a critique of European imperialism*" (italics in the original). Joseba Gabilondo, "Geo-Bio-Politics of the Gothic: On the Queer/Inhuman Dislocation of Spanish/English Subjects and Their Others (for a Definition of Modernity As an Imperialist Geobiopolitcal Fracture)," *Anuario de Literatura Comparada* 4 (2014): 165.

44. Homi Bhabha, *The Location of Culture* (London: Routledge, 1994), 71.
45. Mary Coffey, "Realism, Fantasy, and the Gendered Trope of Colonial Relations in Galdós's Fiction," in Smith and Nalbone, *Intersections*, 177.
46. Coffey, *Ghosts of Colonies*, 267.
47. For more on Galdós's collaboration with *La Prensa*, see Dolores Troncoso, *Galdós: Corresponsal de* La Prensa *de Buenos Aires* (Las Palmas: Cabildo Insular de Gran Canaria, 2020).
48. Pérez Galdós, Prologue to *La sombra*, 6–7.
49. *El Imparcial* was published in Madrid from 1867 to 1933, reaching one of the highest circulations of any Spanish periodical to date, in part due to its accessible price. The literary supplement ran between 1874 and 1933, and included contributions from all the renowned authors of the day: Juan Valera, Ramón de Campoamor, Emilia Pardo Bazán, Jacinto Octavio Picón, and Leopoldo Alas ("Clarín") in its early years, as well as Ramón del Valle-Inclán, Miguel de Unamuno, Pío Baroja, and José Martínez Ruiz ("Azorín") later. For more information, see "*El Imparcial* (Madrid. 1867)," Hemeroteca Digital, Biblioteca Nacional de España, accessed June 6, 2022, http://hemerotecadigital.bne.es/details.vm?q=id:0000189234&lang=es.
50. This is the edition of "Tropiquillos" that is cited throughout the chapter. No page numbers are offered, as the source material does not provide them. Benito Pérez Galdós, "Tropiquillos," *Los lunes de El imparcial*, December 18, 1893, no pagination.
51. Like its literary supplement, *El Imparcial* is not paginated, but the adjective appears in the lead story on the front page of the issue from December 18, 1893.
52. Notable examples include: John Sinnigen, "Cuba en Galdós: La función de las colonias en el discurso metropolitano," *Casa de las Américas* 212 (1998): 115–21; Michael Ugarte, "The Spanish Empire on the Wane: Africa, Galdós, and the Moroccan Wars," in Tsuchiya and Acree, *Empire's End*, 177–90; Coffey, "Realism, Fantasy, and the Gendered Trope"; Julia Chang, "Becoming Useless: Masculinity, Able-Bodiedness, and Empire in Nineteenth-Century Spain," in Murray and Tsuchiya, *Unsettling Colonialism*, 173–202. On the figure of the *indiano* in Galdós, see Luisa Elena Delgado, "El lugar del salvaje (Galdós y la representación del indiano)," in *Homenaje a Alfonso Armas Ayala*, dir. Yolanda Arencibia Santana, coord. Rosa María Quintana, vol. 2 (Las Palmas: Cabildo Insular de Gran Canaria, 2000), 303–13; Eva Maria Copeland, "Empire, Nation, and the *Indiano* in Galdós's *Tormento* and *La loca de la casa*," *Hispanic Review* 80, no. 2 (Spring 2012): 221–42; Surwillo, *Monsters by Trade*; and Dorota K. Heneghan, "The *Indiano*'s Marriage and the Crisis of Imperial Modernity in Galdós's *El amigo manso*." *Siglo Diecinueve* 22 (May 2016): 91–108.
53. Alan Smith describes the protagonist as having accumulated his wealth in America, Africa, and "Oriente" (the East). *Los cuentos inverosímiles*, 148.
54. David Punter and Glennis Byron, "Imperial Gothic," in *The Gothic* (Oxford: Blackwell Publishing, 2004), 47. Coffey notes that this generalization only applies to Galdós's fiction previous to *Tormento* (1884), in which participation in Spanish imperialism denotes a certain level of corruption. Coffey, *Ghosts of Colonies*, 242. In contrast, Galdós's posterior fiction posits *indianos* as possessing "a particular ethical perspective of the world unachieved by residents of the metropolis" (256).

55. Alan Smith, for instance, reads the story as critiquing the entire "orden colonial basado en la fuerza militar, cuyo fin era la explotación de los recursos y mercados que mantenían el imperio, que eran el combustible para la máquina del progreso" (colonial order based on military force, whose end was the exploitation of resources and markets that maintained the empire, that were the fuel for the machine of progress). *Los cuentos inverosímiles*, 167.
56. Surwillo, *Monsters by Trade*, 90.
57. The Sepoy were Indian soldiers serving under British colonial rule.
58. Smith notes the echoes of Poe's "The Fall of the House of Usher" (1839) in this description of the ancestral home's destruction as symbolic of the family's downfall. *Los cuentos inverosímiles*, 152.
59. In the text's first appearance as "Fantasía de otoño," Tropiquillos had additionally included "tribus insurrectas" (insurgent tribes) and "el valor somnoliente y opiáceo de orientales corrompidos" (the sleepy and opiate valor of corrupt Orientals) to the list, making clear both the guilt he assigned to the native population and his pejorative view of them. As the pages of *La Prensa* were unnumbered, no page numbers are provided here. Galdós, "Fantasía de otoño," *La Prensa* (Buenos Aires), December 12, 1884.
60. Bardavío Estevan, "'¡España es también aquí!,'" 190.
61. Bardavío Estevan, "'¡España es también aquí!,'" 190. This tendency also appears in the Spanish realist novel. Examples include Valera's 1879 *Doña Luz* (in which Father Enrique is sent back to Spain to convalesce from maladies contracted in the Philippines) and Galdós's 1888 *Miau* (in which the protagonist Ramón Villaamil returns home ill from the tropics).
62. Bhabha, *The Location of Culture*, 66.
63. Peñate Rivero hypothesizes that Tropiquillos is a lonely gentleman of leisure whose "monótona y mediocre" (monotonous and mediocre) life drives him to dream of foreign adventures in the spice trade. By this reading, not only is the protagonist's downfall imaginary, but his entire identity as a colonizer is an invention. *Benito Pérez Galdós*, 562.
64. In the 1885 article "Furor colonial y otros furores," Galdós seems to echo Tropiquillos's imperialist sentiments upon listing the introduction of wine and beer as one of the many civilizing effects of Europeans in Africa. Benito Pérez Galdós, "Furor colonial y otros furores," in *Cronicón*, 158. Nevertheless, the author's predilection for irony has been amply documented, most notably in Diane Urey's *Galdós and the Irony of Language* (Cambridge: Cambridge University Press, 1982).
65. Since the establishment of the British East India Company in 1600, Great Britain dominated the colonization of Asia, and by the nineteenth century, its predominance in China went unquestioned. Joan Torres-Pou, *Asia en la España del siglo XIX: Literatos, viajeros, intelectuales y diplomáticos ante Oriente* (Amsterdam/New York: Rodopi, 2013), 12. From 1859 to 1863 Spanish forces also aided the French in the Cochinchina Campaign against Vietnam, but as Torres-Pou observes, it received little national attention and was entirely ignored in the literature of the time. *Asia en la España del siglo XIX*, 84.
66. Joyce Tolliver's work is fundamental to the study of Pardo Bazán's literary treatment of Spanish imperialism, particularly regarding the Philippines. See her many publications listed in the bibliography. For more on Pardo Bazán's depiction of the Americas and Spanish colonization there, see Ronald Hilton, "Emilia Pardo Bazán and the Americas," *The Americas* 9, no. 2 (Oct. 1952): 135–48; Rocío Charques Gámez, "El descubrimiento de América en el *Nuevo Teatro Crítico* de Emilia Pardo Bazán," *Actas del III Simposio "Emilia*

Pardo Bazán: El periodismo," ed. José Manuel González Herrán, Cristina Patiño Eirín, and Ermitas Penas Varela (A Coruña: Real Academia Galega and Fundación Caixa de Galicia, 2007): 349–66; María Luisa Pérez Bernardo, "Hernán Cortés en la obra periodística y literaria de Emilia Pardo Bazán," *Tejuelo* 8 (2010): 46–58; and Mercedes Tasende, "Entre la leyenda negra y la leyenda dorada: Emilia Pardo Bazán ante el descubrimiento, la conquista y la colonización española del nuevo mundo," *Anales de Literatura Española Contemporánea* 40, no. 1 (2015): 425–51. On her depiction of Spain's interventions in the Philippines, see María Luisa Pérez Bernardo, "El escenario de las Islas Filipinas en las crónicas y cuentos de Emilia Pardo Bazán," *Revista Filipina* 13, no. 1 (Spring 2009): no pagination, http://revista.carayanpress.com/bazan.html. On Pardo Bazán's depiction of Spain's late empire and the events of 1898, see David Henn, "Reflections of the War of 1898 in Pardo Bazán's Fiction and Travel Chronicles," *Modern Language Review* 94, no. 2 (April 1999): 415–25; Kathleen Doyle, "Gender Violence and Late Colonial Anxieties in 'Piña' by Emilia Pardo Bazán," *Caribe: Revista de Cultura y Literatura* 11, no. 2 (Winter 2008/2009): 7–22; and Bardavío Estevan, "'¡España es también aquí!'"

67. Representative examples of Pardo Bazán's opinions on Spain's late empire can be found in María Luisa Pérez Bernardo, ed. *De siglo a siglo (1896–1901): Crónicas periodísticas de Emilia Pardo Bazán* (Madrid: Pliegos, 2014). Studies that view Pardo Bazán as an imperial apologist include Henn, "Reflections of the War"; Tasende "Entre la leyenda"; and Helena Miguélez-Carballeira, "Teaching Pardo Bazán from Postcolonial and Transatlantic Perspectives," in Versteeg and Walter, *Approaches to Teaching*, 86–92.

68. Lou Charnon-Deutsch, "Racial Theory and Atavism in Pardo Bazán's Short Fiction," *La Tribuna: Cadernos de Estudos da Casa-Museo Emilia Pardo Bazán* 9 (2012–2013): 152.

69. Joyce Tolliver, "Over Her Bloodless Body: Gender, Race, and the Spanish Colonial Fetish in Pardo Bazán," *Revista Canadiense de Estudios Hispánicos* 34, no. 2 (Winter 2010): 286.

70. *La Ilustración española y americana* was a Spanish weekly "marketed as a luxury item" that ran from 1869 to 1921. As the title indicates, the periodical was a pioneer for its use of graphics "printed on high-quality paper," including color photography, which provided a snapshot of modern Spanish life. Valis, *The Culture*, 146. Subtitled "museo universal: periódico de ciencias, artes, literatura, industria y conocimientos útiles" (universal museum: periodical of sciences, arts, literature, industry and useful knowledge) the content of *La Ilustración española y americana* was markedly non-partisan. For more information, see "La Ilustración española y americana," Hemeroteca Digital, Biblioteca Nacional de España, accessed July 19, 2022, http://hemerotecadigital.bne.es/details.vm?lang=es&q=id:0001066626.

71. On a grander scheme, Spanish incursions into the northern Rif zone starting in 1909 marked a growing interest in conquering Morocco in the wake of other colonial losses.

72. All quotes of the story come from the original periodical publication. Emilia Pardo Bazán, "El brasileño," *La Ilustración española y americana*, September 30, 1911, 182–83, 186.

73. He explains, "Claro es que lo consideraba una tontería; pero frecuentemente pensaba en ello. Y será casual, o serán artes del diablo, pero no se explican sólo con hablar de coincidencias" (183, 186; It's clear that I considered it nonsense, but I frequently thought about it. And be it chance, or be it through the devil's art, it can't be explained through coincidence alone).

74. Brantlinger describes imperial gothic works as "stories that are relentlessly masculine in orientation and often overtly misogynistic." Brantlinger, "Imperial Gothic," 158.

75. According to Eduardo Rivail Ribeiro, Tapuya "was how the Tupí-speaking tribes of coastal Brazil referred to their non-Tupí-speaking enemies, mostly inhabitants of the country's interior. When Europeans started exploring the Brazilian coast, most of it was occupied by Tupí-speaking tribes." "Tapuya Connections: Language Contact in Eastern Brazil," *Llames* 9 (Spring 2009): 61n2.
76. Luisa Elena Delgado describes the accusation of cannibalism as one of the key arguments used to justify Spanish conquest and colonization of American lands. Delgado, "El lugar del salvaje," 307. Nevertheless, Pardo Bazán held Bernal Díaz del Castillo in high esteem as a faithful chronicler of the conquest. Pérez Bernardo, "Hernán Cortés," 51.
77. For more on typical characterizations of the *indiano* within Spanish realism, see Delgado, "El lugar del salvaje"; Eva Lafuente, "La figura del indiano y el viaje a América en la narrativa breve de Pardo Bazán," in *La literatura de Emilia Pardo Bazán*, ed. José Manuel González Herrán, Cristina Patiño Eirín and Ermitas Penas Varela (A Coruña: Fundación Caixa Galicia/Casa-Museo Emilia Pardo Bazán, 2009), 411–23; and Copeland, "Empire."
78. Examining José María Cruz in Galdós's 1892 play *La loca de la casa*, Delgado discusses "la racialización metafórica con que se caracteriza su barbarismo" (the metaphorical racialization with which his barbarism is characterized). Accused of "ennegrecer y afear su carácter" (blackening and making ugly his character), Cruz responds by accepting without shame these charges, leading Delgado to conclude that Cruz "asum[e] su condición de 'negro' en una sociedad 'blanca'" (assumes his "black" condition in a "white" society). Delgado, "El lugar del salvaje," 309. Copeland views the *indiano*'s characterization in this same work more positively, as embodying a "hybrid subjectivity . . . with the potential to 'regenerate' Spain." Copeland, "Empire," 225.
79. Delgado, "El lugar del salvaje," 305.
80. Brazil was the world's biggest producer of diamonds from the early 1700s through 1870, when it was eclipsed by Africa. Darcy P. Svisero, James E. Shigley, and Robert Weldon, "Brazilian Diamonds: A Historical and Recent Perspective," *Gems & Gemology* 53, no. 1 (Spring 2017): 2.
81. Interestingly, Christopher Schmidt-Nowara employs the metaphor of the curse in his assessment of Spain's colonial legacy: "What for some Spanish and North American historians was (or is) a virtue of Spanish 'colonial legacies'—the persistence of language, religion, social structures, and cultural practices—was a curse to others, especially in independent Latin America." Christopher Schmidt-Nowara, "Introduction: Interpreting Spanish Colonialism," in Schmidt-Nowara and Nieto-Phillips, *Interpreting Spanish Colonialism*, 3.
82. Charnon-Deutsch and Maria Dorofeeva both view Spain's historical treatment of the Roma thusly. See Lou Charnon-Deutsch, *The Spanish Gypsy: The History of a European Obsession* (University Park: The Pennsylvania State University Press, 2004), 10; and Maria Dorofeeva, "'Lombroso Transformed into Painting': Art, Criminology, and the Re-invention of the Spanish Gypsy," *Nineteenth-Century Art Worldwide* 15, no. 3 (Autumn 2016): 7.
83. Norma Beatriz Chaloult and Yves Chaloult, "The Internal Colonialism Concept: Methodological Considerations," *Social and Economic Studies* 28, no. 4 (December 1979): 86.
84. According to Charnon-Deutsch, "Between 1499 and 1783 Spanish courts issued more than two dozen state interventions. In addition there were twenty-eight royal proclamations and decrees issued by the Council of Castille; twenty-seven laws went into effect in Portugal; and twenty other edicts were issued by the regional governments of Aragón, Cata-

luña, Navarra, Valencia, and Granada. The Catholic clergy accused the Gypsies of pagan practices; the state found them to be too peripatetic for any reasonable control and jurisdiction; and local authorities and tradesmen in the towns where they camped used them as a handy scapegoat for every crime or mishap." *The Spanish Gypsy*, 233.

85. Throughout this chapter, I follow Charnon-Deutsch's lead and use the term "gypsy" to refer to the cultural construct of the Roma as they appear in literature or other media. I use "Roma" to refer to refer to the actual ethnic group behind the gypsy image. Charnon-Deutsch, *The Spanish Gypsy*, 14.

86. María Sierra-Alonso, "Cannibals Devoured: *Gypsies* in Romantic Discourse on the Spanish Nation," in *Enemies Within: Cultural Hierarchies and Liberal Political Models in the Hispanic World*, ed. María Sierra-Alonso (Newcastle: Cambridge Scholars Publishing, 2015), 198.

87. Dorofeeva, "Lombroso Transformed," 6.

88. While the conflation of gypsy culture and the culture of Andalusia inevitably Orientalized the latter, Spain actively participated in this exoticization. As Charnon-Deutsch describes, "the collapsing of the two cultures, Andalusian and Gypsy, also participated in a broader nationalist endeavor to enhance and capitalize on Spain's self-image as a nation with a highly exportable exotic underside" starting in the late nineteenth century. *The Spanish Gypsy*, 184.

89. Dorofeeva, "Lombroso Transformed," 4. Although these anthropological treatises were novel in their approach, they nevertheless served to confirm longstanding ethnic and racial prejudices on "a (pseudo) scientific basis," thus protecting the interests of "the white, male middle-classes." Samuel Llano, "Public Enemy or National Hero? The Spanish Gypsy and the Rise of Flamenquismo, 1898–1922," *Bulletin of Spanish Studies* 94, no. 6 (2017), 992.

90. Dorofeeva, "Lombroso Transformed," 12.

91. Jennifer Smith, "The Gypsy's Curse: Race and Impurity of Blood in Pardo Bazán," *Revista Canadiense de Estudios Hispánicos* 39, no. 2 (winter 2015), 459. Sierra-Alonso makes explicit the colonial link in stating that "the burgeoning discipline of criminology took up the torch of western civilization and dealt with these [gypsy] (and other) enemies within who had had the temerity not to remain in the far-off lands of the colonial world at a reassuring distance from the good citizens of Europe." Sierra-Alonso, "Cannibals Devoured," 192.

92. For more on nineteenth-century visual and literary depictions of gypsies, see chapter 5 of Charnon-Deutsch, *The Spanish Gypsy*.

93. Surprisingly, the gypsy is not commonly associated with Gothic narrative outside of Spain, despite two key Gothic works featuring gypsy characters: the seductive Esmeralda in Victor Hugo's *The Hunchback of Notre Dame* (1831), and the gypsies in service to the Count in Bram Stoker's *Dracula*.

94. Charnon-Deutsch explains that "the Gypsy woman is a threat to the family (in the bourgeois sense), the social system (because of her lax morals), the nation (since she owes allegiance to no one), and even sexuality itself, since the man who falls prey to her seductions is often portrayed as a castrated, feminized figure no longer in control of his actions." *The Spanish Gypsy*, 240.

95. *El Liberal* was a moderately republican publication, self-proclaimed to have the widest circulation of any Spanish periodical starting in 1889. The Sunday editions of *El Liberal* were generally headed by illustrated essays from notable public figures, such as former prime minister Emilio Castelar, or pieces of fiction by renowned authors. By the 1920s, it was the most read periodical amongst the working class "por su lenguaje claro y con-

tundente, su preocupación por los problemas de los trabajadores, sus informaciones rigurosas y exhaustivas y un cierto sensacionalismo" (for its clear and convincing language, its concern for the problems of workers, its rigorous and exhaustive news, and a certain sensationalism), according to María Dolores Sáiz, as quoted in "*El Liberal* (Madrid. 1879)," Hemeroteca Digital, Biblioteca Nacional de España, accessed June 14, 2022, http://hemerotecadigital.bne.es/details.vm?lang=es&q=id:0001066755.

96. *El Eco de Galicia* (1878–1902) was the first major periodical for the Galician immigrant community in the Americas.

97. All citations come from the original printing in *El Liberal*. Although there are no page numbers, the entire story is found on the issue's front page.

98. Early European myths assigned gypsies an Egyptian origin, often conflating them with "the Egyptians of the old Testament, who, Ezekiel prophesied, would be dispersed among the nations." Charnon-Deutsch, *The Spanish Gypsy* 5.

99. Smith, "The Gypsy's Curse," 470.

100. As Antonio Gómez Alfaro observes, the tendency to portray an exoticized gypsy dialect was widespread in nineteenth-century Spanish literature, particularly as a part of *costumbrismo*, the artistic movement to represent scenes of everyday life and traditions considered authentic to Spain. See the chapter "Gitanos en las colecciones costumbristas del siglo XIX" in Antonio Gómez Alfaro, *Escritos sobre gitanos* (Barcelona: Asociación de Enseñantes con Gitanos, 2010). Sebastián Herrero's *costumbrista* sketch "La gitana" (The gypsy) provides a clear example in which the gypsy's jargon, italicized and thus emphasized within the text, is meant to lend both exoticism and credibility to the portrait. Sebastián Herrero, "La gitana," in *Los españoles pintados por sí mismos*, vol. 1 (Madrid: Ignacio Boix, 1843), 289–99.

101. Emilia Pardo Bazán, "Maldición de gitana," in *Obras Completas*, vol. 16, *Cuentos de amor* (Madrid: Administración, 1898), 206.

102. Teresa Bastardín Candón refers to the Andalusian dialect as a "variedad desprestigiada" (disparaged variety) of Spanish speech, the frequent object of jokes in the nineteenth-century popular press. "Creencias y actitudes lingüísticas sobre las hablas andaluzas en la prensa de mediados del siglo XIX," *Boletín de Filología* 55, no. 2 (2020): 306

103. The fear of dining as a group of thirteen arises as the topic of many nineteenth-century Spanish fantastic fictions. Other notable examples include José Selgas's "El número trece" (1876; The number thirteen), and Pedro Escamilla's short story of the same name discussed in Chapter 1.

104. Smith, "The Gypsy's Curse," 471.

105. Smith, "The Gypsy's Curse," 471. In this regard, "Maldición de gitana" provides an interesting contrast with Pardo Bazán's "Los pendientes" (1909; The earrings), in which a virtuous, blue-eyed, blonde Christian woman is the one to foretell a dark future for her inconstant lover and his new half-gypsy, half-Jewish muse.

106. Smith, "The Gypsy's Curse," 460.

107. Smith, "The Gypsy's Curse," 470.

108. Blanca de los Ríos, "La gitana," in Saez de Melgar, *Las mujeres españolas*, 1:597. Lou Charnon-Deutsch describes de los Ríos as an "aristocratic native of Seville and a celebrated writer and critic who collaborated in the ultranationalist periodical *Raza Española*." This background explains De los Ríos's extremely pejorative attitude toward the subject of her article. Charnon-Deutsch, *The Spanish Gypsy*, 188.

109. Bienstock Anolik, "The Infamous Svengali," 171.

110. Hazel Gold, "Illustrated Histories: The National Subject and 'the Jew' in Nineteenth-Century Spanish Art," *Journal of Spanish Cultural Studies* 10, no. 1 (March 2009): 92.
111. Cited and translated in Chang, *Blood Novels*, 9.
112. Margot Versteeg, "Good and Bad Fusion in Emilia Pardo Bazán's *El becerro de metal* (1906)," in Smith and Nalbone, *Intersections*, 110-11.
113. For more on the prominence of Jews in Spanish public debates, see Isidro González García, "España y el problema judío en la Europa del siglo XIX," *Cuadernos de Historia Moderna y Contemporánea* 7 (1986): 123-40.
114. Gold, "Illustrated Histories," 105n6.
115. Versteeg, "Good and Bad Fusion," 108. Joshua Goode discusses Pulido's project in depth in chapter 8 of *Impurity of Blood*.
116. Gold, "Illustrated Histories," 93.
117. Pura Fernández provides a comprehensive overview of Jewish stereotypes in nineteenth-century Spanish literature in "La literatura del siglo XIX y los orígenes del contubernio judeo-masónico-comunista," in Ricardo Izquierda Benito and Iacob M. Hassán, eds., *Judíos en la literatura española* (Cuenca: Universidad Castilla-La Mancha, 2001), 301-51. For more on Galdós's depiction of Jews, see: Vernon Chamberlin, "Galdós' Sephardic Types," *Symposium: A Quarterly Journal in Modern Literatures* 17, no. 2 (1963), 85-100; Sara Schyfter, "The Judaism of Galdós' Daniel Morton," *Hispania* 59, no. 1 (March 1976): 24-33; Dennis A. Klein, "The Jews of Nineteenth-Century Spain According to Historical Fact and Selected Novelists," *Yiddish-Modern Jewish Studies* 15, no. 1-2 (2007): 45-59; and Gold, "Illustrated Histories." On the representation of Jews in Pardo Bazán, see Brian J. Dendle, "The Racial Theories of Emilia Pardo Bazán," *Hispanic Review* 38, no. 1 (1970): 17-31; Beth Wietelmann Baur, "Catholicism, Feminism, and Anti-Semitism in Pardo Bazán's *Una cristiana-La prueba*," *Letras Peninsulares* 8, no. 2-3 (1995-1996): 295-309; Maryellen Bieder, "Negotiating Modernity in Multicultural Spain: Emilia Pardo Bazán's *Una cristiana* and *La prueba*," *Siglo Diecinueve* 16 (2010): 137-69; Maryellen Bieder, "Racial Identity, Social Critique, and Class Dynamics in Pardo Bazán's *Una cristiana-La prueba* and *El becerro de metal*," in Smith and Nalbone, *Intersections*, 91-107; and Versteeg, "Good and Bad Fusion."
118. Joseph Gillet ponders, "Did the tragic figure of the Jew have no appeal for the Spanish imagination? He was a significant figure to Goethe and Shelley, inspired Lenau and Chamisso, filled a wide canvas in Quinet's *Ahasvérus*, but he has never tempted any great, or even a mediocre Spanish poet." Joseph E. Gillet, "Traces of the Wandering Jew in Spain," *Romanic Review* 22 (1931): 26-27. At the same time, Enrique Martínez-López uncovers a tradition of Spanish *literatura de cordel*, cheap booklets of popular reading similar to chapbooks, that features the Wandering Jew in "La leyenda del Judío errante en la literatura de cordel española," *Bulletin Hispanique* 92, no. 2 (1990): 789-825. Pura Fernández further discusses serialized popular literature inspired in the Wandering Jew in "La literatura del siglo XIX," as does Lou Charnon-Deutsch in "'Hatred Alone Warms the Heart': Figures of Ill Repute in the Nineteenth-Century Spanish Novel," in *Engaging the Emotions in Spanish Culture and History*, ed. Luisa Elena Delgado, Pura Fernández, and Jo Labanyi (Nashville, TN: Vanderbilt University Press, 2016), 95-110.
119. It should be noted that Escamilla published two short stories with the same title of "La mosca" in *El Periódico para todos*, one in 1873 and one in 1875. Both stories share the similar conceit of a fly that, dripping with ink, creates the image of a beautiful woman, though only the 1873 text features a Jewish character.
120. All quotes from the story and their corresponding page numbers come from this orig-

inal printing of "El cuadro de maese Abraham." Pedro Escamilla, "El cuadro de maese Abraham," *El Periódico para todos* 2, no. 39 (February 8, 1873), 615–17.

121. The stereotyped nature of Abraham's characterization is particularly evident upon comparison with the main character, also a seventy-year-old Jewish man named Abraham, in Escamilla's "El reloj" (The watch) published a year after "El cuadro." Notably, these characters are not the same, given that one lives alone in the Spanish city of León and the other lives with his granddaughter in Germany, but they are nearly interchangeable. Not only do both Abrahams share a trade of dealing in questionable antiques, an impressive fortune, and a crippling phobia of thieves, but these qualities are described with the exact same formulas across both texts. For instance, in the first text, the narrator claims that maese Abraham "no se hubiera dejado ahorcar por dos millones" (615; would not have let himself be hanged for two million), and in "El reloj" a German friend accuses Abraham, "no os dejaríais ahorcar por dos millones" (you would not let yourself be hanged for two million). Pedro Escamilla, "El reloj," *El Periódico para todos* 3, no. 10 (January 10, 1874), 148. According to Gisèle Cazottes, Escamilla's Jewish figures serve only to symbolize the sly and greedy accumulation of wealth. Cazottes, "Contribución," 25.

122. Charnon-Deutsch, "Hatred Alone," 95.
123. DeLamotte, "White Terror," 27.

CODA

1. Catherine Jagoe, "Noncanonical Novels and the Question of Quality," *Revista de Estudios Hispánicos* 27, no. 3 (1993): 432.
2. Aldana Reyes and Rødtjer, for instance, include Asensi in their study of the Spanish Gothic for *The Cambridge History of the Gothic*. See also Rocío Rødtjer, "Out of Time: Julia de Asensi and the Historical Legend," in *The Modern Spanish Canon: Visibility, Cultural Capital and the Academy*, ed. Stuart Davis and Maite Usoz de la Fuente (Cambridge: Legenda, 2018), 58–71; and Rocío Rødtjer, *Women and Nationhood in Restoration Spain 1874–1931: The State as Family* (Cambridge: Legenda, 2019).
3. Jackson, *Fantasy*, 6.

Bibliography

Alarcón, Pedro Antonio de. "La mujer alta." *La Ilustración Artística* 1, no. 1 (January 1, 1882): 3, 6; no. 2 (January 8, 1882): 10–11; no. 3 (January 15, 1882): 19, 22; no. 4 (January 22, 1882): 26–27.

Alarcón, Pedro Antonio de. "The Tall Woman: A Tale of Fear." In *The Nun and Other Stories*. Translated by Robert M. Fedorcheck, 153–69. Lewisburg, PA: Bucknell University Press, 1999.

"*Álbum salón* (Barcelona)". Hemeroteca Digital, Biblioteca Nacional de España. Accessed October 23, 2022. https://hemerotecadigital.bne.es/hd/es/card?sid=1426014.

Aldana Reyes, Xavier. *Spanish Gothic: National Identity, Collaboration, and Cultural Adaptation*. New York: Palgrave Macmillan, 2017.

Aldana Reyes, Xavier, and Rocío Rødtjer. "The Gothic in Nineteenth-Century Spain." In *The Cambridge History of the Gothic*, vol. 2, *Gothic in the Nineteenth Century*, edited by Dale Townshend and Angela Wright, 285–302. Cambridge: Cambridge University Press, 2020.

Aldaraca, Bridget. *El ángel del hogar: Galdós and the Ideology of Domesticity in Spain*. Chapel Hill: University of North Carolina Press, 1991.

Allen, Virginia M. *The Femme Fatale: Erotic Icon*. Troy, NY: Whitson Publishing Company, 1983.

Álvarez Junco, José. "The Nation-Building Process in Nineteenth-Century Spain." In *Nationalism and the Nation in the Iberian Peninsula: Competing and Conflicting Identities*, edited by Clare Mar-Molinero and Angel Smith, 89–106. Oxford: Berg, 1996.

Álvarez Junco, José. *Spanish Identity in the Age of Nations*. Manchester: Manchester University Press, 2011.

Anderson, Benedict. *Imagined Communities: Reflections on the Origin and Spread of Nationalism*. Rev. ed. London: Verso, 2006.

Andrés Ferrer, Paloma, and Miguel Jiménez Molina. "'Theros,' la cosecha de la vida, cuento inverosímil de Galdós." In *Homenaje a Alfonso Armas Ayala*, vol. 2, edited by Lourdes Acosta González, 75–97. Las Palmas: Cabildo Insular de Gran Canaria, 2000.

Aresti, Nerea. "La hombría perdida en el tiempo. Masculinidad y nación española a finales del siglo XIX." In *Hombres en peligro: género, nación e imperio en la España de cambio de siglo (XIX-XX)*, edited by Mauricio Zabalgoitia Herrera, 19–38. Madrid: Iberoamericana Vervuert, 2017.

Astigarraga, Jesús, ed. *The Spanish Enlightenment Revisited*. Oxford: Voltaire Foundation, 2015.

Austin, Karen. "Don Anselmo and the Author's Role." *Anales Galdosianos* 18 (1983): 39–47.

Baker, Brian. "Gothic Masculinities." In *The Routledge Companion to Gothic*, edited by Catherine Spooner and Emma McEvoy, 164-73. London: Routledge, 2007.

Baldick, Chris. "The End of the Line: The Family Curse in Shorter Gothic Fiction." In *Exhibited by Candlelight: Sources and Developments in the Gothic Tradition*, edited by Valeria Tinkler-Villani and Peter Davidson, with Jane Stevenson, 147-57. Amsterdam: Rodopi, 1995.

Baquero Goyanes, Mariano. *El cuento español en el siglo XIX*. Madrid: CSIC, 1949.

Bardavío Estevan, Susana. "'¡España es también aquí!': Nación e imaginario colonial en los cuentos de Emilia Pardo Bazán." *Castilla: Estudios de Literatura* 9 (2018): 176-203.

Bastardín Candón, Teresa. "Creencias y actitudes lingüísticas sobre las hablas andaluzas en la prensa de mediados del siglo XIX." *Boletín de Filología* 55, no. 2 (2020): 285-310.

Baur, Beth Wietelmann. "Catholicism, Feminism, and Anti-Semitism in Pardo Bazán's *Una cristiana-La prueba*." *Letras Peninsulares* 8, no. 2-3 (1995-1996): 295-309.

Beltrán y Rózpide, Ricardo. "Los congresos del centenario." *La Ilustración española y americana*, December 30, 1892, 458-59.

Ben Slama, Mohamed. "El género femenino como elemento amenazante: 'La mujer alta', de Pedro Antonio de Alarcón, y 'La mujer sin cara', de Emilio Carrere." *Brumal* 4, no. 2 (Autumn 2016): 247-60. https://doi.org/10.5565/rev/brumal.226.

Berger, John. *Ways of Seeing*. London: Penguin Books, 1990.

Bergland, Renée L. *The National Uncanny: Indian Ghosts and American Subjects*. Hanover, NH: The University Press of New England, 2000.

Beyer, Stefan. "Goethean Rhymes and Rhythms in Verse Translations of Faust into Spanish." *MonTI: Monografías de Traducción e Interpretación* 5 (2013): 349-63. https://doi.org/10.6035/MonTI.2013.5.15.

Bhabha, Homi. *The Location of Culture*. London: Routledge, 1994.

Bieder, Maryellen. "Negotiating Modernity in Multicultural Spain: Emilia Pardo Bazán's *Una cristiana* and *La prueba*." *Siglo Diecinueve* 16 (2010): 137-69.

Bieder, Maryellen. "Racial Identity, Social Critique, and Class Dynamics in Pardo Bazán's *Una cristiana-La prueba* and *El becerro de metal*." In *Intersections of Race, Class, Gender and Nation in Fin-de-siècle Spanish Literature and Culture*, edited by Jennifer Smith and Lisa Nalbone, 91-107. London/New York: Routledge, 2017.

Bienstock Anolik, Ruth. "The Infamous Svengali: George du Maurier's Satanic Jew." In *The Gothic Other: Racial and Social Constructions in the Literary Imagination*, edited by Ruth Bienstock Anolik and Douglas L. Howard, 163-93. Jefferson, NC: McFarland & Co., 2004.

Bienstock Anolik, Ruth. "Sexual Horror: Fears of the Sexual Other." In *Horrifying Sex: Essays on Sexual Difference in Gothic Literature*, edited by Ruth Bienstock Anolik, 1-24. Jefferson, NC: McFarland & Company, 2007.

Blanco, Alda. "Theorizing Racial Hybridity in Nineteenth-Century Spain and Spanish America." In *Empire's End: Transnational Connections in the Hispanic World*, edited by Akiko Tsuchiya and William G. Acree, Jr., 84-106. Nashville, TN: Vanderbilt University Press, 2016.

Blanco, María del Pilar, and Esther Peeren. "Introduction: Conceptualizing Spectralities." In *The Spectralities Reader: Ghosts and Haunting in Contemporary Cultural Theory*, edited by María del Pilar Blanco and Esther Peeren, 1-27. London: Bloomsbury, 2013.

Blanco, María del Pilar, and Esther Peeren. "Spectral Subjectivities: Gender, Sexuality, Race / Introduction." In *The Spectralities Reader: Ghosts and Haunting in Contemporary Cultural Theory*, edited by María del Pilar Blanco and Esther Peeren, 309-16. London: Bloomsbury, 2013.

Botting, Fred. *Gothic*. London: Routledge, 1996.
Brantlinger, Patrick. "Imperial Gothic." In *Teaching the Gothic*, edited by Anna Powell and Andrew Smith, 153–67. Basingstoke: Palgrave Macmillan, 2006.
Brantlinger, Patrick. *Rule of Darkness: British Literature and Imperialism, 1830–1914*. Ithaca, NY: Cornell University Press, 1988.
Britt, Brian. *Biblical Curses and the Displacement of Tradition*. Sheffield: Sheffield Phoenix Press, 2011.
Brogan, Kathleen. *Cultural Haunting: Ghosts and Ethnicity in Recent American Literature*. Charlottesville: University Press of Virginia, 1998.
Burdiel, Isabel. "The Liberal Revolution, 1808–1843." In *Spanish History since 1808*, edited by José Álvarez Junco and Adrian Shubert, 17–32. London: Arnold, 2000.
Burguera, Mónica and Christopher Schmidt-Nowara, eds. *Historias de España contemporánea: Cambio social y giro cultural*. Valencia: Universitat de València, 2008.
Buse, Peter, and Andrew Stott. "Introduction: A Future for Haunting." In *Ghosts: Deconstruction, Psychoanalysis, History*, edited by Peter Buse and Andrew Stott, 1–20. London: Macmillan, 1999.
Callois, Roger. "The Fantastic." *Forum* 2, no.3 (May 1958): 51–55.
Calvino, Italo. Introduction to *Fantastic Tales: Visionary and Everyday*, edited by Italo Calvino, translated by Alfred MacAdam, vii–xviii. Boston: Mariner Books, 2015.
Campos Marín, Ricardo, José Martínez Pérez, and Rafael Huertas García-Alejo. *Los ilegales de la naturaleza: Medicina y degeneracionismo en la España de la Restauración (1876–1923)*. Madrid: CSIC, 2000.
Cánovas del Castillo, Antonio. *Discurso sobre la nación: inauguración del curso del Ateneo en Madrid, noviembre de 1882*. Madrid: Biblioteca Nueva, 1997. https://www.cervantesvirtual.com/nd/ark:/59851/bmc6toj6.
Cantos Casenave, Marieta, and Daniel Muñoz Sempere. "Introduction: Otherness and National Identity in 19h-Century Spanish Literature—Spaniards on the Margins." In *Otherness and National Identity in 19th-Century Spanish Literature*, edited by Marieta Cantos Casenave and Daniel Muñoz Sempere, 1–14. Leiden: Brill, 2022.
Cardona, Rodolfo. "1865 Galdós en *La Nación*: 'Variedades.'" In *A Sesquicentennial Tribute to Galdós 1843–1993*, edited by Linda M. Willem, 261–68. Newark, NJ: Juan de la Cuesta, 1993.
Cazottes, Gisèle. "Contribución al estudio del cuento en la prensa madrileña de la segunda mitad del siglo XIX. Pedro Escamilla." *Iris* 4 (1983): 13–37.
Chaloult, Norma Beatriz, and Yves Chaloult. "The Internal Colonialism Concept: Methodological Considerations." *Social and Economic Studies* 28, no. 4 (December 1979): 85–99. https://www.jstor.org/stable/27861779.
Chamberlin, Vernon. "Galdós' Sephardic Types." *Symposium: A Quarterly Journal in Modern Literatures* 17, no. 2 (1963): 85–100.
Chang, Julia. "Becoming Useless: Masculinity, Able-Bodiedness, and Empire in Nineteenth-Century Spain." In *Unsettling Colonialism: Gender and Race in the Nineteenth-Century Global Hispanic World*, edited by N. Michelle Murray and Akiko Tsuchiya, 173–202. Albany: State University of New York Press, 2019.
Chang, Julia. *Blood Novels: Gender, Caste, and Race in Spanish Realism*. Toronto: University of Toronto Press, 2022.
Charnon-Deutsch, Lou. "Evolutionary Logic and the Concept of Race in Pardo Bazán's Short Fiction." In *Approaches to Teaching the Writings of Emilia Pardo Bazán*, edited by Margot Versteeg and Susan Walter, 64–70. New York: Modern Language Association of America, 2017.

Charnon-Deutsch, Lou. *Fictions of the Feminine in the Nineteenth-Century Spanish Press*. University Park: The Pennsylvania State University Press, 2000.

Charnon-Deutsch, Lou. "'Hatred Alone Warms the Heart': Figures of Ill Repute in the Nineteenth-Century Spanish Novel." In *Engaging the Emotions in Spanish Culture and History*, edited by Luisa Elena Delgado, Pura Fernández, and Jo Labanyi, 95-110. Nashville, TN: Vanderbilt University Press, 2016.

Charnon-Deutsch, Lou. *Hold That Pose: Visual Culture in the Late-Nineteenth-Century Spanish Periodical*. University Park: Pennsylvania State University Press, 2008.

Charnon-Deutsch, Lou. "Racial Theory and Atavism in Pardo Bazán's Short Fiction." *La Tribuna: Cadernos de Estudos da Casa-Museo Emilia Pardo Bazán* 9 (2012-2013): 143-53.

Charnon-Deutsch, Lou. *The Spanish Gypsy: The History of a European Obsession*. University Park: Pennsylvania State University Press, 2004.

Charques Gámez, Rocío. "El descubrimiento de América en el *Nuevo Teatro Crítico* de Emilia Pardo Bazán." In *Actas del III Simposio "Emilia Pardo Bazán: El periodismo,"* edited by José Manuel González Herrán, Cristina Patiño Eirín, and Ermitas Penas Varela, 349-66. A Coruña: Real Academia Galega and Fundación Caixa de Galicia, 2007.

Clery, E. J. "The Supernatural Explained." In *The Rise of Supernatural Fiction 1762-1800*, 106-14. Cambridge: Cambridge University Press, 1995.

"Código Civil de 1889." In *La mujer en los discursos de género: Textos y contextos en el siglo XIX*, edited by Catherine Jagoe, Alda Blanco and Cristina Enríquez de Salamanca, 262-88. Barcelona: Icaria, 1998.

"Código Penal de 1870." In *La mujer en los discursos de género: textos y contextos en el siglo XIX*, edited by Catherine Jagoe, Alda Blanco and Cristina Enríquez de Salamanca, 261-62. Barcelona: Icaria, 1998.

Coffey, Mary. *Ghosts of Colonies Past and Present: Spanish Imperialism in the Fiction of Benito Pérez Galdós*. Liverpool: Liverpool UP, 2020.

Coffey, Mary. "Realism, Fantasy, and the Gendered Trope of Colonial Relations in Galdós's Fiction." In *Intersections of Race, Class, Gender and Nation in Fin-de-siècle Spanish Literature and Culture*, edited by Jennifer Smith and Lisa Nalbone, 165-84. London: Routledge, 2017.

Coffey, Mary, and Margot Versteeg. Introduction to *Imagined Truths: Realism in Modern Spanish Literature and Culture*, 3-35. Toronto: University of Toronto Press, 2019.

Cohen, Jeffrey Jerome. "Monster Culture (Seven Theses)." In *Monster Theory: Reading Culture*, edited by Jeffrey Jerome Cohen, 3-25. Minneapolis: University of Minnesota Press, 1996.

Combs, Colleen J. *Women in the Short Stories of Pedro Antonio de Alarcón*. Lewiston, ME: The Edwin Mellen Press, 1997.

Contreras y Alba, María del Pilar. "La solterona." In *Las mujeres españolas, americanas y lusitanas pintadas por sí mismas*, vol. 1, edited by Faustina Saez de Melgar, 360-75. Barcelona: Juan Pons, 1881.

Copeland, Eva Maria. "Empire, Nation, and the *Indiano* in Galdós's *Tormento* and *La loca de la casa*." *Hispanic Review* 80, no. 2 (Spring 2012): 221-42.

Cruz, Jesús. *The Rise of Middle-Class Culture in Nineteenth-Century Spain*. Baton Rouge: Louisiana State University Press, 2011.

Curtis, George W. Introduction to *Modern Ghosts*, edited by George W. Curtis, xii-xiv. New York: Harper Brothers, 1890.

Cuzovic-Severn, Marina. "Imperialist Seductions: A Genealogy of the Femme fatale in

Spanish Literature from Romanticism to Modernism (1845–1908)." PhD diss., Michigan State University, 2014.

DeLamotte, Eugenia. "White Terror, Black Dreams: Gothic Constructions of Race in the Nineteenth Century." In *The Gothic Other: Racial and Social Constructions in the Literary Imagination*, edited by Ruth Bienstock Anolik and Douglas L. Howard, 17–31. Jefferson, NC: McFarland, 2004.

Delgado, Luisa Elena. "El lugar del salvaje (Galdós y la representación del indiano)." In *Homenaje a Alfonso Armas Ayala*, vol. 2, directed by Yolanda Arencibia Santana and coordinated by Rosa María Quintana, 303–13. Las Palmas: Cabildo Insular de Gran Canaria, 2000.

de los Ríos, Blanca. "La gitana." In *Las mujeres españolas, americanas y lusitanas pintadas por sí mismas*, vol. 1, edited by Faustina Saez de Melgar, 589–607. Barcelona: Juan Pons, 1881.

de los Ríos, Laura. "Análisis de los cinco cuentos de esta selección." In *La comendadora, El clavo, y otros cuentos,* by Pedro Antonio de Alarcón, edited by Laura de los Ríos, 53–99. Madrid: Cátedra, 2003.

de Madrazo, Pedro. "La señora mayor." In *Los españoles pintados por sí mismos*, vol. 2, edited by Ignacio Boix, 348–58. Madrid: Ignacio Boix, 1844.

de Mobellán de Casafiel, Sebastián. "Rosa la solterona." In *Las españolas pintadas por los españoles*, vol. 1, edited by Roberto Robert, 93–104. Madrid: J.E. Morete, 1871.

de Paula Campá, Francisco. "Las dos edades críticas de la vida de la mujer." In *Discursos pronunciados en la inauguración de las sesiones de la Academia de Medicina de Valencia en el año 1876*, 19–43. Valencia: Imprenta de Ferrer de Orga, 1876. https://www.google.com/books/edition/_/G3uB1FY8WzgC?hl=en&gbpv=0.

Dendle, Brian J. "The Racial Theories of Emilia Pardo Bazán." *Hispanic Review* 38, no. 1 (January 1970): 17–31.

Derrida, Jacques. *Specters of Marx: The State of the Debt, The Work of Mourning and the New International*. Translated by Peggy Kamuf. New York: Routledge, 1994.

Dijkstra, Bram. *Idols of Perversity: Fantasies of Feminine Evil in Fin-de-Siècle Culture*. Oxford: Oxford University Press, 1988.

Dorofeeva, Maria. "'Lombroso Transformed into Painting': Art, Criminology, and the Reinvention of the Spanish Gypsy." *Nineteenth-Century Art Worldwide* 15, no. 3 (Autumn 2016): 2–33. https://doi.org/10.29411/ncaw.2016.15.3.2.

Doyle, Kathleen. "Gender Violence and Late Colonial Anxieties in 'Piña' by Emilia Pardo Bazán." *Caribe: Revista de Cultura y Literatura* 11, no. 2 (Winter 2008/2009): 7–22.

Duncan, Cynthia. *Unraveling the Real: The Fantastic in Spanish American Ficciones*. Philadelphia: Temple University Press, 2010.

Eastman, Scott. *A Missionary Nation: Race, Religion, and Spain's Age of Liberal Imperialism, 1841–1881*. Lincoln: University of Nebraska Press, 2021.

Enríquez de Salamanca, Cristina. "La mujer en el discurso legal del liberalismo español." In *La mujer en los discursos de género: Textos y contextos en el siglo XIX*, edited by Catherine Jagoe, Alda Blanco and Cristina Enríquez de Salamanca, 219–52. Barcelona: Icaria, 1998.

Escamilla, Pedro. *La casa maldita y otros casos insólitos*. Torrelavega: Quálea, 2015.

Escamilla, Pedro. "El cuadro de maese Abraham." *El Periódico para todos*, February 8, 1873, 615–17.

Escamilla, Pedro. "La mosca." *El Periódico para todos*, February 8, 1875, 611–13

Escamilla, Pedro. "El número trece." *El Periódico para todos*, January 12, 1879, 187–88.

Escamilla, Pedro. *La pesca del diablo y otros relatos extraños*. Madrid: Diábolo Ediciones, 2021.

Escamilla, Pedro. "El reloj." *El Periódico para todos*, January 10, 1874, 148–50.

Espejo Saavedra, Ramón. "El terror y el deseo en 'La mujer alta' de Pedro Antonio de Alarcón." In *Perversiones decimonónicas: Literatura y parafilia en el XIX*, edited by Jorge Avilés Diz, 57–73. Valencia: Albatros, 2018.

Estruch Tobella, Joan. Introduction to *Literatura fantástica y de terror española del siglo XVII*, edited by Joan Estruch Tobella, 9–14. Barcelona: Fontamara, 1982.

Fernández, James. "America Is in Spain: A Reading of Clarín's 'Boroña.'" In *Bridging the Atlantic: Toward a Reassessment of Iberian and Latin American Cultural Ties*, edited by Marina Pérez de Mendiola, 31–43. Albany: State University of New York Press, 1996.

Fernández, Pura. "La literatura del siglo XIX y los orígenes del contubernio judeo-masónico-comunista." In *Judíos en la literatura española*, coordinated by Ricardo Izquierdo Benito and Iacob M. Hassán, 301–51. Cuenca: Universidad Castilla-La Mancha, 2001.

Fernández Díaz, David Félix. "Fisonomías de lo invisible: raza y nación en la literatura decimonónica española (1808–1843)," *Cuadernos de Ilustración y Romanticismo* 25 (2019): 11–25.

Flores, Antonio. "El ómnibus y la calesa." In *Ayer, hoy y mañana o la fe, el vapor y la electricidad*, vol. 2, 333–40. Barcelona: Montaner y Simón, 1893.

Fradera, Josep. *La nación imperial: Derechos, representación y ciudadanía en los imperios de Gran Bretaña, Francia, España y Estados Unidos (1750–1918)*. Barcelona: Edhasa, 2015.

Franz, Thomas. "The Concentrated Metafiction of Galdós's *La sombra*." *Revista de estudios hispánicos* 21, no. 3 (October 1987): 51–66.

Fuentes Peris, Teresa. *Galdós's* Torquemada *Novels: Waste and Profit in Late Nineteenth-Century Spain*. Cardiff: University of Wales Press, 2007.

Fuentes Peris, Teresa. *Visions of Filth: Deviancy and Social Control in the Novels of Galdós*. Liverpool: Liverpool University Press, 2003.

Gabilondo, Joseba. "Geo-bio-politics of the Gothic: On the Queer/Inhuman Dislocation of Spanish/English Subjects and Their Others (For A Definition of Modernity as an Imperialist Geobiopolitcal Fracture)." *Anuario de Literatura Comparada* 4 (2014): 153–67.

Garcia-Balañà, Albert. "Racializing the Nation in Nineteenth-Century Spain (1820–65): A Transatlantic Approach." *Journal of Iberian and Latin America Studies* 24, no. 2 (2018): 265–77.

George, Jr., David R. "'Playing Japanese' in *fin-de-siècle* zarzuela." In *Intersections of Race, Class, Gender, and Nation in Fin-de-siècle Spanish Literature and Culture*, 123–45. London: Routledge, 2017.

George, Jr., David R. "The Tall (Wo)Man: Crossing Heterosexual Gender Identities in Pedro Antonio de Alarcón's *La mujer alta*." *Romance Languages Annual* 7 (1995): 473–77.

Gillet, Joseph E. "Traces of the Wandering Jew in Spain." *Romanic Review* 22 (1931): 16–27.

Gold, Hazel. "Illustrated Histories: The National Subject and 'the Jew' in Nineteenth-Century Spanish Art." *Journal of Spanish Cultural Studies* 10, no. 1 (March 2009): 89–109.

Gómez Alfaro, Antonio. *Escritos sobre gitanos*. Barcelona: Asociación de Enseñantes con Gitanos, 2010.

González García, Isidro. "España y el problema judío en la Europa del siglo XIX." *Cuadernos de Historia Moderna y Contemporánea* 7 (1986): 123–40.

González Mas, Ezequiel. "En torno a *La mujer alta*, de Alarcón." *Salina: Revista de Lletres* 7 (1993): 56–58.

Goode, Joshua. *Impurity of Blood: Defining Race in Spain, 1870–1930*. Baton Rouge: Louisiana State University Press, 2009.

Gordon, Avery. *Ghostly Matters: Haunting and the Sociological Imagination*. Minneapolis: University of Minnesota Press, 2008.

Groom, Nick. *The Vampire: A New History*. New Haven, CT: Yale University Press, 2018.

Guijarro, Marta, and Óscar Peláez. "La longevidad globalizada: un análisis de esperanza de vida en España (1900–2050)." *Scripta Nova: Revista electrónica de geografía y ciencias sociales* 12, no. 260 (March 2008): No pagination. http://www.ub.edu/geocrit/sn/sn-260.html.

Halberstam, Judith. *Skin Shows: Gothic Horror and the Technology of Monsters*. Durham, NC: Duke University Press, 1995.

Heiland, Donna. *Gothic & Gender: An Introduction*. Malden, MA: Blackwell Publishing, 2004.

Hendershot, Cyndy. *The Animal Within: Masculinity and the Gothic*. Ann Arbor: The University of Michigan Press, 1998.

Heneghan, Dorota K. "The *Indiano*'s Marriage and the Crisis of Imperial Modernity in Galdós's *El amigo manso*." *Siglo Diecinueve* 22 (May 2016): 91–108.

Henn, David. "Reflections of the War of 1898 in Pardo Bazán's Fiction and Travel Chronicles." *Modern Language Review* 94, no. 2 (April 1999): 415–25.

Hernández Suárez, Manuel. *Bibliografía de Galdós*, vol. 1. Las Palmas: Cabildo Insular de Gran Canaria, 1972. https://hdl.handle.net/20.500.12285/mdcte/361.

Herrero, Sebastián. "La gitana." In *Los españoles pintados por sí mismos*, vol. 1, 289–99. Madrid: Ignacio Boix, 1843.

Hilton, Ronald. "Emilia Pardo-Bazán and the Americas." *The Americas* 9, no. 2 (Oct. 1952): 135–48.

Höglund, Johan. *The American Imperial Gothic: Popular Culture, Empire, Violence*. Surrey: Ashgate, 2014.

Horner, Avril, and Sue Zlosnik. "No Country for Old Women: Gender, Age and the Gothic." In *Women and the Gothic: An Edinburgh Companion*, edited by Avril Horner and Sue Zlosnik, 184–98. Edinburgh: Edinburgh University Press, 2016.

Iarocci, Michael. *Properties of Modernity: Romantic Spain, Modern Europe, and the Legacies of Empire*. Nashville, TN: Vanderbilt University Press, 2005.

"La Ilustración española y americana." Hemeroteca Digital, Biblioteca Nacional de España. http://hemerotecadigital.bne.es/details.vm?lang=es&q=id:0001066626 (accessed July 19, 2022).

"*El Imparcial* (Madrid. 1867)." Hemeroteca Digital, Biblioteca Nacional de España. http://hemerotecadigital.bne.es/details.vm?q=id:0000189234&lang=es (accessed June 6, 2022).

Jackson, Rosemary. *Fantasy: The Literature of Subversion*. London: Methuen, 1981.

Jacobson, Matthew F. *Whiteness of a Different Color: European Immigrants and the Alchemy of Race*. Cambridge, MA: Harvard University Press, 1998.

Jagoe, Catherine. *Ambiguous Angels: Gender in the Novels of Galdós*. Berkeley: University of California Press, 1994.

Jagoe, Catherine. "Disinheriting the Feminine: Galdós and the Rise of the Realist Novel in Spain." *Revista de Estudios Hispánicos* 27, no. 2 (May 1993): 225–48.

Jagoe, Catherine. "Noncanonical Novels and the Question of Quality." *Revista de Estudios Hispánicos* 27, no. 3 (1993): 427–36.

Jagoe, Catherine, Alda Blanco, and Cristina Enríquez de Salamanca, eds. *La mujer en los discursos de género: Textos y contextos en el siglo XIX*. Barcelona: Icaria, 1998.

Kahn, Andrew. *The Short Story: A Very Short Introduction*. Oxford: Oxford University Press, 2021.

Kingsbury, Karen. "Yellow Peril, Dark Hero: Fu Manchu and the 'Gothic Bedevilment' of Racist Intent." In *The Gothic Other: Racial and Social Constructions in the Literary Imagination*, edited by Ruth Bienstock Anolik and Douglas L. Howard, 104-19. Jefferson, NC: McFarland, 2004.

Kirkpatrick, Susan. "Constituting the Subject: Race, Gender, and Nation in the Early Nineteenth Century." In *Culture and the State in Spain, 1550-1850*, edited by Tom Lewis and Francisco J. Sánchez, 225-51. New York: Garland Publishing, 1999.

Klein, Dennis A. "The Jews of Nineteenth-Century Spain According to Historical Fact and Selected Novelists." *Yiddish-Modern Jewish Studies* 15, no. 1-2 (2007): 45-59.

Kosofsky Sedgwick, Eve. *Between Men: English Literature and Male Homosocial Desire*. New York: Columbia University Press, 1985.

Krauel, Javier. *Imperial Emotions: Cultural Responses to Myths of Empire in Fin-de-Siècle Spain*. Liverpool: Liverpool University Press, 2013.

Labanyi, Jo. Introduction to *Galdós*, edited by Jo Labanyi, 1-20. London: Longman, 1993.

Labanyi, Jo. *Gender and Modernization in the Spanish Realist Novel*. Oxford: Oxford University Press, 2000.

Labanyi, Jo. "History and Hauntology; or, What Does One Do with the Ghosts of the Past? Reflections on Spanish Film and Fiction of the Post-Franco Period." In *Spanish Culture from Romanticism to the Present: Structures of Feeling*, edited by Jo Labanyi, 303-16. Cambridge: Legenda, 2019.

Lafuente, Eva. "La figura del indiano y el viaje a América en la narrativa breve de Pardo Bazán." In *La literatura de Emilia Pardo Bazán*, edited by José Manuel González Herrán, Cristina Patiño Eirín, and Ermitas Penas Varela, 411-24. A Coruña: Fundación Caixa Galicia/Casa-Museo Emilia Pardo Bazán, 2009.

Laqueur, Thomas. *Making Sex: Body and Gender from the Greeks to Freud*. Cambridge, MA: Harvard University Press, 1992.

Lee Six, Abigail. *Gothic Terrors: Incarceration, Duplication, and Bloodlust in Spanish Narrative*. Lewisburg, PA: Bucknell University Press, 2010.

Lee Six, Abigail. *Spanish Vampire Fiction since 1900: Blood Relations*. London: Routledge, 2019.

"*El Liberal* (Madrid. 1879)." Hemeroteca Digital, Biblioteca Nacional de España. http://hemerotecadigital.bne.es/details.vm?lang=es&q=id:0001066755 (accessed June 14, 2022).

Llano, Samuel. "Public Enemy or National Hero? The Spanish Gypsy and the Rise of Flamenquismo, 1898-1922." *Bulletin of Spanish Studies* 94, no. 6 (2017): 977-1004. https://doi.org/10.1080/14753820.2017.1336363.

Lloyd Smith, Allan. "The Phantoms of *Drood* and *Rebecca*: The Uncanny Reencountered through Abraham and Torok's 'Cryptonymy'." *Poetics Today* 13, no. 2 (Summer 1992): 285-308.

López, Sylvia. "The Gothic Tradition in Galdós's *La sombra*." *Hispania* 81, no. 3 (September 1998): 509-18.

López Santos, Miriam. *La novela gótica en España (1788-1833)*. Vigo: Academia del Hispanismo, 2010.

Louis, Anja. *Women and the Law: Carmen de Burgos, an Early Feminist*. Woodbridge: Tamesis, 2005.

Luckhurst, Roger. *The Mummy's Curse: The True History of a Dark Fantasy*. Oxford: Oxford University Press, 2012.

Malchow, H. L. *Gothic Images of Race in Nineteenth-Century Britain*. Stanford, CA: Stanford University Press, 1996.

Mariscal, George. "The Role of Spain in Contemporary Race Theory." *Arizona Journal of Hispanic Cultural Studies* 2 (1998): 7-22.

Marshall, Bridget M. *Industrial Gothic: Workers, Exploitation and Urbanization in Transatlantic Nineteenth-Century Literature*. Cardiff: University of Wales Press, 2021.

Martínez-López, Enrique. "La leyenda del Judío errante en la literatura de cordel española." *Bulletin Hispanique* 92, no. 2 (1990): 789-825.

Martínez Santa, Ana. "La influencia de E. T. A. Hoffmann en *La sombra*." In *Actas del IV Congreso Internacional de Estudios Galdosianos*, vol. 2, 157-68. Las Palmas: Cabildo Insular de Gran Canaria, 1993.

Martín Sánchez, David. *Historia del pueblo gitano en España*. Madrid: Catarata, 2018.

Marx, Karl, and Frederick Engels. *The Communist Manifesto*. Translated by Samuel Moore. London: Pluto Press, 2017.

Marx, Karl. *The Process of Capitalist Production*. Vol. 1 of *Capital: A Critique of Political Economy*, translated by Samuel Moore and Edward Aveling, edited by Frederick Engels. Chicago: Charles H. Kerr & Company, 1906.

Massé, Michelle A. "Gothic Repetitions: Husbands, Horrors, and Things that Go Bump in the Night." *Signs: A Journal of Women in Culture and Society* 15, no. 4 (Summer 1990): 679-709.

Mateos, Ana. "A Black Woman Called *Blanca la extranjera* in Faustina Sáez de Melgar's *Los miserables* (1862-63)." In *Unsettling Colonialism: Gender and Race in the Nineteenth-Century Global Hispanic World*, edited by N. Michelle Murray and Akiko Tsuchiya, 107-33. Albany: State University of New York Press, 2019.

Mateos, Ana. "Fantasies of Race: A Transatlantic Approach to Class and Sexuality in Emilia Pardo Bazán's *La Tribuna*." In *Bulletin of Hispanic Studies* 92, no. 5 (2015): 531-49, https://doi.org/10.3828/bhs.2015.31.

McKinney, Collin. "'Enemigos de la virilidad': Sex, Masturbation and Celibacy in Nineteenth-Century Spain." *Prisma Social* 13 (2014-2015): 72-108.

McKinney, Collin. "How to Be a Man." In *Spain in the Nineteenth Century: New Essays on Experiences of Culture and Society*, edited by Andrew Ginger and Geraldine Lawless, 147-73. Manchester: Manchester University Press, 2018.

McKinney, Collin. *Mapping the Social Body: Urbanisation, the Gaze, and the Novels of Galdós*. Chapel Hill: University of North Carolina Press, 2010.

"Méndez Bringa: la visión de la España de entresiglos." *Descubrir el arte*, April 22, 2015. https://www.descubrirelarte.es/2015/04/22/mendez-bringa-la-vision-de-la-espana-de-entresiglos.html.

Mercer, Leigh. "Shadowing the Gothic: Rosalía de Castro's *La hija del mar* and Benito Pérez Galdós's *La sombra*." *Decimonónica* 9, no. 1 (Winter 2012): 34-47.

Mercer, Leigh. *Urbanism and Urbanity: The Spanish Bourgeois Novel and Contemporary Customs (1845-1925)*. Lewisburg, PA: Bucknell University Press, 2013.

Miguélez-Carballeira, Helena. "Teaching Pardo Bazán from Postcolonial and Transatlantic Perspectives." In *Approaches to Teaching the Writings of Emilia Pardo Bazán*, edited by Margot Versteeg and Susan Walter, 86-92. New York: Modern Language Association of America, 2017.

Miller, Gabrielle. "¡Mi hijo es mío, puñales! Excessive Paternal Devotion in Benito Pérez Galdós's *Torquemada* Novels." *Decimonónica* 17, no. 2 (Summer 2020): 65-80.

Miller, Gabrielle. "Unveiling the *Beata*: Feminine Aging and Subjectivity in *El doctor Centeno* (1883) and *Tormento* (1884)." Anales Galdosianos 55 (2020): 39-53. doi:10.1353/ang.2020.0000.

Moers, Ellen. *Literary Women: The Great Writers*. New York: Doubleday, 1976.
Molina Porras, Juan. Introduction to *Cuentos fantásticos en la España del realismo*, edited by Juan Molina Porras, 9–47. Madrid: Cátedra, 2006.
Monlau, Pedro Felipe. *Higiene del matrimonio o el libro de los casados*. 2nd ed. Madrid: Rivadeneyra, 1858. https://babel.hathitrust.org/cgi/pt?id=ucm.5322558049&view=1up&seq=7.
Monleón, José B. *A Specter Is Haunting Europe: A Sociohistorical Approach to the Fantastic*. Princeton, NJ: Princeton University Press, 1990.
Monleón, José B. "Vampiros y donjuanes (Sobre la figura del seductor en el siglo XIX)." *Revista Hispánica Moderna* 48, no. 1 (June 1995): 19–30.
Moreno Godino, Florencio. "La vieja verde." In *Las españolas pintadas por los españoles*, vol. 2, edited by Roberto Robert, 115–22. Madrid: J.E. Morete, 1872.
Mosse, George. *The Image of Man: The Creation of Modern Masculinity*. New York: Oxford University Press, 1996.
Murray, N. Michelle, and Akiko Tsuchiya, eds. *Unsettling Colonialism: Gender and Race in the Nineteenth-Century Global Hispanic World*. Albany: State University of New York Press, 2019.
Nagel, Joanne. "Masculinity and Nationalism: Gender and Sexuality in the Making of Nations." *Ethnic and Racial Studies* 21, no. 2 (1998): 242–69.
Nalbone, Lisa. "The Legal, Medical, and Social Contexts of the Angel in the House." In *Approaches to Teaching the Writings of Emilia Pardo Bazán*, edited by Margot Versteeg and Susan Walter, 49–57. New York: Modern Language Association of America, 2017.
Oliver, Walter C. "The Short Stories of Benito Pérez Galdós." PhD diss., University of New Mexico, 1971.
Oswald, Dana. "Monstrous Gender: Geographies of Ambiguity." In *The Ashgate Research Companion to Monsters and the Monstrous*, edited by Asa Simon Mittman and Peter J. Dendle, 343–63. Farnham: Ashgate, 2012.
Paquette, Gabriel. *Enlightenment, Governance, and Reform in Spain and Its Empire 1759–1808*. London: Palgrave Macmillan, 2008.
Pardo Bazán, Emilia. "El antepasado." *Álbum salón*, July 1, 1898, 249–50.
Pardo Bazán, Emilia. "El brasileño." *La Ilustración española y americana*, September 30, 1911, 182–83, 186.
Pardo Bazán, Emilia. *Cuentos fantásticos*. Edited by Ana Abello Verano and Raquel de la Varga Llamazares. León: Eolas, 2020.
Pardo Bazán, Emilia. "El descubrimiento de América en las letras españolas: Las conferencias del Ateneo (Primera serie)." *Nuevo Teatro Crítico* 2, no. 21 (September 1892): 17–64. https://www.cervantesvirtual.com/obra-visor/nuevo-teatro-critico--15/html/0295a03e-82b2-11df-acc7-002185ce6064_18.html.
Pardo Bazán, Emilia. "El descubrimiento de América en las letras españolas: (1.a) Libros de Fernández Duro, el p. Cappa y el p. Coll." *Nuevo Teatro Crítico* 2, no. 20 (August 1892): 65–109. https://www.cervantesvirtual.com/obra-visor/nuevo-teatro-critico--12/html/02959896-82b2-11df-acc7-002185ce6064_66.html.
Pardo Bazán, Emilia. "Los hilos." *Apuntes*, July 12, 1896, no pagination.
Pardo Bazán, Emilia. "Maldición de gitana." *El Liberal*, September 5, 1897, no pagination.
Pardo Bazán, Emilia. "Maldición de gitana." In *Obras Completas*, vol. 16, *Cuentos de amor*, 201–07. Madrid: Administración, 1898. https://sirio.ua.es/libros/BEducacion/cuentos_amor/ima0198.htm.

Pardo Bazán, Emilia. "La mujer española." In *La mujer española y otros escritos*, edited by Guadalupe Gómez-Ferrer, 83–116. Madrid: Cátedra, 2018.

Pardo Bazán, Emilia. "Pedro Antonio de Alarcón. Necrología." *Nuevo Teatro Crítico* 1, no. 9 (1891): 22–80.

Pardo Bazán, Emilia. "Pedro Antonio de Alarcón. Las novelas." *Nuevo Teatro Crítico* 1, no. 10 (1891): 20–67.

Pardo Bazán, Emilia. Prologue to *Cuentos sacro-profanos*, 5–11. Madrid: V. Prieto y Compañía, 1899.

Pardo Bazán, Emilia. Prologue to *Un viaje de novios*. Alicante: Biblioteca Virtual Miguel de Cervantes, 2000. https://www.cervantesvirtual.com/nd/ark:/59851/bmckk977.

Pardo Bazán, Emilia. "Vampiro." *Blanco y negro*, no. 539 (August 31, 1901): no pagination.

Pardo Bazán, Emilia. "Vampiro." In *Cuentos completos*, edited by Juan Paredes Nuñez, 2:351–54. A Coruña: Fundación Pedro Barrié de la Maza, 1990.

Paredes Nuñez, Juan, ed. *Cuentos completos de Emilia Pardo Bazán*. 4 vol. Vigo: Fundación Pedro Barrié de la Maza, 1990.

Patel, J. A., F. B. H. Nielsen, A. A. Badiani, S. Assi, V. A. Unadkat, B. Patel, R. Ravindrane, and H. Wardle. "Poverty, Inequality and COVID-19: The Forgotten Vulnerable." *Public Health* 183 (May 2020): 110–111. https://doi.org/10.1016/j.puhe.2020.05.006.

Payán, Juan Jesús. *Los conjuros del asombro: Expresión fantástica e identidad nacional en la España del siglo XIX*. Newark, DE: Juan de la Cuesta, 2022.

Peñate Rivero, Julio. *Benito Pérez Galdós y el cuento literario como sistema*. Zaragoza: Libros Pórtico, 2001.

Pérez Bernardo, María Luisa, ed. *De siglo a siglo (1896–1901): Crónicas periodísticas de Emilia Pardo Bazán*. Madrid: Pliegos, 2014.

Pérez Bernardo, María Luisa. "El escenario de las Islas Filipinas en las crónicas y cuentos de Emilia Pardo Bazán." *Revista Filipina* 13, no. 1 (Spring 2009): no pagination. http://revista.carayanpress.com/bazan.html.

Pérez Bernardo, María Luisa. "Hernán Cortés en la obra periodística y literaria de Emilia Pardo Bazán." *Tejuelo* 8 (2010): 46–58.

Pérez Galdós, Benito. *13 cuentos*. Edited by Esteban Gutiérrez Díaz-Bernardo. Madrid: EDAF, 2001.

Pérez Galdós, Benito. "13-VIII-65. Revista de la semana." In *Los artículos de Galdós en "La Nación,"* edited by William H. Shoemaker, 117–21. Madrid: Ínsula, 1972.

Pérez Galdós, Benito. *La conjuración de las palabras*. Edited by German Gullón. Barcelona: EDHASA, 1991.

Pérez Galdós, Benito. *Cuentos*. Edited by Yolanda Arencibia. Las Palmas: Cabildo Insular de Gran Canaria, 2013.

Pérez Galdós, Benito. *Cuentos fantásticos*. Edited by Alan E. Smith. Madrid: Cátedra, 2008.

Pérez Galdós, Benito. *Los cuentos de Galdós*. Vol. 1 of *Obra Completa*, edited by Oswaldo Izquierdo Dorta. Las Palmas: Cabildo Insular de Gran Canaria/Centro de la cultura popular canaria, 1994.

Pérez Galdós, Benito. "La cuestión social." In *Obras inéditas*, edited by Alberto Ghiraldo, 147–56. Vol. 6 of *Cronicón (1883–1886)*. Madrid: Renacimiento, 1924.

Pérez Galdós, Benito. "Fantasía de otoño." *La prensa* (Buenos Aires), December 12, 1884.

Pérez Galdós, Benito. "Furor colonial y otros furores." In *Obras inéditas*, vol. 6, *Cronicón 1883–1886*, edited by Alberto Ghiraldo, 157–62. Madrid: Renacimiento, 1924.

Pérez Galdós, Benito. *Ocho cuentos de Galdós*, edited by Oswaldo Izquierda Dorta. Las Palmas: Cabildo Insular de Gran Canaria, 1988.

Pérez Galdós, Benito. Prologue to *La sombra*, 5-8. Madrid: La Guirnalda, 1890.

Pérez Galdós, Benito. *La sombra, Revista de España* 18, no. 70 (1871): 269-92; no. 71 (1871): 417-39; no. 72 (1871): 601-23.

Pérez Galdós, Benito. "Observaciones sobre la novela contemporánea en España." In *Ensayos de crítica literaria*, edited by Laureano Bonet, 123-39. Barcelona: Ediciones Península, 1999.

Pérez Galdós, Benito. *The Shadow*. Translated by Karen O. Austin. Athens: Ohio University Press, 1980.

Pérez Galdós, Benito. "La sociedad presente como material novelable." In *Ensayos de crítica literaria*, edited by Laureano Bonet, 218-26. Barcelona: Ediciones Península, 1999.

Pérez Galdós, Benito. "Tropiquillos." *Los lunes de El imparcial*, December 18, 1893, no pagination.

Pérez Galdós, Benito. "Una industria que vive de la muerte." *La nación*, December 2 and 6, 1865.

Pérez Galdós, Benito. "El verano." In *Almanaque de La Ilustración española y americana para 1878*, edited by Abelardo de Carlos, 54-57. Madrid: Aribau, 1877.

"El Periódico para todos." Hemeroteca Digital, Biblioteca Nacional de España. Accessed July 18, 2022. http://hemerotecadigital.bne.es/details.vm?q=id:0003433857&lang=en.

Pierce, Joseph M. "I Monster: Embodying Trans and *Travesti* Resistance in Latin America." *Latin American Research Review* 55, no. 2 (2020): 305-21. https://doi.org/10.25222/larr.563.

Pont, Jaume, ed. *Narrativa fantástica en el siglo XIX (España e Hispanoamérica)*. Lleida: Milenio, 1997.

Pozzi, Gabriela. "Madres histéricas, médicos y la sexualidad en tres cuentos fantásticos de Emila Pardo Bazán." *Letras Femeninas* 26, no. 1-2 (2000): 157-69.

Procter, James, and Angela Smith. "Gothic and Empire." In *The Routledge Companion to Gothic*, edited by Catherine Spooner and Emma McEvoy, 95-104. London/New York: Routledge, 2007.

Puebla, Consuelo. "La deformación del personaje Alarconiano." In *Monstruosidad y transgresión en la cultura hispánica*, edited by Ricardo de la Fuente Ballesteros and Jesús Pérez Magallón, 245-58. Valladolid: Universidad Castellae, 2003.

Punter, David, and Glennis Byron. "Imperial Gothic." In *The Gothic*, 44-49. Oxford: Blackwell Publishing, 2004.

Quesada Novás, Ángeles. "Nuevos cuentos ilustrados de Emilia Pardo Bazán." In *Literatura ilustrada decimonónica: 57 perspectivas*, edited by Borja Rodríguez Gutiérrez and Raquel Gutiérrez Sebastián, 677-90. Santander: Universidad de Cantabria, 2011.

Rabkin, Eric, ed. *Fantastic Worlds: Myths, Tales, and Stories*. Oxford: Oxford University Press, 1979.

Rementería y Fica, Carlos. *El hombre fino al gusto del día, o Manual completo de la urbanidad, cortesía y buen tono*. Madrid: Imprenta de Moreno, 1829.

Reisz, Susana. "Las ficciones fantásticas y sus relaciones con otros tipos ficcionales." In *Teorías de lo fantástico*, edited by David Roas, 193-221. Madrid: Arco/Libros, 2001.

Ribas-Casasayas, Alberto, and Amanda L. Petersen. "Introduction: Theories of the Ghost in a Transhispanic Context." In *Espectros: Ghostly Hauntings in Contemporary Transhispanic*

Narratives, edited by Alberto Ribas-Casasayas and Amanda L. Petersen, 1–11. Lewisburg, PA: Bucknell University Press, 2016.

Ribeiro, Eduardo Rivail. "Tapuya Connections: Language Contact in Eastern Brazil." *Llames* 9, (Spring 2009): 61–76. http://www.etnolinguistica.org/artigo:ribeiro_2009.

Ridao Carlini, Inma. *Rich and Poor in Nineteenth-Century Spain: A Critique of Liberal Society in the Later Novels of Benito Pérez Galdós*. Woodbridge: Tamesis, 2018.

Risco, Antonio. *Literatura fantástica de lengua española*. Madrid: Taurus, 1987.

Roas, David. Prologue to *El Castillo del espectro: Antología de relatos fantásticos españoles del siglo XIX*, edited by David Roas, 5–24. Barcelona: Círculo de lectores, 2002.

Roas, David. Introduction to *Cuentos fantásticos del siglo XIX (España e Hispanoamérica)*, edited by David Roas, 7–36. Madrid: Marenostrum, 2003.

Roas, David. *De la maravilla al horror: Los inicios de lo fantástico en la cultura española (1750–1869)*. Pontevedra: Mirabel, 2006.

Roas, David. "Entre cuadros, espejos y sueños misteriosos. La obra fantástica de Pedro Escamilla." *Scriptura* 16 (2001): 103–18.

Roas, David. *Hoffmann en España: Recepción e influencias*. Madrid: Biblioteca Nueva, 2002.

Roas, David. *La sombra del Cuervo: Edgar Allan Poe y la literatura fantástica española del siglo XIX*. Madrid: Devenir, 2011.

Rodrigo-Alharilla, Martin. "Spanish Sailors and the Illegal Slave Trade to Cuba, 1845–1867." *Journal of Iberian and Latin American Studies* 27, no. 1 (2021): 94–117.

Rødtjer, Rocío. "Out of Time: Julia de Asensi and the Historical Legend." In *The Modern Spanish Canon: Visibility, Cultural Capital and the Academy*, edited by Stuart Davis and Maite Usoz de la Fuente, 58–71. Cambridge: Legenda, 2018.

Rødtjer, Rocío. *Women and Nationhood in Restoration Spain 1874–1931: The State as Family*. Cambridge: Legenda, 2019.

Rueda, Ana. "At the Crossroads of Age and Gender: Widowhood in the Spanish Long Eighteenth Century." In "Intersections between age and gender in Enlightenment society," ed. Hanna Nohe, special issue, *Das achtzehnte jahrhundert* 44, no. 2 (2020): 228–48.

Sánchez Martínez, Andrés. "La cara oculta de la realidad: elementos fantásticos en *La princesa y el granuja* de Benito Pérez Galdós." *Philobiblion: Revista de Literaturas Hispánicas* 11 (October 2020): 121–37. https://doi.org/10.15366/philobiblion2020.11.005.

Santacruz, Pascual. "El siglo de los marimachos." *La España Moderna* 19 (1907): 79–94.

Scanlon, Geraldine. *La polémica feminista en la España contemporánea (1868–1974)*. Translated by Rafael Mazarrasa. Madrid: Akal, 1986.

Schmidt-Nowara, Christopher. "Introduction: Interpreting Spanish Colonialism." In *Interpreting Spanish Colonialism: Empires, Nations, and Legends*, edited by Christopher Schmidt-Nowara and John Nieto-Phillips, 1–18. Albuquerque: University of New Mexico Press, 2005.

Schmidt-Nowara, Christopher and John Nieto-Phillips, eds. *Interpreting Spanish Colonialism: Empires, Nations, and Legends*. Albuquerque: University of New Mexico Press, 2005.

Schneider, Steven J. "Mixed Blood Couples: Monsters and Miscegenation in U.S. Horror Cinema." In *The Gothic Other: Racial and Social Constructions in the Literary Imagination*, edited by Ruth Bienstock Anolik and Douglas L. Howard, 72–89. Jefferson, NC: McFarland & Co., 2004.

Schyfter, Sara. "The Judaism of Galdós' Daniel Morton." *Hispania* 59, no. 1 (March 1976): 24–33.

Showalter, Elaine. *Sexual Anarchy: Gender and Culture at the Fin de Siècle*. New York: Viking, 1990.
Shubert, Adrian. *A Social History of Modern Spain*. London: Unwin Hyman, 1990.
Shulman, Marcy G. "Ironic Illusion in *La sombra*." *Anales Galdosianos* 17 (1982): 33–38.
Sierra-Alonso, María. "Cannibals Devoured: *Gypsies* in Romantic Discourse on the Spanish Nation." In *Enemies Within: Cultural Hierarchies and Liberal Political Models in the Hispanic World*, edited by María Sierra-Alonso, 187–221. Newcastle: Cambridge Scholars Publishing, 2015.
Sinnigen, John. "Cuba en Galdós: La función de las colonias en el discurso metropolitano." *Casa de las Américas* 212 (1998): 115–21.
Smith, Alan E. Introduction to *Cuentos fantásticos*, by Benito Pérez Galdós, 11–28. Edited by Alan E. Smith. Madrid: Cátedra, 2008.
Smith, Alan. *Los cuentos inverosímiles de Galdós en el contexto de su obra*. Barcelona: Anthropos, 1992.
Smith, Andrew. *The Ghost Story, 1840–1920: A Cultural History*. Manchester: Manchester University Press, 2010.
Smith, Andrew. "Gothic Imperialism at the *Fin de siècle*." In *The Cambridge History of the Gothic*, vol. 2, *Gothic in the Nineteenth Century*, edited by Dale Townshend and Angela Wright, 463–81. Cambridge: Cambridge University Press, 2020.
Smith, Andrew. "Hauntings." In *The Routledge Companion to Gothic*, edited by Catherine Spooner and Emma McEvoy, 147–54. London: Routledge, 2007.
Smith, Angel and Clare Mar-Molinero. "The Myths and Realities of Nation-Building in the Iberian Peninsula." In *Nationalism and the Nation in the Iberian Peninsula: Competing and Conflicting Identities*, edited by Clare Mar-Molinero and Angel Smith, 1–30. Oxford: Berg, 1996.
Smith, Jennifer. "(De)Pathologizing Lesbian Desire in Late Nineteenth-Century Spain." *Anales Galdosianos* 56 (2021): 185–203.
Smith, Jennifer. "The Gypsy's Curse: Race and Impurity of Blood in Pardo Bazán." *Revista Canadiense de Estudios Hispánicos* 39, no. 2 (Winter 2015): 459–82.
Smith, Jennifer, and Lisa Nalbone, eds. *Intersections of Race, Class, Gender, and Nation in Fin-de-Siècle Spanish Literature and Culture*. London: Routledge, 2017.
Smith, Jennifer. *Women, Mysticism, and Hysteria in Fin-de-Siècle Spain*. Nashville, TN: Vanderbilt University Press, 2021.
Snow, Joseph. "Viejas marginadas en el patriarcado medieval español." In *Actas del XVI Congreso de la Asociación Internacional de Hispanistas: Nuevos caminos del hispanismo*, edited by Pierre Civil and Françoise Crémoux, 113–129. Madrid: Iberoamericana Vervuert, 2010.
Soria, Mar. "Colonial Imaginings on the Stage: Blackface, Gender, and the Economics of Empire in Spanish and Catalan Popular Theater." In *Unsettling Colonialism: Gender and Race in the Nineteenth-Century Global Hispanic World*, edited by N. Michelle Murray and Akiko Tsuchiya, 135–69. Albany: State University of New York Press, 2019.
Stollznow, Karen. *Language, Myths, Mysteries and Magic*. New York: Palgrave Macmillan, 2014.
Stories by Foreign Authors: Spanish. New York: Charles Scribner's Sons, 1898.
Stott, Rebecca. *The Fabrication of the Late-Victorian Femme Fatale: The Kiss of Death*. London: Macmillan, 1992.
Surwillo, Lisa. "Inscribing *Indianos* into Modern Imperial Histories." In *Empire's End: Transnational Connections in the Hispanic World*, edited by Akiko Tsuchiya and William Acree, 191–203. Nashville, TN: Vanderbilt University Press, 2016.

Surwillo, Lisa. *Monsters by Trade: Slave Traffickers in Modern Spanish Literature and Culture.* Stanford, CA: Stanford University Press, 2014.

Surwillo, Lisa. "Pituso en *blackface*: Una mascarada racial en *Fortunata y Jacinta.*" *Hispanic Review* 78, no. 2 (Spring 2010): 189-204.

Svisero, Darcy P., James E. Shigley, and Robert Weldon. "Brazilian Diamonds: A Historical and Recent Perspective." *Gems & Gemology* 53, no. 1 (Spring 2017): 2-33. https://www.gia.edu/gems-gemology/spring-2017-brazilian-diamonds.

Tang, Wan S. "'Yo no soy un hombre': Masculinity, Monstrosity, and Gothic Conventions in Galdós's *La sombra* (1871)." *Hispanic Review* 88, no. 3 (2020): 243-63.

Tasende, Mercedes. "Entre la leyenda negra y la leyenda dorada: Emilia Pardo Bazán ante el descubrimiento, la conquista y la colonización española del nuevo mundo." *Anales de Literatura Española Contemporánea* 40, no. 1 (2015): 425-51.

Todorov, Tzvetan. *The Fantastic: A Structural Approach to a Literary Genre.* Translated by Richard Howard. Ithaca, NY: Cornell University Press, 1975.

Tolliver, Joyce. *Cigar Smoke and Violet Water: Gendered Discourse in the Stories of Emilia Pardo Bazán.* Lewisburg, PA: Bucknell University Press, 1998.

Tolliver, Joyce. "Colonialism, Collages, and Thick Description: Pardo Bazán and the Rhetoric of Detail." In *Imagined Truths: Realism in Modern Spanish Literature and Culture*, edited by Mary L. Coffey and Margot Versteeg, 215-35. Toronto: University of Toronto Press, 2019.

Tolliver, Joyce. "*Dalagas* and *Ilustrados*: Gender, Language, and Indigeneity in the Philippine Colonies." In *Unsettling Colonialism: Gender and Race in the Nineteenth-Century Global Hispanic World*, edited by N. Michelle Murray and Akiko Tsuchiya, 231-53. Albany: State University of New York Press, 2019.

Tolliver, Joyce. "Framing Colonial Manliness, Domesticity, and Empire in 'Página suelta' and 'Oscuramente.'" *Revista de Estudios Hispanicos* 46, no. 1 (March 2012): 3-24.

Tolliver, Joyce. "Over Her Bloodless Body: Gender, Race, and the Spanish Colonial Fetish in Pardo Bazán." *Revista Canadiense de Estudios Hispánicos* 34, no. 2 (Winter 2010): 285-301.

Tolliver, Joyce. "Pardo Bazán and Spain's Late Modern Empire." In *Approaches to Teaching the Writings of Emilia Pardo Bazán*, edited by Margot Versteeg and Susan Walter, 93-98. New York: Modern Language Association of America, 2017.

Tolliver, Joyce. "La voz antifeminista y la amenaza 'andrógina' en el fin de siglo." In *Sexualidad y escritura (1850-2000)*, edited by Raquel Medina and Barbara Zecchi, 105-19. Barcelona, Anthropos, 2002.

Torres-Pou, Joan. *Asia en la España del siglo XIX: Literatos, viajeros, intelectuales y diplomáticos ante Oriente.* Amsterdam: Rodopi, 2013.

Tosh, John. "Hegemonic Masculinity and the History of Gender." In *Masculinities in Politics and War: Gendering Modern History*, edited by Stefan Dudink, Karen Hagemann, and John Tosh, 41-58. Manchester: Manchester University Press, 2004.

Trancón Lagunas, Montserrat. *La literatura fantástica en la prensa del Romanticismo.* Valencia: Institució Alfonse el Magnànim/Diputació de València, 2000.

Trigo, Beatriz. "El espacio fantástico en tres cuentos de Emilia Pardo Bazán o la reafirmación de la sociedad patriarcal." *Cuaderno Internacional de Estudios Hispánicos y Lingüística* 2 (2002): 109-34.

Troncoso, Dolores. *Galdós: Corresponsal de* La Prensa *de Buenos Aires.* Las Palmas: Cabildo Insular de Gran Canaria, 2020.

Tsuchiya, Akiko, and William G. Acree, Jr., eds. *Empire's End: Transnational Connections in the Hispanic World*. Nashville, TN: Vanderbilt University Press, 2016.
Tsuchiya, Akiko. *Marginal Subjects: Gender and Deviance in Fin-de-Siècle Spain*. Toronto: University of Toronto Press, 2011.
Turner, Harriet. "Rhetoric in *La sombra*: The Author and His Story." *Anales Galdosianos* 6 (1971): 5–19.
Ugarte, Michael. "The Spanish Empire on the Wane: Africa, Galdós, and the Moroccan Wars." In *Empire's End: Transnational Connections in the Hispanic World*, edited by Akiko Tsuchiya and William G. Acree, Jr., 177–90. Nashville, TN: Vanderbilt University Press, 2016.
Urey, Diane. *Galdós and the Irony of Language*. Cambridge: Cambridge University Press, 1982.
Valis, Noël. *The Culture of Cursilería: Bad Taste, Kitsch, and Class in Modern Spain*. Durham, NC: Duke University Press, 2002.
Valis, Noël. "Homosexuality on Display in 1920s Spain: The Hermaphrodite, Eccentricity, and Álvaro Retana." In *Freakish Encounters: Constructions of the Freak in Hispanic Cultures*, edited by Sara Muñoz-Muriana and Analola Santana, 190–216. *Hispanic Issues on Line* 20 (2018).
Valis, Noël. Review of *Pedro Antonio de Alarcón (prensa, política, novela de tesis)*, by Ignacio Javier López. *Hispanic Review* 78, no. 3 (Summer 2010): 449–51, https://www.jstor.org/stable/25703541.
Valis, Noël. *Sacred Realism: Religion and the Imagination in Modern Spanish Narrative*. New Haven, CT: Yale University Press, 2010.
Versteeg, Margot. "Good and Bad Fusion in Emilia Pardo Bazán's *El becerro de metal* (1906)." In *Intersections of Race, Class, Gender and Nation in Fin-de-siècle Spanish Literature and Culture*, edited by Jennifer Smith and Lisa Nalbone, 108–22. London: Routledge, 2017.
Vialette, Aurélie. *Intellectual Philanthropy: The Seduction of the Masses*. West Lafayette, IN: Purdue University Press, 2018.
Von Tschilschke, Christian. "La crisis de la masculinidad como crítica al colonialismo en *Aita Tettauen* (1905) de Benito Pérez Galdós." In *El otro colonialismo: España y África, entre imaginación e historia*, edited by Christian von Tschilschke and Jan-Henrik Witthaus, 149–70. Madrid: Iberoamericana Vervuert, 2017.
Weber, Max. *Ancient Judaism*. Translated and edited by Hans H. Gerth and Don Martindale. Glencoe, IL: The Free Press, 1952.
Weller, Krisztina. "The Mysterious Lady: An Enigmatic Figure in the Fantastic Short Story of Nineteenth-Century Spain." *Scripta Mediterranea* 8–9 (1987–88): 59–68.
Whitford, David M. *The Curse of Ham in the Early Modern Era: The Bible and the Justifications for Slavery*. New York: Routledge, 2009.
Wolfreys, Julian. *Victorian Hauntings: Spectrality, Gothic, the Uncanny and Literature*. New York: Palgrave Macmillan, 2002.
Wolters, Nicholas. *Masculine Figures: Fashioning Men and the Novel in Nineteenth-Century Spain*. Nashville, TN: Vanderbilt University Press, 2023.
Zorrilla, José. Prólogo a "La pasionaria." In *Cantos del Trovador*, vol. 3, 7–8. Madrid: Ignacio Boix, 1841.

Index

Page numbers in *italic* refer to figures.

Alarcón, Pedro Antonio de
   fantastic short fiction and, 4, 5
   Jewish characters by, 133–34
   Pardo Bazán and, 11–12, 72, 148–49n44
   realist fiction and, 11–12
   See also "mujer alta, La" (Alarcón)
Alas, Leopoldo ("Clarín"), 10, 32, 80, 81, 172n49
Álbum salón (periodical), 26
Alcalá Galiano, Álvaro, 32, 34–35, *35*
Aldana Reyes, Xavier, 149n49, 163–64n73
All Is True (Furst), 145n1
Allen, Virginia, 160n39
Álvarez Junco, José, 147n28
"amigo de la Muerte, El" (Alarcón), 12
Anderson, Benedict, 9
ángel del hogar (angel in the house), 56–59
ángel del hogar, El (Sinués de Marco), 158n8
Animal Within, The (Hendershot), 86
"antepasado, El" (Pardo Bazán)
   compared to "Los hilos" (Pardo Bazán), 33, 38
   intersection of class, gender, and race in, 143
   middle-class identity in, 19–20, 24–25, 26–31, 54

narrative perspective in, 27
publication and reception of, 26, 32
Apuntes (weekly), 32
Arenal, Concepción, 58
aristocracy
   in "El antepasado" (Pardo Bazán), 26–30
   as evil and deviant in Gothic fiction, 25–26
   modernity and, 20–21
   See also middle class (bourgeoisie)
Asensi, Julia de, 25–26, 32, 71, 143, 152n32
"Así y todo" (Pardo Bazán), 152n34
Austin, Karen, 165n88

Baker, Brian, 80
Baldick, Chris, 108
Bannerman, Anne, 160n37
Baquero Goyanes, Mariano, 7, 145n3
Bardavío Estevan, Susana, 116
Baroja, Pío, 172n49
Bastardín Candón, Teresa, 177n102
becerro de metal, El (Pardo Bazán), 134
Bécquer, Gustavo Adolfo, 5, 25–26, 64, 126, 134
Beltrán y Rózpide, Ricardo, 104–5
Berger, John, 67
Bernaldo de Quirós, Constancio, 126

Bhabha, Homi, 111–12, 116
Bienstock Anolik, Ruth, 81, 132
blackface, 103
Blanco, Alda, 168–69n4
Blanco, María del Pilar, 24, 53, 156n79
Blanco y negro (periodical), 91, *93*, 97–98, *99*
Blasco Ibáñez, Vicente, 126
Blood Libel, 134
bohemianism, 125
Borges, Jorge Luis, 146n11
Botting, Fred, 13–14, 152n31
bourgeoisie. *See* middle class (bourgeoisie)
Brantlinger, Patrick, 111, 114, 174n74
"brasileño, El" (Pardo Bazán)
    compared to "El cuadro de maese Abraham" (Escamilla), 135–36
    compared to "Maldición de gitana" (Pardo Bazán), 124, 127
    curse and racialized Others in, 102, 110–12, 118, 119–24, 139–40
    narrative perspective in, 109–10, 119, 122–24
    publication and reception of, 118–19
    slavery in, 120, 123–24
Britt, Brian, 108
Brooks, Peter, 146n17
"buen judío, El" (Pardo Bazán), 134
Burdiel, Isabel, 150n3
Burgos, Carmen de, 64
Butler, Judith, 162–63n61

Callois, Roger, 146n13, 146n15
Calvino, Italo, 5
Campá, Francisco de Paula, 71
Campoamor, Ramón de, 172n49
cannibalism, 121
Cánovas del Castillo, Antonio, 106
Capital (Marx), 23, 45
Caprichos (Goya), 63–64, *65*, 73
Cardona, Rodolfo, 157n91
"casa donde murió, La" (Asensi), 32, 71
casta (caste), 105
castas pardas (free Americans of African ancestry), 106, 110

Castelar, Emilio, 176–77n95
castizos, 9–10
Castle of Otranto, The (Walpole), 25
Catholicism, 5, 105–6, 147n20
Cazottes, Gisèle, 12
"Celín" (Galdós), 6–7
censorship, 4
Chamisso, Adelbert von, 7
Charnon-Deutsch, Lou
    on de los Ríos, 177n108
    on Pardo Bazán, 118, 149n48
    on periodical press, 149n54, 160n41, 166n98
    on race (*raza*), 104
    on Romani people, 175n82, 175–76n84, 176n88, 176n94
cholera, 46–50
Christmas Carol, A (Dickens), 23
class
    in "El cuadro de maese Abraham" (Escamilla), 137
    in "Maldición de gitana" (Pardo Bazán), 127–28
    nation building and, 9–11, 141–44
    See also middle class (bourgeoisie)
classical antiquity, 59–60
Coffey, Mary, 111, 112, 113, 146n17
Cohen, Jeffrey, 60
colonialism, 110–12. See also *indianos*; indigenous peoples
Communist Manifesto (Marx), 23
Conde Lucanor, El (Juan Manuel), 138
Congreso Geográfico Hispano-Portugués-Americano (Hispanic-Portuguese-American Geographic Conference, 1892), 104–5, 168–69nn3–4
conjuración de las palabras, La (Gullón), 161n45
conjuros del asombro, Los (Payán), 7–8, 147n23
Constitution of 1812, 9–10, 20–21
Contreras y Alba, María del Pilar, 75
Copeland, Eva María, 123
Coronado, Carolina, 166n96

"Corpus" (Pardo Bazán), 134
Correspondencia de Canarias, La (periodical), 161n43
Cortázar, Julio, 146n11
Cortes de Cádiz, 9
"corza blanca, La" (Bécquer), 126
"Creed en Dios" (Bécquer), 152n32
"crimen científico, Un" (Fernández Bremón), 81
criminal anthropology, 107, 125–26
cristiana, Una (Pardo Bazán), 134
crones
    characteristics of, 63–64, 65, 70–72
    in "La mujer alta" (Alarcón), 55–56, 61, 62–63, 72–80, 82, 94, 99
Cruz, Jesús, 150–51nn9–10
"cruz del diablo, La" (Bécquer), 26
"cuadro de maese Abraham, El" (Escamilla)
    curse and racialized Others in, 102, 134–40
    Jews in, 134–40, *138*
    narrative perspective in, 109–10, 134–39
    publication and reception of, 134, 137–38, *138*
cuento español en el siglo XIX, El (Baquero Goyanes), 7, 145n3
"Cuento futuro" (Alas), 81
cuentos (short stories), 3–4
Cuentos de amor (Pardo Bazán), 126, 129
Cuentos de terruño (Pardo Bazán), 91
Cuentos negros o historias extravagantes (Serrano Alcázar), 149n47
Cuentos sacro-profanos (Pardo Bazán), 4, 7, 12, 26, 32
"cuestión social, La" (Galdós), 45
Culture of Cursilería, The (Valis), 75
curse
    in "El brasileño" (Pardo Bazán), 102, 110–12, 118, 119–24, 139–40
    in "El cuadro de maese Abraham" (Escamilla), 102, 134–40
    Jews and, 134
    in "Maldición de gitana" (Pardo Bazán), 102, 124, 127–32, 139–40
    racialized Others and, 103–4, 108–10
    in "Tropiquillos" (Galdós), 102, 110–12, 113–18, 124, 139–40
Curse of Ham, 108
Curtis, George William, 72, 146n9

Dacre, Charlotte, 160n37, 170n28
de los Ríos, Laura, 163n64
Degeneration (Nordau), 107
DeLamotte, Eugenia, 107, 137
Delgado, Luisa Elena, 123, 175n76
delincuente español, El (Salillas), 126
Derrida, Jacques, 23, 29–30
"Desde afuera" (Pardo Bazán), 147n22
desheredada, La (Galdós), 148n37
diario de Las Palmas, El (periodical), 112
Diario de un testigo de la Guerra de África (Alarcón), 133–34
Díaz del Castillo, Bernal, 121
Dickens, Charles, 23
Dijkstra, Bram, 63, 161n49
Disaster of 1898, 112
Discurso sobre la nación (Cánovas del Castillo), 106
Don Juan Tenorio (Zorrilla), 84
Doña Luz (Valera), 173n61
Dorofeeva, Maria, 175n82
Dracula (Stoker), 25, 55, 81, 160n37, 176n93
Dreyfus affair, 133
Duncan, Cynthia, 3, 61, 78

Eastman, Scott, 110
Eco de Galicia, El (weekly), 126
education, 21
Egypt, 109
"encubierto, El" (Asensi), 152n32
Episodios nacionales (Galdós), 147n20
Escamilla, Pedro, 12–13, 71, 134. *See also* "cuadro de maese Abraham, El" (Escamilla)
Escenas fantásticas (Selgas), 149n47
Espejo Saavedra, Ramón, 163n63, 163–64n73

Estébanez Calderón, Serafín, 126
Estruch Tobella, Joan, 7
ethnicity. *See* race (*raza*)

"Fall of the House of Usher, The" (Poe), 173n58
fans, 72, 74–75, 77–78
fantastic short fiction
   as counterpoint to realist fiction, 1–2
   nation building and, 11–12, 141–44
   reception and scholarship on, 2–8
   Todorov on, 2–3, 8, 11, 12, 13
   See also specific tropes, authors and works
Fantastic Worlds (Rabkin), 5
Faust (Goethe), 81
Fedorchek, Robert, 160n33
Female Gothic, 101
femininity
   bourgeois models of, 56–59
   in "Maldición de gitana" (Pardo Bazán), 126, 127–28
   middle-class identity and, 28
   motherhoodand, 57, 63–64, 70–71
   See also gender nonconformity
feminism, 58
femmes fatales
   characteristics of, 63–64
   in "El verano" ("Theros") (Galdós), 55–56, 61, 62–63, 64–70, 79–80, 82, 99
   gypsies as, 126
Fernández Bremón, José, 81, 171n40
Fernández Díaz, David Félix, 169n11
flamenquismo, 125
Flores, Antonio, 43
Fontana de Oro, La (Galdós), 46, 165n83
Fortunata y Jacinta (Galdós), 32, 103, 106
Frankenstein (Shelley), 81, 86
Franz, Thomas, 165n88
Fuentes Peris, Teresa, 46, 168n115
"Furor colonial y otros furores" (Galdós), 173n64
Furst, Lilian, 145n1

Gabilondo, Joseba, 171–72n43
Galdós, Benito Pérez
   on fantastic fiction, 6–7
   Jewish characters by, 134
   on modernity and class, 10, 22, 25, 32, 153n45
   realist fiction and, 11–12
   See also specific works
Gender and Modernization in the Spanish Realist Novel (Labanyi), 10–11
gender nonconformity
   men as mad scientists and, 56, 81–91, 92, 99–100
   men as vampires and, 56, 61–62, 80, 81–82, 91–101, *93, 99*
   as monstrosity, 55–63, 80–81
   nation building and, 9–11, 141–44
   women as crones and, 55–56, 61, 62–64, 70–80, 82, 94, 99
   women as femmes fatales and, 55–56, 61, 62–70, 79–80, 82, 99, 126
George, David R., Jr., 73
"Gestas, o el idioma de los monos" (Fernández Bremón), 171n40
ghost stories. *See* spectrality
Ghosts of Colonies Past and Present (Coffey), 111, 112, 113
Gillet, Joseph, 178n118
Gimeno de Flacquer, Concepción, 58
"gitana, La" (de los Ríos), 132
"gitana, La" (Herrero), 177n100
Gloria (Galdós), 134
Goethe, Johann Wolfgang von, 81
Gold, Hazel, 133
Gómez Alfaro, Antonio, 177n100
Gómez de Avellaneda, Gertrudis, 167n111
González Mas, Ezequiel, 163–64n73
Goode, Joshua, 102–3
Gordon, Avery, 19–20
Gothic (Botting), 13–14, 152n31
Gothic & Gender (Heiland), 60
Gothic fiction
   aristocrats as villains in, 25–26
   fantastic short fiction and, 13–14
   ghost stories and. *See* spectrality
   imperial curse stories and, 111–12, 114, 119. *See also* curse

Jewish characters in, 134
  masculinity and femininity in, 55, 60–61. *See also* gender nonconformity
  nation building and, 142
  origins and evolution of, 4
  racialized Other in, 107–8
Goya, Francisco de, 63–64, *65*, 73
Great Round-Up (1749), 125
Groom, Nick, 50
Gullón, German, 161n45
Gutiérrez Díaz-Bernardo, Esteban, 161n45
gypsies, use of term, 176n85. *See also* Romani people
gypsyphilia, 125

Haggard, H. Rider, 160n37
Halberstam, Jack, 60
Heiland, Donna, 60
Hendershot, Cyndy, 86
hermaphrodites, 60
Hernández Suárez, Manuel, 161n43
Herrero, Sebastián, 177n100
Higiene del matrimonio (Monlau), 56–57, 81, 159n26, 167n102
"hija del diablo, La" (Asensi), 152n32
"hilos, Los" (Pardo Bazán)
  illustrations for, 32, 34–35, *35*
  middle-class identity in, 19–20, 24–25, 31–39, 54
  narrative perspective in, 32–33, 36–38
  publication and reception of, 32, 147n22
Hispano-Moroccan War (1859–1860), 133
Historia verdadera de la conquista de la Nueva España (Díaz del Castillo), 121
"History and Hauntology" (Labanyi), 37–38
Hoffmann, E. T. A., 4, 5, 7
hombre fino al gusto del día, El (Rementería y Fica), 77, 162n54
Horrifying Sex (Anolik), 81
Hugo, Victor, 176n93
Hunchback of Notre Dame, The (Hugo), 176n93
hypnosis, 36

Iarocci, Michael, 36, 146n14
Idols of Perversity (Dijkstra), 63, 161n49
Ilustración Artística (periodical), 72, 77, 160n33, 162n57
Ilustración española y americana, La (weekly), 64, 118–19
imagined communities, 9
Imparcial, El (periodical), 113, 172n49
imperial curse stories, 111–12, 114, 119. *See also* curse
Impurity of Blood (Goode), 102–3
indianos
  in "El brasileño" (Pardo Bazán), 122–24
  in Galdós's novels, 123, 172n54
  in "Tropiquillos" (Galdós), 113–18
  in "Vampiro" (Pardo Bazán), 93–94, 96–97, 98–99, 111, 114
indigenous peoples
  in "El brasileño" (Pardo Bazán), 102, 119–22
  in North American Gothic fiction, 107–8
  as racialized Others, 102–3, 110–11
  in "Tropiquillos" (Galdós), 102, 116, 117
"industria que vive de la muerte, Una" (Galdós)
  middle-class identity in, 19–20, 24–25, 39, 44–54
  narrative perspective in, 47–48, 50–53
  publication and reception of, 46
internal colonization, 124–25
Italian, The (Radcliffe), 160n37, 170n28
Izquierdo Dorta, Oswaldo, 161n45

Jackson, Rosemary, 11, 144
Jacobson, Matthew, 104
Jagoe, Catherine, 10
James, Henry, 152n36
James, William, 150n1
Jews
  in "El cuadro de maese Abraham" (Escamilla), 102, 134–40, *138*

Jews (*continued*)
    as racialized Others, 102–3, 132–34, 138
    in realist fiction, 103
Juan Manuel, Don, 138
judío nigromante (Jewish necromancer), 138
Juif errant, Le (Sue), 134

Kirkpatrick, Susan, 9
Kosofsky Sedgwick, Eve, 28

Labanyi, Jo
    on *Fortunata y Jacinta* (Galdós), 169n7
    on ghosts, 37–38
    on middle class, 150–51n9
    on nation building, 9, 148n34
    on realist fiction, 10–11
    on women's bodies, 63
Labra, Rafael María de, 165–66n91
Laqueur, Thomas, 56
Lewis, Matthew, 134, 160n37, 170n28
Leyendas (Bécquer), 25–26
Leyendas y tradiciones en prosa y verso (Asensi), 25–26, 143
Liberal, El (periodical), 126
liberalism, 19–21
limpieza de sangre (purity of blood), 103, 105–6, 132–33
literatura de cordel, 178n118
Lloyd Smith, Allan, 14
loca de la casa, La (Galdós), 123
López, Sylvia, 165n83, 166n93
lunes de El Imparcial, Los (literary supplement), 112, 113

mad scientists
    in *La sombra* (Galdós), 56, 81–91, 92, 99–100
    as trope in Gothic fiction, 55, 81, 86
Madrazo, Pedro de, 77, 78, 162n54
majismo, 125
Making Sex (Laqueur), 56
Malchow, H. L., 107

"Maldición de gitana" (Pardo Bazán)
    compared to "El cuadro de maese Abraham" (Escamilla), 135–36
    curse and racialized Others in, 102, 124, 127–32, 139–40
    intersection of class, gender, and race in, 143
    narrative perspective in, 109–10, 127, 129
    publication and reception of, 126, 129
Mapping the Social Body (McKinney), 22, 155n69, 155n75
Marginal Subjects (Tsuchiya), 59
"marido verdugo, El" (Coronado), 166n96
marimachos ("butch" women), 59, 73, 167n111
Marquard, Leopold, 125
Marshall, Bridget, 46
Martínez Campos, Arsenio, 113
Martínez Ruiz, José ("Azorín"), 172n49
Martínez-López, Enrique, 178n118
Marx, Karl, 23, 45
"máscara, La" (Pardo Bazán), 32, 147n22
masculinity
    bourgeois models of, 56–59, 80–81, 119
    in "El brasileño" (Pardo Bazán), 119–20
    in "La mujer alta" (Alarcón), 75–77, 80
    See also gender nonconformity
Massé, Michelle, 166n100
Maturin, Charles, 134
Maupassant, Guy de, 152n36
Maurier, George du, 134
McKinney, Collin, 22, 58, 155n69, 155n75
meigas, 164n80
Melmoth the Wanderer (Maturin), 134
men. *See* masculinity
Méndez Bringa, Narciso, 91, *93*, 97–98, *99*
Mercer, Leigh, 32, 154n66, 166n93
"Mermaid, The" (Bannerman), 160n37
Miau (Galdós), 80, 173n61
Middle Ages, 60

middle class (bourgeoisie)
   in "El antepasado" (Pardo Bazán), 19–20, 24–25, 26–31, 54
   in "Los hilos" (Pardo Bazán), 19–20, 24–25, 31–39, 54
   in "Una industria que vive de la muerte" (Galdós), 19–20, 24–25, 39, 44–54
   models of masculinity and femininity and, 56–59, 62, 119. *See also* gender nonconformity
   modernity and, 19–26
   in "El número trece" (Escamilla), 19–20, 24–25, 39–45, 54
   in realist fiction, 22, 32
Miller, Gabrielle, 162n56, 163n62
miserables, Los (Sáez de Melgar), 103
"miserere, El" (Bécquer), 152n32
Missionary Nation, A (Eastman), 110
Mobellán, Sebastián de, 77
Modern Ghosts (Curtis), 72, 146n9
modernity, 5, 19–26, 29–31, 54
Moers, Ellen, 101
Monk, The (Lewis), 134, 160n37, 170n28
Monlau, Pedro Felipe, 56–57, 81, 159n26, 167n102
Monleón, José B., 152n36, 157n97, 163–64n73, 164n80
Monsters by Trade (Surwillo), 59, 102
monstrosity
   gender nonconformity as, 55–63, 80–81
   men as mad scientists and, 56, 81–91, 92, 99–100
   men as vampires and, 56, 61–62, 80, 81–82, 91–101, 93, 99
   women as crones and, 55–56, 61, 62–64, 70–80, 82, 94, 99
   women as femmes fatales and, 55–56, 61, 62–70, 79–80, 82, 99, 126
Moreno Godino, Florencio, 163n70
moriscos, 103
Morocco, 133
"mosca, La" (Escamilla, 1873), 134

"mosca, La" (Escamilla, 1875), 32, 178n119
motherhood, 57, 63–64, 70–71
Moyano Law (1857), 21
"mujer alta, La" (Alarcón)
   crone as monster in, 55–56, 61, 62–63, 72–80, 82, 94, 99
   ideal woman in, 62
   intersection of class, gender, and race in, 143
   masculinity in, 75–77, 80
   narrative perspective in, 61
   publication and reception of, 12, 72, 149n49, 160n33, 162n57
mujer fría, La (Burgos), 64
mummy fictions, 109
Mundo invisible (Selgas), 149n47

Nación, La (newspaper), 46
Nagel, Joanne, 58
Narraciones inverosímiles (Alarcón), 4, 72
nation building and national identity
   fantastic short fiction and, 1, 8–10, 11–12, 141–44
   models of masculinity and femininity and, 58–59
   race (*raza*) and, 102–8, 110–12
   realist fiction and, 10–12, 142
Native Americans, 107–8
Nodier, Charles, 7
Nordau, Max, 107
Novelas cortas (Asensi), 143
nuevas teorías de la criminalidad, Las (Bernaldo de Quirós), 126
"número trece, El" (Escamilla)
   middle-class identity in, 19–20, 24–25, 39–45, 54
   narrative perspective in, 39–41, 42–43
   number thirteen in, 177n102
   publication and reception of, 39
"número trece, El" (Selgas), 177n102
Nuñez, Juan Paredes, 92–93
nymphomania, 161n49

"Observaciones sobre la novela contemporánea en España" (Galdós), 6, 10, 25
Ocho cuentos de Galdós (Izquierdo Dorta), 161n45
"ojos verdes, Los" (Bécquer), 64
"omnibus y la calesa, El" (Flores), 43
Orientalism, 125

Palacio Valdés, Armando, 126
Pardo Bazán, Emilia
   Alarcón and, 11–12, 72, 148–49n44
   Catholicism and, 147n20
   colonialism and, 116, 118
   on fantastic fiction, 7
   feminism and, 58
   Jewish characters by, 134
   Los lunes de El Imparcial (literary supplement) and, 172n49
   on middle class, 10, 21–22, 32
   periodical press and, 18
   race (*raza*) and, 105
   realist fiction and, 11–12
   See also specific works
"pasionaria, La" (Zorrilla), 5
Patmore, Coventry, 158n8
Payán, Juan Jesús, 7–8, 147n23
Peeren, Esther, 24, 53, 156n79
Peñate Rivero, Julio, 52, 64, 156–57n88, 173n63
"pendientes, Los" (Pardo Bazán), 177n105
Peninsular War (1808–1814), 9
periodical press, 3, 4, 10, 17–18. *See also specific periodicals*
Periódico para todos, El (weekly), 39, 134, 137–38, *138*, 154n64
Philosophy of Money, The (Simmel), 36
physiognomy, 159n25
Picón, Jacinto Octavio, 172n49
Pinzón, Martín Alonso, 105
pobres vergonzantes (shameful poor people), 41, 53
Poe, Edgar Allan, 4, 7, 173n58
Polidori, John William, 81
Porras, Juan Molina, 72
power
   in "El brasileño" (Pardo Bazán), 120–21, 139–40
   in "El cuadro de maese Abraham" (Escamilla), 137, 139–40
   curse as interracial exchange and, 104, 108–9
   in "El verano" ("Theros") (Galdós), 67–70
   in "Maldición de gitana" (Pardo Bazán), 124, 127–28, 130–31, 139–40
   in "Tropiquillos" (Galdós), 115–16, 139–40
   in "Vampiro" (Pardo Bazán), 62
Pozzi, Gabriela, 28
Prensa, La (periodical), 112
Procter, James, 111
"promesa, La" (Bécquer), 152n32
Properties of Modernity (Iarocci), 146n14
prueba, La (Pardo Bazán), 134
publishing industry, 22
Puebla, Consuelo, 163–64n73
Pulido, Ángel, 133

Quesada Novás, Ángeles, 153–54n50

Rabkin, Eric, 5
Racconti fantastici dell'Ottocento (Calvino), 5
race (*raza*)
   in "El brasileño" (Pardo Bazán), 102, 110–12, 118, 119–24, 139–40
   conceptualizations of, 102–8
   in "El cuadro de maese Abraham" (Escamilla), 102, 134–40
   curse and, 103–4, 108–10
   limpieza de sangre (purity of blood) and, 103, 105–6, 132–33
   in "Maldición de gitana" (Pardo Bazán), 102, 124, 127–32, 139–40
   nation building and, 9–11, 141–44
   national identity and, 102–8, 110–12
   in realist fiction, 103
   in "Tropiquillos" (Galdós), 102, 110–12, 113–18, 124, 139–40

Radcliffe, Ann, 4, 101, 160n37, 170n28
raza castiza, 142
Real Academia Española (Royal Spanish Academy), 133, 153n45
realist fiction
   fantastic short fiction as counterpoint to, 1–2
   gypsies in, 126
   masculinity and femininity in, 56
   middle-class identity in, 22, 32
   nation building and, 10–12, 142
   race (*raza*) in, 103
   reception of, 6
Realist Vision (Brooks), 146n17
Red and the Black, The (Stendahl), 145n1
Regenerationist movement, 107
Regenta, La (Alas), 32
Reisz, Susana, 11
"reloj, El" (Escamilla), 134, 179n121
Rementería y Fica, Carlos, 77, 162n54
República de las Letras, La (periodical), 64
Revista de España (periodical), 83, 160n34
Revista Moderna, La (weekly), 64, 153n49
Ribeiro, Eduardo Rivail, 175n75
Ridao Carlini, Inma, 41, 152n29
Ríos, Blanca de los, 132
Risco, Antonio, 148n40
Roas, David, 4, 7, 12, 154n64, 171n32
Rodrigo-Alharilla, Martin, 167n110
Rodríguez Arroquia, Ángel, 168–69n4
Romani people
   in "Maldición de gitana" (Pardo Bazán), 102, 126–32
   as racialized Others, 102–3, 106–7, 124–26
"rosa de pasión, La" (Bécquer), 134
"Rosa la solterona" (Mobellán), 77
Rueda, Ana, 162n55

Sab (Gómez de Avellaneda), 167n111
Sáez de Melgar, Faustina, 103
Sagasta, Práxedes Mateo de, 113
Sáiz, María Dolores, 176–77n95
"Saletita" (Pardo Bazán), 167–68n112
Salillas, Rafael, 107, 126

"santa de Karnar, La" (Pardo Bazán), 71
Santacruz, Pascual, 59, 73, 167n111
Schmidt-Nowara, Christopher, 175n81
seigneurial jurisdiction, 21
Self-Help (Smiles), 165–66n91
Selgas, José, 12, 177n102
"señora mayor, La" (Madrazo), 77, 78, 162n54
Serrano Alcázar, Rafael, 12
Sexual Anarchy (Showalter), 58, 59
Sforza, Galeazzo Maria, 152n35
She (Haggard), 160n37
Shelley, Mary, 81, 86
Showalter, Elaine, 58, 59
Shubert, Adrian, 21, 154n65, 155n72
Shulman, Marcy, 165n88
Sierra-Alonso, María, 125, 176n91
Simmel, Georg, 36
Sinués de Marco, María Pilar del, 158n8
sirens, 60
Six, Abigail Lee, 164n80, 166n93
slavery and slave trade
   in "El brasileño" (Pardo Bazán), 120, 123–24
   Curse of Ham and, 171n35
   Spanish racial superiority and, 110
   in "Vampiro" (Pardo Bazán), 96–97, 98–99
Smiles, Samuel, 165–66n91
Smith, Alan, 66, 156n85, 172n53, 173n55, 173n58
Smith, Andrew, 155n71, 171n37
Smith, Angela, 111
Smith, Jennifer, 129, 131–32, 161n49
Society for Psychical Research, 150n1
"solterona, La" (Contreras y Alba), 75
sombra, La (Galdós)
   compared to "Vampiro" (Pardo Bazán), 92
   ideal woman in, 62
   mad scientist as monster in, 56, 61–62, 81–91, 92, 99–100
   narrative perspective in, 61, 83–90, 99–100
   prologue to, 160n41

sombra, La (Galdós) *(continued)*
  publication and reception of, 6–7, 64, 83, 149n49, 160n34
  publication of, 112
"sombra de don Luis Arce, La" (Asensi), 152n32
Spanish-American War (1898), 107
Specters of Marx (Derrida), 23
spectrality
  in "El antepasado" (Pardo Bazán), 19–20, 24–25, 26–31, 54
  colonialism and, 111
  in "Los hilos" (Pardo Bazán), 19–20, 24–25, 31–39, 54
  in "Una industria que vive de la muerte" (Galdós), 19–20, 24–25, 39, 44–54
  modernity and, 19–26
  in "El número trece" (Escamilla), 19–20, 24–25, 39–45, 54
  popularity of ghost stories and, 19
  racialized Others and, 107–8
  in *La sombra* (Galdós), 84
Stendhal, 145n1
Stevenson, Robert Louis, 55, 81, 86
Stoker, Bram, 25, 55, 81, 160n37, 176n93
Stollznow, Karen, 108
Strange Case of Dr. Jekyll and Mr. Hyde, The (Stevenson), 55, 81, 86
"Su retrato" (Escamilla), 71
Su único hijo (Alas), 80
Suárez Casañ, Vicente, 159n21
Sue, Eugene, 134
suicide, 36–37
Surwillo, Lisa, 59, 102, 167n109, 167n110

taxation, 21
"té de las convalescientes, El" (Pardo Bazán), 154n42
"tesoros de la Alhambra, Los" (Estébanez Calderón), 126
theater, 33–35, *35*
"Theros" (Galdós). See "verano, El" ("Theros") (Galdós)
Todorov, Tzvetan, 2–3, 8, 11, 12, 13

Tolliver, Joyce, 18, 173n66
Tormento (Galdós), 123
Torres-Pou, Joan, 173n65
Tosh, John, 80
Trancón Lagunas, Montserrat, 7
tribuna, La (Pardo Bazán), 103
Trigo, Beatriz, 100, 168n116
Trilby (Maurier), 134
"Tropiquillos" (Galdós)
  compared to "El brasileño" (Pardo Bazán), 118–19, 120, 121
  compared to "El cuadro de maese Abraham" (Escamilla), 136
  compared to "Maldición de gitana" (Pardo Bazán), 124, 127, 130
  curse and racialized Others in, 102, 110–12, 113–18, 124, 139–40
  narrative perspective in, 109–10, 114
  publication and reception of, 6–7, 112–13
Tsuchiya, Akiko, 59, 149n48
Turner, Harriet, 165n88

Unamuno, Miguel de, 172n49
universal male suffrage, 21
Unraveling the Real (Duncan), 3
Urrutia, Mariano, 137–38, *138*

Valera, Juan, 172n49, 173n61
Valis, Noël, 75, 148n44, 150nn7–8, 153n44, 154nn62–63, 155n77
Valle-Inclán, Ramón del, 172n49
vampires
  as trope in Gothic fiction, 81–82. See also *Dracula* (Stoker)
  in "Vampiro" (Pardo Bazán), 56, 61–62, 80, 81–82, 91–101, *93*, *99*
"Vampiro" (Pardo Bazán)
  ideal woman in, 62
  illustrations for, 92, *93*, 97–98, *99*
  indianos in, 93–94, 96–97, 98–99, 111, 114
  intersection of class, gender, and race in, 143

narrative perspective in, 91–92, 95–96
publication and reception of, 91, 149n49, 160n35
vampire as monster in, 56, 61–62, 80, 81–82, 91–101, *93*, *99*
"Vampyre, The" (Polidori), 81
"verano, El" ("Theros") (Galdós)
   compared to "La mujer alta" (Alarcón), 75, 79–80
   femme fatale as monster in, 55–56, 61, 62–63, 64–70, 79–80, 82, 99
   narrative perspective in, 61, 66–70
   publication and reception of, 6–7, 64, 66
Versteeg, Margot, 146n17
viaje de novios, Un (Pardo Bazán), 147n19
Vialette, Aurélie, 155n77
"vieja verde, La" (Moreno Godino), 163n70
Visconti, Bianca Maria, 152n35
volkgeist, 104
voting rights, 21
"voto, El" (Pardo Bazán), 167–68n112

Walpole, Horace, 25
Wandering Jew, 134
Weber, Max, 171n33

Weller, Krisztina, 66
werewolves, 60
Whiteness of a Different Color (Jacobson), 104
Wolfreys, Julian, 54
Wolters, Nicholas, 158n11
women. *See* femininity; motherhood
women's rights, 58
working class
   in "Una industria que vive de la muerte" (Galdós), 44–46, 52–53
   middle-class identity and, 24, 32, 142
   in "La mujer alta" (Alarcón), 77–78
   nation building and, 9
   in "El número trece" (Escamilla), 42–44
   women and, 58, 103

yellowface, 103

"zapatos viejos, Los" (Pardo Bazán), 126
Zofloya (Dacre), 160n37, 170n28
Zorrilla, José, 5, 84

www.ingramcontent.com/pod-product-compliance
Lightning Source LLC
Chambersburg PA
CBHW030652230426
43665CB00011B/1061